the DEATH *of* PRIMROSE WHITTAKER

KERRY CHAPUT

Black Rose Writing | Texas

ISBN: 978-1-68513-670-3
LIBRARY OF CONGRESS CONTROL NUMBER: 2025937412
PUBLISHED BY BLACK ROSE WRITING
www.blackrosewriting.com

Printed in the United States of America
Suggested Retail Price (SRP) $23.95

The Death of Primrose Whittaker is printed in Minion Pro

*As a planet-friendly publisher, Black Rose Writing does its best to eliminate unnecessary waste to reduce paper usage and energy costs, while never compromising the reading experience. As a result, the final word count vs. page count may not meet common expectations.

the DEATH of PRIMROSE WHITTAKER

Chapter One

Portland, Oregon, 1924

It's a good thing I'll be dead by tomorrow.

"Primrose!" Mother pokes her wooden fan into my low back. "Sit up, you dreadful girl."

Her insults grow nastier as I fade into fatigue. The days are long when you carry the weight of the future. "I don't want to sit up. I do not wish to be here at all."

"You've only done two readings today, and you're turning off customers with your sour attitude."

"It's probably this gaudy costume you have me in." A thrown-together spiritualist act, my flowing black robe barely covers the slip Mother thinks passes for a dress. Mismatched buttons clatter on my sleeve as I wave my arm. "This getup grows more ridiculous by the day."

Lined up on the waterfront with the other swindlers and beggars, Mother competes for coins like the director of a penny arcade at an amusement park. "Step right up! Hear your future… if you dare." She hisses and claws at the air as people ignore her and stroll past. It's mortifying.

"Must you act like a feral cat?" I ask.

"People want a show. We give it to them." She pulls my bracelets higher on my arm where they press into my skin. Mother thinks the bangles give me an exotic allure, but she's just fashioned them from cracked beads and fishing wire.

"Why don't *you* parade around in undergarments and read futures, then? I'm tired of all this." I try not to stare at her trembling arthritic fingers as I say this.

"You are ungrateful. You've inherited the perfect act, and all you do is complain."

I never wanted the perfect act. I would have settled for normal parents and a friend or two, but that would be too much to ask for. When you possess psychic powers, that's all anyone can see.

Thick, pewter clouds hang over the Portland sky like smoke trails caught in a net that clings to the city. A September storm will shut down our setup soon enough, but until then, there are secrets to expose.

"My complaints are warranted. Standing on a windy street corner to manipulate grieving widows? It's torture."

I pull the bangles down to my wrist where they don't pinch my skin. Mother slides them back up. "Well, your torture is in high demand right now. Best grab those coins while desperate women toss them right into your palms."

It's bad enough that Mother exploits the brokenhearted. Forcing me to fabricate messages from the afterlife is unforgivable. After so many people died from The Great War and Spanish flu, you couldn't take two steps without stumbling over a crying widow, and my unscrupulous mother pounced.

I can see their past and future from only a touch, and still, our act is lies, lies, lies. All I see is their soul, their past and future selves. I haven't a clue what their loved ones think from the great beyond.

Still, each reading leaves me lethargic and teary, like a newborn assaulted by the terrifying world. A simple handshake often leads to the ugliest places. The only way I've been able to tolerate this life is knowing I'll die at midnight on my twenty-second birthday. *Tonight.*

Mother won't listen. She says these repeated dreams of death are nonsense. Nothing more than a fight against my destiny. I can't make her listen any more than I could turn her skin green, so here I sit on this rickety stool—hands propped on the paper-mâché folding tray table once used to hold discount perfumes at our neighborhood pharmacy—and count down the hours until my death.

"Oh, here comes a prospect." Mother's eyes light up. "Her fur stole oozes money." She pinches the fine hairs on my neck, which aggravates me to no end, as I'm already paying attention.

The ones with the greatest need speak with me the moment our eyes meet. A whisper between souls. I sense them by the grip on my chest and the urgency in their eyes. How their emotions seep into me like groundwater. It's hell, knowing I'll see her greatest pain, yet be powerless to stop it.

The woman fiddles with her brooch, emerald and sapphire stones in a platinum circle. Waterman's Jewelry displayed one like this in their window once. It cost as much as a year's rent at our townhouse on Gale St. The woman pretends to watch people meander along the riverfront but sneaks a glance my way. Wealthy folks frown on black magic, until they burn for answers the non-magic world refuses to give.

"What do we have here?" the woman asks. "Are you the daughter of that green-haired fellow?"

Father's bright green getup was hair dye, while my silver locks are a genuine metaphysical phenomenon. No one seems to care about truth, so long as I give them a future that helps them sleep at night.

"Yes!" Mother guides the woman closer. "Come, meet Silver Lily, the best fortune-teller in the Pacific Northwest." She looks to the sky and spreads her palm wide. "A psychic extravaganza."

I've always despised that opening. Hair like Christmas tree tinsel and a fear of bodily contact while being exploited by my own mother. Can't imagine why I welcome death.

Mother smiles widely, pulling out the folding chair she's painted gold, covering the chipped areas with her hand.

"Well, I suppose I could try." The woman lowers slowly, fanning her skirts. She hesitantly hands me a quarter, which Mother swipes and tucks into her brassiere. Tiny moisture droplets sit on the woman's raven hair from the almost rain. She smiles at my silver locks the way you stare at an ugly baby—with horror and pity.

I may not speak to the dead, but people show me the darkest, ugliest corners of their mind… the thing their soul is thirsty to tell. And I'm the sorry sap who listens. All my attempts to ignore their whispers have been futile. I need them as much as they need me. Without visions, I suffer the most intense physical ailments and an indescribable loneliness.

I let the woman's inner mind beckon me. Mother kicks my shin under the table, and I try not to roll my eyes. To make her happy, I wave my hands stupidly over the crystal ball as I pretend to massage the air to summon my visions. As if I need such theatrics.

All I need is contact. I reach for her hand, and the vision begins as it always does—a crawling ache like spiders under the skin of my forehead. With one bit of touch, the whisper will grab hold, and I'll enter her soul for the briefest of moments, satiating my aching hunger for the spirit realm.

An itch only a vision can reach.

My heart rate quickens, and my stomach tightens as I split in two. While my physical body sits frozen in a trance, my psychic body plummets through the familiar dark wind toward an invisible barrier. I break through with a snap and await the reward at the end—the blissful quiet of the other world.

The place where truth doesn't hide.

A gilded sky directs me along a path of golden honeycomb lined with vibrant emerald grass. Tall poppies sway in the breeze, their papery, tomato-red petals tickling my ankles as I pass. My honeycomb path ends, and in a dive, I throw my arms out to fall into the stars. The twinkling lights cradle my body and tingle my skin. The woman's story unfolds, clear as words in a book.

While every soul appears different, the comfort of the stars remains constant. A welcome universe of truth far away from life as a lonely silver girl in a very human world. I hope death takes me to an infinite poppy field surrounded by love.

How I wish I could stay here, swimming through the cloudless sky where my body floats weightless. But alas, I've seen all there is, and my body beckons my return. I tumble into the blackness and back into my physical body, where an agonizing headache greets my return. The blissful quiet of my stars is the squishy middle, bookended by the harsh, painful ride to and from her soul.

Just as in life, there is no good without suffering.

"Well, what do you see?" The woman pets the fox tail draped over her shoulder. Her eyes flick repeatedly up to my hair, squinting with every glance.

"Oh, your loved one must have much to say," Mother says. "Silver Lily, what have you seen?"

"Please," the woman says. "We've had so much loss."

The desperation in her voice breaks me. I saw her future from the stars. A new husband and twin babies who will die at eight months from typhoid. Their plump cheeks will turn blue as their last breaths escape their little mouths. Her first husband's death was clear, but there were no messages of peace and love.

And since I live in the knowledge of what pain awaits people on this hellish earth, I do the only thing I can. "Your husband sends word that he loves you," I choke out. "He is happy and not in pain."

"Oh." Her strained smile seems to bleed with terrible memories. "That's wonderful news."

Her dead husband's story played out in the stars. An artillery shell blasted his neck while in a *Montfaucon trench. No one ever speaks to me from the beyond, but that's all anyone wants to know about. "Charlie," I say. "He had bushy eyebrows and snorted when he laughed."

She smiles and seems to hate herself for it. "Yes, that's him."*

"There's more, if you'd like to hear."

"Yes," she says as she leans toward the front of the chair.

"You will remarry. His name is Edward, and you will have twin babies." I leave out the dreadful truth of those little girls or how Edward will leave her.

She dabs a handkerchief to the corners of her glassy eyes. "Two girls?"

"Yes, ma'am. Two beautiful, healthy babies. You'll be carrying by next year." Mother clears her throat, narrowing her eyes with a warning. "Charlie is sending you a new family, so you can live happily ever after."

He is doing nothing of the sort, but this is a tried-and-true lie, proven to soothe every weary soul.

The only physical touch I know is a brief brush of skin that leads to misery. I lie, withholding the terrible parts of my visions. I keep them in my heart where they churn and bleed. Lies may momentarily comfort, but the whole truth waits in the dark to ruin everything.

"Well, that is a wonderful vision, indeed," Mother says. "For an added quarter, Silver Lily will read your fate in tarot cards." She shoves the crystal ball aside and splays out a deck of cards.

"Oh, that would be lovely," the woman says.

"No, I—"

Before I can protest any further, mother pinches the back of my arm. She's done this so often that thumb-sized bruises live on my skin. My vision narrows. "I can't."

"She must have powerful visions of your future." Mother fiddles with the peacock feathers on my head, repositioning them as a stray silver lock falls in my face.

"Your hair," the woman says. "It shines like my silver tea set. Remarkable."

I much prefer rude comments to gawking, as their pitiful stares make me want to scream.

Briefly as a child, I was a lovely plain brunette, until one day silver bled out of my scalp like poured mercury. Then, instead of school and friends, my parents capitalized on my peculiar coloring and troublesome visions. Psychic powers have leached life from me ever since.

Mother fastens the errant lock with a pearl pin. "It proves she's special. Just look at her eyes. Magic lives inside our Silver Lily."

Almost as if she loves me. At the same time my hair turned, my cobalt blue irises disappeared, leaving clear orbs lined with a ring of sapphire, like an agate. I wipe the corners of my eyes as they ache and water in daylight. Yet another thing that makes life unbearable.

"What else do you see, Silver Lily?" The woman leans forward, holding her breath. When I don't speak, she grabs my sleeve, which makes me want to cry.

"No, I can't do this." I stand, knocking the folding stool to the ground.

"Silver Lily, this woman has paid us," Mother says through gritted teeth.

A familiar ball presses into my chest so tightly, I dig my knuckles into my sternum until it stings. I've always assumed this was all the lies that live deep inside me. Any attempts to interfere with visions only stir the worst possible scenario, turning me into the cause of someone's hurt. If only I could have known someone like me to help navigate this mess of a life. Instead, I am an anomaly. A true outcast.

"I'm sorry."

Pale light filters through the heavy clouds. I'm having trouble standing. Trouble breathing. Mother's voice cracks as loud as shattered glass. "Silver Lily, get back here!"

I run straight for the water. Faux black pearls bounce against my chest as coin-sized metal embellishments on my robe jangle in the wind. My feet halt at the shimmering edge of the Willamette River as I clutch the pain in my chest and think of all the horrible images I've swallowed over the years. They're part of me now. Like wallpaper.

I never had a chance with silver hair and crystalline eyes, riding on the coattails of my infamous medium father who died too young. My death on the eve of my twenty-second birthday has seeped into my dreams most every night. I've spent the years wondering why the spirit world chose me while not offering one bit of guidance. I suppose none of that matters anymore as death hovers near enough to taste.

Mother's voice yanks me back to the present. "Stop this nonsense, Primrose." She hobbles toward me on her creaking joints, cheeks burning red. "That woman offered a dollar for her fortune, and you're going to give it to her."

"Her future is horrid." My gaze remains on the lapping water.

"Who cares," Mother says. "This dollar could buy a tincture for my pain. Would you deny me that?"

Her knobby knees and fingers always look so painful, and every time I want to throw something at her, I remember her arthritis, and it fills me with guilt. I hang my head. "No, I wouldn't."

"Oh, the things I could do with your talent. You waste all your potential on self-pity instead of grabbing life by the throat."

I get nothing from these visions other than a countdown to the afterlife. "As you have done, mother to the talent? How does the view look from behind me?"

She slaps me swiftly across the cheek. Arthritis has twisted her hand like a claw, but her palm still finds contact with my cheekbone. "Don't blame me. You inherited this legacy from your good-for-nothing father," she snaps.

My father. A charlatan I barely knew, whose drug-fueled antics linger like a nightmare. "You shoved me into this hell."

Again, she rolls her eyes. "You think life comes with sunshine and rainbows? Nobody cares about truth or lies. You either take the opportunities or fall apart. Just like Vanessa," she spits.

Her sister Vanessa, the real psychic who could have guided me. Mother kept her far away, claiming she'd confuse me with obligations to truth and all that other nonsense. "You took the opportunity, all right. Put me to work as the youngest psychic in the country before I knew how to tie my shoes."

She growls before glancing back at the eager woman waving a dollar at us. "That's the price one pays for having a gift," she says.

"Not that you'd know anything about that."

Mother threatens me with another slap. She would give her right hand for my life, but no, the visions had to skip her and land on me like a bomb. "My weak bones won't let me work." She rubs her elbow and grimaces. Her guilt is her own form of magic. "Now stop complaining and tell that woman about her perfect future."

And just like that, my sympathy for her evaporates. "Only because you asked so nicely."

"You're especially insolent today."

"Well, I'll be dead in a matter of hours, and that sort of thing leaves a girl grumpy."

"Not this again. You're always so dramatic." She puts on her best whiney voice. "I haven't any friends or boyfriends. I'm going to die soon. Blah blah."

"I'm so glad my life is a mockery to you." Smoky clouds hover over us as drizzle floats from the dark sky. "Her babies will die," I say. "I can't tell her that."

Her eyes widen, her lips stiffen. "Then lie."

Maybe she wouldn't have a hobbling walk or swollen knees if she laid off the gin. I follow her, just as I always do. For years, I was too scared and too busy keeping my parents alive to consider another life. Why change now? Just a few more hours.

When we return, the woman pleads for a fortune. "Are you well, darling? I'd so like to hear more. I'll be a mother someday?" Her voice catches on a bubble in her throat.

It's all I can do not to throw my arms around her and cry for her unborn babies, but that will only lead to more miserable visions. If I had any power, I would prevent all the pain. I'd be a changemaker, altering the future to prevent every tragedy. But no, all I can do is lie and hide anything ugly from lost people searching for hope.

I stare into the woman's eyes, ignoring these ridiculous tarot cards. "I see an easy birth. Two healthy, pink girls in white dresses. Baptized at St. James."

"Oh my, that's our church," she says.

I shuffle past the visions of blue, lifeless faces. Her weeping over their tiny bodies that will die one hour apart. How this woman will attend her twins' funeral at the same church where they were baptized, and how she will kill herself exactly one year later.

"Ruby and Anna," I say.

"My two favorite aunts." She shakes her head, tears in her eyes.

Mother reaches for the woman's hand. "Silver Lily sees all."

She hands Mother two dollars and smiles. "What joy you've given me."

"You'll be a wonderful mother," I say, willing myself not to snarl at my own sorry excuse for a parent.

The sky opens, dropping fat raindrops over our table, as *Silver Lily, psychic extravaganza*, closes shop for the last time. Mother smiles at the money in her brassiere, unwilling to believe my death is imminent. I imagine the life I could have had. The good I could have done with a little guidance or even one friend like me. Then, in an instant, that watery image slides into my heart, where it burns like acid.

Chapter Two

We walk through downtown, wheeling our setup under the black clouds. Mother is on a mission to waste today's funds on some new herbalist she's frequented, and I've got nothing better to do, so I tag along. Black velvet covers our wagon, a faded silver lily painted on the fabric. A nod to my father's traveling act, the Emerald Poppy, where he donned green hair and a faux poppy in his lapel. His shows were pathetic lies, where his little girl read fortunes, and he took the credit. We've survived by riding infamy ever since.

People stare as we drag ourselves up Fifth Street. We pass Meier & Frank department store where they sell Ouija boards for ninety-eight cents. Piercing the veil between the living and dead has become a household pastime. People love the novelty of the spiritual realm, yet shun people like me.

"Here we are," Mother says. She opens the apothecary door as a brass bell chimes above. We shake out our umbrellas, leaving them against the doorstep as the wind howls strong enough to carry them away.

"Mrs. Whittaker. Lovely to see you today." The chemist stares at us with heavy eyes, an odd expression for a man in his late twenties. "Come in out of that nasty weather."

"Mr. North." Mother saunters to him. "This is my daughter, Primrose." She doesn't stop to allow an introduction. "I need a tincture. My joints are so awful."

Her hand still found a way to slap me. Besides, her tinctures and balms never do a damn thing, and she'll resort to guzzling gin by sunset.

"Well, then." He smooths back his thick black hair, shooting me a quick, pained smile. "Let me see what we have."

He ducks behind his curtain where glass bottles clink together. I run my hands along the potions and liniment bottles in the window. Dried herbs hang from the rafters, presumably to lessen the rancid smell that lingers through the shop. Gold and pewter dishes hold soaps and tablets and crystals for old world healing.

He returns and hands my mother two bottles. "Here you are, Mrs. Whittaker."

Mother discovered this new apothecary and has been here every day this week. Mysterious and brooding, Russell North is a different kind of character. Red lines encircle his pale, cloudy blue eyes, which he closes as he speaks, more like an ailing grandfather than a young man.

What has this haggard man gone through, and what awaits him in the coming years? I shake away any crazy notion of dipping into his soul, though his darkness tugs at me.

Mother smiles insincerely and nods, searching the shelves for potions to waste our money on.

He smiles, an unnerving desperation in his eyes. "Can I help you with something?" he asks me.

"I'm well, Mr. North. My mother is the one who needs help." *In more ways than one.*

His voice drags. "Call me Russell. May I call you Rose?"

"Absolutely not," I say.

He stifles a smile, and I swear I see a spark of light glint off his opaque blue eyes. "Are you in search of something in particular?"

"I don't believe there's anything in your shop that will heal me." Not unless he possesses a way to inject me with the power to alter the universe.

He examines my hair and eyes, as if he doesn't believe my declaration. As if all my hidden pain sits on my skin on full display.

He wears a peacock feather in the breast pocket of his windowpane suit. Green and blue circles like vibrant eyeballs. I pull away, afraid he'll touch me, and I'll see what's inside his sadness. I turn around and search the store for anything interesting, avoiding the uncomfortable air of this odd chemist.

"You might be interested in these." Russell ducks behind the counter and returns holding a pair of boots. Shining silver and pointed at the tips with a dainty spool heel. In the light, they reflect rainbows of green and blue.

Intrigue takes over. Something in these witchy boots makes my heart race. "I do like those."

"I thought you might," he says.

"Why would you think that? We just met."

"They match your hair." Russell's eyes glint with a flicker from the prism hanging in the window. "We could all use a little sparkle to remind us of the beauty in the world."

"They're just shoes."

A twitch of his eyebrows leads to a half-smirk. "Are they?"

His stare unnerves me. It's too intense, too familiar. "What's a chemist doing with flashy boots?"

"A customer died. This is all that's left of her."

"What a story!" I almost laugh but realize he isn't joking. "Did one of your potions kill her?"

He dips his head but drags his eyes up. "Not one of *mine*, no."

His pale eyeballs appear milky. Not quite clear like mine, but it still gives me pause. Patchy red bumps on his neck give him a feverish, wild look. "I don't delight in wearing a dead woman's shoes, Mr. North."

"Russell." He rubs his fist into his sternum, digging his knuckles into his skin until he winces.

I've never met another person with eyes like mine, let alone knuckles their sternum as I do. Could he have visions too? Have I really met another clear-eyed psychic mere hours before I die? Figures.

"My gift to you." Russell hands me the boots. "I hope they ease your loneliness."

What's with this guy? He speaks like one of the smarmy acts my parents worked with.

High-ankle lace-up shoes with sterling shimmer and sleek lines. My reflection shines back at me like a mirror, only my eyes are wide, and my cheeks glow a rosy red. Perhaps I've gone mad, but brightness flickers inside me, as if a pair of boots can change anything.

Mother appears. "Primrose, stop dawdling." She notices the boots. With a gasp, she snatches them from his hands. That woman would give her body for anything free. "Oh my, these are something special."

Desperate for that feeling of light once again, I yank them back. "These are mine." I hold them to my chest with a quick nod to Russell. He could be full of it, but these sparkly things just may lighten my final hours.

Her smile turns into a sneer, cartoonish in its curves. "What does a dead girl need with new boots?" Mother lumbers to the door and taps her foot impatiently.

I glance back at the mysterious chemist as we pass under the chiming bell. He clutches his chest again and I shake away the nagging voice that tells me we share the mystic wonders of starry nights. I can't entertain the notion that he could understand me. The potential hurts too much, and death awaits my arrival.

Outside, the wind blows unusually strong. Twisty and angry, the storm tosses paper lilies from my hair. Through the window, Russell buries his head in his hands. Smarmy people don't do that. I would know.

Without time to indulge the idea of a kindred magical spirit, I follow Mother into the windstorm. We stumble through hail and raindrops the size of houses.

Eight blocks later, at our freezing one-bedroom duplex just outside the bustling streets of downtown, Mother kicks the radiator and bangs on the wall we share with the landlord. "Fix this heat, you lousy no-good lowlife!"

"You do have a way with people, don't you, Mother?"

"If you would just pop over with your blouse hanging open, he'd jump to it in no time."

"Or you could pay the damn rent." I cover myself on instinct. "And gross. The man is eighty and walks with a cane."

"Don't be such a prude, Primrose. This is how you get somewhere in life." She grabs a flask from behind one of the framed pictures on the mantel. Pathetic faded magazine clippings haphazardly stuck behind chipped glass and framed as if we know these people. She swigs the gin she trades heaven knows what for with the neighbor who brews it in his basement. "Your figure could do more for us if we show it off."

"I already play into your circus. Leave my figure be."

"Your psychic allure is one thing. Your unique appearance is entirely another. You could be famous—make every man fall at your feet, if you'd just try." She runs her finger along the picture of Coco Chanel. "Coco says that beauty is a weapon."

As if I care about men falling at my feet. That's her dream, not mine. "I don't need any more weapons." The darkness inside me is weapon enough.

She waves her hand and glugs from her flask, collapsing on the ripped Davenport under the wall clock that stopped ticking in 1918 that we never bothered to fix.

Her gnarled hands remind me how she lives with pain every day. My visions tell me she'll live to seventy. Thirty more years of swindling after I'm gone. What with her sneaky ways and aggressive flirting, she'll manage just fine.

"I see you staring at my witch fingers, my little mystic. I once was pretty, before you came along." She twists her hair around her finger. "If I had my sister's witchy beauty, I could have mesmerized any man in the world. But no! I had to be born boring and predictable."

"I hate that you kept me from your sister. Aunt Vanessa could have taught me how to deal with this silver disaster."

Mother snarls. "The only thing Vanessa could have taught you is weakness. That girl had the chance to make us famous, but she gave that up for what? Love?" She waves her hand with a *psht* sound from her snarled lips. "You should be a force in the entertainment world. If only you'd care as much as I do."

I do care. Too much. Just not about what she thinks I should.

Mother gulps from her flask, eyes closed and blissful in her pain. "I'm going to bed," I say. I should tell her I love her, but we've never said those words, so why start now?

I slink back to my room in the basement and remove the layers of lies. The fraud of rouged cheeks and hoops that dangle from my ears. I unpin my hair, as silvery locks tickle my bare back.

The reflection in my vanity mirror could have been conventionally beautiful, in a different life. Creamy skin, big round eyes, full, pink lips. I leave the string of faux pearls around my neck, enjoying how the cool stones drape over my breasts. With a stretch, I run my hands through my hair to loosen the strands.

"I'm sorry," I say to my hair. "For hiding you under hats and feathers and scarves." Even hair dye does nothing to affect the platinum gleam. My obstinate hair refuses color, mocking me with its silvery persistence.

I don't know why I refused Mother the boots, seeing as how I'm hours from death. But now that they sit shiny and poised, witchlike and dark, I want them on my feet, to carry me somewhere magical.

I hold them up again to examine my reflection. A defiant Primrose whispers back, *Don't give up.*

Could there be such a world, where my powers help people? Where I'm not a lonely oddity in a sea of un-psychic normals?

Memories plague me. One day in second grade, I befriended a girl. When she held my hand, my psychic body flew through her soul—before I learned how to resist each whisper. Her poppy garden grew from fissured, parched earth, and her stars fell around me like broken glass. Once back in my physical body, I begged her not to go home because her father had died, and shock would send her tumbling down the stairs. She ripped her hand away and ran screaming. I tried to stop her, but she somersaulted past the teacher and down the school's concrete stairs. My vision turned real before my eyes.

She ended up in a wheelchair. They did, in fact, find her father dead at home later that day. The school reported my dangerous delusions and erratic behavior, so Mother yanked me out to capitalize on my "talents." Father had been gone a year, and we had nothing, so I've worked as Silver Lily ever since. The truth never sets you free.

"I will only hurt people," I say to my reflection. The vision fades, and I slip my feet into the silver sparkly boots, knowing this is my last moment before I escape this hellish existence. No love, no friends, and not one person's caring touch. Not one.

I pull out a hidden flask stolen from my mother, and stare at its faded steel and chipped paint. I've avoided booze this long, since watching my parents pass out drunk every night, but my lingering death makes me nervous. This stuff turned both my parents wild. Perhaps it will numb the fear that bubbles inside me.

I drink and dance naked, save for my pearls and boots, twirling to Bessie Smith on the radio and dreaming of the afterlife. No more keeper of secrets. No more lies. A burning sadness rips through me at the thought, which makes absolutely no sense. Psychic visions are the root of all my suffering. Competing emotions shoot through my mind, a riot of confusing voices, so I quiet them with a long gulp of liquor that may as well be gasoline for how it burns. I start to understand what she sees in this stuff as my head swims in the perfect fuzzy numbness.

The growing storm beats against the windows of my basement room, wind howling like a frantic whistle. Portland rarely storms. It's more like constant wet air that weeps, but tonight, we expect a downpour. Rain and hail pound the pavement as the wind tosses newspapers and pebbles against the glass. The intensity pulls me to the window, the ground seeming to shift as I walk. I climb onto a chair and grip the cold cement, unable to grasp what I'm seeing through the thrashing storm. It couldn't be.

A… peacock?

I've officially drank too much.

I push the window open as the storm blasts me. His feathery tail taunts me, but I can't open my eyes against the deluge of rain. Still naked and unable to shut the window, I shiver in the frigid air. Wind wraps around my head like a snake, lifting my hair straight toward the ceiling.

The storm shoves me back as if it's grown hands, dangling me by my pearls as I teeter off the back of the chair on my heels. The wind thrusts me backward, knocking my head against the floor with a sickening crack. I reach for the peacock, but he's disappeared. Ice pelts my body until the storm quiets.

The ball of lies I've spent a lifetime ignoring knocks against my chest. Through my fading vision, my boots spark silver, hinting at possibility. "I change my mind," I scream. "I don't want to die."

A puff of icy wind blasts my face as my sleepy voice mutters, "I want to help people."

The dream that drags me to the other side begins with familiarity. I stare through the prism of sunlight, eyes squinted, death hovering above me. Exhausted and weary, I wait for my heart to cease beating and the darkness to take me, despite the odd regret that begs for life.

Reality floats away, into the great abyss of night as a fierce wind howls. I'm lifted from the black into a vast white emptiness. No vibrant poppies, no spongy honeycomb. Floating through the gauzy white stillness, my feet dangle from my limp body.

"Primrose," a voice sings.

Hanging by death's grip, I stare into a blinding gold light. A translucent orb takes shape and drips like a teardrop from the sky. "I need your help," a woman's voice echoes.

A cocoon of spiderwebs pins my limbs tight against my legs. "I'm so tired of living with everyone's pain."

"I know, dear, but you're needed on Earth."

My mind swirls, trying to understand. "This is the night I die."

"You're going back." A powder-like gold dust falls over death's grip and the web loosens. From the floating orb, a bright voice like a song. "*He* needs you."

"Who needs me?"

"The man with three colors. It's imperative you save him," she says. "When you do, you'll discover the reason you have this gift. A life of good deeds awaits."

No way. Too good to be true. I struggle for footing, but I find only air. "What's the catch?"

"You've always been smart, Primrose." She nods as if answering a question no one asked. "Just because you haven't seen me doesn't mean I haven't been watching. Now, the one rule is you must tell the truth of your visions. No more lies."

"I'll return to the human world to save some tri-colored man by telling the stupid truth? What kind of racket is this?" Memories crawl back to me of that girl's twisted legs at the bottom of the stairs. Her screeching cries. "That's torture."

"That, my dear, is the deal."

"What deal? You decide and I obey?" I reach for her, but the light flares bright as the sun.

Death releases my arms but hovers near. Half of me wants the apparition to squeeze me until I disappear, while the secret, vulnerable part of me wishes to slip back to Earth and fix every person in pain.

"You've always wanted to help people, and now you can save them all," she says. "Trust your visions."

"Dying sounds easier." This is not happening. "I can't hurt people like that."

"You can no longer run away," she says.

"And if I refuse? If I lie about what I see?"

"That would bring you a lifetime of sadness. Fear of visions and lack of touch. More of what you hated so much you wished for death."

Tears gather in my eyes. "I didn't ask for this."

"No, you didn't." The orb grows larger, then smaller. "But sometimes we're capable of more than we can imagine, and we need a little push."

I lean toward the circle that seems to hum, a faint familiarity in her voice. "Who are you?"

The orb floats down, bouncing as the gold circle turns clear, revealing a woman dressed in a tight, black beaded gown smiling through bright red lips. A gold and emerald crown twinkles atop her silver curls that cascade to her waist. She taps her shoe with a shining scepter of light. "I am Gwendolyn, your spirit guide."

She must be kidding. Twenty-two years I've struggled with not one whisper of help. "It took you this long to show! You're supposed to guide me, right? You're terrible at your job."

When she laughs, her gown flickers red and back to black. "You can have everything you dream of." The orb glows so bright I wince.

Frigid air floats me through the stars splashed onto an inky sky. *What the hell is a man with three colors?*

My physical body wakes with a gasp. Pounding headache, naked and shivering, unable to breathe, my room drenched in offensive sunlight.

"Primrose!" Mother yells from upstairs. "Don't think because it's your birthday you'll get a rest. Hurry it up, child!"

I stand on wobbly legs and scratch my face slowly, hard enough to draw blood.

"Are you listening to me?" She flings the door open, standing at the top of the staircase, mouth and eyes wide open. "We're late."

I can only imagine how I must appear. Naked, save for silver boots and a strand of pearls. A scratched face, my silver hair matted to a frizzled mess, held prisoner by my first hangover.

"Primrose, what in the devil?"

Teeth gritted, I say, "Get out." She hesitates. "Out!"

Mother stumbles back and slams my bedroom door. The noise grips my head like a vice and my neck could collapse under the weight of my skull. How does Mother live through this every morning?

I run to the mirror, breathless and desperate to prove Gwendolyn and this deal have all been a dream. A drunken, mind-bending mistake. A bright red scratch from my temple to the corner of my mouth drips blood down my cheek. Real blood on my real body. I'm still here.

The psychic staring back at me faces an impossible task. Live with no secrets—difficult enough for this lonely fortune-teller, I've built a life around lies, but now I must become the angel of misery. Still in shock, I tighten the strand of pearls around my neck until it stings.

Oh, God. I'm twenty-two. And very much alive.

Chapter Three

I want to vomit in my sparkly boots.

I can't tell if it's the aftereffects of an entire flask of gin or the notion that I must face another day of visions—this time, with truth. Could this all have been a terrible misunderstanding? A gin-fueled mania coupled with misperceptions of my dreams?

Mother has me scheduled for a reading today at a speakeasy. Drunk patrons love a show, and the money in the darkness of hidden bars is better than in daylight.

Out of nowhere, my spirit guide appeared to ruin my death plan. All to help some three-colored man—whatever that means. I might imagine a new beginning, where visions lead to truth and truth leads to an altered universe… if I wasn't about to faint from nausea.

Mother throws the door open. "Get a little zozzled last night?"

"I'm fine."

"You're looking more and more like your old mom." She sighs. "Get yourself together. Drink some water and pickle juice. You'll be fine."

I stare at the silver pointed shoes and consider running anywhere but here. I would too, if it weren't for Gwendolyn's one-sided, forced, unfair deal. Truth or live in misery. What a bunch of bullshit. Still, these boots, like a hug for my feet, sparkle in the morning light. As soon as the room stops spinning, I throw on a dress and drag myself upstairs, longing for the death I should be enjoying right now.

Mother pinches my cheeks. "The sauce doesn't agree with you, Primrose. You resemble the walking dead."

"Funny, that's exactly what I am."

She eyes my boots. "I want those."

"Why do you care?" I look down. "They wouldn't even fit you."

"Vanessa had a pair just like them." She purses her lips and growls. "That witch always thought she was better than me."

"Where is she now?" I ask.

"Who knows? Somewhere wasting her potential. Now, give me the boots."

It takes me a moment to form the word, but even a hangover can't dull my defiance. "No." She leans closer, eyes bulging. The old me hesitates, but the new Primrose has nothing to lose. "I said no. Russell gave them to *me*."

Her cheeks glow red. "What's yours is mine. You owe me."

"What do I owe you for? Being born? Stealing your beauty?" I rock back on my heels, swallow to clear my voice, then glare into her eyes. "If you want these boots, you're going to have to rip them from my feet."

Mother glares at the shoes as if they're the answer to her unexceptional existence—no psychic powers, arthritic joints, a drinking problem, and a daughter who refuses fame. "Watch your tongue, young lady." She throws a scarf around her neck and a black cape around her shoulders.

She reaches for her flask, and I know what that means. A day of drinking until she passes out, and I must clean her up. I can't do it, not today. Still enamored with these unique shoes, I tap my toes together and remember Gwendolyn's promise. If this wasn't drunken delusions, that means I can live a life with purpose if I save some unknown man. Psychic visions with the power to help people.

Now, how do I find a three-colored man?

✳✳✳

I drag my tired legs behind Mother fifteen torturous blocks into town. Every time I stop to let nausea roll through me; she clicks her tongue like she's calling a horse. The cool October breeze feels like heaven on my cheeks. We pass piles of dried leaves and rustling newspapers in a narrow alley. Lines of laundry dangle above us as families chatter and laugh, preparing a Sunday full of normal goings-on, with no peacocks or fortunes, or near-death hallucinations while doused in bathtub gin.

She knocks three times on a metal door.

Gwendolyn's "deal" nags at me like a festering blister. Maybe it wasn't real. "Mother, I don't think you want me to do this today."

"I told you that silly notion of death wouldn't come true. You'll just have to saddle up and deal with the world of the living like the rest of us. Now get on with it and stop complaining."

A window in the door slides open. "Password?"

"Duck soup," Mother says.

He slides the window shut and the door clicks open. We step into a black hallway, my hands feeling along a brick wall. I can only imagine what will happen when the truth tumbles from my readings. "Don't say I didn't warn you."

She ignores me. Sconces flicker amber light over the sticky floor in the narrow hallway. A deep drumbeat and tinkling of piano keys travel through the walls. The man leading us flings the velvet curtain aside and extends his hand into the hidden recesses of gin-soaked secrecy where powdery perfume mixes with smoke.

"We need to primp," Mother says to the man. "We'll head to the powder room."

The man smacks her on the backside. She squeals and pretends to swat his arm. If I wasn't so sick, I would slap them both.

The man winks at me and reaches to tap my behind. I grab his wrist and squeeze hard. "Hands off the goods, Mister." Dammit. I touched the bastard.

A barely there smile hints from behind his heavy mustache. "You're a sassy thing."

"You have no idea. Touch me like that and I'll ruin you."

He laughs. "What are you gonna do? Fight me?"

This lost soul wears his secrets on the surface. No starry night or poppy path. "No. I'll tell your wife you like men. The petite type with skinny hips."

He straightens up, eyes wide. Coughs then looks around. "What the hell?"

"You dress them in red lipstick and pearls, like little dolls. How unique."

He loosens his collar.

"Oh, what's that? You buy them lingerie and take pictures? You naughty man." I smile, very amused by this whole interaction.

"Silver Lily," Mother sings from the bathroom, then lowers her voice to a growl. "Get over here."

The man grabs the fleshy part of my arm hard enough to sting. "Keep your mouth shut."

I let my eyes fall to his hand and glance back up at him until he releases his grip. "Your secret is safe with me. But don't threaten me again."

I've seen it all in my visions and nothing surprises me. From the intriguing to outrageous, the fantastical to the strange, and everything in between.

As I stare in the cracked mirror in the ladies' room, Mother pins strands of black velvet and fake lilies in my hair. "How am I to fit through the doorway with all this?" I ask.

"Duck."

"I don't need this. Neither do they. Don't you get it? Nobody cares about my stage name and the jewelry and the makeup."

She runs shimmering eye powder over my eyes. Silver to match my hair. "Nonsense. Nobody wants you as you are. Women wear red lips and pointed brassieres. We flutter our eyes and laugh at men's pathetic jokes. Life is acting, Primrose."

"It shouldn't be." I sink into the chair, staring at the paper lilies as large as my fist perched on the top of my head.

"Do you think this is the life I asked for?" Mother says, her back to me.

This is the life she forced on me.

Mother scoffs. "Vanessa used her visions to make men love her while she could have made us the show of the times, selfish wench. Where were *my* powers of persuasion?"

Again, with this story.

Vanessa's reputation as a seductress has been family lore for as long as I can remember. Mother simultaneously admired and hated her sister for possessing what she never could—men's attention.

The makeup pouch clunks when she drops it on the counter. "Your father loved me once." She throws her bag of baubles next to the makeup and catches herself. "But he chose morphine and whisky. And a host of other women."

"The doctor injected him with morphine to help the shakes. It isn't his fault he took too much too fast."

"You won't find me touching the stuff," she says.

She's convinced herself it's the arthritis, but the gin certainly doesn't help. And I'm certain crystals and herbs do little to address her shaking limbs.

She's spent two decades using me and drinking away the past. I don't know why she can't celebrate who she is—a woman who was lucky enough to avoid the burden of seeing futures.

"I have a bad feeling about today," I say.

"Give these people a fortune and leave them wanting more." She straightens up and rubs her knuckles. "If the men grab you, just smile and laugh. It's better that way."

Over the years, the getup and costume jewelry have changed, but the message remains the same—be the lie. Even if your powers are real.

Mother prepares a table in the middle of the room, pushing everyone aside like Charlie Chaplin is about to arrive. Sorry, folks, it's just her spinster daughter.

A bartender cleans sticky champagne coupes lined up on the mahogany bar. His eyes reflect the sconce light. He must not notice my silver hair in this dark room as he smiles through his groomed mustache, slicked to peaks on the ends.

Mother grabs me, slaps me into a chair, and rings a cowbell. "New addition to our performance," she whispers.

"What's next, shall I ride in on an elephant?"

The crowd gathers around to examine this wild woman and the girl with lilies on her head. Women smoke long cigarettes, hanging on men in tailored suits, all swaying to the quiet timbre of the piano.

"Today we have a special treat for you." Mother sticks two fingers in her mouth and whistles as if she isn't already the most conspicuous thing in the room. "Her visions will mesmerize you. Her fortunes will answer your deepest questions. Be prepared to experience the wonder of the supernatural. Step up for your moment with Silver Lily!" Her voice booms. She extends her arm and splays her knobby fingers wide like the ringleader in a circus.

The meager crowd claps and gathers around to examine me as if I'm a goldfish in a glass jar.

"Step up! Who's first? One dollar per reading."

She's raised our prices. She must be taking advantage of their illicit activities in this illegal bar, holding them over their heads like ransom. Prohibition only made everyone thirsty for more of what they can't have.

A man steps up, grabs his lapels. "Let's see what you got, Silver Lady."

Mother rests her hand on his shoulder. "Silver *Lily*."

He shrugs. Sits down opposite me and slaps a dollar bill on the table. Mother grabs the money, tucks it into her brassiere with a closed-mouth smile, and slides the crystal ball to me.

I shudder at the idea of what I might see. What I must say. Dammit, Gwendolyn. I could have retired into the stars, but no, here I am peddling fortunes once again. Why would she force me to tell the truth after ignoring me for decades? Unless it really was a dream. My intuition knows last night was real, but my mind's all jumbled today.

"Well lady, what do you see?" the man asks.

Perhaps I could lie and see what happens. "Shh," I say. I need to think. Tightness builds in my chest, as if a giant burp of magic might release the pressure. I toy with the idea of telling the truth. I wear the magic boots now—at least, I'd like to believe they're magic.

The man coughs, then sighs, then coughs again.

Memories taunt me of all the times I've toyed with the truth. The girl I paralyzed, or when I correctly warned my father that he would go to sleep and not wake up. The first boy I kissed. I warned him he would end up in prison for murdering his neighbor in a drunken brawl. Years later, when he beat that guy with a baseball bat and landed in the penitentiary, every person in a five-block radius reported me to the cops. Mother convinced them it was merely an act. Cheating is in our blood, you know.

If I thought it was rough before, being turned into the neighborhood witch made me lonely *and* untouchable. It was only manageable because I'm supposed to be dead by now. Who am I kidding, it was torturous the entire time.

A shadow moves across the table, then winds up the piano and climbs the wall as it morphs into a hovering orb, like a gleaming golden egg. Through the dark, I hear, "Primrose, we made a deal."

No escaping now. Her voice is proof it was much more than a dream. "No Gwendolyn, *you* made a deal."

The man furrows his brow, wondering what strange vision I'm speaking to.

"I'm sorry it has to be this way," Gwendolyn whispers in my ear. "Remember, speak the truth, or suffer a lifetime of misery with no end."

Mother's pleading eyes beg for me to carry on. No one sees or hears Gwendolyn except for me, the mad psychic conversing with her invisible spirit guide.

The man laughs. "What, nothing to see, miss? Just a lousy swindler, huh?"

Anger thunders through my limbs. I am many wrong things, but I'm not a joke. I place both my hands on the crystal ball but slide my foot to touch his under the table to access his secrets. Pulled through a portal, my mind nears the stars of this man's world. His path of poppies releases gold coins as they shake in the wind. The grass flutters, shreds of crisp green bills. I vault off the honeycomb path like a diving board and swim through the blackness as his memories and wishes wash over me. A drop from the stars, a thundering headache, and I'm back in this shitty bar.

My eyes shoot open. "You've been wanting to invest in the railroad."

He sits tall, flickers his eyes left and right. "I've not told a soul."

Mother places her hands on her hips and smiles.

"Impossible times will befall this country." I hesitate, knowing that in nine years, America will crumble. Banks will close, people will starve. I only must tell his fortune, I remind myself. "You'll invest in the Great Northern Line. Because you're wily and do not trust a soul, you'll hide your cash in wells and under floorboards. And because of that, you'll be very wealthy. Lonely as can be, but wealthy."

He thuds against the back of his chair, breathless.

"That is your future," I say. "Next."

Mother guides him up. He stumbles to the bar with a childlike grin plastered on his face.

This isn't so bad.

A woman lowers to the chair with a giant inhale from her cigarette. "Well, what've you got, little lily girl?"

I *hate* when they mock me.

I push away the ridiculous ball and throw the tarot cards on the floor. Mother gasps but I shoot her a look to warn that if she pushes me, I might throw her to the ground as well.

My body aches and my mouth is so dry I have trouble speaking, but I grab the woman's hands and squeeze. Into the world of stars I go. Through the tight, black tunnel, I land on her yellow road. One lonely poppy bends and twists to find the sun. The sky swirls, but this time a drum thumps in the background. After a brief trip through the stars, I'm back in my human form, staring at the flapper who yanks her hands from mine.

"You dance here during the day, and sneak into secret clubs after your children fall asleep."

She laughs. "That's no mystery, everyone here knows that. You're a fraud." She sneers. "A tacky one, at that."

As if she personifies class.

I grab the edge of the table with what little strength I have. Shake my head no. The woman snickers. "Bartender," she yells. "Mix me up a Gin Rickey, will ya', doll? This cheat is wasting my time."

Mother slams her hands on the table and lowers to my ear. "What're you doing? Give the woman a fortune."

The flapper laughs heartily, beckoning others to join in. Their laughter seeps into me. Crawls in every crack and eats away at me like maggots. Reading through anger is never a good idea.

"You stupid fool," Mother whispers. "Do it or I will."

Behind the veil of closed lids, Gwendolyn's voice appears for only me. "Just tell the truth and trust your visions. It will set you free." I try to open my eyes, but she holds them shut until I agree.

"Silver Lily, what is happening to you?" Mother says. "Is it another vision?"

Through the visions of tears and screams emerges one shining star among the wreckage. What if I can help someone?

My eyes fly open. I want to fall on the floor and beg the underworld to swallow me. "Fine!" I yell.

The flapper, no longer in her chair, has draped herself over a barstool. "Honestly. Where do you find these pathetic swindlers?"

When I stand, the chair flies out from behind me. I knock the crystal ball to the floor, where it shatters into a dozen pieces. Mother gasps while I inhale the sweet scent of triumph. She wants the truth? I'll give her the truth.

Sauntering to the bar, I take a seat next to the woman. I keep my voice low. "You're someone's mistress," I whisper.

Out of the corner of my eye, I see her shift and lower her drink.

"Can I get you anything, miss?" the bartender asks.

With a smile, I respond. "Coffee."

"You're like a sideshow at a circus," the woman snaps.

"Is my vision ringing a bell, darling? Well, of course it is. Your secret fella has a wife and three daughters who sleep upstairs while you make whoopie in the basement. He likes it rough. Oh! Look at that. So do you, it appears."

The woman gathers her shoulders like a pintuck skirt.

"I haven't said it loud enough for the rest of the bar to hear, though I'd be happy to announce it again." This woman bathes in touch, getting her body absolutely slathered in hands and lips. She doesn't see how lucky she is.

The bartender slides me a mug of coffee. Bounces his eyes between the two women at his bar, then settles on me with a deep breath that puffs his chest against his crisp white shirt.

"No, I hear you," she mutters. "I think I should leave now." She stands, straightens her dress, her neck flushed a dozen shades of crimson.

I grit my teeth and swallow the lump in my throat. "One more thing you should know. You're not the only plaything in that basement. He has four others." I shake my head. "One even hid in the closet and watched him spank you."

She runs into the darkness, her sobs trailing down the hall and behind the velvet curtain.

The bartender looks at me, eyebrows raised.

I shrug. "This is why I have no friends."

When he licks his lips, they gloss like cooked sugar. "Cream?"

"Black is fine." The hot, bitter coffee burns a trail down my throat.

Mother stomps over, eye bulging. "What has gotten into you?"

"You got your fortunes. Now leave me alone."

"You don't tell the truth, you stupid child. You lie!"

"Haven't you noticed? I'm no longer a child." I rip the paper lilies from my head and throw them at her. "And Silver Lily is dead. Chase my father's shadow yourself."

Her breathing deepens. "You selfish girl." She examines the lilies, on the brink of tears. "I've built all this for you. Lord knows you couldn't have lived a normal life."

"You did this for you. This entire act keeps you in oils and crystals while you guzzle gin and fall for any man who looks your direction."

She wipes her eyes and gathers the crumpled paper lilies. "Cool off. Don't even think of returning home until you've come to your senses."

I lean toward her. "I'm done with this act."

She looks angry enough to spit. "You are not prepared for the ways of this world, Primrose. Men will use you, then leave you broken and empty. I'm all you've got, kid."

My fear of touch came from my attempts to help gone awry, but Mother's remarks about my defects and men's horrid impulses strengthen every worry in my heart.

"You use me worse than anyone."

She runs her tongue across her teeth and clucks at the bartender who pretends to clean glassware. "You spiteful girl. You'll regret crossing me." She steps back, gathers our wagon, and pathetically wheels it out of the secret bar.

"Are you always this intense?" the bartender asks.

"Yes."

As Mother hobbles away, I remind myself that I can't hold up my end of this stupid deal while she's forcing me to lie.

"Sure you don't want something stronger?" He gestures to my coffee.

"No. I'm not one for the hooch." Thank God. My entire childhood existed against the background of booze, cigarettes, and used syringes in the bathroom. I have to be better than them, but my resolve just took one hell of a hit.

He watches me as I remove the rest of my hair decorations and cheap bangles. "Toss these for me?"

"Sure." He slides them off the bar into a metal can. "What's your real name?"

"Primrose."

"Nice name."

"Not really, but thank you." I search his face and clothing, his hair and eyes and fingernails. Even his clothes are black and white. No three colors anywhere. Of course it wouldn't be that easy.

He lowers to his elbows, leans close to my face. "So, how did you know all those things?"

I hold back a sigh. "I might look like a phony, but I assure you, my visions are real."

"Why play along with your mother's act? Why not go at it on your own?"

Such a simple question with such a complex answer. "My life has never been mine. Not for one day."

He smells of smoky cologne and Ivory soap. I gulp the coffee, trying to burn away the aching need to press my face into his neck and run my fingers through that loose curl that hangs at his forehead. When you've been starved your entire life, men begin to look like a lifesaving meal. Lust and empty touch could fill my belly, and for only a moment, oh, wouldn't it taste good.

"I find your look mesmerizing," he says with a grin that makes my thighs quake.

"Careful, you can't touch me. I'm like a black widow who siphons your happiness with one bite."

"I doubt that."

His dark eyes plead with me.

Please don't ask me. Please don't ask me.

I decide to cut him off. "If you ask me for a vision, I'll tell you the truth. Even things you don't want to hear."

"I don't care what you see in those beautiful crystal eyes."

I don't even need to know his name. Just a press of lips could satisfy me for a while. I've waited so long and been so skilled at ignoring loneliness. Now, I can't protect myself or anyone else, so what's the point?

I slip my cape over my shoulders, my heart thumping in my chest. I smile, dragging my fingers along the bar top and over the edge, forgetting everything I know to be true. Though my eyes remain locked with his, I step through the curtain and into the dark hallway. Back pressed against the rough bricks in the shadowy darkness, I wait.

When he touches me, my head swims, but I manage to resist a vision. Not much is stronger than lust. He presses his chest to mine, his hands gripping my hips. I grab his suspenders and pull close, tasting those glossy lips for one luscious moment while a kiss suspends any psychic existence. How a loveless kiss can feed my soul is terrifying, but needed in a primal, animalistic way. One moment is all I get before his mustache tickles my upper lip, distracting me enough to send me flying, sucked through a tunnel of frigid wind.

I land in my vision not on my feet, but on all fours, breathless. My bright yellow path has turned amber, covering me in sticky honey. I shake my hands and the honey splatters onto a swarm of bees hovering over the poppies. The bees drop to the grass as their buzzing turns silent and the poppy petals wither to gray dust.

My chest tightens. The honey river turns to a slide and sends me face first into the depths of blackness below. I fall, waiting for the stars to catch me, but I tumble so fast I can't scream.

My hair catches on something. I hang over the void, seeing only darkness. My head throbs from my taut hair. This man's soul stares back at me. His future. His dark secret.

Please no.

I reach for his image, color shooting from my hands. Strips of red and purple and green cast like a net over him, but just before the colors land on his image, something yanks me backward.

I somersault and scream as the world pulls me back into my body where I yank back from the bartender's kiss with a yelp.

He runs his fingers through my hair. "Did you see something?" he asks.

No. Not this.

"You see my future, don't you? Please, tell me."

I exhale and push him away, tears in my eyes. "I'm so sorry to do this to you."

He recoils, arms resting at his sides. He doesn't want to touch me anymore. They never do.

I rub my palms into my eyes so hard they sting. I click my toes together, desperately hoping this is all a big mistake. Tonight. This moment if there is any humanity left in this world. "You get very, very sad," I say. He doesn't move. "You test your skin sometimes, to see if you can feel anything through the sadness."

His chin trembles. He's curious, so he moves closer. "Yes."

"Sometimes cigarettes, sometimes… blades."

A tear leaks from his eye. "I think about death all the time."

They're drawn to the darkness in me. As if they know a kiss with the broken human but fully alive psychic will match the empty home they've always known. I know the game. We use each other, leaving us both more alone than before. My eyes have adjusted to the dark. I see the lines in his forehead. The freckles on his nose.

The lump in my throat could choke me, it's so large. "On a sticky fall evening under a harvest moon, you'll take a kitchen knife." I search for any way to avoid this, but Gwendolyn's hum wavers in the distance. "You'll drag the blade across your neck left to right, until a cascade of bright blood douses your chest. Your death will take less than sixty seconds."

The piano picks up as people dance behind the curtain and laughter bubbles through the hidden bar.

He straightens, aware he's opened the door to truth. His eyes light up, almost relieved by my vision.

"You can't do it," I say, my voice trembling.

"It appears I can."

"Please, don't," I beg. It's too late to change the course of his life. Like always, I'm useless, watching catastrophe unfold. But this time, I've handed him the knife.

I've given him the strength to kill himself. It's intolerable.

Redness fills the whites of his eyes. "You should go."

I tap my toes and cry. I have no power, no magic to fix what's broken. Just the excruciating truth to swallow me whole.

Sounds of joy distract me as couples breathe in each other, touching and swaying to the music. I tighten my cape, slip on the hood and slink toward the door. When I look back, the bartender mutters to himself, "Sixty seconds."

Words stay locked in my mind for fear that I'll say something to hasten his future. I fight the urge to burst into tears. A couple pushes past me, eager to dip into the forbidden waters of gin and underground secrets, where they can touch and laugh and kiss under the murky light.

The only way I've ever been able to help is by lying, and now I can't do a damn thing but watch the destruction. The worst of it all? My longing for touch has only intensified.

The bartender crosses his arms and nods to the door, his steely eyes frighteningly alive.

The dreary afternoon drops a film of moisture on my face and neck. Raindrops quiver the water puddled at my feet, each drip pulsing out concentric circles that glimmer silver from my reflection.

As my chest tightens and squeezes, darkness creeps into my heart. My first attempt at truth and I've embarrassed one and given another license to die. This is so much worse than I anticipated. I used to dream of preventing pain, back before I learned you can't change anyone.

I've spent so long waiting to die, I have no idea how to live.

Chapter Four

As I watch the sunrise, images of the bartender's last moments hold a grip on me—the sliced flesh, the life draining from his eyes. I can't wait for this elusive three-colored man. It's too painful. If there's a way to help these lost souls, I have to find it. I wait on Russell's doorstep, huddled against the cold glass in the blustery spring morning, hoping beyond reason that he can explain my visions.

Off in the shadows, a basement window reflects an odd image. Tripod claws tap their way along the pavement, a long green tail brushing the ground. I turn in all directions, but I see no peacock.

If my life has taught me anything, it's that nothing is ever too strange to exist.

The door behind me moves, swept open suddenly, and I find myself flat on my back, staring up at the jingling gold bell.

"Primrose? What are you doing?" Russell motions me inside and shuts the door.

After hours on the cold pavement last night, the warmth of his shop makes me tremble with gratitude. As raindrops slide down my cheeks, I stare at him, a little too needy for my liking but I'm panicked. "Can you help fix me?"

"Come in." He guides me behind the curtain, past his workshop, where pots boil on the stove and herbs and animal hides hang from the fireplace mantel.

A collection of chicken feet cover the table. Dried to a crisp, their tips look like mangled witch's hands. "You have quite the laboratory here."

"Those heal dry skin," he says.

I shudder at the thought of chewing on a stick of dried bird feet. "Oh, that's… strange."

"I experiment with nature. Everything from toadstools to pig's blood."

"To cure ailments?" I ask.

"Well, yes. And for… other things." He motions with a pointed finger to my feet. "I see you enjoy your boots."

"They're a perfect fit." Curiosity taps at my shoulder. A peacock, some mysterious three-colored man, and my first visit from my spirit guide. All since wearing these boots. I have so many questions.

Russell turns to the back of the room and opens a door into a small apartment. "Come in."

"You live here?"

"Yes." He points to a chair near the fireplace. I bend down to look through the flames. His workshop boils and steams away through the opening, carrying the odors of rotting mushrooms and roasted innards. I fight the urge to cover my mouth.

"Tell me," he says. "What's this about fixing you?"

Nerves jitter through my limbs. Face to face with another psychic who could understand me. I don't speak. I want to hold the possibility a bit longer, in case I'm wrong and he's nothing more than an odd chemist with milky eyes and indigestion.

"Are you… I mean, do you have…" One deep breath and I decide to dive in. "Do you see things?"

He doesn't seem surprised. "What makes you think that?"

The scent of boiling meat turns my stomach but doesn't dampen my excitement. He didn't say no.

"Your eyes. They're like mine," I say. "And the way you rub your sternum. I do that when I bottle up the things I see."

He rubs his chin and slides his hands down his neck.

"I'm a fortune-teller who reads visions and flies through souls," I say. Nothing like a little desperation to force out one's truth. I wait for a sign of confusion, disgust, intrigue, but I see… understanding.

"It's a painful life, isn't it?" he asks.

I bite my lip to stop the barrage of questions about to tumble out. "You *are* like me."

He turns away and slicks his hair back. "My hair turned black when I tried to cure my visions."

"You can do that?"

"I wouldn't recommend it."

Gwendolyn gave me a way out, but is this what I'll look like? Aged a few decades with hollow eyes and a wasted body? While I consider Gwendolyn's promise, the idea of living without my starry nights leaves a hollow pit in my soul.

Thick, muddy liquid bubbles away in a copper pot over the fire. His heavy, fatigued eyes and painful grimaces—is this how it looks to live without powers? "I must tell the truth of the awful things I see with no way to help."

He slips his hands in his pockets. "That's the curse of it all, isn't it? We avoid touch and truth, pulling away from the people we're desperate to help."

My throat thickens but I swallow against it. "I've been strong most of these years. Avoided all of it. But now I can't. I'm twenty-two and my need to have someone close is damn near killing me." I wish it had killed me.

He drops his head and slides his hands into his pockets. "Yeah. That's the worst part for me too."

He's broken and sad, yet carries on with this shop, creating noxious brews and outrageous remedies. "Can you cure it?"

"No," he says without hesitation. He blinks hard, lifting his forehead to stretch his heavy eyes wide open. "I imagine you've tried to avoid visions before and discovered how awful that feels."

He's right. The headaches, the racing heart. The tremors. I'd hoped he had answers for me, as if he's some all-knowing magician. "What I really want is to help these people. The cosmos gave us something incredible that only seems to bring pain for everyone. There must be a better way."

He wilts right before my eyes. "I've not found a better way. Not yet."

Despite looking half-dead, he somehow knew enough to gift me something sparkly that could change my life. He did something good. "Why did you give me the boots?"

He shrugs. "Someone should enjoy them. They do no good collecting dust in the corner of my shop."

I don't believe him. He knows things. Rain drips down the tiny window, casting a watery shadow on the barely visible sunrise. Water seems to hold this city in its grip, even in early autumn. "Strange things have happened since you gave them to me. Are they magic?"

"There's magic in everything, I would think."

I'd like to believe they hold power, like some child's rhyme or fable. How a pair of boots could change the way I see myself seems like nonsense, yet also wildly plausible. The familiarity when I slip them on, as if I've worn them before, and the dazzle of silver reminds me that beautiful things shine.

"Visions are easy as breathing. I suppose there's magic in that." I spin a dangling stained-glass pendant, sending flashes of rainbow light around the room. "Do you tell people about your powers?"

"No. I've hidden my gifts." He walks past me to stir the swampy stew over the fire. "I've never worked as a fortune-teller to, you know, avoid telling fortunes."

"Fair point." I stand and pace the room, past my reflection in a cracked mirror propped on his writing desk. Mussed hair like a knotted pile of silver necklace chains. Black shadows line my eyes, the mixture of petroleum jelly and soot meant to darken my lashes. "I've never had a say in my life." A dancing monkey at the circus, that's all I've been. "Father made a living selling my visions."

"What happened to your money?"

"It went into bottles of liquor, and then into his veins to lessen the effects of the alcohol. Whoever decided you could treat one addiction with another?" A tapered candle drips yellow wax in a slow stream and gathers in a pile on the table. I stick my finger in the warm wax and watch it cool and harden. "I've refused touring ever since, though Mother pushes every day. Anyway, everything changed last night."

He taps the spoon on the edge of the pot and rests the sludge-covered wood on a glass plate. "That storm was something else."

"It wasn't just the storm. Based on twenty years of dreams, I'm supposed to be dead," I tell him. "Instead, I'll live a life sentence here on Earth, care of my spirit guide."

He shakes his head, a look of shock plastered to his face. "You can see your future?"

"I thought so."

"That's not right. We can only see others, not our own."

A twirling seed of doubt grows in my gut. I've always doubted my dreams. They aren't visions, after all. "Shit. I must have been wishing so hard to escape this life I conjured a pretend escape."

He dabs the sweat beading on his temples with a thinned rag he hangs on a hook near the stove. "Our spirit guides are never wrong. Who do you think sends you the visions?" He scratches at the red bumps on his neck.

"I thought they were inside me."

"We're merely a conduit to the information of the universe. If you're still in this earthly body, it means you haven't yet learned your ultimate lesson."

"That means you haven't either."

He nods with a pained smile. "You're smart."

"Not smart enough to use our power for good." I peel the wax from my finger and roll it in a ball, then drop it back to the liquid pool near the candle's flame and watch it melt. "She tells me I can learn to do good with these visions, but I have some weird riddle to solve. You ever heard of a man with three colors?"

"Can't say that I have. But things are rarely as they seem. Lessons and riddles aren't about the prize at the end, they are about the journey."

"I've been on this journey since the day I realized I couldn't touch people."

"It is the worst part of it all, isn't it? Knowing when your partner begins to fall out of love with you, or how you disappoint your family." He turns back around to stir though the soup though I doubt it needs attention. "Some truths are better left hidden."

"Do you have a spirit guide?" I ask.

"We all do, even the non-psychics. We're simply better at listening."

I never believed anyone was on my side.

It's all too strange how my life has transformed since yesterday. Excitement and fear and disbelief compete in my heart like popcorn kernels over heat. Which will be the first to pop? I run my hand along a brass framed picture of a teenage boy with silver hair. He stands in front of a steaming lake. "Is this you?"

"Yes."

"Where was this taken?"

"Nowhere." He drops the spoon onto the floor. My flowing black dress jangles with coins and beads as I reach for the handle, but he beats me to it. I stand tall and stare at him, wondering what he's hiding. "Where did you learn all this?"

"I learned from others."

"Others? There are more like us?"

"More than you'd think."

I roll a cracked bead from my getup between my first and second finger. I've always been an outsider, but could I be more? "Where are they?"

He clears his throat, cleaning up the stinky mess as he gathers his thoughts. "In hiding. Like me. Trying to find answers."

Russell heads to the sink to wash up. I turn back to the picture, wondering how a lake can steam like that. A jeweled box sits next to the picture. Its emerald glass panels catch the light of the pendant in the window and bounce rainbows across the room. When I pick up the delicate box, I note an inlaid metal plate stamped with the words *Hot*

Lake Hotel, La Grande, Oregon. A tiny town at the base of the Blue Mountains east of here. Why would anyone go there?

"Don't touch that." Russell snatches the box from me, holding it firm against his chest.

"I'm sorry. The colored glass called to me." A couple walks past the tiny window, casting a momentary shadow over Russell's face, though rainy daylight appears in his eyes just as quickly. "What is Hot Lake?"

"Don't ask questions you aren't ready to hear the answers to."

"How do you know I'm not ready?" The rancid smell returns to the air as bubbles from the stew pop and spray. "Are there psychics there?"

"It's a resort. The hot springs treat ailments, and the place attracts many eccentrics. Some ride horses along the trails and dance into the night in the ballroom. Others look for something to cure their woes." Russell places the box gingerly back under the window and readjusts the picture.

"Is that why you were there? Were you sent there as a kid?"

He squints, scratching his hairline as patches of his skin turn pink. "Listen to me." He faces me, brows lifted. "Stop looking outside yourself for answers. You have this gift for a reason, and only you can discover why."

"If there's a way to live with this…" Sadness swoops through me at the loneliness that has bruised my every memory. "I could finally touch people."

"I've been where you are. There are no simple answers, and none of this is an easy journey," he says while rubbing his sternum with two fingers.

"Yeah." I lift my arms in a shrug, sensing he's done sharing. "Journeys never are."

I think about all the things I see in my poppy-lined paths of honeycomb, and how badly I want to fix every hurt I come across. Perhaps being helpless is just as painful as what happened on the stairs all those years ago. Heal a man with three-colors to become a powerful psychic who heals all, a future I hadn't imagined until I nearly died.

"Thank you, Russell. It's nice to know there's someone out there like me." I smile and plug my nose as I run past the drying animal intestines into the frosty morning where my journey awaits.

Hot Lake. A place of boiling water that treats ailments and houses silver psychics. I don't care what Russell says. Painful or not, I must move forward. A spark of life found me after decades in hiding. Maddening as it is, it's left me wanting more.

***

I creak open the door to our townhouse. Mother stares at me, puffing out a ring of cigarette smoke. "Well, what do you have to say?"

I need money, and she's the keeper of the coins. Any pride still clinging to me gets knocked off like barnacles drenched in acid. "I'm… sorry."

"That's more like it." She swipes her unruly hair from her tired, bloodshot eyes. "And you'll give me the boots?"

"Never."

"They're just shoes, Primrose." Her acrid, gin-soaked breath puffs into the air as she sighs. "My sister wore ones like this every day while I tottered around in ripped loafers. She had all the glitz I deserved. Don't you think it's my turn?"

They aren't just shoes. They're the first moment I realized I didn't want to die. I claw at the sides of my dress, yanking a flattened penny off a loose string. "Use some of your gin money to buy your own boots. Not everything I earn is for you."

"Don't judge me for how I deal with my painful body." Her hands tremble as she grabs her flask and glugs enough to ruin any chance of a sober day. "I just want to look pretty again." She tosses back the rest of the flask with a gag at the end. A loud, wet burp brings her back.

"You have no idea how difficult my life is."

I flick the penny to the scratched parquet floor where it lands in a sticky mess of spilled booze no one has bothered to clean. I imagine more people like me. Could I have friends or people to guide me? It's too wild to comprehend.

"I know you're terrified, darling. It's why I've created all this for you. No one will love you if you can't touch them. Remember the last time you hugged your father? You predicted his death that night and you felt so responsible when he never woke up."

I was seven. The syringe was still sticking out of his bruised elbow.

She steps close, her breath like rotting fruit. "You'll never leave me. I want the world for you, and you know it."

So many strings dangle from that promise. Put to work telling fortunes enough to pay for booze. Fill her need for attention and fame. But I want no part of the attention she craves. I simply want to make sense of this supernatural existence. "I'm going to take a bath, and then I'll dress for Silver Lily."

"Good girl." She fumbles in the cupboard for another hidden bottle, and I retreat to my basement.

I run myself a bath to scrub away the smeared makeup and any remnants of my first truthful readings. I rub until my skin glows red. Slipping under the water, I blow bubbles and let the warmth wrap around me.

A vision.

Two women strapped to a table, woozy and crying. Bright lights. Metal clangs in the distance. Death waits near to suck the life from them.

I shoot out of the bathtub water, my fingers tight against the edge of the tub, scraping the smooth porcelain until I catch my breath. I wrap myself in a towel and slide to the wet floor, rocking to make the vision go away.

Is this what awaits on my quest to find the three-colored man? No, Russell told me we can't see our own futures. This vision felt real. If it isn't my future, then whose is it? What choice do I have but to release the lies I've held like secrets and search for the psychics who know more than I. If I want magic, I first have to believe in it.

After a rushed attempt to get dressed and braid my hair, my cheeks are so flushed they require no rouge. I choose a powder blue dress with a dropped waist, lined with white lace at the sleeves and neck. Nothing Mother would allow for Silver Lily. I cover myself with a thick, flowing cape, the tip of my silver boots staring at me from below. I drag myself up the stairs to the kitchen.

"Don't you look… plain."

"Mother, psychic work gives me headaches and makes me the loneliest person in the world."

"Nonsense. We're all lonely. Might as well do something worthwhile with this gift."

All I am is the keeper of lies in a tacky sideshow.

She offers me the flask, but I shove her hand away. "Suit yourself." She covers her shoulders with her ripped shawl. "You can't imagine what it's been like, surrounded by exceptional people with powers. And here I am, dull and dowdy, and alone." She glances at my boots. "Just like my sister, you take and take and leave me with nothing."

A knock from the tip of a cane rattles the door. "Ms. Whittaker!" our landlord shouts. "You're two months late on rent. Again."

Mother rolls her eyes. "That old curmudgeon just won't leave me be." Before she opens the door, she turns back. "You'll read fortunes today. But so help me, if you tell people the truth, I'll slap you ten ways to Sunday."

Something in me snaps. The hope I've held grows so large I can't help but let it in. Some kind of answer waits for me at a boiling lake in the Blue Mountains.

I stuff a change of clothes and some toiletries in a poplin cinch bag and shut the door on my basement room. While Mother's distracted, I grab a knife, using the tip to pry open the lock on her vanity. Strands of faux pearls and teardrop earrings, hair rosettes, and lace ribbons. All tacky baubles to make her appear wealthy.

Sitting on her wobbly chair, I examine the ghostly white powder and various makeup tins. Mother uses a pencil to draw a beauty mark below her left eye, but the Portland rain always rolls a black stream down her cheek.

Under the tray hides a velvet bag, lumpy and full. I've always suspected it was here.

I pull the strings apart and gasp. Not just a few coins… handfuls of money. Dollars and quarters and even a gold watch. "That miserable woman." Mother and the landlord are still in conversation, so she hasn't heard me shuffling through her things.

I stuff half the bills in my pocket and wrap up the coins. The watch can stay. I leave her enough money for rent and food for a while. Crushed paper lilies decorate the room. Ripped and wilted, they remind me that this part of my life is over. I stab the kitchen knife into the vanity, straight through the center of the silk bloom.

No need to say goodbye. She'll only convince me to stay. I crawl out her window, convinced this is the right choice. The only choice. Excitement tingles through my hands, my spooled heels clicking the pavement in time to raindrop patter.

The train station is only a ten-minute walk. I scan every stranger for a sign of three colors. Not that I know what to look for, but it seems something like that might be fairly easy to spot. Waiting for my ticket, I glide my hand along my silver braid as it rests over my shoulder.

A woman beside me whispers, "I grayed young too. You know, a transformation can cover that right up." She smooths her chestnut-colored *transformation*. It's a wig, but apparently women need to be transformed.

Her wavy curls are the color of gingerbread instead of a silvery moon. My problem is far larger than a few graying hairs. "Thank you, but I quite like the color." That's a first, but it's true.

"I said, that will be two dollars. I haven't got all day," the elderly man behind the counter says.

"Yes, of course." I hand him two dollars and nod to the woman who can't stop gawking at my hair. Her stare doesn't make my skin crawl like usual.

"Your train leaves in five minutes," the man barks. "Mind you don't miss it."

I gather my bag and ticket, and slip away with visions of healing waters and psychic friends. I choose a quiet spot on the train, grateful no one's soul has beckoned me today. In a matter of hours, I'll be at some mysterious resort with people who look like me. My mind races far too easily toward the notion of a hidden family and a place of belonging.

The train rumbles and shakes as it rolls away from Portland, where Mother must realize I'm gone. No more fortune-telling. No more show.

Hope fills my heart, but visions dance like a prickly whisper on my skin. Russell's sickly face, his warnings against looking too hard for answers. There's something darker at this resort, I feel it in my bones. And I do have a weakness for all things dark.

The train clacks across the rails, sending thunder through my legs and into my chest. A slate-colored cloud hovers in front of the sun, shifting the light in the train car, pulling the warmth from the windows.

With a lurch, the train grows in force, heading east toward a boiling lake. The healing waters could cure me, but my hope rests in something bigger, something I've long since given up on. I could be more than a hapless fortune-teller. If I'm correct about Hot Lake Resort, I'll learn what to do with these visions from spirits. I'll change lives because the rest of my people will show me how. And that is worth all the journeys in the world.

Chapter Five

I've never ridden a train before.

For all the things I've seen in my visions, I've lived very little outside my basement on Gale Street. I suppose I didn't need to see the world, as I've been waiting for death. Until death wasn't an option.

Greenery flies past my window like a watercolor painting. Bright like Russell's glass case and dark like the soles of my boots. Giant maple trees shade the sun as raindrops trail down the windows. All I've ever known is a concrete and stone city, and a dark river polluted with trash and memories.

"Pardon me, miss."

A tall young man smiles down at me, wearing a perfectly tailored, double-breasted pinstripe suit, navy blue and white, not a wrinkle on him. He smiles wide and free as dimples pucker his cheeks while he examines the oddity before him.

After an uncomfortably long pause, I say, "You wanted my pardon, sir?"

"Ah, yes." He removes his fedora, naturally a matching navy blue, and holds it to his chest. "I hoped you could tell me if I'm on the right train."

I point at the whooshing scenery. "It's a bit too late even if you are."

He pulls out a pocket watch attached to a gold chain and examines the timepiece with a scowl. "I'm afraid I don't know where I'm going."

"You look to be a man who knows exactly what he's doing." I cross my hands in my lap, hopeful he won't ask for a reading.

He lowers onto the seat in front of me, leans against the window and turns his head. "I loathe leaving the city." He turns to face me, his eyes alight. "Can I tell you a secret?"

Oh joy. I love secrets. "Okay."

"My father sent me on a journey of sorts. A test, if you will."

"A test?" I ask, already invested.

"Yes. I'll take over for my family's real estate company." He nods in affirmation to himself. "Father sent me here, but I've spent the past forty-eight hours in a gin-soaked haze in Portland, and now must find one of our troubled locations out in the godforsaken desert."

"I didn't know buildings could be troubled. I thought that was reserved for people."

He smiles, sensing my mystical aura, no doubt. "You're quite funny. I didn't catch your name." He nods and raises his eyebrows, waiting for my reply.

"Primrose Whittaker."

"Pleasure to meet you." He stares again like I've cast a spell on him. "Anyway, I must get to Hot Lake before nightfall."

People often trust me and share intimate details. I wish I could be trusted. "You're going to Hot Lake also?"

"Oh, that must mean I'm on the correct train. What a relief." He runs his hand over his golden hair that reminds me of straw drenched in sunshine. "What are you going there for?" He drapes his arm over the seatback.

I want to blurt out the truth of searching for psychics and the potential for a family of like-minded mystics, but I think better of it. "Vacation."

"Well, that's lovely. Won't your family miss you?"

"No." I pull my silver braid over my shoulder. "You say your father owns the resort?"

"I'm set to inherit many of these odd locations all over the US. But first, I need to handle the issues, just as he instructed me. So many neglected resorts off causing trouble, and I'm to turn them profitable if I want to be more than a playboy whose only talent is offending women." He shrugs. "His words."

I understand the pain of falling short in your parents' eyes but can't say he offends me. "I'm sure you'll prove your worth, Mister…?"

Just as he's about to tell me his name, a loud explosion sends my heart into my throat. A screech follows as the train slows, bumpy like the wheels have turned from round to square. I grip the seat next to his hand, but quickly slide away. Even during an accident, I carefully avoid any wayward brush of skin. Squealing brakes struggle to slow the metal beast as screams fill the car.

We bounce and thrash around like hail in a storm, so I hold tight to the chair railing, my cheek pressed against the cool leather.

The train comes to a thudding halt as steam clouds the windows.

"That can't be good," the tall man says. He stands and dons his hat. "I'll check. You stay here."

I don't take orders from anyone, especially not some real estate mogul I just met. I stand, my knees a bit wobbly. But once they steady, I march down the stairs.

At the front of the train, three men stare at a blown-out cage, copper wiring flying out like steaming squid tentacles. I spot a trail that runs along the tracks, worn by feet and wheels and hooves.

"Boiler explosion," a man says to another. "This train is out of commission not even thirty minutes outside Portland."

The man in the pinstripe suit asks, "And how are we supposed to get to our destination?"

The conductor rubs his forehead. "You wait here for the trolley that will take us back to the city, or you walk to the next station, but that would take hours."

Mister navy blue suit retrieves his leather satchel from the unloaded luggage.

I walk away from the worried passengers and approach the trail alongside the tracks. My boots glow as a flutter of sunlight skips along the dirt and lights up the ferns. An obvious sign to move toward an unknown stop deep in the Oregon forest. Have these signs always been here, but I was too mired in pain to notice?

"What do you say, boots? Shall we?" They don't speak back, but I do amuse myself.

The man from the train yells for me. "Miss, wait!"

I don't listen. I speed up, noting how the ferns crowd either side of the trail like feathers on the purses of women in the speakeasies, soft and pretty and bright.

"Wait." He catches up with me. "What're you doing?"

"Walking. I thought that was obvious."

He stares down at my feet in a sort of wondrous awe. "Those are some boots."

His tone is mocking, but I'm well used to that. I flip my silver braid and carry on.

"I'm sorry, I've just never seen anything like them." He fumbles along behind me like a puppy. "Wait, I'll go with you."

I stop and release a loud sigh. "Why?"

He gasps, hand to his chest. "You can't walk through the forest alone."

"I assure you I can." I've been alone for the entirety of my life.

"Let me try again." He grabs his lapels and clears his throat. "Another train won't run for hours, if at all. The next station may be a trek, but we can travel together. I may be dreadfully hungover, but I'm still decent company."

My instinct is to do this alone, but he does seem to know more about this resort than I do. "I suppose I can't stop you."

"I will take that as an invite," he says.

We walk along the trail that winds us through a woodsy forest of hemlocks and red cedars. Rain drips off their leaves to bracken and thistle below.

"I never caught your name," I say.

"Sterling. Mr. Ash Sterling."

"Ash… Sterling? That's an odd name."

"Isn't it though? Ash was my mother's father, and we take our grandparents name in our family. Ridiculous and charming, if I do say so myself. What's even more ridiculous than two names in shades of gray?" he asks. "Three!"

"Three shades of gray?" A tingle patters up my neck.

"My mother's maiden name is now my middle name. Go on, ask me." He doesn't wait for me to ask. "Silver! My name is like a party trick. Ash Silver Sterling at your service." He bows, his hand behind his back.

"You're kidding. A name of three colors?" With his fancy suit and family money, this *can't* be the man I'm to save. Then again, looks often mean nothing. The man who appears to have it all could hold dark secrets.

"What is it?" he asks.

I shake my head and force myself to keep walking. "Nothing. Tell me about the resort. Why is it troubled?"

"The resort is losing money. The first and second floor are luxury guest rooms, and the dining room and ballrooms are always a hit, but we've been bleeding money for two years now. To get in the black, we leased out the third floor to a doctor who uses the mineral springs for medicinal purposes. I suspect the medical goings-on are off-putting to the guests."

"What sort of medical things do they treat?" I've heard of women getting thrown into places like this for being overly sexed or just plain mouthy.

"Who knows?" His offended scoff suggests he's too squeamish to have even evaluated the doctor or his practice. Amateur.

"And your father sent you to do what, exactly?"

He hesitates. "Well, I'm to provide a full report. I'll give recommendations for how to make Hot Lake profitable again."

I wonder if he knows about the psychics who lurk in their midst. Russell didn't need to give me details, that photo told a story. Nothing seems odder to me than a sanitorium right above the wealthy set drinking and dancing the fox trot.

"Look." He reaches for a low bush with bright red domes like gumdrops. "Thimbleberry," he says. "We used to pick these at the lake when I was a boy. We spent summers at our Providence summer home." He pulls a cluster from their stems. Ash holds one up to the sunlight to admire the ruby color.

Without realizing, I've begun to rub my temple. A full day without a reading has already set in.

"Are you unwell?" he asks.

I drop my hand to my side. "A minor headache. They happen from time to time."

"Ah. I've never experienced one myself, but I understand they are quite bothersome."

"You need not concern yourself with my ailments. I've lived with them for years, and your sympathy only aggravates me."

Despite my unnecessary gruffness, he manages a smile, his eyes clear and bright. "Yes, I apologize. I know how aggravating I can be."

I open my mouth as if I could take back the insult, the sharp-tongued whip of a wounded girl who has never had a casual conversation in her life. For once, someone has approached me without the silent tug of darkness. Everyone wants to tear through me with their teeth, chewing what they need without regard to the human attached to their visions. Ash may be the first to let me breathe.

When I step back to the dirt trail, a glowing gold beam shoots from my foot. The forest floor lights with amber light as gold particles float up into the air, then fall like dust. When they land, yellow flecks fade back to the damp, dirt-lined path of a few moments ago.

"Are we ready?" he asks.

An apology rests on my tongue, too afraid to tumble out. "Yes."

We walk for hours. We weave in and out of rainforests and through tunnels of bent trees, over wooden bridges and glittering blue streams. I ask about Ash's life in New York and his travels across the country, trying to discover how I can help him. His older, successful brothers rattle his confidence. One is a lawyer, another a banker. Ash is the only one willing to take over his father's business, but the family disappointment hasn't yet proved himself.

I don't say much, avoiding questions about telling fortunes or my near-death two nights ago. The less he knows, the better.

As afternoon light drops low in the sky, we pass a towering pine tree with a weathered trunk of flaking bark. Ash looks up, hands on his hips. "Douglas fir. They can live for up to seven hundred and fifty years."

"That sounds like a punishment."

"I don't know. There's so much joy in this life. I wouldn't mind another few hundred years."

"Spoken like a rich man."

"You don't like me much, do you?"

"I don't know you, Mr. Sterling. I'm simply protecting myself." Like I do with everyone I meet.

"Understood." He nods like a wise old man. "Who do you trust?"

Not one name or image pops into my mind. Not my selfish mother who brings home a different man every other week, or my father who spent his days owned by a quest for fame and found only the bottom of a syringe. Certainly not Gwendolyn for abandoning me all these years. "No one." I dare to meet his eyes. "I don't trust a single soul."

"Oh." His eyes of pity turn up a wave of shame deep in my belly. "I suppose that isn't the fault of the girl with headaches, but the world who failed to fix them, no?" He smiles, full of surprising innocence. "Under the green light of this forest, your eyes look like a cat's. Faded green, but almost like I can see through them."

He doesn't stare at me as a novelty. The concern in his eyes frays my resolve to keep him at arm's length. He thinks my headaches are an unfortunate malady, and not my own doing. "Perhaps this lonely world does have something to do with my headaches, Mr. Sterling."

"Please, call me Ash."

"A reminder that my name is Primrose and if you call me Rose or Prim, I might just leave you to fend for yourself in the forest." Well, I can't expect to change in one day. This sharp tongue has decades of practice.

He smiles, tucks his hands in his pockets. "Understood."

We continue forward as night descends on this wooded trail that never seems to end. The air swirls around me. The skin on my arms turns to goosebumps and I stop walking.

"What is it?" Ash asks.

"Something's watching us."

Ash crouches and flicks his eyes in all directions. "I don't see anything."

"No, I don't see it. I feel it." Subtle purring buzzes in my ear. The purr grows louder and faster as a headache tightens around my forehead. The sun dips below the horizon, leaving a sea of shadows that swim around us like sharks.

"There," he says. He points to two bright, glowing orbs, yellow like the centers of a chamomile plant. "Oh, hell. I'm city folk. We don't mess with wild animals."

I try to make out the shape around the orbs. A curved hump behind, two points like triangles on top. A puff of hot air clouds from below the eyes and the purring ceases. Silence.

"It's a cougar," I whisper.

The beast dips his head, eyes focused. She bends her legs, prepared to pounce. Ash steps back but I look into the cougar's eyes, and I listen. I've never read an animal, but it's as if the creature has deposited something in my mind.

"Her baby is near." My heart races, thundering in my ears.

Ash spins frantically in circles. "Do we run?"

"Don't turn around," I say. "If you turn your back, she'll pounce."

"How do you know?"

"I just do." Cougar readings, this is new. I've been too busy grappling with my fear of human touch to listen to animals. But here I am, in the Oregon forest on a chilly fall night, next to a strange man, staring at the eyes of an animal that could tear us to shreds in an instant. And somehow, I can feel *everything*.

I step forward and pause. The giant cat dips her head lower.

"We don't want your baby," I say.

Ash mumbles behind me, leaned against a tree trunk. "We're going to die."

"Tell me what to do," I whisper to the fierce, beautiful creature.

The cougar crouches, then hesitates. I forego my no-touch policy, figuring I'd rather read a mountain lion than let her slash her giant claws through my skin.

Trust your visions.

With a trembling hand, I reach for her. Ash grunts behind me.

"What are you doing?" he scream-whispers.

The giant cat launches through the air, claws spread, teeth bared. She screeches—part growl, part hiss—stopping just shy of my feet. My back pressed into the tree, I quiet my breathing, and bite through my fear.

This vision isn't the same. No stars or veil, no yellow road. Just her soul on bare display, offered up for anyone who wishes to look. She escaped a trap a few days ago. The picture is clear in my mind. She can smell humans from far away and has tracked us for the last two miles, teaching her young one how to stalk. She doesn't care to eat us as a family of bunnies hides nearby. I look to the right, indicating where she should follow until she finds the scent.

The cougar, head tilted, licks her lips. She yawns and turns around. Tucked in the shrub behind her, a cub cries for her mama. She saunters to her baby and nudges her to follow. The cat stares at me over her shoulder with one slow blink.

Ash huddles against the tree, face buried in his hands. I gather my footing and catch my breath. "She's gone," I say.

Ash stands, head leaned back against the tree. "What happened? I think I blacked out."

"She changed her mind. Decided we didn't look as tasty as she thought." I stare at my boots that glitter in the moonlight. Who knew reading animal souls was this easy?

"My father is a hunter," he says. "I should have learned how to shoot. If I listened to him and always carried a pistol, I would have known what to do."

"No." My head throbs again, a subtle pounding in my temples. "We wouldn't have killed her. I wouldn't have let you."

Did I do it? Did I save the man with three colors? I presume the answer to that is no, as nothing is ever that easy.

"We can't keep going. It's too dangerous out here." He looks around as if he can see through the inky night dancing with shadows.

My boot's tips flicker pale gold, illuminating an impression in the ground. A circle surrounded by three points pointed forward. I take a step to see another one, and another one.

"Some sort of bird left a trail," I say. I imagine the peacock from Portland but the idea of a peacock loose in the forest would be ridiculous.

"We're going to follow the directions of a bird?" he asks.

"Where's your sense of adventure, Ash?" I veer off the trail and follow the claw prints down a hillside and around boulders. We push through the center of ferns and over rotting logs. A stone cabin sits in the hollow, overgrown with ivy. A bright moon illuminates the house and stream that runs past the crumbling structure.

"Perfect," Ash says. "We can sleep here for the night."

I eye him, hands on my hips.

"I promise, I'll stay far away from you."

"Just remember what the tip of these boots would feel like rammed into your shin. I'll be wearing them all night."

"Noted."

He ascends the stairs, and I follow. The railing feels slick under my hands, the stones stained green as if they're now part of the forest. Through an arched door we enter a room with four walls covered in crawling moss and ivy. Where a roof should connect the peaks, the trees have grown over, branches winding together and dripping with lichen.

"It will have to do," Ash says. He gathers leaves into a pile in the corner. "You can sleep here."

"Alright." I curl on my side on the crunchy leaves and listen to him walk the space to find his bed for the night.

After a few minutes of silence, I say, "You haven't commented on my silver hair. Everyone does."

"Not everyone, it seems."

"Aren't you curious, why my hair shines like polished silver and why my eyes lack any color?"

"Of course. But once you tell me the answer, I won't be curious anymore. And where is the fun in that?"

An owl hoots from a tree branch above as if he's speaking to us. His hoot sounds like, *Who cooks for you,* and I think about my life in a cold basement when there is so much wonder in the world. I would love to be the kind of person who looks at a Douglas Fir and wonders how to live for seven hundred years. The kind of person who wants more life, not less.

"That cougar could have killed us," Ash says. "You didn't seem afraid."

That's because trusting my vision with a territorial cougar is far less terrifying than trusting a vision on any human. "I'm not supposed to be here," I blurt out. "The other night, I hit my head and almost died."

"But here you are."

"Yes, here I am." I roll to my back and stare at the ceiling of trees shading the glittering moonlight.

"Sounds like you *are* supposed to be here," he says. "Perhaps you need a reminder that there is joy in every day, if you look for it."

Cool moss provides a soft cushion for my cheek. The wind whispers through the crumbling stone cottage as I think about Ash's words. I don't see the wonder in the world around me. At least, I haven't until today. And today is as good a time as any to start.

✳✳✳

I wake fully rested after dreams of fairy woodlands and forest sprites, peacocks and steaming lakes.

The cottage is empty.

Maybe Ash carried on by himself. The man has three colors in his name. Does this mean I must trail after him like a puppy, on the lookout for every potential danger? How exhausting.

"Good morning." Ash yells from the stream below.

More exhausting hovering, it appears.

I walk down the steps and take in the clear morning. The foliage drips and rustles and cracks—like the forest has its own language. Ash is freshening up with the icy water.

"Do you get the feeling this forest is special?" I ask.

He shakes his hands and pats his face. "Special? A cougar tried to kill us, and we slept on a bed of greasy stones that stained my suit. And that scuffle yesterday made me lose my favorite fedora. So, no."

My dress remains powder blue and smooth.

"We need to get to the resort," he says. "Father will be furious that I'm late."

"It isn't your fault the train broke down."

"Everything is my fault." He sighs. "You ready for another day of walking?"

Much as I want to stay in this magical nook of trees, I have a journey to take. "Ready."

Ash limps for a few steps.

"Are you okay?" I ask.

"Blisters. Damn shoes are shiny and sleek but are not meant for forest treks." He points to my boots. "I would think your feet would be screaming, walking in those things. They look like witch boots."

"Perhaps they are." I turn from him and clamber up the hill to the path. All the bird prints are gone this morning, leaving the pale morning light pooled on the dirt path.

Ash grunts and slides back several times as I stifle a laugh watching him struggle. A bird bounces on a thin branch next to my head. He lets me rub his head, unafraid of human touch. Bright yellow light shoots from the tip of my boots, and a watery image appears. A farmhouse, white with a large porch, and a young man in a rocking chair who stares at his feet.

The image evaporates. For some reason, my chest aches. Am I reading forest animals and conjuring my future now?

"Another day on this wretched trail." Ash wipes his hands on his pants.

"Shall we?" I ask.

We walk again for hours, Ash searching every corner for wild animals. Other than an owl hooting from a ponderosa branch, the walk is uneventful.

"I think we'll come across a farmhouse," I say.

"In the forest?" He swats away a dragonfly.

"Just a feeling."

Ash leans against a tree to catch his breath. "You must be in desperate need of a holiday to travel all this way by yourself."

"Indeed, I am." I peel a slab of bark from a trunk and crumble it in my fingers. "This elusive doctor might be able to help some aches and pains." And mental exhaustion from my feckless psychic powers.

"In a way, he's my answer too," Ash says. "Father demands I turn a profit, and the doctor's practice brings in money, so I must work with him."

I've flown through many visions of want and desire, and I know that for most people, there is never enough money. Ash wants more than riches though. He needs approval. He seems like a lost little boy in the body of a strapping young man.

We navigate over boulders and under vine maples with the slightest tinge of red at their leaf tips. A waterfall rushes somewhere nearby as we breathe in the chilled misty air in this shadowed patch of forest hidden somewhere in the Hood River Valley.

"You look to be enjoying this," he says.

"I am also a city girl. Not really by choice." I should have lived out here with the animals and the trees. No one asks me for anything out here.

We follow the well-worn dirt trail, the only indicator that we aren't meandering in the wrong direction. The trail leads us to a stream which Ash uses inlaid stones to step across to the other side. He extends his hand to help me across.

I stare at his hand, knowing that his touch will change everything. I will see into his soul and discover something terrible to fix and it's too soon for that.

"It's only a little water." I take a running leap across the stream, my boots landing in a patch of feather grass dotted with drops of moisture like teardrops.

Ash straightens his jacket. "I was merely trying to be a gentleman."

Honestly, why are men such fragile creatures? I ignore him and trudge through the tall waving grass. As we crest a hill, we meet endless rows of plants. Taller than the two of us combined, the giant creeping greenery climbs up around stakes planted in the ground.

"Ah," Ash says. "A hop farm. Splendid."

He enters a row, and I follow, staring up at the golden and lime-colored leaves and their soft cones dangling from the vines. We pass through the hops to rows of corn stalks and a grove of apple trees.

A scarecrow stands among the stalks, arms propped up by poles. Ash examines the straw-stuffed figure. "Poor chap. They couldn't even paint his eyes straight."

Through another endless row of corn, I glimpse a farmhouse. White with a wraparound porch, just as in my vision. "Maybe they'll know how to get to Hot Lake."

I speed up, my boots taking on a life of their own. The man sits on the rocking chair, just as I knew he'd be. "Excuse me," I say as we approach the steps, but the boy doesn't move. "Hello?"

He still doesn't move. Is he sleeping? I gingerly step onto the porch. Silence. The farmer seems near my age. The sun has tanned his skin, and his caramel tinted hair falls over his cheek, hiding his face.

"Excuse me." I soften my steps and creep closer. "What's your name?"

His high cheekbones catch the light. My stomach tightens at the site of his profile. I want to move his hair and tuck it behind his ear, but I know better.

He turns to me, shoulders slumped but gaze fierce. One blue eye. The other green and brown.

Another three-colored man.

Chapter Six

Soft pink blossoms from a crabapple tree shade the boy's face, but they do little to soften his intense stare. His hair resembles an overgrown shrub that needs pruning, and his multicolored eyes could be glass marbles for the way they reflect the light. Something flips in my belly, a yearning I've rarely felt. Maybe this time, I'm drawn to *his* darkness.

I can't seem to turn away. Neither can he.

"My name is Primrose Whittaker," I say. "We're in need of a place to rest."

He stands slowly and lifts an ax in the air which sends my heart into my throat, but he lays the handle on his shoulder. One more long stare and he walks around me, down the steps past Ash without a glance, and into the orchard.

"Chatty fellow," Ash says.

I lean over the wood railing and watch his shoulders tighten and ripple as he slings the ax. Sweat beads on his tanned neck. He stops chopping and glances over his shoulder, directly at me. My heart leaps into my throat, and I spin away to catch my breath.

Ash climbs the steps, fanning his flushed cheeks. "Nothing like a brisk walk to get your heart pumping."

The screen door creaks open and a tall man in overalls steps out. "Morning," he says.

"Good morning, kind sir," Ash says. "We're on an adventure that has quickly turned long and uncomfortable. Would you allow us a brief rest here?"

He nods. "Come in. I've got plenty of cider."

"Splendid." Ash takes an exaggerated step forward into the house.

I sneak another glance at the man with the messy hair.

"His name is Finn," the man says.

He stands next to me at the railing, and we watch him chop wood like a machine. No grunts, no rests. He doesn't even stop to throw all that copper hair out of his face.

"Is he all right?" I ask.

"In a matter of speaking. Finn came to live with me last year."

I don't push him. I don't need to touch either of them to know this entire house functions under a cloud of sadness. The sun-drenched field isn't enough to offset the past these two men carry around their necks.

"He's my nephew." He sighs, which fades to a grimace. "We lost family."

My chest aches for him. I watch the way Finn chops without emotion, and realize he isn't a machine. He's angry and hurt. "That's heartbreaking."

"My brother is gone." He rubs his eyes which redden but do not produce tears. "So now Finn lives here. He's a fine farmhand, but he doesn't speak much. And he refuses to cut his hair."

I've seen people try to wade through this kind of tragedy—their souls are so quiet and cold. The pain of their past is too great. Sometimes their starry night has turned to ice, an eternal winter. I need to help him thaw. Help him find the light in all that darkness.

I have no power. Not yet. "Thank you for offering your home to us."

"Come in, cider is nice and warm."

We enjoy spiced apple juice from mason jars and fresh biscuits with whipped butter. A welcome treat after nothing but berries and river water.

"Where're you two headed?" he asks.

"Hot Lake Resort," Ash says.

"There are hot springs that treat various ailments," I say.

"Is that what you're going for?" he asks.

Among other things. "I have headaches."

"It's no doubt with those eyes of yours. Clear as crystal. They must let in all the light."

Most people just stare, slack jawed. I appreciate his forwardness. "Yes, they're uncomfortable."

He stretches and rests his thumbs in the straps of his overalls. "We all come to this world exactly as we are meant to be."

A farmer with an old soul. I bet his starry night is calm and bright. I want to peek inside. Why I burn to fly through souls is puzzling. Nothing but pain rests there, yet the truth of the stars is close to home. I suppose I hope to find the ones with joy—but they never seem to call me.

"And why are you going to the hot springs?" he asks Ash.

"Oh me?" He swigs the last of his cider and slams the glass to the table a little too loudly. "I'm the money. I'm going to check on my, um, my father's investment."

"Hmm." The farmer stands and watches Finn from the window. "I've heard of Hot Lake. The Natives called it the Valley of Peace. Healing waters meant no one was to fight on that land."

I lean back in my chair and glimpse Finn who's stripped to his white tank top. He slides his hand through his hair, and I tip back in the chair farther, teetering on two legs so I can trace the line of his muscular shoulders. He cracks the ax into a stump and walks off. Before I realize how I've twisted my torso to watch him go, I fall to my backside, my chair crashing to the floor.

"Careful, now," the farmer says.

Ash rushes to my side.

"I'm fine," I say. I stand and straighten my dress, cheeks flushed hot and mortified.

Finn thuds into the kitchen from the back porch. He stares at us without expression, watching me stand and fix the chair. When his gaze settles on me, I detect the slightest shift in his expression. An almost imperceptible head tilt, as if he wants to laugh at me.

"Finn, these fine folks are headed east. To see a doctor at Hot Lake Resort." The farmer hands him a mason jar of cinnamon-spiked cider.

Finn says nothing. He returns to the back porch and shuts the door behind him.

"Do you think the resort could help my nephew?" the farmer asks. "I don't know what I believe about healing water, but he needs people his age. He deserves more than working my farm until his fingers bleed."

"All walks of life enjoy the baths," Ash says. "There's dancing and horseback riding." Ash is looking to stuff his hotel with every willing person he meets. He'll do anything to impress his father, even bilking this poor man out of cash. But Ash places his hand on his chest and bows. "He can be my personal guest. I'll make sure we have a room for him free of charge. I'll even cover his meals."

Nobody offers things like that without a motive, do they?

Ash clears his throat. "That is, if he wants to join us?"

We glance out the window at the back of Finn's head. "I think deep down we all want more friends," the farmer says. "And a break may do him good." He claps his hands together. "Now, you'll stay here for the night. I've got plenty of room and I can't send you back out there without a proper supper."

"Thank you," I say. "We never caught your name."

"The name's Uncle Henry. That's what everyone calls me."

***

As afternoon peaks and the sun lowers in the sky, I slip onto the back porch to watch the birds swoop over the fields. Two men, both three-colored. One in name and the other in eyes. By trying to force an answer to my problem, I walked right into the riddle. And now I have two potential men to save and even fewer answers than before. I twirl the blue ribbon holding my braid, remembering Finn's gaze and how I fell to the floor staring at him. What is wrong with me?

The trees rustle in the late afternoon breeze that carries the soft scent of jasmine. So different from the city with all this space and greenery and fruit.

The door opens. Uncle Henry wipes his hands on a blue and white checkered dish towel. "Would you mind going around back to the cellar to grab a jar of peas?"

"Certainly."

I step down into the cellar slowly. The dark, cool underground reminds me of my basement room on Gale Street. I tap the stone walls in search of the shelves, carefully patting my hands around in the dark. Damn clear eyes.

I blink a few times until my vision adjusts. Ah, shelves. Through a shadow, Finn steps into the light of the cellar, hammer in hand.

My heart lurches. "Finn. You scared me half to death." What a ridiculous saying that is. I've been nearly dead for years. "Uncle Henry sent me for peas."

He reaches past me for a glass jar on the highest shelf, the heat from his chest radiating close to me in pulses. He hands me the jar without a smile.

"Thanks." I grasp it, careful not to touch his fingers.

He doesn't look away.

"Did you want to say something to me?"

He shakes his head no. His eyes still glow bright and glassy. From his copper hair to his sun-kissed skin, it's like he's been dipped in gold. I should walk away and leave him to his work, but the cool air is comforting. His silence is almost like its own conversation.

"You know, most people talk too much," I say. "Most never know when to shut up."

He doesn't quite smile but something shifts in his eyes.

I almost touch his hand just to get a glimpse of his starry night. Two whole days without a vision leaves me with an odd itch to once again walk a honeycomb road. Besides, my headache is thumping something fierce now.

"I fled Portland to find Hot Lake Resort." Shut up, Primrose. He doesn't care. "Have you heard of it?" He doesn't react but oh, those eyes.

He shakes his head.

"I just found out about it." I swing my foot side to side, glancing down at the way my boots sparkle in the dark. When I look back up, he's tucked his hair behind his ear. I've never noticed someone's cheekbones before but his rest high and pronounced, like a little shelf to display his eyes. "I'm very grateful for the rest here though."

Ash stumbles past the cellar, swatting away flies. Finn points to him with a questioning look.

"Me and Ash? No." I shake my head, trying not to scream that he has it wrong. "No. Just friends on a journey."

He examines my hair and furrows his brow. I would usually run my fingers through the tips and make a smart comment to shame them for staring. Not with him. I *like* his stare. I never want it to stop.

That's a new one.

He doesn't need to hear your life story. "Well, I'll leave you to your work. Thank you for this." I hold up the jar.

Finn returns to his project.

Hand shading my eyes, I peek at the ground to find my way back to the house. We're somewhere in Hood River, only an hour from the city, but the sun is nothing like the dreary gray skies of Portland. I bring the jar to Uncle Henry in the kitchen. He's preparing stew for supper and smiles when I arrive. "Thank you, kindly."

I lean against the window as he cooks. "You have a beautiful property here."

"It's been in my family for quite some time. I like to think this land holds a bit of magic."

With Finn's eyes and the apricot sunshine, I'm inclined to agree. "How far are we from Hot Lake?"

"Oh, quite a way. You have a bit of a journey left to take, don't you?" He winks and I'm unsure how to take it.

Uncle Henry removes his towel from his shoulder and wipes his hands. "Finn's been so hard on himself. I hear him on the rooftop some nights." He throws the towel down and rubs his temples. "I want more for him."

"Maybe he just needs to trust the world again." I say it as if it's easy, or even possible.

The familiar spider crawl skitters across my forehead. *Oh no.*

"I'm all the poor kid has left."

Uncle Henry's soul beckons me. His aching forehead becomes mine. His pounding heart thumps in my ears. That itch I felt earlier demands to be scratched. I touch his hand and for a moment, I think maybe I've lost my powers. But then, his soul sucks my psychic self through the colorless tunnel, hard and fast until my boots pierce the film into my vision.

I land on the spongy yellow beeswax and I'm home, this time with the sweet scent of apple trees and cinnamon cider. I don't see an end to my yellow road, so I meander through the trees and touch the feather-light poppy petals, as their black centers seem to wink at me. The sun is bright, but my eyes welcome the color.

Pink blossoms fall from the trees, and I never want to leave. But then the yellow road ends. I teeter on the edge, staring down past my toes to the great expanse of stars below my feet. Uncle Henry's voice echoes, "Finn? Finn?"

Like every itch, you can only ignore it for so long. Arms out, I swan dive into the golden twinkling of light. My stars welcome me home.

A vision emerges through the black. Finn and myself in a room of emerald light and green marble. I run my fingers through his hair. He brings my hand to his cheek and whispers my name. *Primrose.*

My head swims and fingertips tingle, more than usual while floating in the stars. My chest expands like a hot air balloon.

Uncle Henry appears. A watery figure in the distance. "He's ailing from a broken heart," he says. "I'm not sure it will ever mend."

Finn leans to kiss me, but the stars drop me back to the dark, where I tumble and bounce until I'm spit out and shot back to my body, hand on Uncle Henry's. Breathless, I struggle for words, my hot neck suffocating all my thoughts.

"Are you okay?" he asks. "You went silent for a moment there. Your eyes rolled back in your head."

I've always known my visions turn me zombie-like for a few moments. It usually scares the life out of people. But not Uncle Henry. "Fine, thank you." Why did I see myself in this farmer's vision?

He pulls out a chair. "Please, sit. You're flushed."

"Uncle Henry?" He tilts his head, patiently waiting for my question. "Don't you get lonely out here?"

"Oh, well." He puffs out his lips with a big exhale. "Hard to be lonely with all this life around. I have critters and creatures to keep me company and crops to tend to. Birds whistle me awake while the creaks in this old house remind me of all the family and friends who've passed through here on their way to something special."

"That's lovely." I've always taken solace in the starry nights of souls for which there is no love or family.

"Here's the thing, Miss Primrose." His gray wisps of hair flutter at his temples as the breeze flies through the open window. "Home is a feeling, not a place. It's a little corner of Earth you carve out for yourself where the goings-on of the world rest far away. This farmhouse has been home for many travelers. I hope that for even one night, they'll know a touch of the peace I live in."

"Can't say that I've ever been home, then."

He smiles with the softness of a man who's seen devastation but chooses not to let it break him. "You will."

Ash barrels through the door. "Why are there so many god-forsaken flies here?"

"They like to harass the city folk." Uncle Henry winks at me before returning to chopping carrots. "Don't seem to bother me none."

Ash checks his watch, which he's done every two minutes since arriving. "My father must be beside himself that I'm out here gallivanting while I should be working."

"Gallivanting? Aren't you fleeing cougars and fending off God-forsaken flies?" I bite back a smile.

He points a thumb toward Uncle Henry. "Like he said, I'm city folk."

Uncle Henry drops the knife on the butcher block. "Heard from the neighbor that the train was up and moving again. I think you can catch one tomorrow after a good night's rest."

Can't this be my adventure? I could watch the sunshine flood the fields from the inviting rocker on the porch. The warm scent of chicken stew and thyme fills every corner of this farmhouse like a welcome sign.

"Fine," Ash says. "But I shall stay indoors for the remainder of the day."

"That's probably best," I say.

At our late afternoon supper, the open windows carry the sweet scent of pine. Ash tells us of his father's gun collection while Uncle Henry nods along. I try not to watch Finn, so quiet and stoic, but I'm pulled to him like a rushing river down a waterfall—no choice but to tumble down.

"Finn here has the best eye for weather." Uncle Henry holds his spoon in mid-air, stopping to swallow his recent bite, as if he has all the time in the world. "He's worked hard and helped me rest my old bones. I've very proud of him."

Finn looks up at us through the strands of hair. After a glance around the table, he nods once. A subtle acknowledgement of Uncle Henry's compliment.

Ash clinks his fork to his plate so gently I almost don't notice that he's staring at the two men in admiration. "Nothing better than that." His voice breaks, a little higher than normal.

We continue in silence, scooping up big bites of stew and cornbread, washing them down with iced apple cider. Some leaves outside the kitchen window have turned. Butter yellow and apple red. A delicious warmth spreads through me. There is no darkness at this table to beckon my mind, leaving me open to taste the sweet silence of togetherness.

After dinner, we all move around the kitchen, clearing plates and wiping crumbs from the table. Finn almost brushes my arm, and I nearly let him. With the kitchen clean, Uncle Henry shoos us to the front porch for a bite of divinity candy made by his neighbor at the next farm over.

We bite silently into this cloudlike ball of sugar as a warm wind flutters the leaves on the apple trees, blowing a few stray yellow ones to the dirt. Uncle Henry plays a sad tune on his harmonica. No one person is staring at my hair. All these men are too busy looking off into the orchard, lost in their own dreams and regrets.

"The quiet does nothing to distract my thoughts," Ash says.

"That's exactly why I love it." Uncle Henry lowers his harmonica to his lap and enjoys the last piece of candy, making sure we all had our fill first.

Finn leans back in his chair which creaks against the old porch. He stretches his arms and places his hands behind his neck, his satisfied sigh indicating he agrees with Uncle Henry. He likes the silence too.

Ash leans forward, elbows on his knees, contemplating this place. "What say you, Primrose?" he asks. "Does the silence heal or hurt?"

All eyes turn to me in silent waiting. I dust my hands of the sticky divinity and look at the three men. "Both."

We retire to our bedrooms for a long rest. Just after sundown, a knock rattles my door. I open it to find Ash, scratching his temple. "You don't find this quiet unsettling?"

Still stuck on our earlier conversation, he seems to need my reassurance out here in the dark of night. "I don't know, I find this place entirely homey."

He shakes his head. "Some bug keeps rattling in the trees, and I'm fairly certain animal paws crunched hay outside my window. That cougar stole my fedora, and what am I to do now without a complete suit? We must get on that train tomorrow and find civilization." He slicks back his hair. "Before we encounter something truly ridiculous, like flying monkeys."

"Your blue fedora might be gone, but I'm sure Uncle Henry has a spare cowboy hat you could borrow."

He chuckles with raised eyebrows. "A cowboy hat? With this jacket? No, no, no. I want my fedora back. It was quite expensive."

"I'm certain it would block the sun just the same."

"It's not at all the same."

He's lonely, I surmise. This young aristocrat probably sleeps with an entire staff underfoot, ready to attend to his every need. Here, we really are alone with our thoughts. "Are you going to be okay tonight? Do I need to read you a bedtime story?"

He cocks his head, but I understand him. He wouldn't want me remarking on his fear or identifying the lonely boy he seems to hide under a fancy suit and big opinions. So, I chose humor, and I think it works.

"Childhood rhymes are more frightening than silence." He grimaces, an exaggerated attempt to make me smile. It works.

"Good night, Ash. And I'm glad you're along for my adventure."

He smooths his lapels and bows. "Perhaps you are on *my* adventure."

I shut the door and think of the fantastical creatures I've encountered thus far. How and why did I develop the ability to interpret the unspoken words of cougar? The world felt different the moment I laced up these boots. Still, the question lingers… who must I to save? Ash or Finn.

I tap my toes together, remembering the almost-dead Primrose of three nights ago. A cluster of light appears out my window. Sparkly and dancing, the emerald-colored dots seem to wink at me, so I crawl out to the balmy night with the crickets and beetles and hooting owls.

The buoyant creatures flicker into the cornfield with long rows of tall, green stalks as far as the eye can see. I tiptoe after them, hoping it's Gwendolyn with some sort of wisdom for me… though I'm not holding my breath.

I'm standing in a swarm of dragonflies. Their bodies seem to catch the moonlight, which I find curious because I've never known them to glow in the dark.

Bright metallic spots cover the ground and cornstalks, then dance into the sky. I extend my hand to grab one, but they move like fish caught in a current, as they bounce and quiver. They're playing with me.

A smile takes hold as I spin in their light. I skip up and down the row of corn as the cool breeze tickles my neck. My boots flicker through the luminescent night, and I think my heart could dance like this forever.

In one swift thud, the light disappears, leaving me alone in a field with no insects to speak of. I could have dreamed it, but the joy felt so real.

Down the long row of corn a silhouette hovers of the farmhouse backlit by the giant silvery moon. In the center of the circle, the figure of a lonely man.

Finn.

Drawn to his perch high above the farm, I find the ladder leaning against the second story roofline. I consider leaving him alone, but my boots seem to carry me up the rungs. When I step onto the roof, Finn's eyes grow wide. He uncrosses his arms, pressing his hands into the roof shingles.

"Can I sit with you?" I ask.

He nods.

I lower next to him, the wood slats creaking under our weight. We stare together at the fields behind the house, lined by trees with fading leaves. "Fall is here, it seems," I say. "The colors here are something else."

I turn to see him staring at my hair. He inspects it, looking from the moon and back to me.

"That's the one good thing about this hair." I pull a lock through my fingers and watch it float in the balmy air. "In the moonlight, I positively glow."

Finn smiles for the first time since I've met him—a closed-mouth grin that changes the shape of his cheeks.

"Would you believe me if I told you my silver hair and clear eyes give me a mirror into your soul?"

He grins for the second time in thirty seconds, and I think I've found my new purpose in life—to make him smile. He props his elbows on his knees and takes in the heady spring air.

"Are you happy here, Finn?"

He shrugs, an answer in itself. He looks at me and raises his eyebrows.

"Me? No, I've never been happy." I catch myself. "I mean, not really."

He nods in understanding.

"Your Uncle Henry thinks you might want to join us at Hot Lake."

He turns away and stares at the ground below.

"We'd be happy to have you with us. The eccentric resort could be good for you." I lean forward to catch his eyes. "If that's what you want."

My heart catches in my throat with a soft flutter. His eyes turn serious. If I were bold, my hand might wander to his temple, where my fingers would glide through his thick mop of hair.

His starry night isn't beckoning me. No, I *want* to touch him. I ache for it. Of all the emotions I've feared, I never imagined I'd get to experience this one.

It's somehow too much and not enough all at once, so I stand and lose my footing, but recover just as he reaches for me, nearly touching my hand. "Clumsiness and rooftops don't mix," I say with a nervous laugh.

On a flat section of roof over the attic window, we face each other, staring into each other's eyes. He's close enough that I can smell his skin. Crisp pine from all that wood he's chopped. His cheeks glisten under the moon, and his blue eye catches the light.

"Good night, Finn."

He hovers close to me without breaking his stare, but then he exhales and softens his shoulders. "It's not that I can't talk. I just choose not to." He shrugs. "Everything is easier that way."

His voice rings high and clear, not the deep sound I expected. He spoke to me because he wanted to.

"I hope you'll be on the train with us tomorrow. It would be a lonely adventure without you."

Feeling soft and fragile and not at all like I welcomed death the other night, I step away and descend the ladder, catching a final glimpse of his smile on my way down. My chest pulses and I begin to see how life is full of surprises when you aren't marching toward death.

I crawl back through my window and turn off my oil lamp. My cheeks hurt from smiling so hard. I hear a tap at my window and dip my head out to see dragonflies spread far and wide, like a thousand metallic eyes blinking at me. Their lit bodies migrate together and flicker into the orchard.

Uncle Henry is right, this place is magic.

I fall into a soft, hazy sleep, holding tight to the enchantment of this farm. My thoughts hover on the lightness of fantastical creatures and a quiet man backlit by moonlight. I don't let myself exhale because the next breath might bring me back to Earth.

Chapter Seven

As I drink in the last of the orchard-kissed breeze from the front porch, I imagine what this Hot Lake will look like. Boiling lake water to rid ourselves of ailments. Why are there psychics there, and why didn't Russell want me to go? The lifelong quest for a community, friends, some kind of knowledge over the wild of psychic life—it all awaits to unfold. How I wish to stay here at this farmhouse, drinking cider and watching the days roll by. Alas, I remind myself, there is no peace while my powers control me.

Uncle Henry prepares a delicious breakfast to send us on our way. Finn doesn't come downstairs, and I want to hold on to the feeling I had last night on the rooftop. His voice and his smile and the way I swooned like a silly teenager.

Ash steps onto the porch and takes a deep inhale. "Goodbye dirty, dusty, fly-infested nature. I will not miss you." He turns, expecting me to smile. When I don't, he says, "Well, the people I might miss."

I lean back and stretch my arms against the railing. "We can tolerate anywhere if the ones we love are there." Imagine having people to love.

"You haven't complained of a headache this entire time. Are you certain you need healing?"

I crawl my fingers along my silver braid. "There's a universe of things you don't see or understand, Ash."

"I admit that I find women to be… an enigma."

"We aren't so complicated. We just want to be seen, like you do."

He nods, an accepting, contemplative motion. "Do you think Finn will join us?"

My vision showed us at the resort in a near-kiss. "I hope so."

Ash props his foot on the base of the porch railing. "A week at a Sterling resort should perk him right up. Hotels and relaxation are our game."

He's become a caricature before my eyes. His stance, his forced posture. The ridiculous tagline. "Ash, your father isn't here. You can be yourself."

He drops his foot to the porch, smoothing the lapels of his cream jacket with the pang of embarrassment in his eyes.

Uncle Henry steps onto the porch. He sighs and shakes his head an exaggerated no. "Finn doesn't want to be a bother."

He'd rather stay here in his prison of silence on his lonely rooftop. But we had a moment. He looked at me. And my visions are never wrong. I steady my voice, hoping my cheeks haven't blushed. "He would be a welcome companion."

Uncle Henry hands me a basket. "I prepared some food for your trip. My late wife always did this for guests, and I don't want her disappointed with me from the beyond, so here you go." He hands me the lidded basket with a gingham towel peeking out the side.

"I'm sorry about your wife, Uncle Henry."

"Oh, well. Em's the reason I keep going. She loved that boy in there." He sighs and turns so Ash won't hear. "I wish he'd take a break from this place for a little while."

I reach for his wrist. This is the beauty of my brand of magic. Once I see inside his starry night, I can touch for a short while as a normal person would. Nothing new to see… until there's something new to see.

Uncle Henry nods and jangles the keys in his pocket. "Ever been in a model T pickup?" he asks Ash.

"No, sir. We're more of a Rolls-Royce family. But if it carries me to an enclosed train out of this sun, I'm certain I will love it."

"Come on, son. Let's get you back to civilization."

I peek through the windows and fight the urge to go grab Finn and force him to come with us. *Stupid Primrose, you can't force anyone to do anything.* But I can't leave without saying goodbye.

I walk around the back of the house just as Finn steps outside, my heart thumping in my ears. He meets me in the patch of groundcover at the foot of the steps, then leans against the railing, arms crossed, and head hung low.

"You aren't coming with us?" I ask.

After a glance past me, he shakes his head.

"Oh." I swallow against the lump in my throat, clinging to my vision but not wanting to scare him. "I came to say goodbye then."

He untangles his arms. I linger my gaze on his deep copper hair and his tanned skin against those eyes that remind me of a postcard I bought once of Crater Lake on a summer's day. Vibrant grass alongside placid water. I don't want to leave him.

He reaches for my hair, and I panic. What is he doing? Doesn't he know what will happen? No, of course he doesn't. I can't leave without a peek into his soul, so I don't flinch when he pulls a pink blossom from my hair. I reach for it and allow my fingers to curve around his surprisingly soft hand. His soul tugs at me as his starry night whispers and sings. I don't let go.

My psychic body flies into a vision, through the black tunnel. But this time, it's sprinkled with light. No howling wind or frigid air. I land on my spongy honeycomb, petals of apple blossoms floating around my feet. The bright red poppies grow tall—as tall as me. They arch overhead, forming a tunnel. Blooms drop by elongated stems and tickle my face. One pushes my back until I stumble forward. Another pushes me, and another, until the tunnel grows smaller, forcing me on hands and knees.

I crawl until I reach the end of the road, the poppies taking over my vision like bursts of red flames. Through the stems, I fall into the stars. The flickering lights bounce and toss me into the dark. I fall fast and land with a thud, but something catches me.

Finn. Tricolored eyes, a giant smile, and hair trimmed.

"I'm here," he says. "Stay with me."

He holds my hand, and we walk along my road that is no longer honeycomb, but bright yellow bricks the color of sunshine, not a red poppy in sight.

"Where am I?" I ask.

"You're home, where the truth doesn't lie. Now hold on and don't give up on me."

The ground gives way, and I plummet through the darkness again, until I'm back on the very real Earth, my hand still on Finn's. Remnants of my fall through the stars pound like a hammer to my skull.

My stomach aches, and my heart hurts, and all I want is to keep him close. Why is my mouth dry? I squeeze tight against the crushed blossom that burns hot in my hand.

"What just happened?" Finn asks.

Breathless, I can't slow my heart rate. That vision felt like it was happening to me. "I just…" I swallow against the dry ache in my throat. "Nothing. A little lightheadedness."

He shifts one step closer. "You don't need me tagging along on your adventure."

Oh, but I do. "You wouldn't be tagging along. You'd be a welcome friend."

He looks to the treetops, squinting in the sunlight. "A week at soaking pools, playing croquet and pretending to know how to fox trot sounds tedious." He sighs. "But you aren't tedious. I enjoy talking with you."

"Don't come along for me." Please do. Please stay close and fill my days with smiles and heart flutters. "Come because you deserve a break. You work nonstop here."

He shrugs. "I'm comfortable here."

Uncle Henry honks the horn, so I gather myself. I want to convince him, but there could be psychics there with answers. I need to focus on myself. That's hard to do when touch suddenly seems possible. I smile through a hitched breath. "Goodbye, Finn."

I stumble to the front of the house, leaning against the peeling paint of the wood slats to steady myself. I lift the basket from the porch and drop the crumbled pink petals to the dirt. Ash motions for me to sit up front with Uncle Henry between frustrated glances at the sun. I get in and hold back tears.

I guess Finn isn't the one to save.

The truck rumbles and bounces even though we haven't moved yet. Uncle Henry fiddles with something under the hood. A door slams. Finn stands on the front porch with a sack slung around his shoulder.

Uncle Henry shuts the hood and slides into the driver's seat. "Looks like someone changed his mind."

Finn jumps on the truck bed next to Ash. He glances over his shoulder and flashes me a closed-mouth smile.

I bite my lip, trying to control the joy that balloons in my chest. The yellow leaves of fruit trees wave in the breeze and the stalks of corn and hops fade toward their winter slumbers. I could breathe here. Uncle Henry drives away from the farmhouse.

Finn told me I was home. Perhaps I could be.

＊＊＊

After a short, bumpy ride along the Oregon side of the Columbia River, we arrive at a no name station as Mt. Hood's snow-tipped peak sparkles in the distance. With a working rail line, Hot Lake is mere hours away, and lingering questions about these three-colored men hover over me, warning that answers must be found.

Ash and Finn look around in contemplative silence while I watch their body movements and subtle changes to their expressions, hoping beyond reason to discover which of them I'm to save without having to fly through their sad, sad souls.

"Here we are," Uncle Henry motions to the platform of the train station with one bench under a rusted tin shade, and an empty booth with long gone windowpanes. As if time has forgotten this place. "I've purchased tickets for all of you," Uncle Henry says.

"Thank you, that's very kind," I say.

Uncle Henry scratches at his cheek and motions to Finn, who sits on a bench staring toward the field beyond the tracks. "Please take care of him. He's all I have left."

Finn's hands rest together on his lap, the muscles in his arms lean and pronounced. The unease in his eyes. "I will."

Uncle Henry points to Ash, who glances between his shiny gold watch and down the length of the railroad, impatience returning to his every breath. "Think Mr. Real Estate will find what he's looking for at Hot Lake?"

"I hope we all do," I say.

A train thumps along the curve from beyond the trees, screeching into the tiny station. A thick metal hook connects five compact cars with faded green velvet curtains tucked behind tall windows. The conductor waits at the helm, eyes firmly on his watch.

"Go on, now." Uncle Henry extends his hand to the door in the first car. Ash steps up first and reaches for me, but I cough and clasp my hands together.

"Fine, yes, I know." Ash rolls his eyes. "You're capable." He turns and I follow into the empty car. Warm air sticks to my skin. Clean leather seats appear untouched, their nail head trim shining in the light.

Ash falls into a seat, and I sit across from him. I open the window to watch Uncle Henry say goodbye to Finn.

"You come home any time you want, son."

Finn nods. He looks at me and I smile, hand above my eyes to shade the blinding light. "Thank you."

"Remember," Uncle Henry says. "Underneath all the ugly of this world hides a little something beautiful. You just have to find it."

Finn embraces his uncle but remains tall and rigid. He pauses at the train before stepping into the car.

Ash waves him over. "Come on, Finn. Let me tell you about the resort."

Finn lifts his chin and looks Ash straight in the eyes. He walks down the aisle with an exaggerated heel to toe, his boots tapping the metal floor in perfect rhythm.

I scoot toward the window and glance at the seat next to me. Finn lowers himself down and leans back against the leather. His jaw twitches as he clenches his teeth, seemingly overwhelmed with the train and his new friends who are eager to get to know him.

I almost touch Finn's knee to settle his nerves, but catch myself just in time, pretending to stretch my arms out. What the hell? I don't go around touching people like a normal person.

If Finn notices my slip up, he doesn't let on.

I lean out the window and smile at Uncle Henry as the train rumbles forward. He holds his palm up, his arm still as we roll out of sight. I remember the last train that exploded into copper tubing and grab my seat reflexively. Speed increases, and wheels clack along the rails, but the inside ride seems to glide along like butter off a hot spoon.

Gold braid trims the curtains that flutter in the breeze. Stained inlaid glass panels cast a subtle pistachio hue over the car interior. Dangling from the tassels are vibrant green and blue beads… in the shape of a peacock feather.

Ash clears his throat. "Scenery does not interest me." He leaps up and moves to the seat in front of us. "Want to know a secret about the resort?

We both lean closer.

"The doctor that leases the third floor has some odd practices. Things we haven't seen anywhere." Ash crosses his arms over the seatback and rests his chin on his hands. "The hot springs treat all sorts of things. People soak in them for rheumatism and drink them for stomach ailments. He brings experimental drugs from all over the world." He leans back. "So the rumors say."

"Do his practices work?" I ask.

"Who knows? We call him The Wizard."

Ash doesn't seem to know that psychics gather there. I hope they do. "And what are you going to do when you meet this wizard?" I ask.

Ash stretches his arms. "I'm going to find out why occupancy is down, and I will—" He scratches his temple then remembers his thought. "Act accordingly."

I can only assume those were his father's words. I hope he can see he is more than his father's view of him. He's also the kind man who didn't mock my appearance. He's the kind of man to offer Finn a free stay at his resort.

A mysterious doctor who uses volcanic water and strange drugs. I try to imagine what Russell went through, and how he came to live with hooded eyes and chest pain. Perhaps that's the price we pay to change who we are.

"I'm curious to see this boiling lake," Ash says. "How does such a thing happen?"

Finn clears his throat. "Water seeps into deep underground pools where it's heated by magma."

Ash smiles. "You spoke," He slaps him on the shoulder. "Well done, chap."

"I speak fine. I simply choose my interactions carefully."

"Well, I can appreciate that." Ash considers him. "Magma heated water? Who ever heard of such a thing?"

"You can't live in Oregon without having at least heard of them," I say. "I dipped in Breitenbush once when we were on tour."

Their raised eyebrows make me instantly regret my big mouth. I never slip like that.

"On tour?" Ash shimmies his shoulders. "Are you a musician or dancer?" He gasps with excitement. "A Vaudeville performer?"

Still reeling, I consider lying to hide anything personal, but that has only ever made me miserable. "Not that impressive." I search for a way out, a partial truth I can tell, but Finn's welcoming eyes pull the truth right from my depths. "My parents had a traveling show. The Emerald Poppy. My father had green hair and told fortunes while I tagged along to taverns and communes, but most of the time we peddled our fortunes on street corners."

Ash's eyebrows lift. He turns to me, speechless, then looks to Finn, who asks calmly, "Why?"

I smile, as I asked myself that every day of my childhood. "Mother believed she was meant for fame and riches. My father eventually had one good year when we hit the fair and circus tours. Even a few theaters. He made a killing as a novelty act." The novelty was me, feeding him visions.

"You didn't attend school?" Ash asks, mortification spread across his face.

"Yes, until... It didn't go well." Drastic understatement. It wasn't Father's death or both drinking day and night that ruined me. The worst of it all was sending that girl down the stairs. The moment I discovered I would never rise above any of it. How could I? I was born a girl with a gift that takes more than it gives.

"How did you learn?" Ash catches himself grimacing and forces a steady face.

"Books. Life. You'd be surprised how much you can learn with simply your eyes and ears."

Finn chuckles silently as they both lean back to their seats and watch the golden landscape whir past the windows. I lean my head against the glass and count the pine trees as they flick past. Truth is, I slipped because I felt safe. With these three-colored men, I'm something more than a psychic with silver hair.

After three hours of sleepy warmth in the empty yet cozy train car, we arrive at our destination. The train comes to a stop with a puff of smoke around the windows. We gather our belongings and step down onto the platform.

A sign sticks out of the dirt, faded and leaning at an angle with a questioning tilt. Painted white with a green glove pointing east, it reads, *Hot Springs This Way.*

With my satchel around my shoulder, I tighten my grip around the handle of the basket, and we set a course down the dirt road at the foot of the golden hills. Our unlikely trio follows the curves around bitterbrush and gnarled twisted limbs of juniper skeletons. Painted green rocks and boulders guide the way like mile markers.

I silently curse my clear eyes as they leak tears under the beating sun. For once in my life, I long for the gray Portland sky. We stop to enjoy Uncle Henry's offerings, sharing lemonade in the shade of a willow tree that sways in the wind.

"Ash, are you planning to kick the doctor out of the hotel?" I ask.

"If I have to." He nods as if to remind himself he's the boss here. Funny, when he postures like that, he looks more childlike than ever. "Something is making us lose customers."

I steady my face to hide the creeping need to ask about the doctor. I sense he has something to do with Russell's past, and why psychics convene in his hospital.

"The man built a surgery viewing center," Ash says.

I'd sooner go flying through the darkest of souls than view an open abdominal cavity from above. "Why would anyone want to watch that?"

Ash rolls his eyes. "People love a show. Especially the bloody kind."

I tuck my knees toward my chest, hugging my legs close. "Our traveling show often followed a dentist who removed diseased teeth right there on stage for a dollar a pop. He wore them on a chain around his neck and called himself the Dandy Dentist."

"That's a lie," Ash says.

"It's true! He'd yank one loose and drop it in a bucket to wash and string up later."

Ash throws his head back, laughing at the ridiculous idea. I laugh because it's just ridiculous enough to be true.

Finn's blank stare suggests we're acting too childish, but then he brings the lemonade to his mouth, stopping just shy of his lips as he says, "That's one tooth fairy I don't want to see under my pillow."

We lose it, laughing until Ash snorts, causing Finn to spit out his lemonade. We hold our gaze for a long moment, his smile brightening the color in his cheeks. This lonely girl went in search of answers and picked up two friends along the way.

Once we are full of laughs and lemonade, we continue over a wooden bridge and through a field of white feather grass taller than even six-foot-tall Ash. Anticipation rests on the surface of my skin like a chill. A black crow beats his wings loud enough that we all turn. He swoops down to us and lands on Ash's shoulder. "Damn nature! Get this thing off me." Ash windmills his arm, but the bird hangs on.

I try to swat him away, but Ash's flailing sends me over a rock and onto my backside.

Finn makes a *shhh* sound and extends a steady hand. Ash recoils, but the crow blinks his black, inky eyes and curls into Finn's palm, balled into a small mass of black feathers.

The bird opens one eye, which rolls around like a black pearl, turning to look directly at me. His dark eyes pulse with gold ribbons of light from the reflecting sunshine. A dark wave rolls through me like a warning. The crow turns his tiny head back to face Finn, and after two slow breaths, closes his eyes to fly away into the hills.

"Well, that was unpleasant." Ash straightens his jacket then slaps Finn on the shoulder. "Thank you, Finn. I'm very glad you joined us on this peculiar journey."

Finn reaches down for me. I hold his hand as he lifts me to standing, his hand lingering on mine. Another vision yanks at my consciousness, but I drop my arms, already regretting that I can't move closer to him. "Did you… talk to that crow?"

Finn shrugs, a glint in his blue eye. "I simply let him know I see him and respect him. Crows are incredibly smart. They live in families, just like us."

"Like some of us."

He furrows his brow but thankfully doesn't dig deeper. If he did, I may have turned and run the other way. Finn seems to understand the power of silence better than anyone I've ever met. He kicks a green bean-colored stone down the road, and sneaks a smile over his shoulder.

I take stock of my current gifts. Friends on a journey, seeking answers at the end of the sepia road. Magic boots and the whispers of secret stars. My persistent ball of pressurized light finds a momentary reprieve as I travel with these men who, though they may have three colors, have also depths of soul and no attempts to use me.

"Do you smell that?" Ash asks.

We approach a broken white church on a hillside, leaning as if the wind has contorted the frame over the years. It's faded white and vaguely pretty, like a forgotten memory. At the base of a large bluff, a sulfurous marsh poisons the air as steam unfurls like a wicked breath from a ghost's whisper.

"I think we've arrived at Hot Lake," Ash says.

Black gates greet us. Their decorative scrolls curl like fingers, beckoning us inside with their gnarled, knotted knuckles.

The gates creak as I push them open. A wooden walkway seems to suspend over the water, a long, flat path to the sprawling brick resort, with no railings to protect us from slipping into the fiery lake.

Rocking back on my heels, I tap my glittering silver toes together. I wait for them to light the way, like they did when the path first lit with golden sunshine, but nothing happens. Maybe these boots aren't magic after all.

The nervous twitching below my eye tells me this place holds secrets, but I continue along the boardwalk. Here, I'll overcome fear and save one of these men. Learn the limits of my psychic power and conquer the darkness. But at what cost?

A sign prominently sits at the walkway toward the front door that reads "Hot Lake Sanitorium." Ash gasps, his hand extended toward the sign. "What is this? A sanitorium? We did not approve this." He stomps toward the door, hands balled into fists.

At the grand entrance to the hotel, I take a deep breath of hot, wet air. A sanitorium? I've read of those places. Women land in facilities for being oversexed or not sexed enough. If they like girls, or if they're dying of consumption. The pit in my chest just grew to giant proportions.

Something prances over my feet. A peacock trails his long, feathery tail over my boots then twists his shimmering blue neck in my direction.

A middle-aged woman shaped like a broomstick throws the door open and empties a pail of dirty water in the pond outside the entrance. Not very resort like.

Ash steps forward with a grand bow. "Greetings. I am here to evaluate our investment." His voice drops lower than I've heard him speak.

She scowls at us. Her hair is wrapped in a tight bun and round spectacles balance on her nose. She rolls her eyes when she sees my hair. "The doctor isn't taking new patients."

"We aren't patients." Ash bristles, hands on his lapels. "My father owns this building, and the doctor refuses to respond to our inquiries. Please make up three rooms for us immediately."

"And if I say no?"

Finn and I grimace to each other, watching the two battle for the last word. "Then I shall pull all money and have you fired. You'll be closed by the end of the week." He leans toward her and enunciates every syllable in the word, "Evicted."

The woman practically growls. "Fine." She holds the door open, eyes narrowed like a hawk.

"Are you aware," I say, "that a peacock just walked over my boots?"

"Otto."

"He's a pet?"

She smirks. "We keep all manner of animals here. Milking cows, and dozens of chickens, horses, and pigs. The peacock, though, he keeps the whimsy alive."

"Naturally." Another oddity to this fantastical journey. The peacock seems to soften the worry around this place. A smile among the whispers of darkness.

We step into a chartreuse foyer. Walls of green marble speckled with white. A glass skylight floods the room with filtered prisms of forest colors. Giant, waxy leaves of a houseplant crawl into the corners near a fountain that trickles water the color of algae.

"It's like the forest exploded in here," Ash whispers.

"Wait here," the woman barks. She disappears behind swinging doors of shining mahogany.

"Green water? Unruly houseplants? It's no wonder the place is losing money." Ash shakes his head and examines the peculiar touches. "An abomination." He's particularly fascinated by a jade goblet of cooled hot spring water, so the sign reads.

Through the back wall of windows, I glimpse someone. The wavy green glass obscures his figure, but he seems young and timid with a lowered head and careful steps.

I walk along the windows until I find a door with a jeweled emerald handle. I click it open and step outside to the back of the hotel that faces the bluff. He's not a boy, but a young man. He wipes the sweat from his brow, startled when he notices the silver-haired girl speechless in front of him.

Olive skin, speckled with patches of white and pink.

Christ.

Three-colored skin.

Chapter Eight

Ten minutes I watch him push a creaking wheelbarrow full of chicken feed, backing into the shade of the covered porch so he doesn't catch me staring. Three tri-colored men. This must be a joke.

This one isn't three-colored in eyes or name but wears his like a sign for the world to see. No hiding. My feet step forward of their own accord before I force them steady. No one wants to be approached because of the way they look. Especially when one is different. I stroll across the patio, smelling the coral and red rose bushes, pretending not to investigate him from afar.

His name, his story. I need details. He could be the one to save, and the tug at my heart suggests a vision could change everything for him or for me. Forget the strange green hotel. I'll be searching for this man's story.

He pushes his wheelbarrow along the dusty road, back toward the farm and stables. Ash knocks on the window behind me and waves me back inside.

Back in the office, Ash's face has reddened, and Finn looks around with overwhelmed eyes. This hotel is a lot to take in, even for a jaded gal such as myself. We walk down a faded brick hallway after the oh-so-unfriendly woman. We pass a functioning post office, and a barber sleeping in his chair, feet propped up, decked out in an emerald suit and matching shoes. A confectionary sells green chocolate and popcorn the color of Brussels sprouts.

"Is this some sort of weird theme?" I ask Finn. "The gothic exterior of this place doesn't match the joke that's inside."

"It's definitely strange."

"Why is that woman dressed in all white though?" I motion to the one leading us to our rooms.

Finn examines a jeweled mirror on the wall, watching a couple laugh through the reflection. I turn over my shoulder to see a young man and woman holding hands, sharing a milkshake. "Thank goodness the ice cream is a normal color." I catch Finn's eyes in the mirror.

"Oh." He turns to me and nods. "The woman up there is the nurse for the sanitorium. She had the clerk find us three rooms and is grilling Ash about why he's here."

Ash shakes his head as we walk, hands clasped behind his back. Pipes braced to the ceiling seem to hum and rattle. We all look up. "What is that?" I ask.

"The thermal water to heat the resort," Broomstick says.

I can almost hear the water shooting through the metal tubes, drumming along like a heartbeat.

At the base of a staircase, a sign reads, *Keep your voices low and be sweet.* "What's up there?"

She whips around. "We don't disturb the medical patrons."

The faint smell of burnt wood wafts down the stairs, followed by a deep, gurgling moan. Finn and I grimace at each other.

A silver flash shoots past me, so I stop at the empty ballroom as the others walk ahead. Just inside the wallpapered dance hall a young girl, perhaps ten, crouches under a potted fern, giggling.

Excitement shoots through me like a meteor. "Hello?"

She jumps up, revealing her silver pigtails and dress to match. Like tin foil mixed with silk. A silver girl. The first one I've ever seen outside my own mirror.

The girl gasps. "I… I knew you were here. Finally."

Well, this is unnerving. Another psychic has info on me. "Where are your parents?"

"What parents?" She creeps past me, pressing her back against the wall. "We've been waiting for you."

Warmth floods my chest. Her sweet face. Her silver hair. I resist the urge to ask her a thousand questions right here. "Waiting for me? Did you see me in a vision?"

"Marion told me. She sees everything." She darts to the doorway, pulling back when a guest strolls past the door.

"Who's Marion? Wait, please. Don't go."

She pops her head back in to say, "Better hurry, Miss Strauss doesn't like guests speaking with us. But you aren't a guest of the first floor, are you? At least, not for long. My name is Clara. I see through walls."

By the time I reach the hallway, she's gone. "A silver girl," I mutter. I fight the growing concern that this little girl lives in a sanitorium with psychic visions and no parents, adding her to my list of potential people to save. She sees through walls?

I find the group at a rotunda of stained-glass windows. A marble table stands lonely in the middle, topped with a vase of sunflowers, like an art piece.

"You may stay in these guest rooms," the woman says with a snarl. "Do not think you have the run of the place."

"I will move around as I please," Ash barks. His attempts to sound intimidating only come out like a petulant child.

Three doors with jeweled handles stare back at us. We approach the center of the room where shadows mimic creeping through a grassy field at dusk.

Ash forces a low, controlled voice. "Thank you, Mrs.—"

"*Miss* Strauss."

Ash takes a breath to calm his frustration. "*Miss Strauss*, I demand to see the doctor at once."

The tightly wound woman taps her foot, her steely stare boring through Ash. "I don't respond to demands, young man."

Ash bristles, his face growing puffy and red. "My father sent me here to fix the problems in this crumbling excuse for a resort and that is what I shall do. If you do not find me a moment with the good doctor, I will break the door down and find him myself."

The woman's face darkens, which in this light resembles avocado skin. "Very well. Come with me," she says.

Her pristine white leather shoes stomp back down the hall as Finn and I stare at each other.

"Well, this is not your typical hotel," I say with a nervous laugh.

Finn runs his hand through his hair while pushing his door open, then shoots me a closed-mouth smile. "Primrose, why are you here?"

Because I have psychic visions that turn me into a lonely mess of a person, and I need to find people like me to guide me in this thing called life. "I guess I'm looking for a way to be happy." True enough.

"Yeah." He smiles, nods his head in agreement, then backs into the door to his room, pushing it open.

"Don't get lost in a sea of chartreuse in there." The door shuts and I shake my head. Primrose, you fool. You've never flirted a day in your life.

I enter my room, bedecked in lime-colored bedding and a crystal and emerald chandelier. My mind reaches for what life might be like when I meet those girls upstairs, when I find answers to all my painful questions. An instant pang grabs my chest. The girl I sent tumbling down the stairs screamed *help me* over and over, so loud I still hear it in my sleep from time to time. She changed my life, and I can't even remember her name.

I slide open the window to smell the sulfur that lingers in the moist air around the hotel. Behind a row of hedges, the man from earlier walks past, making eye contact with me. I wave, but he turns away, pulling his sleeve down past the white patches on his wrist.

Too many of us struggle to love. To give and receive affection freely. We arrived here looking for something to heal our lonely hearts. How I long to touch Finn and fly through his quiet soul.

I bend down to examine the rustling flowers as something pushes through the center. A sharp beak hits me on the nose and shoves me to my backside.

Through the greenery, a tall shining blue neck appears with a warble.

Otto, the pet peacock. "Did you have to beak me?"

He doesn't seem remorseful.

He crawls onto my window ledge, blue puffs on his head waving like antennae. His gaze narrows as he opens his silver beak to a stream of fog that unfurls behind him, carried on the wind from the lake.

I rise to my knees so we're eye to eye. His breath whistles and his tiny heart flutters in his chest. I hear no words, but somehow, I understand him.

"You're a pet. A novelty of colorful feathers. Everyone loves you but you're trapped alone in the Oregon mountains, not another peacock soul around."

I pet his silky neck, eliciting a tremble from his blue feathers. "You just want to be with birds who look like you, don't you?"

He rubs his hard beak on my hand.

A knock on my door. When I open it, Ash steps inside, face red as those thimbleberries in the forest. "That madman refuses to speak with me!"

"What happened?"

Ash points to Otto. "Is there a peacock in your window?"

"Why wouldn't there be?"

Fists to his eyes, he groans. "This place is madness!" He flops against my doorway. "Braun wouldn't even open his door. He opened a metal slit, so all I saw were his eyes. That charlatan told me to leave and never return."

"I assume you threatened him."

"Of course I threatened him! Father tells me never back down. Never. I am to demand what I want."

"Ash, when has that ever worked with anybody?"

"It works for my father. He's harsh, but he always gets what he wants."

I don't say that he seems to have much to learn. He'll never be the angry businessman who can push people around. He's too soft for that. "Let me try," I say.

"Oh, you can do better than me?"

"Not better, just different." Besides, it will give me a chance to find that girl and whoever Marion is. Psychics, right under this roof. My heart flutters high in my chest.

Ash softens. He stares into my eyes, again mesmerized as if they truly are crystal balls. "You seem to see things, don't you?"

Oh no, don't ask me for a vision. Don't see me for the psychic I am. He steps near, but Otto squawks shrill and loud.

Ash steps back, hands raised in the air. "Sorry. Didn't mean to upset the exotic bird."

Miss Strauss marches down the hall, her starched white nurse uniform swishing at her knees.

"Oh, bloody hell," Ash says. "Here she comes again."

I love how he sounds British when he loses his cool. He's surprisingly endearing, this daddy's boy who'll never become who he's aspiring to be.

"What did you do?" Her hands on her hips look like wire hangers, elbows sharp as arrowheads.

I step in front of Ash. "He's merely trying to get answers. He owns the resort."

He yells over my shoulder, "Answers to why you've turned our resort into an emerald-themed circus!"

Finn steps into the rotunda, his eyes wide.

"Dr. Braun is a brilliant man, and you've offended him," she snaps.

"I don't care if he's Houdini himself," Ash says. "The man owes us answers."

Strauss's stare looks as if it could slice him in two.

"Everyone calm down." I lift my hands. "Miss Strauss, I would very much like to see the doctor. I won't ask about money."

"We have enough silly little silver girls already. The great doctor has much work to attend to."

Ash steps up beside me. "There are more women with silver hair here? Did you know this?"

I shake my head, hoping he doesn't ask more questions. Miss Strauss looks ready to kick us all out of here. In a panic, I blurt the first thing that comes to mind. "Russell North sent me."

She straightens up. "Oh." Not soft, but not angry either, her voice hints at concern.

"Who is Russell North?" Ash asks.

"He's a friend. He's been here before."

Strauss lowers her hands with an exhale and shakes her head. "In that case, you may come."

Finn peeks out from the doorway, hair newly brushed, but still hanging in his face. "Everything okay?"

"Yes." I smile, grateful to have friends who care what happens to me. "Ash, you stay here. Let me go." He throws his hands up. I bet he's already worried about calling his father.

Strauss grunts, but nods once, hard and fast. "Follow me."

We walk through the winding hallways and past the dining room where guests laugh. We pass the sign that instructs us to *keep our voices low and be sweet*, and up the green carpeted staircase for two flights. Strauss reaches to unlock a thick metal door, but first shoots a glance back at me. "Do not upset him, understand?"

"I have no intention of upsetting him," I say in all honesty. "Are the silver girls okay?"

A near-twitch by her right eye puts me on high alert. She doesn't want to speak of them. "They are well cared for." She squares her shoulders, eyeing me up and down. "Russell sent you?"

I nod, unsure why she's asking me again.

"Very well."

Once inside the medical ward, those women reach for me, whoever they are. They hide away in these walls and know things about me. The faint sound of bubbling water gurgles a steady rhythm in the distance.

The quiet hallway hides chatter and singing and prayer behind walls I sense somehow, though I don't hear it. Emerald globe lights cast shadows like sea kelp on the walls. We pass a slightly ajar door, a woman's eye visible for only a moment before she slams it shut.

Miss Strauss knocks on a thick slab of a door in the center of the hallway. The mail slot opens, and just as Ash said, the man's eyes appear in the rectangular opening. Just a man. I'd half expected him to be a beast with eyes of flames.

"What is it?" he asks.

"This silver is here to see you."

"My name is Primrose." I am not simply a silver. He grunts, then slams the metal slot closed.

She knocks again and leans down to the metal to speak. "Russell sent her."

After a long pause, the door clicks open, and a voice from the darkness says, "Let her in."

"Well go on," Strauss says. "Remember. Do not anger him. Or you'll have *me* to deal with."

I wanted to meet the women, not this doctor. Though he is connected to Russell and may help me discover some things. I smooth my dress and step into the doctor's office. A constant tick beats like the loudest clock in the world. Thick velvet drapes block out the sunshine and a dimly lit lamp ekes a drop of light on his desk. The man stands like a shadow in the darkness.

"Welcome." His voice rumbles low, like an organ note. "What brings you here?"

I strain to see his outline. He's tall and lean with a thin face and oval wire spectacles. My chest thumps and my head pulses, his soul teasing me. He doesn't want me inside, but he has secrets to spill. Dammit, I'm not ready for a mad doctor's poppy road.

"I need your help," I say. My voice catches, the heaviness of the room making my head spin.

"What kind of help? Rheumatism? Stomach pain?"

I shift my weight to one foot, crossing my arms and legs at the same time. "Not that kind of help."

The doctor removes his glasses and taps them on the table. "We don't cure psychic delusions here." He hasn't let go of the spectacles, still tapping the frames on the desk as he examines me.

I don't move, unsure of what comes next. "Why would I want to cure anything? I just want answers."

He snarls, displeased with my answer. "You may leave," he says.

"Wait." I rub my temples as the crushing need to jump into Braun's soul climbs through me. But that's the last thing I want.

The doctor steps forward to examine me.

"I'm just like Russell," I blurt out.

Dr. Braun's breathing deepens with a long, whistled exhale. He walks to the window and throws open the curtain. Blinding light shocks me, and I cover my eyes with the back of my hand.

Braun examines my watery eyes and fully silver hair as a deep, sinister smile creeps across his face. The corners of his mouth lift like a marionette's limbs.

"My full name is Primrose Whittaker."

His face twitches. One eye shuts, then opens again, like I've just said something offensive.

He clears his throat. "You interest me, Miss Whittaker," he says.

He paces the room in long, exaggerated steps. As my eyes adjust, I see his sloped nose and his dark brown hair slicked back with pomade. Wrinkles pucker the corners of his eyes, his skin aged beyond the forty-something doctor he most likely is.

"You want to learn about your affliction?" he asks.

"I don't know if I see it as an affliction." That's a lie. I've seen it as a disease my entire life. A disease I want to love.

"Miss Whittaker, visual and auditory hallucinations fill your brain." He holds up one finger, a twinkle in his eye. "You see and hear things we mortals can't."

Whether the storm was an escape from death or a predestined bump, I'm right where I belong. "My visions are a hell of a lot more than just sight and sound."

He silently gasps, leaning back to examine my eyes from afar, and I worry I have said too much. "I will help you. Under one condition."

Oh Lord, not this again. I've made enough deals to last a lifetime. "What is it?"

"You must get rid of that man you came with. Mr. Sterling."

"Get rid of him?" I ask.

"We're doing important work here. Healing people of pain and psychological disturbances. Mr. Sterling has threatened to evict us and sent his useless son to do his dirty work. I won't allow it."

Ah. Ash's father sent him here to prove his strength. Deal with the medical facility in person, to Dr. Braun's face. Or turn this place profitable, which, by the looks of it, may be impossible. It's a sanitorium inside a very odd resort.

"I'm not sure how to do that."

"Come." Braun throws open his office door, bumping Strauss in the backside which causes her to blush five shades of red. He ignores the embarrassing encounter, and directs us to a room where he knocks and waits.

"Yes?" a raspy voice says.

"Open the door please. We have a visitor."

She complies. A young woman, barely out of her teenage years. Pale skin and giant milky eyes. Once silverish hair dulled to somewhere between strawberry blond and gunmetal gray.

I step forward to look at her. "You're like me."

"Yes," Braun says. "The world doesn't understand you, do they? They use you and mock you."

She's right here. A psychic woman with a shared experience. I can't tear my eyes away for fear she'll turn into a mirage. "Why are you here?"

"Same as you," she says. "We're so thrilled you've arrived."

"Why do you all keep saying that?"

"Marion," she says. "She saw your future. We've seen it too. This is going to be hard for everyone, Primrose."

I step closer. "What does that mean?"

"Thank you, Judy." Dr. Braun leads me out of the way, undeterred by my resistance. Judy shuts the door.

She's a silver woman who knows things. She's read my future without touching me, and it's so enticing I want to burst through this door and make her tell me everything.

"Primrose, here we learn about your gifts *together*. We explore the limits of your mind and capabilities. Here, I allow my patients to be the wild psychics of their dreams."

"I'm uncertain why the others are here, but I don't need any more wild."

Judy says through the closed door, "Primrose, take the deal."

Excitement tingles on my skin at the prospect of spending time with women who have answers. Darkness taps at my heart, a deep-held memory of my father's feet sticking out from under a fallen dining table. Tall with legs like stilts and arms to match, his lifeless bones twisted unnaturally, with a syringe sticking out of the crook of his elbow.

Almost as if he can read my mind, Braun says, "I know the darkness you carry is terrifying. We need to examine it. Understand it. *Control* it."

A nurse walks past us with a rolling tray of little white cups full of pills and lined up syringes of emerald liquid. I won't allow some doctor control anything about my life. The only people I want access to are the ones with silver hair.

"I'll work on Mr. Sterling. But I want to spend time here. I want to talk with your residents."

Braun ekes out a knowing smile. My stomach tightens in reaction, but I can't register that fear. There are kindred spirits mere feet from me.

"Fine," Braun says. "Strauss!" He snaps his fingers without looking away from us. "I will see you tomorrow."

"Dr. Braun?" He waits impatiently for me to speak. "Why have they been waiting for me?"

He scratches at his temple. "We all have." And he's gone.

Strauss nods and motions for me to follow. Near the staircase, I hear a loud crash, followed by a scream. "Oh dear, not again," Strauss says. "Stay here and don't cause any trouble."

I consider going back to Judy, but a pale green shadow snakes across my hand, causing my entire arm to pulse. I follow the shadow to a different room, one where the door rests ajar. "Come in," a voice says.

A woman sits in the window, warm sun flooding her face. Tiny ankles peeking out from under a blanket. Frail hands. She opens her mouth to speak but freezes as her parted lips twist into a relieved smile. "I'm so happy you're here."

I step inside, sliding my palms against my skirt. A woman no older than Braun whose frown lines don't match her clear, golden skin. Crystal clear eyes like ice. Silver hair cropped to her shoulders. The contrast is so striking, I can't even blink. I look out the window. Her view overlooks the boiling lake which shimmers blueish green. "I've been looking for people like me for years. And here you are."

"Here we are." She joins me in gazing out front. "A few of us, anyway."

"That's a few more than I ever dreamed of." The breeze picks up outside the window as a few pale-yellow leaves sway up to our view then back toward the ground. "Marion, is it? You've seen my future. How? We've never met."

"I see everything, even when I wish not to." There's a pained honesty in her voice. In her eyes.

"Your hair," I say. "It hasn't lost the silver like Judy's has."

"Some strands still hang on."

I have a million questions and not enough time. "What will happen to me here?"

Strauss bursts through the door. "What did I tell you?" She grips my arm so tight that my knees buckle. I try to wriggle from her grip, but she claws deeper.

I look over my shoulder at Marion. She has no reaction but nods once. Strauss drags me out of the room, down the hallway. As she does, I feel something. No poppies, no stars, just a vision of Miss Strauss. And it's a doozy.

"Get off me," I say.

"There are rules! The doctor told you to come tomorrow. This isn't social hour."

I glance back and see that little girl Clara smack dab in the middle of the hall, watching with intrigue. Strauss tugs me so hard that I yelp. "Hands off, you witch."

Strauss releases me but puffs her cheeks out and looks into my eyes. "You won't last long here. Dr. Braun is more powerful than you could ever be."

You'd think dealing with clairvoyants would make her hesitate before threats. I exhale and step to Strauss's ear. "You threaten me one more time, and I'll tell the doctor your little secret."

She freezes, pulls her shoulders back. "What secret?"

I pause to let the silence twist in her chest for a while, worry corkscrewing deeper with every second. "You watch him. From windows and behind furniture. Sometimes while he sleeps. When he showers, when he lies with a woman. You're always there, watching with such desperation you can hardly see straight."

She steps back and runs her bottom lip along her teeth.

"Certainly, I'm not the only one here that sees your soul? Can you imagine if I asked these women what they know about you?"

She clears her throat. "None of them would dare threaten me. We own them."

The edges of my vision blurs and pulses as my heart beats so fiercely in my temples, I struggle to steady myself. "No, you don't. I'll make sure they know that too."

Strauss holds the door open. "You're all too broken, Miss Whittaker. The world has shunned you, disregarded your strange little mind and weakened body. Your chest hurts and head thumps, am I right?" When I don't respond, her cheek twitches in silent triumph.

"You watch the darkest moments of someone's soul and wade through that waste every day. You live in hell, and we give you a way out. Who is stronger here?"

My visions have always been my defense. I can knock down anyone with one glimpse into their future or past. This place sees my psychic powers as a disease to be attacked. For the first time, I don't believe I can separate the two. I am my poppy road, and I can either accept that or let the world rip me apart one claw at a time.

They can leave me in shreds and my powers will remain intact. I turn my back to Strauss and look at the women staring at me from along the hallway. Some silvers, some brunettes. All women with terrified eyes. Even Marion has wheeled out of her room. They've been waiting for me. Maybe it isn't the three-colored man I should focus on.

I walk past Strauss with a wink and out of the medical ward. "A battle of wills is what you want?" I ask. "Fine then. See you tomorrow."

Everyone needs saved. Even me.

Chapter Nine

Mere hours after my time in the medical ward, I'm mired in questions with no answers. As I lie on my bed in the bright moonlight, I consider the deal that brought me here.

Ash Sterling, pompous yet charming rich boy who can't seem to think for himself. I'd save him from his father's clutches. Finn, handsome farmer with eyes like green and blue sea glass whose touch turns me weak. I'd heal his broken heart. And the unnamed caretaker of Hot Lake's animals, whose skin is unlike anyone I've ever seen. I have no idea how I would save him. Not yet.

One of these men holds the key to a new life. The role they each play in this adventure unfolds in a blurry mess. I haven't slept and the fresh air calls to me, so I slip out my window into the crisp fall night under a hovering moon.

Early morning here looks nothing like the city. Hints of fading moonlight skitter across the starry sky. Mineral-drenched steam breathes into the pre-dawn shadows as the wind rakes through my silver hair like fingers.

Answers. I need answers. "Gwendolyn, you could make up for lost time and help me out," I whisper into the quiet. "Guide me, dammit."

A flicker the size of a seed grows into a giant mass of hovering gold. Inside, Gwendolyn cracks her neck sideways as her dress flutters between crimson and jet black. "You called?"

"I did, but I didn't think you'd listen." She hasn't for the past two decades.

Gwendolyn stabs her scepter into the orb. She glides like a bat, arms splayed, black wings billowing. Once she lands next to me, her wings disappear, and her dress shimmers tight against her curves. "This journey has shown you a glimpse of your powers."

"Is it the boots? Are they magic?"

"They could be."

"I don't understand." I pace back and forth in front of her. "One minute I'm ready to die, and the next, I'm wearing flashy boots and begging to live."

Gwendolyn lifts into the air and spins as the crystals on her dress clink together. When she comes to a stop, she's wearing my same dress. Same silver boots, same long silver hair. I don't like this mirror.

"How do you feel when you look at me?" she asks.

"Angry."

Her hair flutters into the air like a wisp of wind. "Why?"

"I never asked for this life."

"But have it you do," she says.

"You left me to falter in this unbearable human world, only to return to keep me from the one thing that would give me peace. You made a deal against my wishes and gave me no guidance."

She spins again, coming to rest as myself as a child, hair brunette at the tips and pewter at the roots. "I've always been with you. You didn't call for me until the night of the storm. You never saw me, even when I appeared."

She snaps her fingers, and she is again Gwendolyn, world's worst spirit guide. I rack my brain for any memory of her, but I come up with only hazy images of my mother laughing through a drunken stumble onto a radiator, or my father sneaking around backstage with a much younger singer, holding his finger to his mouth to remind me to stay silent. One fractured, hazy image comes back to me from when I was twelve and I felt a presence, but I shoved it away, convinced it was my imagination.

"I didn't know I had a spirit guide. It was my fault I couldn't see you?"

She exhales with a saddened gaze. "Oh, Primrose. Some things aren't anyone's fault. They simply happen."

"I could have—" I fight the tightness in my chest. "All this time, I could have had a friend. A mentor?"

"Darling, your life started when you decided not to wait for death. I'm here now. So are you."

I grind my heels into the soft, marshy ground. "Give me some guidance. Please."

Her eyelashes grow five times their size, flashing tiny emerald jewels at their tips. When she blinks, they release waves of green light. "Save the three-colored man."

"Which one? You never told me there were three!"

"You must discover that yourself."

The terms of the deal linger at the edge of my consciousness, testing my deepest fears. "Tell the truth and discover how to help people. Can't you just tell me how?"

"You know that is not how life works." Her scepter produces a gold ball of light that balloons like bubbles in a hot bath.

"Wait," I beg. "I'm afraid."

She holds her hand to the orb, freezing it next to her. "Fear keeps you from seeing the real you." She exhales, a puff of rose-tinted mist.

"What do I do now?" I hate how desperate my voice sounds.

"The truth is always a good place to start."

The orb scoops her like a spoon through ice cream and floats her into the sky. Black beads drop from her dress like moonbeams to the ground. All the light dissipates, as her jewel-toned image transforms into white steam.

"Good-for-nothing spirit guide," I say to myself as I stomp back to the gardens behind my room.

Before heading inside, an amber glow from the window of the barn catches my eye. I push the barn door open with a creak and follow the light to the corner of the stable, in a converted stall. I find the caretaker on a mattress on the floor, reading Emily Dickinson by the light of a lantern.

"You like poetry?" I ask.

He throws his book aside and presses his back into the wall, as a chicken clucks next to him.

"I didn't mean to scare you. I'm sorry."

He looks around, mouth open. "It's all right. What are you doing here?"

"I was out for a walk, enjoying the silence. Do you want me to leave?"

"No." He stands up and rubs his palms on his thighs. "I wake before the animals," he says. "In case they need me."

Up close, I see that his cheek displays a pink patch in the shape of a heart. "That's nice that they have you."

I lean against the wall opposite him. His pale patches of skin reflect the shadows of the lantern. The large pink heart stretches across his left eye, with spots extending down his neck and mottling his arms. "My name is Oliver." He rubs his neck and leaves his hand splayed across the largest patch on his neck.

"It's nice to meet you. I'm Primrose."

"I'm not here to treat my skin," he says with resolve. "That's what everyone thinks, so it's best to get that out of the way when I meet someone."

It's best to start with the truth, Gwendolyn said. "That's good. I don't want Dr. Braun to change me either."

He swings his arm, twisting his torso and making him appear younger than he is. "The other silvers come here wanting to be normal."

I step forward so my face is in the light. "So many things make people different. It's a wonder there's such a thing as normal."

He smiles and brings his other hand to his neck.

"Did you know Russell?" I ask.

He looks up, eyes bright. "Of course I did."

"He's the one who sent me here."

"I hope he's happy."

"Me too." Though I suspect he's far from it.

"Russell taught me how to play poker, and how to make a poultice to treat a head cold. We both spent a lot of years here. I'm glad he got out."

"Why did he leave?"

A cat meows as he walks into the stall and rubs his side on Oliver's leg. He lifts the cat and holds him close to his chest. "Dr. Braun treats everything. Lots of rheumatism and stomach problems."

"Sounds odd for a resort."

"The wealthy folk love it. Warm baths are just weird enough to believe in. But the silver girls, they came one by one after Russell, who constantly left to meet with shamans and healers. They never cured him, so he came back, often with another psychic in tow, begging Braun to fix him."

Why didn't I ask him more questions before I left? Silly girl was in too much of a hurry to begin the adventure. Now I've cornered this man in the pre-dawn light looking for answers. "I'm not like the other ones. I came here to meet people who look like me. To find out the truth of my powers."

"But what does the truth matter when you're the wrong colors?" He winks.

The world that lives by brunette or blond, olive or pale. Blue eyes or brown. A world where touch is merely a touch. "I bet everyone is wrong, and our colors are just right."

"Maybe." He grins, finally looking his age. "I wish I could convince you to turn around before things get bad. Braun and Strauss have a way of manipulating everyone."

The skin across my temples starts to crawl and itch. He's trying to tell me something. I blink hard, fighting a vision.

"It's okay," he says. "You can read my mind. I've seen how much it hurts your kind to ignore your powers."

It does hurt. Like I'm on fire and the water that can put out the flame is right there, if I just reach out and touch it. "Are you sure?"

He laughs and extends his hand. "I've already seen it all. Go ahead."

I wrap my fingers around his where the pads feel more like a nail file than a hand. All that hard work has given him calluses.

His soul sucks mine through the colorless tunnel of wind. I land not on my footpath, but in a pool of amber water. So hot that my skin hurts. I swim to the edge and crawl through the poppies as smoke rises from their centers. Dripping with thick, steaming water, I crawl through the green grass. The ground shakes and cracks down the middle. I slide on my belly, dropped into a dark cavern where stars catch me. Below, I see Oliver, being treated in the pools and mud baths. Braun watches him scream as they submerge him in hot water. Tears leak from his eyes when they scrub yellow oil on his naked body.

He walks from the bright yellow pool, out toward the horses and pigs and feral cats who await his return. They lick the oil off his skin. The ground opens and sucks me down into the black.

I land back into my pounding body that holds Oliver's hand. I can't breathe. "You came here to fix your white and pink patches."

His hand slides from mine. "It's called vitiligo." He swallows and looks up to the cobweb-covered eves. "Braun rescued me from an orphanage and brought me here for medical experiments. Turns out turmeric does the trick. He mixed it with the hot springs to make a paste."

"You stopped though." His animals welcomed him home. They are why he stays.

"The things we do to ourselves trying to be something different." He shakes his head. "In the mirror, I looked like someone else, and I didn't like that. So, I walked out."

"Braun let you?"

"He works off consent, and I said no. He let me stay because the animals need tending."

The wind bounces the barn door on its rusty hinges, creaking and scraping against the pebbled dirt.

"He left me alone, but I worry about the rest of them." He looks toward the hotel, even though there's a barn wall and a night of darkness between. "They still consent to his madness."

Marion, Judy, Clara. They must not understand the consequences. "Thank you, Oliver. No one ever lets me read them like that, without fear."

"Did you see my future?" He keeps scratching the cat's head with long strokes as he sleeps in his arms.

"No, just your past."

He shrugs. "They've told me the same thing. A hazy future."

His past and his present, but no future in sight. Something's blocking me and I can't see past his now. I nod, but I won't be able to let this go until I discover why my visions with him remain broken. As I turn to leave, he says, "Poetry is pretty." He holds up the book.

"Yes, I suppose it is."

"That's not why I read it though. It gives me a place for all these feelings I'm not supposed to show."

I smile before stepping over the chicken to leave the stall. Daybreak hasn't arrived, but it marches near. I can tell from the way the black sky bleeds into gray like an hourglass.

If Oliver is the three-colored man in Gwendolyn's deal, I'm already ten steps behind.

Chapter Ten

Oliver lingers on my mind for the rest of the morning, holding tight even as I drifted off to sleep for a few hours. As I woke late, breakfast had been cleared from the dining room, and the men were nowhere to be found. At the doorway to the confectionery, the smell of caramel and vanilla fills the air with sweetness, a welcome change from the sulfurous marsh outside. I don't know about green chocolate, but a girl has to eat.

I trade a nickel for a small bar of chocolate and lean against the doorjamb to watch the guests stroll past in their vacation best. White lace and pastel chiffon. Crisp garden party dresses and plaid suits. Matching hats and glossy, lacquered nails. I brought two faded dresses and a bag of coins. But I don't need fancy threads, I remind myself. I need to save one of these three-colored men and hopefully, find some answers along the way.

Ash drags himself around the corner, hands in his pockets, head hung low. Like a sweet puppy who's just had his nose whacked with a rolled newspaper. Otto taps his beak on the window just in front of us. "Ah, again with the bird."

"His name is Otto," I say.

Ash sighs, turning from the window and leaning his shoulder against the wall next to me. "I phoned my father this morning."

"And?" I ask.

"He's furious. He thinks I'm having a holiday around Oregon wasting his money."

I must choose every word wisely if I want him to leave of his own accord. "Strange place to take a holiday." I show him the wrapper of my green chocolate bar.

He rolls to his back, eyes locked on the tin-paneled ceiling. "Sometimes I wonder if I'll ever know the right thing to do. If it's possible to make my father really see me."

"He may never see you, Ash. Will kicking the doctor out of this place change anything for you?"

Ash nods to a pretty woman who walks past. She lifts her bare shoulder toward her chin and smiles with her eyes like a professional flirt. Her face drops into horror when she glimpses my hair. Ash doesn't notice how she gawks at me as he's too busy strumming his fingers on his chin in deep thought.

He's blissfully unaware of everything. It makes my forehead tingle, wanting to see inside his soul. "Why is this so important to you?"

"We all have to take a stand somewhere in life, Primrose." The shift in demeanor is palpable. "Prove ourselves to everyone who looks on with greed and daggers in their eyes."

"What?" Even his voice has changed. All I can think of are the women upstairs with answers. The ones with hair like mine and eyes that can see through souls. My connection to belonging waits a mere two floors away. The only thing that stands in my way is the man before me.

Before Ash can say one more word, and before I talk myself out of it, I grab his arm with both hands. I don't fight. He looks at me with a confused smile and just like that, I'm shot into an icy darkness as a chill races up my spine.

My boots pierce the veil, and I tumble forward. I land splayed on my stomach on a blanket of stars. The twinkle of an endless glittering sky stares back at me.

The stars roll me to my back, as honeycomb hovers over my head. Flowers grow downward like blood droplets. A child sits with a paper airplane in his hand, staring up at his father's bent spine and wagging finger. The father says, "You must fight, my boy. They will take everything if you let them. Be fierce. Be angry, and handle everyone with greed and daggers in your eyes." Little boy Ash falls from the yellow sky, landing in space as his adult self, tethered by strings. White paint covers his face, with black diamonds for eyes, and a hollow, puckered look to his dimples.

He bounces, suspended in the stars like cobwebs.

"What's the matter with you?" I ask.

His black eyes blink over and over, his face expressionless. Green tears leak from his eyes and the same color sludge pours from his mouth. The strings pull his arms up and down and shift his head side to side.

"Your father doesn't own you, Ash." But the puppet does not hear me. One poppy grows thin and silver and morphs into the shape of a sword. It drops from above, slicing through Ash's head before falling to the blackness below. Ash's skull splits open and, like an empty coconut shell, lands in two pieces, one in each of his hands.

The stars bounce, and I know my time here is over. Ash's headless body tumbles forward, his bloody neck knocking me from my cradle of light. I fall through the cavern with a spinning stomach, and slam back into my body, my hands still squeezing Ash's forearm.

He stares at me with concern. "You froze and your eyes rolled back."

A crack shoots through my chest, but I force a few deep breaths.

"Primrose?" Ash asks.

"What?" My head feels as if it's stuffed with straw.

"You're trembling."

Any dismissal I've felt for Ash dissipates when I stare into his worried eyes. I need to convince him to leave Hot Lake so I can have access to the medical ward, but all I see is a scared little boy dominated by his abusive father. I shake away my vision of an empty skull and his bloody neck.

He must develop a way to think for himself or he'll die in service to a father who does not love him. I didn't see his death as certain, written in the stars. I saw a warning. "Does your father see how kind you are?" His shoulders drop. "How deeply you care for others?"

He pulls away with a tug at his sleeve to straighten the fabric. "Kindness is a weakness."

"No, it isn't." He's a little boy playing with a paper airplane, asking someone to love him. "It's your greatest asset."

He runs his fingers along a marble sculpture of a woman pouring from a jug of water. He taps her stone hand and presses his palm into the curve of her fingers.

Finn arrives eating an apple. "Fruit and pastries just sitting out on platters for guests." He bites the last of the flesh and tosses the core in a nearby bin. "This place isn't so bad."

Ash knocks on the pillar seemingly to check its sturdiness. "I have too much to evaluate. Will you both help me?"

Inside, an entire monologue awaits, convincing Ash to let go of this hotel, leave the doctor alone, and find somewhere to drink his troubles away. But I can't bring myself to say it. "Sure. Why not." There are still a few hours before Braun will allow me access upstairs.

"Splendid. We start with the soaking pools. Come along."

A cold metal elevator descends to the basement as we rattle around inside. When it thuds to a halt, Ash slides the gate aside and we're met by Miss Strauss and all her judgment.

"Miss Strauss," Ash says, elongating the miss. "Shouldn't you be attending to the medical patients?"

"The doctor insists I monitor you three." She eyes me. "Don't want you wandering anywhere you shouldn't be."

"Need I remind you that I am the money here?" Ash squares his shoulders. "I could shut you down today. Right this very moment." He lifts his hand and points to the floor. "Now step aside before I throw you out of my way."

She considers, then steps aside, extending her arm to allow us to pass.

"Now, we will evaluate the bathing facilities. Scurry on back to your strange little doctor now." He shoos her along. Once she has slammed the door and we're alone in the hallway, Ash grabs his lapels with both hands. "Well then."

"Soaking pools," Finn says. "Inside."

"This place was a thriving success a few years back," Ash says, yanking on each door with more force than is necessary. "Now look at it. A green monstrosity that stinks of eggs." He finds an unlocked door. "Ah. Here we are."

The salty smell of pumped lake water thickens the air. Steaming water puddles along hexagon-shaped tiles. A row of baths lines the far wall. A couple, eyes closed, soaks in the far bath which look a bit more like giant buckets than bathtubs. Ash points to dressing rooms.

I slip into a women's room with a closet of knit one-piece suits in the corner. I hang my blue dress on a hanger and pull on a suit that fits well enough. The tiles warm my bare feet. This is more skin than I've ever shown to a man in the light of day.

Finn is already in a bath. Ash has claimed one as well, but he's busy inspecting the room and making notes on a clipboard to notice me. No open baths, so Finn slides back to make room in his. I dip into the hot, steaming water which sends a chill across my arms.

"Healing waters, huh?" I ask.

Finn slides his hair from his face, leaving a streak of dripping water down his cheek. "Good for the skin and muscles."

He props one arm on the edge of the bath behind me which sends my heart racing. The steam gives him a glowing, dewy look. "You seem relaxed. Not like back at the farm."

I sink lower in the water to keep myself from touching his face. "Farmwork isn't relaxing," he says.

"Are you happy there?"

"Sure. I guess." He stares up at the ceiling, taking a deep breath of the billowing steam. "As happy as I can be."

His elongated neck highlights the hard line of his jaw. "Why did you decide to come with us? I mean, I'm glad you're here. But what are you looking for?"

His eyes trail down to my mouth and back to my eyes. His heartbeat is audible. Or is it my heart I hear? "I've been asking myself that same question." He drops his arms and splashes a palmful of water over his hair to slick it back.

"And?"

His skin reddens along the hollow of his cheekbone. "When you stepped onto the roof with me, I didn't want you there."

I try not to shrink away. "Oh. I'm sorry."

"I've lived in my mind for so long, I didn't want to share my nighttime silence. It's like there's a wall I can see through but can't break."

"I pushed you. That was selfish of me." I wanted more of him. More of the feeling that erupts when he meets my eyes.

"Dammit!" Ash slaps the paper against the clipboard which has softened and curled from the heat.

I return my attention to Finn, considering how to run out of here before I die of embarrassment.

"The thing is…" Finn leans his arms on the seat next to me, leaning close. "Lying in bed that night, I couldn't stop thinking of how you wandered into our life, our house, and how I didn't want you to go."

My head thumps, both light and heavy.

"Why I'm here is because of you. You're on this journey for reasons I can't understand, but your interest in our lives makes me believe I can care again too."

I inspire him? "The interest in life is a new feature for me." He smiles and I might faint. "Finn, you need to understand who I am."

"Okay. Tell me."

It's best to start with the truth. "I should have died a few days ago, but I lived, and it's made me question everything."

The slight tilt of his head sends me into unknown territory. I don't just want to kiss him. I want to *know* him. "What do you mean, should have died?"

"I spent years believing I'd die the night I turned twenty-two. I was wrong." I glance over my shoulder. The couple still hasn't moved, and Ash is busy inspecting the pipes. Back to Finn where my desire to live and love grows to unmanageable levels. "I see things as a clairvoyant." I drop that first bomb and let it settle. "There might be more of my kind here and I had to find them."

He doesn't look shocked. "You've been lonely, searching for a family. That's not so strange."

"I have silver hair and clear eyes, and if I touch you, I will see your future, your past, your true feelings. Everything about me is strange."

He leans closer while watching Ash but focuses back on me. "That must make touch terrifying."

"Even when I want it."

"I wish I knew honesty. Uncle Henry treats me like I'm made of glass. The neighbors smile but talk about the quiet man who hates people." He bites his bottom lip. "Maybe that's why I followed you here. You may be the most honest person I've ever met."

"It's a lonely life."

"Will you read me?" he asks.

Why did you have to ask me that? No way out. "Finn, I have to tell you what I see. Even if it's awful."

"I've already lived through awful." He holds out his hand. "If you want to touch me, here I am."

His darkness doesn't crawl toward me or tug at my fear. I lay my hand on his. His other hand appears, and I grab that one too. My head thumps but his stars don't call me. They wait, just out of reach. "Nothing yet," I say, both terrified and exhilarated. "I think I need to be closer."

His right hand releases mine. I think he's going to back away, but his shoulder drops and his hand slides to the small of my back. His touch is so soft, yet he pulls me close with enough firmness that I gasp.

Our heartbeats drum together. He closes his eyes but keeps my body against his. As if my heart leads the way, his soul pulls me by the chest. No tunnel this time. When I open my eyes, Finn is still holding me, now in a pool of amber honey, stars twinkling above our heads.

We're safe, together in this vision.

The smear of water on his cheek has turned to drops of honey. I wipe them with my thumb, gliding slowly across his cheekbone. "It scares most people that I can see inside their minds."

"It doesn't scare me."

The sun pulses into a green sky but off in the distance, a black cloud rolls in behind my waving field of blood-red poppies. "I do love it here, where truth doesn't lie." I close my eyes to savor his warm breath on my cheek.

"Deep down, I want to feel again," Finn whispers. "But it's all so terrifying."

Understanding waves like a thread between us, a knowing of loneliness. "Are you afraid of me?"

He pulls me tighter, his hand spread across my back. The honey drains away, and we hover in a pool of gold light. My heart races here in my stars and in my physical world, like two bodies tumbling through a rush of rapids.

"Oh," I say, feeling his thoughts. "Afraid you'll never have a home again."

His intense eyes seem to smile. "What good is home if it hurts to exist?" The air chills as the charcoal clouds rumble toward us, blacking out all color. Finn squeezes me into a hug, lips to my neck as he whispers, "We're both running from pain."

Beneath my fingers, his shoulders fade to emptiness. The vibrant color of my honeycomb world has faded, and the stars hold me back as Finn tumbles into darkness below. His past unfolds as I watch the tragic story.

Finn locked his family in the cellar and ran to save their little dog. They lived in Kansas when a tornado came through. Windmill blades flew apart and shattered the house. He hid in the well, unaware their lantern started a fire, and I didn't find them until it was too late. He didn't even save the dog.

The stars release me back into my overheated body, Finn's lips close to mine. Pain hammers my temples, so hard I squint. All I can do is groan, aching at every joint, every inch of skin.

"It hurts to come back," I say. My stomach tightens, and the pain he's carried fills my insides. "Your family." I don't need to say anything more. "You haven't forgiven yourself."

"And I never will." The thumping in my body slowly recedes and Finn looks into my eyes. "Fear always wins," he says. As he steps out of the bath, I want to hold his hand. I want to stop him from running away. I saw what happened and I don't blame him. But none of that matters when we see ourselves as broken, half-dead, and incapable of love. So, I let him walk away from the painful remnants of our trip through the stars.

***

Finn disappeared after the soaking tub, and I was too busy thinking of how to manage Dr. Braun to go looking for him. I'll find a way to spend time with the medical residents, even with the doctor in the way.

With cool skin and a clean powder blue dress, I sit in Braun's office listening to the tick of the metronome. He opens his door and takes three elongated steps inside, with his lanky legs that match his thin, bony fingers.

Strauss at Braun's heals, narrows her eyes at me. "Can I help with anything, doctor?"

He waves her away without a glance, so she crawls out of the room like a cockroach.

"Mr. Sterling is still here," he says.

"Yes, he is." He doesn't pace, but simply stares at me. "I tried to convince him to leave you alone."

One finger on the bridge of his glasses, he pushes them up on his nose. "Why don't I believe you?"

"I don't care if you believe me." I stand but don't have the courage to walk away. There are silver-haired psychics on this floor.

"You want answers, yes?" He motions for me to sit.

My knees soften as I lower back to the loveseat. "Something like that."

Rhythmic ticking once again fills the silence. He scrapes his chair across the linoleum and sits, facing me. "You want to know why you have these visions, what it feels like with other psychics, and why the spirits chose you."

He knows more about my psychic powers than I do, and I hate it. Dr. Braun understands the secrets and hidden passageways in my mind which scare the wits out of me. "I don't want answers from you."

Braun leans back in his chair. "I've studied these residents for years. I've discovered things about your brain no one else knows." The thinned skin under his eye trembles with each eyelid twitch. "Every one of you wants to know why you're different."

I want to know why I can't see who to save when I look into Ash and Finn and Oliver's souls. I want to understand how to live with this gift and not want to die. "My brain? That seems like something only a doctor would care about."

"You could have all the answers your heart desires or live in fear of the burden you carry." He crosses his arms tight against his chest. "It's up to you which way that goes."

A second pair of spectacles sits on a pile of papers on his desk. Medical degrees decorate the walls on both sides of the room. "Oh," I say. "I could provide you answers, is what you're trying to say." He wants to study me.

"I'm so close," he says. A rare moment of excitement where control slips from his grasp. "I've treated Marion's delusions. When I find the missing piece, I can help more people just like you."

Everyone here has been waiting for me. "How do you know I can help?"

He puffs his lips then tucks them in tight. "I work with psychics, Primrose." As if that is enough of an answer.

"Tell me something, Dr. Braun. Why are you only experimenting on women?"

"Men hide their delusions better. Women aren't capable of that."

"Is that so?" I exhale, counting the squares in the plaid curtains. "You must think I enjoy your company then, what with this smile on my face. Since we're so terrible at concealing our erratic feelings."

One quick sniff and he's already rattled. "My work could heal all the pain associated with your delusions."

Delusions sounds so fantastical. My visions are very real. "Did your work fix Russell?" I ask, knowing full well he might pop a vein in his head. "Seems as if you made him worse."

He grips the chair handles so hard his knuckles turn white. "Russell had so much potential, but he was weak." My mother's words bubble back to me, how Vanessa and I couldn't find the strength to hurt people. Why does everyone see that as weakness?

He closes his eyes to calm his frustration. "You and Finn shared a moment."

"You watched us?"

"I promise you I did not."

That means Clara watched us, that wide-eyed little girl who seems to have visions without touch. I don't like her watching us and I loathe that she seems to report to Braun. "You could fall in love, Primrose. You could touch without seeing things you don't want to see."

"First you want me to get rid of Ash, and now you want me to be a test subject. Make up your mind."

"I still want Mr. Sterling out of my way. But now that you've shown me how badly you want a family, I believe we could do incredible things."

I've never cared much what anyone else wants. Come to think of it, I've never put much energy into what I wanted either. A family. Sure, I ached for connection, but never once tried to fix it. I never believed I could. I resist the urge to glance at the door. "What kind of tests?"

"Cognitive and metaphysical. I examine your gifts as only a doctor can."

Braun opens a cabinet, the key in the lock a high-pitched clang of metal that sends shivers up my limbs. He turns, a glass vial in his hand. The liquid inside shines like a frog's skin.

"Here is your chance, Primrose." Braun paces back and forth, rubbing his chin. "I've invented a new drug. Lessen the pain that comes with psychic visions. Darken your hair and bleed the color back into your eyes." He places the vial on a metal tray where the liquid catches the light. The glass sits next to an empty syringe.

"Erase my power."

"No." His spectacles sit low on his nose. "No drug can change who you are." He still paces back and forth, steps slowed now. "I can end your suffering. Your headaches, the nervous disposition you all seem to share. Even change how you appear to the world."

"Sure sounds like you want to cure us." His message is enticing. Provocative, even. A psychic who can turn on and off as they please. But all I see is that needle prepared to slide through skin. Complete destruction.

"There are still limitations," he says. "I need more subjects to gather crucial data." He catches me staring at the syringe. When we lock eyes, he walks to his door, opens it, and calls me over. Braun points down the hall, slowly raising his arm in front of my face. Marion sits in a wheelchair in the window, catching the sunshine. "Do it for her."

Her bony cheeks and frail fingers haunt my mind. "What's wrong with her?"

He drops his arm to his side. "She isn't responding well. I rescued her from a troublesome hospital, so she is safe now, but the weakness seems to keep progressing."

My mouth suddenly goes dry. "So, stop giving her that medicine."

"Without it, she flies into dangerous delusions. She hurts herself."

Panic grips my stomach. I've often wondered how to cut out the pain, but never had the strength to try it. This gift came with me, for reasons unknown, and I've fought to give it purpose. Even though I've mostly failed. Gwendolyn's hum spins through the air. A warning. I should be focused on the three-colored man, but this woman reveals so much pain I can't help but hurt for her. I could have been her.

"You can help without taking the drugs, Primrose." He steps between my view of her. "That is the beauty of Hot Lake Sanitorium. Here, your treatment is your choice."

Is anything ever really our choice? Marion looks at me with cloudy, teary eyes. I move to step closer to her, but Braun makes a tsk sound.

"Participate and you'll have full access to anyone in this ward. Those men don't understand you, do they? They can never see you the way other psychics do. Here, you could have a home."

All these years, I've lived as the monster that girl at the bottom of the stairs saw me as. I've waited for a death that wouldn't come. I've slept on any chance at hope. "No meds."

"It's always your choice." Braun steps aside to let me stare at Marion again.

I can do more. Save the three-colored man, learn about my gifts, and wrap my arms around this silver woman with the eyes that want to live and a body that won't cooperate. I can do so much more.

Chapter Eleven

The solarium pulses with light, so I sit in the corner, near the warmth from the windows, but tucked away in the shadows to shield my eyes. As I warm my skin and listen to the chatter around the room, pressure builds on my chest. How can one hotel hold so many people that require help? With a heart full of worry, I flood my mind with the people who have forced me to wake up and feel. Ash, Oliver, Finn. Silver-haired psychics Marion and Judy. Now I just need to know how.

Ash finds a table in a darker corner and waves me over. He slides out a chair for me. "Have you found your answer yet, Ash?"

He sits and smooths out his jacket. "Yes. This should be a state-of-the-art resort where the wealthy come to play and relax, and instead the doctor has turned it into a circus."

Green. He's turning this into a place to sell his medication. A resort where hot springs and emerald liquid cure all. I don't verbalize this realization for selfish reasons. I need the doctor right now.

Ash lifts a menu, examining the options as a server approaches. "What can I get you?" he asks.

"I'll take the chicken special. As long as it isn't green." He extends his hand to me, and I nod in agreement. "Make that three specials, and three glasses of Bordeaux."

The server's eyes widen. "Sir? Alcohol is no longer served since Prohibition."

"Oh, nonsense. I don't see any coppers around here, do you?"

The poor server looks as though he may faint. "Water is fine." I shoot a disapproving look to Ash. "I don't drink."

Ash shrugs. "Fine. Water it is." The server takes away the menus. "Finn should be along shortly. He was a bit cagey about dining with us."

Once I know someone's story, they can't go back to the person they were before a psychic opened the door to their secrets. Usually, it's a mix of fear and gratitude. We've entered an agreement of sorts, where I protect their darkest truths and they, in turn, walk away. A barrier which protects us both and leaves me in solitude. Only this time, I don't want protection. Not from him.

The waiter delivers the water, then accepts a crisp dollar from Ash before leaving the solarium.

Ash swirls the water as if it's whisky, ice clanking against the glass. Women smile at him yet he's too preoccupied to notice. His bright skin and dimples give him a boyish charm, while the expensive suit and easy body language remind everyone of his wealth. "Ash, have you ever been in love?"

The question turns him flushed-cheeked, fiddling with his napkin. "What a ridiculous question."

"It isn't ridiculous. Every woman looks at you like some sort of rare sight. They can't stop staring at your face. Some men, too." I pause to see if he reacts. I've seen every sexual preference in my travels and all anyone ever wants is someone to love them.

He scans the room for the most beautiful woman. Young, dark hair. Pretty smile. He marks her for later, I can see. "I love women."

"That is not what I asked."

He stretches back in his chair, eyeing me with agitation. "I don't know. How does anyone know if they've been in love?"

"You would know." Not that I've experienced it, but I have felt wounded hearts in my visions. I assume love and broken hearts go hand in hand.

The way he loosens his collar tells me he lives on the fear side of love. It is a weapon to yield, a tool to utilize. And something he can't buy with daddy's money.

He softens, and I know this moment won't come around many times. "I've only ever seen sex and lust and power. Men aren't gentle and wanting, lying vulnerable in a woman's lap."

"They could be."

He exhales, eyes on me to avoid the beautiful women around the room. "You've met them?"

How to show him what I've seen? What words can express the longing I've felt in most every human—woman and man and child—that lies deep in their soul. "I've seen people in a way you never will, Ash." He connects with me for a long, intense moment, where he seems to understand. "It's the one thing we all share. A need to be seen for who we really are. Loved, not despite our oddities, but because of them."

One prolonged look, and it's gone. His vulnerability has been locked down hard and tight. Another glance at that young woman brings him back to his father's son, a man who proves his worth with loveless sex and detached power.

"This damn hotel. It's not as if I care one bit what they do here, but I must fix their problems. I don't understand why I see flashes of a silver-haired child scurry about, but I imagine it has something to do with why you are here."

Ah, deflection. Men like Ash live by a code of avoidance. Hidden under all that bravado is a kind man who hasn't yet seen how powerful he could be. "I suppose we are all here looking for answers.

Finn enters the solarium, standing with hesitation in the arched doorway. Ash catches me staring. "Have you been in love, Primrose?"

I swat him with my napkin and lift my hand to wave at Finn. He lowers his chin and checks the room before walking over to meet us.

"Finn!" Ash slaps the table. "Welcome. Here we have plain but cold water, which is not at all a luscious Bordeaux, but will wash down the chicken just the same."

Finn lowers to the chair. "Sounds good."

We catch eyes. A tenuous moment hovers between us, the kind that has always kept me distant and afraid. I see his fear all too well.

"This blasted place is hemorrhaging money. The furnishings all need refreshed, and every wall needs a de-greening," Ash says. "How was your experience in the soaking bath?" He looks between us for any sort of answer.

"Hot," I say.

"Very helpful, dear."

Finn's posture stiffens as he sips from the water glass. "It helped my shoulder," he says. "Work at the farm has given me a few aches and pains, but the soaking tub seems to have eased them." He flashes me a grin as he clears his throat. "They don't hurt as much today."

"I refuse to believe water here differs from anywhere else, but this is helpful. Thank you, Finn." The waiter arrives with three plates of food. They look fine to me, but Ash turns his nose up. "After this fine meal, I propose we try out more of the facilities. The dance hall calls to me. That is, if you dance?" he asks Finn.

"I can, yes."

"Ah, well, one can never assume." He attacks his lunch with gusto, examining the wallpaper and ceiling between bites.

"How was your meeting with the doctor," Finn asks.

"Informative."

Ash clangs his fork to his plate. "Did you tell him I am not going anywhere until this place is up to snuff? The ledgers are abysmal."

"He knows." I hesitate but know I can't avoid the truth for too long. "I'll be spending some time on the medical ward." Both men stare at me with worried eyes. "Don't start with me. There are silver-haired women who won't come down here and I want time with them."

Ash huffs. "I don't like this at all."

"I agree, Primrose." Finn leans forward in his chair. "It seems dangerous."

"I've spoken to Oliver, the man who manages the farm. He ensures Dr. Braun is a medical professional and will respect my wishes of not wanting treatment."

"Treatment for what?" Ash asks. "Your silver hair? Please, it is the most interesting thing about your appearance. I quite adore it, don't you, Finn?" He winks at him, causing us both to blush.

I decide not to tell him the truth. To him I am simply an interesting, slightly odd woman he finds entertaining.

Strauss appears at our table. In the fading evening light, her cheekbones glint like razor blades. "The doctor has a message for you, Miss Whittaker."

"I see, what is it?"

She hands me a note, but before I can reach for it, she holds it to her chest. "I will not be sending him any notifications from you, understand? I am not your assistant, Miss Whittaker."

"Of course you aren't. I would never hire you."

The men laugh under cover of tightened lips. At least we can all agree she is wretched. I snatch the note from her hand.

"Do not test me," she says. "We are doing important work that will not be derailed by the likes of you." She folds her hands together. "Now, return to your painting and leisurely strolls. Good day."

She teeters off. "Lovely temperament on that woman," Ash says. "I had a nanny like her once. She lasted three days before I ran her out of the city."

I unfold the note. *3 p.m. My office.*

"I will meet you for evening dancing," I tell them as I tuck the folded paper in my pocket. "I have something to do first."

Finn tilts his head. "You're going to the medical ward?"

"I've managed myself for several decades now. Honestly, it's as if you both find me incapable."

Finn slides his hands across the table, stopping just short of touching my arm. "The man keeps women like you locked upstairs. It's him we don't trust."

"I will come with you," Ash announces.

"No." That's all I need. Dr. Braun would have us both removed from the premises. "I'm simply going to have a chat with a woman named Marion. Really, I'm fine."

The men aren't buying it. Ash crosses his arms. "If you don't meet us at five sharp, we will knock down the doors to come find you."

A warm rush of air floods my arms and neck and I want to wrap my arms around them both. I've never had protectors. Ash stands and grabs his lapels. "Finn, would you inspect the boiler room with me? Apparently, they heat the place with boiling water. Can you imagine? I know little about pipes and things."

"Sure."

Ash eyes the pretty brunette. "I'll be just a moment."

Ash walks off and Finn walks me to the hallway. "I have a bad feeling about Braun," he says.

Truthfully, I do too. But I can handle him. "I've waited years to understand this thing that lives inside me. The psychic power that prevents me from ever fully living. Now is my chance."

He slides his hands in his pockets and leans against the carved decorative paneling on the wall. "The farm changed everything for me." His arms remain stiff, his shoulders high. "I don't know, animals, trees, crops. A house with neighbors and travelers. My Uncle. I sit on the roof because the moon reminds me life keeps moving. The world keeps spinning, and I'm still here."

"That place felt special to me too."

"Do you think it's possible to find that feeling inside us, regardless of where we are?" His cheeks glow red as he shakes off his comment. "Never mind."

I step closer. I don't have a plan for what to say next, only that I want his green and blue and brown eyes to see that his thoughts are safe with me. "You told me that fear always wins. Do you believe that?"

"I used to." He drops his voice to a whisper. "But fear doesn't stop bad things from happening." We stare in an intense, fully charged moment of understanding. We both live with fear, but now, we fear for each other.

"Finn?" I'm close enough that our toes touch. "I'm very glad you're here with me."

He wraps me in his arms, holding me in a hug so tight my heart could break my chest wide open and fly away. I rest my head on his shoulder as his wild bronze hair tickles my cheek.

Not one vision reaches for me. Not even a whisper. I'm too busy feeling *good*.

Finn grabs my shoulders and looks me deep in the eyes. "Promise me you won't let that doctor hurt you."

I can do this. A few tests, some conversations with the psychics, and I'll be done. "I promise." His hands slide from my arms, and he smooths his hair back. "You haven't forgiven yourself for that accident, but I saw your soul. You are kind and good with a future full of love."

He looks out the window to the golden bluff behind the resort with a deep sigh. When he looks back at me, it's as if a layer of his hardened silence has disappeared. "I hope you're right."

"Will you dance with me tonight?"

"Tonight, and tomorrow, and tomorrow again. I'll be waiting, silver girl."

I wait for him to look back over his shoulder, which he does with a sneaky smile. Outside, Otto puts on a display with a puffed blue chest and shining eyes. He tilts his head, a friendly gesture to remind me he is here. As he claws away in a strut, my reflection takes shape in the window. A golden ball of light radiates from the center of my chest, and it feels something like home.

✳✳✳

The medical ward is locked. My head is still buzzing, and I won't be able to stop thinking of Finn until I see him tonight. Right now, I must lock down my armor to deal with Dr. Braun.

After several rounds of knocking and a twist of the doorbell handle, still nothing. Footsteps come up the stairs behind me and I find Oliver holding a crate of milk bottles.

"What are you doing here?" I ask.

"The doctor likes fresh milk for his coffee. I keep bottles in his office so he can avoid coming down to the kitchen."

"Oh. That's nice."

He clears his throat. "Here. Let me." He lowers the box to the floor and unlocks the door to the medical ward. In the crate, a book peeks out of the space between bottles. "You carry books with you for milk deliveries?"

"Oh." He holds the door open with his boot and lifts the handle, stuffing the book farther down. "Um, it's for Marion. She likes to read."

"That's very kind of you."

He nods once and quickly, opening the door for me to enter. The familiar smell of ammonia and sweat hits my nose, dampening any notions of romance I felt earlier with Finn. I follow Oliver to Braun's office, sneaking glances at the scowl-faced nurses and various medical tools in the hallway. A sign above a metal door reads "Viewing Area."

"I don't like it here either," he says. "I only lasted one week when I first arrived."

"Was it awful?"

His face twists, as if a memory has grabbed at his insides. "The treatments didn't hurt. The constant feeling that I deserved to be locked away from the world to change something I was born with—" He shakes away the rest of that sentence.

Clara peeks out her door with a wave at Oliver. He points to the crate, and I lift the edge of a towel. An apple, a few candies from the confectionary, and a strip of ribbon. "Are these for the women here?"

He unlocks a door in the middle of the hall and attaches the key ring to his overalls. "They need something fun to look forward to in this depressing place."

"Do you bring them gifts because you feel sorry for them?"

"Primrose, the only person I feel sorry for is me." He covers the items again and places the milk bottles in a kitchen of sorts attached to Braun's office. After making sure the lock is secured from the inside, he shuts the door, holding the handle longer than is necessary. "The gift you silvers have is special. I've tried to convince them to leave, but they tell me I don't understand."

He stays for the animals and the residents. But what does he do for himself, and why can't I see his future? Questions swirl over which man lands me the deal of a lifetime. Oliver could be the answer to everything. "Most people fear our visions, Oliver, which means they're terrified of us. Not everyone is as kind as you."

There's an ease to him that settles me. I touch his forearm without hesitation. A gesture of thanks, but the words don't come. My peach skin next to his brown and pink and white reminds me of a watercolor painting. He smiles. "They tell me my soul isn't scary like most people's." He places his other hand atop mine and squeezes. "It's because of the women I met here that I could walk away. Who needs a changed appearance when I already have so much joy?"

Tears gather in my eyes. "Yes."

My hand slides away without a hint of a vision. "You all can do great things, once this world lets you in," he says.

He walks toward a room I haven't been to yet. No Braun in sight, and I'm not waiting around. I sneak to Marion's room and knock on the door.

"Come in." Her voice is high and clear.

Once again, she's in her wheelchair, staring out the window at the people meandering below. "Hello. May I sit with you for a minute?"

She nods a few times. "I'm thrilled you're here." My heart rate quickens. A strained smile suggests secrets. She holds them inside just as I do. "You have questions."

Oh, how I've dreamed of this moment. "How do you see things? I only have visions when I touch people."

She considers the question. "This may shock you." Oh, dear. What does that mean? "You can have visions anytime you want."

"No, I can't."

She tucks her hair behind her ear. "We are born with that gift. You've created such a barrier around your power that your mind only allows it when you touch people. You've managed normalcy by avoiding touch. Problem is, you've moved farther and farther away from your purpose."

"No, that's not right. I dream of touch. I've wanted nothing more than someone to hug me or hold my hand." The room has turned unbearably hot. I step out of the sunshine and rub the back of my neck.

"Oh, Primrose." Her brow tightens in sorrow. "That's the human side of you interfering with the psychic side."

My mouth turns completely dry. "How could you know this?"

"We've all read you. We've seen your future because it's entwined with ours."

"How—" No. My mind can't grasp this. "Did you read my soul before you met me?"

She wheels closer with a very labored push of the wheels. "I saw the vision years ago."

"How is my future entwined with yours?"

Her deep breath holds a twinge of regret. "You're here to teach us."

"I don't know anything. Marion, I am not the one to ask for guidance. I'm supposed to be dead right now."

"It's a horror, isn't it? Knowing every awful thing that will happen in the world. Have you seen what's coming in the 1930s, and then another world war?" I nod in solemn agreement. "We just lived through the last one."

"I have no notion to rid myself of visions. I just need to discover how to cope with them. How to live in harmony with something that powerful. I came here to save a man with three colors. Whoever that is." I hang my head. "I sound mad."

Oliver knocks on the door, Marion's book in hand. "Primrose, Braun sent me a message for you." He places the book on Marion's bedside table. "Come back tonight at midnight."

"Midnight?"

"He's busy right now."

A deep sadness ripples under Oliver's smile. Pity, perhaps. He slips out the door where Strauss awaits. "Whittaker. Get out before I drag you back downstairs."

Marion grabs my wrist with surprising strength from her skeletal fingers. "Go on."

I'm so stunned I don't have time to fight the vision. Her soul pulls me so hard and fast my breath leaves my chest. Blood plummets from my head as my vision goes black. Shot like a cannon onto a road of yellow bricks that crack my knees and bruise my palms. I stumble face first onto the hot clay which sears my skin and sends me rolling into cornfields.

A black cloud rolls in, its belly angry and pulsing. Despite my stinging skin, I run down the narrow lane created by towering stalks as they dry to a crisp around me. Back over my shoulder, the blackness grows in force, howling and licking the tips of my silver hair. I run faster, harder, hoping my clumsy feet don't stumble. There's no end in sight, but I run anyway until my lungs sting.

The evil catches me.

The ground disappears, and the storm shoves me off into the starless sky. Nothing to catch me, I plummet. Terror rips through my core as easy as a nail through old fabric. As I disappear into the abyss without a star in sight, I grasp for any sign of joy, of hope. A glimmer appears below. The light expands toward me, growing, growing, until I land with such force I wonder if I have died.

I breathe through the pain and scream, realizing I'm in a dark hole, sitting in a pool of black, oily water. Next to me sits Marion, a calm smile on her face. "Hello, Primrose. I've been waiting."

"What the hell, Marion?" I try to stand but my legs don't cooperate, and I collapse back into the water where tears flood my eyes. "Why does your soul feel like this?"

"The end has been coming for a while. You'll help me." Her wasted body slowly slides under the surface.

"Help you how?" I reach for her, but my fingers rake through a murky handful of water. "I'll save you, I promise."

"No, Primrose. You aren't here to save me, you're here to release me of the pain so I can die."

"No." She sinks farther and farther as I reach for her and come up empty. "Marion, stop. Please. Stay here with me.

Just as she slips under entirely, I scream. A spindle of a red poppy shoots up from the surface and blooms right in front of me. The petals morph into a hand that grabs my wrist, forcing me underwater. I can't breathe, though I kick and thrash. I'm going to die in her soul, in the darkness of my making.

Like a spit from the outer world, I land back on Earth, wrist in Marion's hand, trying not to faint. My head could split open for how it aches.

"You saw?" she asks.

I take a deep breath to ensure oily water hasn't filled my lungs. "You hand me knowledge and then you'll die. This can't be right."

"It is right. You'll know you're on the right path when you see purple tears."

"Purple tears? What are you talking about? If I come across one more riddle—"

"I'm ready. I'm so tired, Primrose." She slides her hand from my hot skin. "Fight to make my death quick, okay?"

Strauss marches in, grabs my arm and pulls, but I can't handle another vision. I may break. I yank away. "Get off me!" Through gritted teeth and heaving breaths, I acquiesce. "I'll go. Just don't touch me."

I follow Strauss out the door with a glance back at Marion. She's calm, she's accepted this. Braun has been slowly killing her in the name of science and she willingly offers her arm for the needle.

Oliver was right. How do you save someone who walks into the fire with free will and eyes wide open?

Chapter Twelve

As I eat alone, I watch the couples laugh around me. I imagine their non-psychic minds and souls blissfully engaging in a meal without the eyes that see beyond their ease. They can simply eat and laugh and hold hands, discussing the mundanity of the weather and their newest hat, while a woman at this table for one with silver hair and eyes into the soul can have a life with purpose, but at the cost of killing one of my own. I shudder at the notion that my power could ruin far more than just Marion, as men like Dr. Braun spread their snake oil to the masses.

Ash and Finn arrive fresh out of their inspection of the inner workings of the hotel. Ash pulls up a chair from another table and flips it around. He thumps into the chair and rests his arms on the back. "The place is crumbling," he says with an odd smile.

Finn slides over a chair to the tiny table. "Busted pipes. Rusted pumps. Exposed wires pose a serious fire risk."

The state of this place concerns me not at all, but these two men warm my heart. Finn has even combed back his hair tonight. "Can you close it down?"

Ash extends his arms and leans back, taking up all the space he wishes to. "I could. We'd take an enormous hit, and I'd have to return to Manhattan with my tail tucked between my legs."

Finn leans forward, arms on the table. "Why care so much about your father's approval?"

"Finn, my good man, you just evaluated an entire operation based on the pipes and wires." He smooths his jacket. "I don't even manage my bank account." He catches our confused glances. "Money simply arrives, and I spend it."

"That is a problem I would like to have," I say.

Finn shakes his head. "Not me. I am owned by no one."

Ash snaps for the server's attention. "I need a glass with ice." The man scurries over to an ice bucket and returns with his requested glass. Ash removes a flask from his pocket. "No, Finn. You are only owned by your grief." Ash unscrews the cap and glugs the liquor into his tumbler, noticing our stunned faces. "I do not know what you've been through, Finn, but whatever it is clearly haunts you. My father's reign of terror is no different."

"I guess we're all just broken glass trying to hide our cracks." I instantly recoil. That sentiment was deep down, hiding in its safe little space in my heart. I guess the pain found its way to the surface because these two men attempted strength but found softness instead, and coaxed mine out too.

Ash guzzles his drink and slams the glass onto the table. "This hotel needs to be rebuilt and the madman in the sanitorium is our primary income. I will not solve this tonight, so let us dance." The way he flips in and out of reality boggles my mind.

The barber and post office have closed for the night. Some remain in the sitting areas for a quiet evening or gather in the solarium to play cards. We climb the stairs to the second floor that houses rooms, an art studio, and a dance hall. Musicians tune instruments as people flow into the ballroom. Sheer drapes flow with grace along the wall of windows that stretch the twelve-foot ceilings. Three glittering chandeliers cast prismed light over the guests who shine in silk and velvet evening gowns. Women with lacquered lips and beaded fringe. I stare down at my basic blue day dress and long, silver hair. Finn has gone to help an older woman navigate the crowd to a seat in the corner.

Ash slides up next to me. "Don't look at them." He sips from his flask and watches the room for signs of beautiful women. "It's easy to wear layers of money and call yourself classy. It is quite another to be unique. That, I fear, may be the most difficult and beautiful thing of all."

I pull my shoulders back, yes, because his kindness has helped me, but also so he knows his words matter. "How can a pompous man with a delicate ego have such a pure view on the world?"

"I am many things, dear Primrose, but complicated is not one of them. I want it all. The money, the status, the undying affection of every beauty in the world." He smiles at a woman, different from yesterday, with white gloves up to her elbows. "None of this changes the fact that I am a lost boy who will never stop searching for home."

I smooth my hair in place and catch my reflection in a mirror. Though the strands shine a shocking silver, they may be the silkiest around. By the time I turn my head Ash is gone, already across the room wooing the woman in gloves. Finn walks toward me, his hair slicked away from his eyes and resting in a wavy mess at his shoulders. "Do you like to dance?" he asks.

"I do, but I rarely act upon it. Complications, as it were."

He nods in agreement. "If we dance, will you have a vision?"

"Probably." I want to tell him everything about Marion and Braun's drugs, and how this decision may break me forever, but I withhold it. It would be a shame to ruin this night with my terrible thoughts. "I want to dance with you." Oh, how I want that.

"I'm going to reach for your hand, and then your waist," he says. "When you hold me back, let the vision come as it may. I won't let go until it passes, and when you're done, we can dance or talk, or simply hold hands in silence."

"Why?"

"Because no one should live in fear of touch."

A woman gasps as she walks past, her companion shushing her, his cheeks aflame with red. "Some fear me but others find me fascinating, as if I am something wild like a horse who changes color."

"Forget them. Look at me." His arms remain at his sides. My heart thumps in my chest, a reminder that my psychic self does not stop me being human.

I force a terrified, overwhelmed nod. Marion said I can see things without touch, but that seems impossible. I stare down at my boots and remember Russell. He said there is magic in everything.

Finn slides close, his belly mere inches from mine. As one hand slides into my palm, the other wraps around my low back. He waits. Nothing yet. He lifts my hand to our shoulders and threads his fingers through mine. "I'm here," he says with hesitancy. "I'm here."

His words leave me confused enough that his soul creeps in. He's present in life, I suppose. And I'm learning the same lesson. The rush overtakes me. I pierce the film of reality and stumble onto a clearing of yellow daisies. Hundreds of them. An eerie calm spreads through me as sound buzzes in the distance.

I reach down to pluck a flower from the ground and twirl its stem in my fingers. Another hand reaches for the flower. Finn. We stand in the same position as my human form. "Something is coming," I say.

"It has been coming since the beginning." His face is his, but his voice sounds hollow. "And we're all here for you."

"I don't understand." His hand warms mine as real as we're still in the ballroom when I was a smitten girl wanting a dance. "I'm here to save someone. Perhaps you."

"Could be. Or maybe you will save yourself."

Finn lets go. He walks backward with a reassuring smile that holds a warning. The daisy is still in my hand, the petals bruised and torn. Yellow turns red, and every flower I see becomes a sea of poppies. Sleep drags me down, slowly yanking me toward the ground. I fight off the urge and rotate my hand, looking at the palmful of poppy petals. They buzz and shake. I try to drop them, but I can't move. My hand pulses with pain as bees swarm from the center of my palm. In front of my eyes, they hover and bulge, as giant, sharp stingers grow from their abdomens.

I stumble back, wondering how long the venom of a hundred bees would take to kill me. They grow three times their size, buzzing so loud I cover my ears. Their bloated bodies rear back, pointing their stingers toward my face, puffed and trembling.

Instead of cowering, I hold up both my hands and scream, so frustrated with these visions I could spit. A wall of amber light encases me and the bees smash into it, falling to the ground, where they wither into a pile of dead flies.

The light evaporates. I'm standing in a glass shield, the bees and coercive poppies frothing with anger outside my bubble. One threatens to sting me, the other to drug me.

The field disappears and I drop, through the stars and past an image. A needle of green liquid injected into an arm as Finn bangs on the window outside. I reach to snatch the needle just as I land with a screech back in my body.

Finn hasn't moved. His face doesn't look scared, his palm is not sweaty. "I'm still here," he says.

"My father died of a drug overdose." I can't imagine what else to say in this moment except to stick to Gwendolyn's advice to trust my visions and start with the truth. "My mother drinks booze all day every day. The one thing I've always known is that I won't be like them. I won't use those things." I force myself to focus on his eyes. "But now the drug is in my life, everywhere, and I have to stop it, or I lose everything, including you."

"You saw your future in my soul?"

"I think so, though I can't understand how. We aren't supposed to see our own future."

He presses me to his belly and squeezes my hand a little firmer. "Maybe it isn't your future, but just a warning. Sounds like our lives are intertwined. We better start dancing."

While I try to decipher how he possibly wants to dance with me after I laid my secrets bare, he's busy swooping me onto the dance floor. The music thumps out a jumpy tune as a man smashes the piano keys from a standing position. We twirl past couples so consumed by their laughter they don't notice the silver whir gliding past. Ash stands in the corner, flipping some woman's hair and kissing her neck.

Though neither of us know these steps, we live in the reverie of spins and laughter, in smiles and the unbelievable elation of touch. Pure touch, without side effects.

Cymbals crash as the music peaks and stops as a rush of energy flows through me. I grab Finn's hand and duck outside the ballroom to catch my breath. "I need some air." We step onto the balcony where Otto sits like a jeweled statue, his long tail cascading down the white stone pillars under the railing.

As if I were a normal woman, I still hold Finn's hand, and let my heart beat fast enough to slip my mind to the uncharted idea of romance. I don't simply want to touch him. I want to feel him.

"Why aren't you scared of me?" I ask.

"My entire family died at my hands. Nothing is scarier than that."

He says that as if it's a truth and not a tragic accident. "Finn, I provide people with the blades to cut their own skin. I give them license to walk into their dark end every time I reveal their almost always bleak future. Does that make me to blame?" A pain twists in my gut. I've always believed I am darkness searching for light, without a question that he is good. How does anyone turn that kindness on themselves?

"I don't know about blame. I just know there's a darkness in you I understand." As usual, they seek me out, those who need to see the ugly side of things. "They've been gone for two years, but somehow, I've learned to exist. I chop wood and harvest crops. I stargaze, and sometimes I sleep. Since you've come along, an unfamiliar feeling has settled in my chest."

"Fear wrapped in hope with a dash of horror?"

"Exactly." He breaks a smile, a sight of unmitigated happiness.

I wrap my hands around his neck, his skin softer than I imagined. We breathe together. Big, heaving puffs of balmy night air under an indigo sky. "It's like the lonely parts of ourselves act as magnets."

He spreads both hands across my upper back, looking down at my face through his loosened hair. "I'm not sure I can do it all again. Feel, that is."

"Seems too late for that." I tip my head up and pull him close, pressing my lips to his. A calm, euphoric mind, and a body of jolting energy sets me off kilter. Unsteady enough to press harder and glide my lips and tongue over his. He balls the back of my dress in his fists and kisses me with an unsatiated hunger.

We are both starved, feasting on the sweet escape of our hearts.

He pulls away, eyes closed, pressing his forehead to mine. Otto honks, as loud as a trumpet's bell pointed at my ear. We jump, cracking our foreheads together. "Shit," he says, lifting my chin up. "Are you hurt?"

"No." Luckily, no bump or headache. "Was that our punishment for such a great kiss?"

A smile tugs at the edge of his lips. "Worth it."

I lean forward to kiss him again, but Ash flies out through the door, startling Otto, who patters toward him with an angry squawk. "Holy hell, don't eat me!" Ash hides behind us, peeking out at Otto who waits at the door, his head cocked to the side, staring at Ash.

"I've never heard of a peacock eating anyone," Finn says.

"Leave it to me to be the first." Ash shoos Otto. "Go away, you feather-headed fowl. There are dances afoot."

Otto hops onto the rail of the balcony, jumps to the next one, and trails himself down the stairs toward Oliver's barn.

"Well, that was unpleasant." Ash shakes out his jacket. "The Charleston has started, and I would very much like to watch you both let loose. You're far too serious, the lot of you."

"Wait, what time is it?" I ask.

Ash shakes away his sleeve and lifts his watch. "The Rolex indicates ten minutes till midnight. Plenty of time to scoot the blues away."

"I can't. I'm meeting Dr. Braun."

The men exchange glances. "No, you aren't, Finn says." I'm about to remind him I need no one's permission to do as I please, but he lifts his hand. "Not without me."

"I can't imagine he would be interested in anything you have to say, Finn. Truly, I am fine."

Ash buttons his jacket. "I will attend as well. I would like a word with that madman."

"This can't go well."

Finn elbows Ash. "What about your admiring ladies waiting for a dance?"

"They are beautiful. And quite the bore. It is all about luncheons and teas with that lot. Dreadful." He opens the door with an extended arm. "Let us spend our midnight in the sanitorium as only sane people do."

"You are very good at irony." I slip past, tugging at Finn's fingers to follow.

Up the stairs to the third floor, the smell of burning pine grows in intensity. Ash swigs from his flask again, bangs on the door, and readies his stance as if he's off to battle. The door creaks open as Finn and I peek out from either side of Ash's shoulders. Strauss wears an unsurprised reaction, only breaking the silence with one, hard sniff.

"Follow me."

An entire floor of ailing humans produces a sort of haze of despair. I imagine the many dark souls wish to reach for me, but the men seem to sense it too. Finn's shoulders rise to his ears as we pass doors ajar into darkness and moans from somewhere unseen.

Strauss opens a door at the end of the hall. "In here." Once we're all inside, she shuts the door and crosses her hands in front of her belly. We examine this strange, windowless room. A glass table sits in the middle, where emerald beams shine through the green-paneled skylight overhead.

Braun steps through a hidden door that looks like part of the wall's marble slab. "Hello, everyone." He steps heel to toe toward us as precise as an incision, a glass orb in his hand. It reminds me of my crystal ball, only green.

"Welcome to my sanctuary." Braun sets it down on a metal ring on the table with his clawlike fingers. "What do you see?" he asks us.

Ash stares at him. "A delusional doctor with his own sanctuary."

Strauss growls from the corner like a rabid dog, but Braun holds his hand to steady her. "Skepticism is good. We need to question everything." His staccato pauses between sentences unnerve me. "It's how I came to a pivotal moment five years ago, right in this very room."

Braun steps behind me and places his hands on my shoulders. My body begins to pulse and ache, my forehead about to burst. I fight the gnashing vision reaching for me and push away the whispers of his soul.

"Russell stood here with me," Braun says. "He struggled and struggled and wanted to die, his visions were so powerful."

"Visions?" Ash asks. "Is that some medical term for headaches?"

The man can't be that obtuse.

"Something like that," Braun says. "He was right here, begging me to kill him. I wouldn't, of course. And not just because I'm a doctor." His fingers press into my flesh, not sharp, but heavy and deep. Hold on. I can't let him pull me in. "I had to save him. And I'd been working with gems for years. We mixed air-dried poppy powder with alkaloids in the hot springs water, which slowed unwanted effects of headaches and lethargy. We had discovered an opium tincture powered by healing waters."

I can't hold on. His touch seems to reach into my chest cavity, pulling me toward the darkness more with every passing second.

Braun senses my tension, I know he does. Finally, Ash grabs Braun's hands. "Unhand her, you lunatic."

Braun laughs, undeterred. "That tincture was one thing, but do you know what we found right here?" We don't dare speak. "When powered by this emerald light, the medicinal powers grew."

"Is this why you've decorated the place in green? Why you've changed the name to Hot Lake Sanitorium?" Ash throws up his hands.

"Our dignified hotel will not become a charlatan's ruse where we sell emerald liquids and call it medicine."

"And why not, Mr. Sterling? People love a sensation. Some of our guests may have shunned away, but many love the odd nature of what I am doing here." Braun rubs his hand over the crystal ball. "I've dabbled in the occult." He shoots a glance toward me.

Finn steps closer, pressing his shoulder into mine for grounding comfort. "Primrose isn't something to be studied," he says. "Find your patients elsewhere."

Braun grins like a maniac. "I suffered from stomach ailments," he says to me. "Nothing worked. I tried everything, including my emerald water. But it wasn't until Russell found the cause. My well had been poisoning me. Arsenic, apparently."

"Russell can see disease," I mutter. "Is that why he works in alchemy? He wants to find another way to cure all the sickness he sees?"

Braun slaps his hand on the glass tabletop. The green light of the orb sucks the color from his face, turning his narrow features sickly and sallow. "Russell has a talent, just like you do, Primrose. But that which makes him special also turns him weak and broken. Debilitating headaches. Daily retching. Russell took my emerald medicine three years ago and began to lose his visions."

"But at what cost?" I ask. "Look at the rest of them on this floor. They're sicker than they ever would be with visions."

Ash grunts. "What are these vision you speak of? Mediums? Seances? Consorting with the dead and seeing disease. Nonsense." With hopeful eyes, I plead for him to believe the unbelievable.

"Maybe you didn't hear me, Braun." Finn puffs his chest, stepping closer to the doctor. Will he punch him in the nose? It wouldn't matter. Nothing will stop him just as nothing will stop me.

"Relax, cowboy. I won't force your little sweetheart into anything she doesn't want to do." He points to Strauss. "Bring her in."

Strauss opens the door for Clara, the nine-year-old snitch. She walks hesitantly up to Braun and looks at us.

"Our young Clara here, she has an untainted gift." Ash bends down, hands on his knees to examine her. "You have silver hair. And the same eyes as Primrose."

I expect him to turn and look at me with a knowing in his eyes, but the poor man can't grasp what he is unwilling to see. There's no magic in Ash's world.

"Clara can see in the dark. Through the dark. Through walls and floors and black skies. She can see anything she wants."

"Isn't that a lovely fairy tale," Ash says.

"It's true," she says. "I watched you shave your chest hair this morning."

Ash pulls back and crosses his arms. "Well, it is quite rude to spy on someone. I shall make sure my windows are closed so little girls can't see something they shouldn't."

She steps to Finn. "You ripped hair from your head. Through tears, no less. I presume it's over guilt for touching that one." She points to me. "You can't be happy. Not yet."

Braun smiles, watching the exchange.

"And you." She steps closer, a grand smile on her face. "Otto likes you, which means I like you. But the way you grimace after a reading. You'll never be a brilliant psychic with that level of fear."

She isn't afraid of the truth, I'll give her that. I bend down to meet her eyes. "What do you want with that kind of power?" I ask.

"How am I to know?" She shrugs. "All I do is see things. Judy speaks with the dead and Marion is the one to see the future."

"Who are these people?" Ash asks.

"Oh, Marion's the one with all the surgeries and the detailed messages from spirit. Her visions are told in golden threads woven into a picture. Primrose, if you ever get your act together, you could teach her a thing or two."

"Spirit shows her the pictures?" Shock immediately follows and the notion that this little girl who sees through walls would call me a teacher.

Ash pushes us back away from Braun and Clara. "Enough of this circus. Visions? Golden threads?" He picks up the glass orb and shakes it. Gold dust floats through the green liquid like a galaxy. He shoves it into Braun's chest. "Take your black magic and find another place to spread havoc. I am evicting you."

His voice certainly does quiver when he declares things.

"Ah." Braun bops his head back and forth as if there is music playing for only his ears. "What would daddy think of this?"

Ash's face hardens. His cheeks burn red. "This is my decision."

"Well, I am paying three-quarters of the expenditure here. You don't want to lose my money."

"We've lost customers because of your madness! You must pay most of the cost because your antics have scared off sane vacationers."

"I'm doing important work!" He balls his fists then quickly regains his calm. "What I've discovered could change medicine forever. I've dabbled in the occult, using my residents' powers to guide my discoveries." He grins at us. "Just like Primrose has agreed to."

I've agreed to some tests. I am not like the rest of them. Ash and Finn look at me as if they want to drag me out of here. "It's the only way I can spend time with the psychics up here. Besides, I can stop anytime I want, right?"

Finn leans to my ear. "Trust nothing."

"You have my word," Braun says. He bends down near Clara who whispers in his ear. Braun smiles with a quick glance to Ash, then reaches into his pocket. He hands Clara a hard candy, and she skips past us, waving to me as if she isn't his little spy. What did she tell him?

"Emerald butterscotch," Braun says. "She loves them."

Ash breaks first. "Come on, we don't need one more minute up here with emerald medicine and crystal balls. Madness, it is." He grabs us both and drags us toward the door.

"I'll make you a deal," Braun says.

"Ash, don't." I have psychic powers to deal with Braun's lunacy. Ash has nothing but a hot temper and an insatiable need to prove his worth.

"Don't worry," Braun says. "You're going to like this game."

"This isn't a competition," Ash says with a tug toward the door. His soul whispers for me, so I turn quickly to force his hand from mine as I reach for Finn.

Braun rubs his chin with his thumb and forefinger. "But… what if it were?"

Ash stops at the door near Strauss. He doesn't move. Doesn't speak.

"I know of a high stakes card game close to here."

Ash's hand slides from my arm and then from Finn's. It's the card game. Ash's face transforms from dismissive to dark intrigue and I know exactly what Clara told Braun. She knows he loves gambling.

"Big players," Braun says. "The biggest in the northwest. Ranches and fortunes have been won over this table."

Ash freezes and closes his eyes, willing himself to walk away. But he doesn't.

"Just think, you could have your own fortune. Return to your father with bigger investments than this little resort."

"I have nothing to wager," Ash says.

"Ah, I see you are bluffing already." He paces the room with a devious smile. "Clara saw your land deeds and business titles. Why did you bring them here, Mr. Sterling?"

Ash looks in our direction but doesn't make eye contact.

"Ah," Braun says. "We've found your little secret. You stole your father's financial records. I wonder what could have made you do that?"

I guess we all do enjoy our little secrets.

"Well, it would be a shame for your father to find out about your theft, wouldn't it? He would be oh so disappointed."

Ash stares at the green panel in the ceiling for a long while. "Put my name in." Ash doesn't shake his hand, or even look at him as he walks toward the door.

"Tomorrow night in the Pendleton underground," Braun says. "I'll book you a spot at the table. If you win, I'll vacate the resort. If you lose, you crawl back to your father, tail between your legs, because you've handed over the sanitorium to me."

Strauss smiles, a wicked, hideous grin.

Braun strokes the top of the crystal ball. "Like I said, everything we do here is voluntary."

Ash waits in the hallway, hands tightening into fists. The door to the sanctuary bangs shut behind us.

"Ash, are you sure you want to do this? He's setting you up to fail."

"I'm a card player, one of the best. It's the only thing I'm good at, and it's been my way out of every mistake in Manhattan. This is how I prove to my father I'm resourceful. I'll shut this place down *and* add to our fortune." His eyes transfix on us in a possessed, wild stare.

Oliver pads down the hall to meet us. He grabs Ash's arm. "Mr. Sterling, Clara told me what Dr. Braun did. You don't know what you're getting into. Braun sends me to the underground to buy ingredients for his potions."

Ash throws his hands up. "Oliver, is it? You don't know me, or my skills. I could save us all and buy this place." He looks past us, into some dreamy scene in his mind. "Patients set free, a thriving resort where you, Oliver, can tend to animals, and I can deliver Finn and Primrose safely out of here. Yes, I can do this. I need to prepare." He disappears down the hall as Clara snickers from behind her door.

Dammit, this could be the moment Ash needs me. A three-colored man delving into an underground for a secret card game with his fancy linen suit.

Oliver shrugs and slips through the doorway, back to his barn, I presume. I wonder what he was doing up here at this time of night.

Strauss shoos us out, shoving us into the stairwell. She slams the door shut.

"Finn, we have to stop Ash from walking into this trap."

"You know, for someone who wanted to die, you sure do have a lot of heart."

"Too much heart doesn't make you love more, it makes you intolerable of all the hate."

Chapter Thirteen

The once grand hotel creaks against the night's cool air. Through the dark, the brass panel of the door handle shines from moonlight finding its way through the midnight. One hour ago, I walked away from Finn, who had asked me why I needed any of this here at Hot Lake. I shrugged and said I don't know. Now, as the night will not release me to sleep, I can't stop thinking of the answer to that question.

When morning hits, Ash will head into the lion's den, blindly shooting for the stars, and I must somehow prevent his crash. Oliver, Ash, Finn. The only way to keep them safe is to keep them close, though heaven knows how any of us find safety against a madman with psychics on his side. I'm also wrestling with the idea that he convinced the psychics to take part in his game.

A knock on my door pulls me from my wandering thoughts. Whoever it is, they're a welcome reprieve. Mother's voice shrieks into my mind, asking me to show skin to manipulate men. I reach for the hotel silk robe and wrap it tightly around me as I push the door ajar to find Finn, eyes wide and bright.

"I can't sleep," he says.

"Me either." As if some alternate woman has taken over my body, I push the door open with a brazen invitation to come inside. He does, looking around in nervous anticipation.

"I wanted a break from farm work." He runs his fingers along the glass lamp on the desk to buy time, or to avoid eye contact. "But truly, deep down, I came here because the loneliness damn near killed me."

His cheeks shimmer under the gleam of a satin sky. "Loneliness has a way of doing that." I click the door shut as quietly as possible, not wanting to scare him away. "I'm a twenty-two-year-old-psychic who has mistakenly avoided touch, thinking she could stop the destruction. Nothing could have stopped it."

"Wait, you were wrong about touch?"

I kick the air like a child, I know, but I might throw him against the wall in the world's most passionate kiss if I don't stop myself now. Lord only knows what kind of psychic eruption that would lead to. "I don't know. A woman upstairs read me. She said I made up the idea that touch leads to visions."

"How do you get visions then?" he asks.

"Apparently, I can see them all the damn time. That's all I need, souls grabbing at me from every passerby. I'll never leave the house." As I stop ranting to catch my breath, I notice he's stepped closer. "I'm sorry, I just took over this entire conversation."

He strides closer still. We're in the dark but bright night floods the room with silver illumination. His multicolored eyes look straight into mine without a flinch. "I don't like talking about myself," he says.

"Clara said you pull your hair."

Finn looks down and shakes his hair loose to reveal patches of red scalp where he's plucked the hair. I glide my hand through his thick locks slowly, tenderly, wanting to make the painful parts stop hurting. No crawling on my head this time, only a deep pounding in my chest.

"That's why you grow your hair long? To hide this?"

"I do it less since I met you. Shit, I sound like a kid." He pulls away, but I keep my hands on the back of his head.

"No, you don't." His soul felt frozen and hollow. I saw the tornado and the fire, and how deep his regret is. "I avoided touching people for two decades. We all do some terribly wild things to avoid hurt."

He slides his hand around my waist. "Funny thing is, I didn't avoid one second of hurt."

I run my fingers along his jaw. His cheekbones. "I'm so sorry about your family."

"My sister had red hair and brown eyes and burped louder than any of us." He cracks a smile thinking about her, which instantly dries up. "I don't know what comes next, but the past few days have been some of the strangest experiences of my life."

For some reason, the bartender jumps into my mind. How he will slice his neck on the night of a harvest moon. He was many in a string of men who served a purpose. I would take their souls into mine and read their future for the short-lived exchange of long-awaited touch. A hard, hurried kiss. Sometimes more. I would strip down, keep my eyes closed, press my naked body to theirs, and lie still after, staring up at the ceiling, more desperate than ever.

Right now, I stare into Finn's hungry eyes, his full red lips, and I don't want to hurry. I don't want rough and cursory. I only wish to hug him hard enough to make the hair pulling stop. He kisses me, pressing me against the wall, our bodies smashed together, our hands exploring exposed skin. His belly. My thigh.

My heart thunders in my chest. Louder and angrier, until it hurts with a delicious dip into the freedom of lust. No visions call to me because I'm not resisting. This is authentic emotion. No yellow bricks. No poppies or stars. Just life.

Chapter Fourteen

After Finn left my room last night, I fell into the kind of sleep that rarely finds me and awoke to a burst of sunshine over my face and neck. The hotel is quiet. Eerily so. After pressing an ear to Finn's door and hearing gentle snores, I dress and grab a buttered roll in a mostly empty dining room. As I wait for someone to answer the medical ward's door, I catch a glimpse out the front window as a sleek white car arrives for Ash. The driver hands him the keys and carries on toward the path that leads to the train. Ash runs his hand along the curves of the hood with a smile.

I don't have time to think of his journey to the underground because Strauss clears her throat in the open doorway. "What do you want, Whittaker?"

I resist the urge to growl back. "I'm here to see Marion."

"No." Just like that. Decisive and unwavering.

Answers. I need answers above all else. "Fine, then let me in to see Braun. Go on, tell him I'm here."

She doesn't need to think about it. She knows he's been waiting patiently for me to come begging for his all-knowing doctor mind. As if I need some man with a degree to tell me what I already know. My special mind could end me.

Strauss throws the door open and walks away as I hurry to get inside. I peek over my shoulder. Clara sits cross-legged on the floor playing Jacks while Judy watches over her. Marion's door is shut.

Miss Strauss knocks three times. The mail slot eventually opens to Braun's wild, mistrusting eyes. "What?" he barks.

"Miss Whittaker here for you." Her sour face may be the expression that lives there at rest.

He shuts the slot. I wonder if I can make a run for one of their rooms, but the door opens, ruining any wild ideas. "Come in," he says.

Not hidden in the shadows today, he wears a freshly pressed white lab coat, care of Strauss, no doubt, and a tweed vest buttoned incorrectly. His hunter green tie completes the look of a doctor portraying a showman... or the other way around.

I step in and watch the door as it shuts. A metronome taps in the corner. "Why the metronome with no piano?" I ask.

"Helps me focus." He points to an exam table with worn leather corners that squeaks when I sit on it.

He looks into my eyes and presses my forehead with both his bony thumbs.

"Ouch." I shove his hands away. "I can assure you, jabbing your fingers into my skull will not help either of us."

"I studied at the Mayo Clinic," he says, aghast that I dare question him. When I don't respond, he points to his Harvard medical degree, framed and askew on the wall. He bristles but carries on. He presses into my shoulders, my neck, my jaw, as if I'm a raw steak to be massaged before searing in a cast iron pan.

"Sir, there's a human attached to these parts."

He stops, furrows his brow. "Many of you have body aches. Bands of muscle rigidity, distended abdomen. Headaches and hypersensitivity to light." He looks down his nose over the spectacles. "Have I gotten close?"

"My abdomen is not distended." I assume that means swollen and that, at least, I do not have. He listens to my heart, my lungs, looks in my ears. "Aren't you going to ask me how long I've had these visions? What they've done to me?"

He taps his pointer finger to his chin in time to the metronome. "I already know those answers. You are certainly no different than the rest of them."

For some strange reason, the idea that I am no more special than every other silver-haired girl that has crossed his path fills me with the same rage as being laughed at. The same fury as when I'm mocked. "You know so little about things outside your medical books."

"I know plenty." He takes elongated steps in a circle, hands clasped behind his back like a villain from a child's rhyme. "You loathe and love your power. You know you're special. A chosen one by the universe or spirits or God. But the pain of it all has left you bereft and lost. You've avoided touch as some way to control that which owns you, and now that you're falling in love and meeting friends, you need answers. Does that about sum it up?"

What at first looked to be a scar on his brow reveals itself up close to be a deep wrinkle. "You missed a few key elements."

"Ah, yes. Clara heard you say you should have died. You know, everyone's spirit guide looks different. Their visions unique to them. What do yours look like?"

I consider what he wants from me and tread carefully. I wouldn't dare tell him about Gwendolyn. "A yellow road lined with poppies. That's where I feel their emotions. I see their story as I dive into a sea of stars."

Perhaps too much truth, but how else can I keep him wanting more?

"Fascinating." He removes his spectacles and holds the corner to his mouth, tapping his bottom lip while in thought. "Clara sees and hears all. Judy speaks with the dead. What is your ability?"

"I just, I see things."

He sniffs in annoyance. "Surely you don't think that is all."

I decide to turn the tables. "What about Marion?"

"What about her?" He snarls with agitation. Impatience for my mistrust. "She is sick. Has been for a very long time."

"What is her ability?"

"She understands intimately every person who will come into her life and what their purpose is. She sees every future in detail. Who will protect or hurt her. And eventually, they all hurt her."

I force my eyes to remain on him and not glance at the door as I want to do. "That means you will hurt her too." So will I, but I keep that to myself.

"Yes." No remorse. "She is giving her body and mind to science. It's a noble feat. One I will not stand in the way of."

"You say she consents, but what choice does she have?"

"Ah." His evil grin makes me want to throw something at him. "You should know more since you've read her. Your visions do not reveal everything. Interesting."

I should know more, be more, read faster and deeper. It all flies through my mind like a whir. Nothing but nonstop failures. This is what he wants. Destabilize me. As if I had much stability to begin with. I don't know, even a thread of resistance feels like more than these women have.

"What more do you need from me?"

He flops into his chair and scribbles notes as the metronome goes tick tick behind him. Without looking up he says, "I need nothing more from you today. Leave me to work."

I slide from the table, my boots hitting the tiles with a satisfying clang. They still reflect the light and somehow, still tap into some part of me that believes in magic. Even in this sterile room with a cobweb hanging over the door.

I let myself out. In the hallway, Strauss's glare is nowhere to be found. Judy's door is ajar. I knock and she patters up to the doorway. "Primrose."

"Judy. You read the dead?" No time for niceties.

She nods and looks behind me. "Strauss will be along soon."

"Why are you here? Don't you want to leave this place?"

"No." She places her hand on her chest. Her forearms are brittle and twiggy, just like Marion's. "This is my answer."

"What answer?"

Her nervous twitches make me want to read her vision. She scratches at her neck. "He's going to cure me. The voices are all but gone. Isn't that incredible?"

"The voices of dead people?"

She grabs my arms while I fight off every speck of whispers from her soul. "They wake me up and stand at the foot of my bed. They want messages to their loved ones." Thank God she releases me and begins pacing. "There's money under the floorboard. I never told her how proud I am, tell her who killed me." Her breath wavers and her fingers jolt in every direction. "It's too much, I can't stop them." Her eyes focus on me with tiny, pinpoint pupils. "They haven't spoken to me in three days."

"Oh." Her body is so frail I consider pulling over a chair, but Clara runs into the room, spinning circles around us.

"Don't do it, Primrose," she says. "Dr. Braun wants to inject you too."

Her innocent little face doesn't match her role as spy in this hellhole. "I won't let him."

"That's what Judy said too." She continues dancing but looks over to Judy who is now rocking in place, staring at a pocket watch. "He gets you all to break."

I lean down to look in her big, blue eyes. They're almost as clear as mine. "What does he offer you?" I shudder with possible answers to this question.

"Candy, of course!"

Judy keeps rocking but finds her voice. "Clara is homeless."

"Not anymore!" she announces with a smile. "Butterscotch and a warm bed and all I have to do is snitch."

"Braun isn't a good man, Clara."

"Don't you think I know that?" Her screechy voice sends me back upright. "But someday I'll get the drug too, when I'm old enough, and I can stop snitching."

"Don't you all see how crazy this is?" I try to catch their attention, but Judy is rocking and Clara is dancing. "He's killing you one sick day at a time and none of this makes you better."

"It will," Judy says. "Dammit, nurses! You're twenty minutes late." Her weak little body certainly found a voice. "Listen, Primrose, you haven't lived with the nonstop, unrelenting hell we have, okay? I'm holding on to Braun's medicine. It's going to fix me. I know it."

I open my mouth to scream that no, the medicine will not fix her, but a nurse arrives rolling a tray. "Out of my way, Prima Clararina!" As if this is some nursery school. She passes me with a *tsk*. "Strauss will kill you if she finds you in here."

"Why is Judy like that?" I follow behind her, noting the sweat streaming down Judy's temples.

"It happens when she doesn't get her dose on time. Sorry, Miss Judy, I had a bleed to attend to." The nurse prepares her arm and measures her heart rate.

Judy grabs me, pulling me close. "Primrose." Her breathing is so fast, she has trouble speaking more than a word before trembling. "I see him. He's here."

"Who?" Clara has pranced her way out of the room, but I see no man.

Judy sobs. "Hurry." The nurse carries on at the same speed, unfazed by the frantic cries that make my chest seize. "Your father," Judy says.

The nurse holds up a syringe, its emerald liquid like the mildew that grows around the fountain in Washington Park back home. Flashbacks of the syringe come back to me; the needle stuck straight out from the crook of my father's elbow. They say to remember them as they lived and not how they died, but that's hard to do when both versions of my father—alive and dead—involved vacant eyes and needle in his veins.

The nurse slides the needle into Judy's arm and presses the green liquid into her body with the push of her thumb. Instantly, Judy settles. She breathes steadier, and leans her head against the chair's back.

"Strauss will be through with rounds any minute. You better git."

I watch color return to Judy's skin and how her hands lay relaxed in her lap. "How do you do this to them and not feel like an awful person?"

"If I don't keep up with their schedule, they go out of their mind. How would you enjoy vomit and diarrhea at the same time while your body is slick with sweat and your heart beats so fast, you're certain you'll simply up and die?"

"You justify this, but you created it."

"Patient wishes." She pushes past me with a shove into my arm. An instant vision with no yellow road. The woman watched her mother suffer melancholia. This little girl had to tie her down and splash cold water on her face. It scared the wits out of her, and here she is, injecting a slow death on innocent women. I consider screaming at her, but it seems like no use.

Judy has drifted to sleep.

I step out to the hallway which is surprisingly quiet. Marion wheels herself toward me looking stronger. "Primrose, watch." She plants her feet and reaches her hands out. I hold her palms. She pulls on me to bring herself to standing on wobbly legs. "See? I'm better."

Her skin is soft but papery. She appears to be around forty, yet her body looks closer to seventy. "Great work," I tell her. Now that she's standing, I see that swollen belly Dr. Braun mentioned. The morning sun isn't strong enough to overpower the desperate gray of the windowless sanitorium. "Aren't these places supposed to offer fresh air and sunlight?"

"We go outside every week for a little while. We scare the guests though."

"I scare everyone." My attempts to lighten the mood fall flat.

She plops back into the chair looking as if she's run a mile. "I know what you're thinking. Why bother trying to walk again if I'm half dead?"

"I don't know. I spent the night I thought I would die spinning naked in my bedroom and getting drunk on bathtub gin."

That elicits a smile. Thank God. "Did you know our bodies rally a good effort before we die? Your presence has given me something to look forward to."

"I don't want to know too much." This, I know, is a giant lie, but I can't trade information for her life. I just can't.

"Too bad. You don't have a choice." She takes a deep breath. "You will become the strongest psychic in the world and stop him from making this medicine legal. He'll kill thousands. Maybe millions."

"You're taking the damn stuff, Marion."

"Only long enough to bring you into the fray. Did you know you were put here to save an entire generation of innocent people?"

"My spirit guide told me I could save many." All I can say is Gwendolyn better get her sequined ass back here pretty soon to help me.

Judy walks out of her room, surprisingly bright and calm. "Primrose, I never finished telling you what your father said."

"That wasn't just a drug frenzy?"

"No. He told me to tell you how good this stuff feels. Even his death felt like drifting off to the calmest sleep he's ever had."

"That's what he said? Not sorry for being a lying womanizer, or swindling his way through my childhood? No mention of ruining my entire life and stealing my visions, leaving me with nothing but confusion over my weird little brain?" I rub my eyes a little too hard and my vision goes black and starry. "He should apologize for keeping me from my aunt. Instead, he only cares about drugs, even in the afterlife."

"Some of the dead speak just so I will listen, not because they have anything helpful to say." Judy yawns. "Have you told her yet?" she asks Marion.

"Told me what?"

"We're also intertwined with your three-colored man." She curls her finger to bring me closer so she can whisper. "Whoever he is, you must save him. He's the link to stopping Braun."

"I don't understand."

Judy joins the huddle, on the lookout for any prying eyes. "I need this stuff now, but only until I'm healed, then we're free. Marion's mother came to me to say that you are on this adventure to find a man with three colors, and it's so he can stop Braun's plans to drug every psychic, mystic, and shaman he gets his grubby hands on."

So, the three-colored man will stop Braun. Poor Judy believes this drug will cure her. "Why does Braun want all this?" I ask.

"I think you know that answer," Marion says.

"Yeah. Infamy. Still, we're missing something." A shuffle in the medicine room causes us to whisper even more. "If I save this person, will that stop you from dying, Marion?"

"No," she says. "Setting me free is how you do all this."

"Kill you, you mean."

"Carry on my powers in your own life and release me from this horrid body that has only ever turned on me. That's exactly what I want."

I shake my head, pushing down my shock and anger for these two. "Both of you need to get the hell out of here. I'll help you."

Marion's smile somehow shames me without a single word. "I don't want to leave. Neither does Judy." Judy forces a nod, suggesting she's less manipulated than Marion. "The closer you get, the more we'll learn. Remember, trust your visions."

"I still can only feel them when I touch people."

"You've been so cut off from your calling, you'll have to learn how to find your peace again."

"I don't find psychic readings powerful."

"And that is your first error." Marion continues on as if Judy isn't twitching and clearing her throat next to us. "Remember your childhood. The voices that came to you in quiet moments. The spirits that were there. Somewhere along the way, you cut them off. They are part of you, you just have to find them."

"I can't handle more voices, Marion. The few readings I do leave me terrified and sleepy."

"Well, then you're doing it wrong. Your strength and power lie in the things you're afraid of. Listen more. And go save that three-colored man."

"I won't do it."

"You will," Marion says with absolute declaration.

Judy shrugs. "I've tried to convince her to fight, but this is what she wants."

"Right, because here at Hot Lake Sanitorium, we always have free will." A decision crafted by an almighty wizard who forces us to believe any part of this is our choice.

Chapter Fifteen

By the time I've reached the bottom of the staircase, I want to tear down the stupid sign telling me to keep my voice low and be sweet. They're killing people up there.

I must save this elusive man with three colors so he can stop Braun, and this will lead to Marion's death and Judy's freedom. It's all too convoluted.

As guests walk past me and meet my eyes with the usual look of horror, I open my ears. I hear nothing. Not the women with linked arms or the man smoking a pipe. Not the young lady fanning her neck, or even the rare gentleman who smiles at me without a laugh. Soul silence.

I need Gwendolyn and a plan.

In the foyer near the front office, Otto quivers next to me, as his long, green tail shimmers with gold. "Good morning, Otto." He lets me pet his head, a strange sensation if there ever was one. "The stakes are so high, my little friend. I'd like to believe I could have power over these visions, but this is all so complicated."

Otto rubs his head into my hand. It isn't an answer, but my fears still soften under his silky blue feathers. I'll take it.

Ash struts into the foyer. "Oh dear, you're petting the bird."

"He's sweet." Otto has had enough and struts his long tail toward the door as a guest allows him through. Truly unlike anything I've ever seen.

"My car has arrived." Ash stares out the window at the very expensive behemoth of a vehicle. "Well, it's not *mine*. Someday I'll own a dozen of those."

"Why would you need a dozen cars?"

"It's not about need, Primrose. You should start making decisions based on want." He narrows his vision and leans in. "What exactly do you want?"

That question seems so easy to answer. There's something sweet and innocent about our friendship. He sees me as a woman with a few oddities. I quite like it. He'll figure out soon enough that I'm a clairvoyant. "To not be afraid."

"Afraid of what?"

Never using my power for good, being unloved and lonely. Hurting everyone by trying to save them but watching them fall apart and die at my hands. "Everything." Seems like a safe answer.

Ash reaches for my shoulder. "Let me take you home."

Home. What is home? A place where my true self lives, unbruised and undeterred from her most enlightened self? I haven't yet found home.

"Primrose," Ash says. "You really can lose attention sometimes."

I pull away and tuck my hair behind my ear. "I can't go back to Portland."

"Is it really so difficult?" he asks. "Can't you just choose to be happy?"

I withhold an eye roll. Says the man with more money than I'll see in a lifetime. "Ash, you have all the wealth and women you could want. Has it made you happy?"

He sighs, "Point taken."

I long to live in the truthfulness of the stars, held and comforted, away from the consequences of Earth. But I'm stuck in this human body, hair and eyes marking me as an untouchable mystic. "They all see me as a peculiar mistake." I lift a hand toward the stares that I almost don't notice anymore, as they're as common as the stink from the sulfur springs around here.

"What do they know?" Ash lifts his chin and eyebrows as if he has forced his body to cooperate with the confidence that flows inside him. "Perhaps they are all odd, and you are the silver magician of our perfectly plain little world."

"You don't believe in magic."

"Ah, yes. But I do believe in you."

I long to ask why, and what part of this mess does he seem to admire, but somehow, his adoring smile is enough.

He shifts yet again, as he is wont to do. "This ridiculous emerald show of Braun's needs to stop. Scaring away guests and keeping troubled patients hostage. I'll put an end to all this. And we will find a proper doctor to help those poor women."

He doesn't see it—he's as troubled as the rest of us.

He smiles at yet another young woman and slaps his hands together. "I need to prepare for my card game tomorrow."

"About that. Please find another way. Braun is unpredictable, and guaranteed to swindle you."

"Of course he'll try," he says. "But I have something on my side that he doesn't."

"What's that?"

"Money. Lots of it." He struts away as I wonder how to save him from this disaster. He's the only one of the three men facing trouble, and I'll have to assume he's my answer to lifelong peace and spiritual power.

I step outside as the geyser spews like a fountain, the water shaded with hints of white and blue and green. A boy sits cross-legged holding a stick in the water, underneath the sign that reads *Danger*.

"What are you doing?" I ask.

He pulls the stick from the water and points to a mesh bag with three eggs inside. "Lunch."

"Oh, of course."

The boy returns to boiling his lunch. In a lake. This place is truly bizarre.

I walk the perimeter, past cobweb thistle stems as tall as me. The dried, sharp reeds wave in the steamy afternoon. I wonder if their stems were once purple and bright. Not too many thistles grow in the concrete ground of Portland.

Steam envelops me as the wind carries the hot springs heat across the flattened clearing. I consider calling Gwendolyn, but worry someone may hear. I can't see farther than an arm's reach in this white haze.

Before my mind decides, I'm pulled into the steam, into what feels like a vision, but no one is around me. No tunnel at all, and there's no wind to speak of. Just stars—thousands splashed across a cobalt sky. They illuminate when I swipe my hand through them, dropping gold dust like petals from a spring tree. They're brighter and softer than the ones I usually see. I want to stay here forever.

A blob of light expands from the endless night, growing closer and brighter, until Gwendolyn appears before me in a simple, silver gown, her hair a finger wave bob of chrome. She reaches for my hand, which I take without hesitation. We drop through the sky in an easy exhale and land on a giant poppy bloom, red all around.

"Whose vision am I in right now?" I ask.

She grasps my hands in hers. "Yours, my dear."

"I can't read my future. Can I?"

"You called me earlier as you whispered a need into the world, and here I am. We are not in your future, we are in your mind. We're safe here to discuss the troubles in your heart."

So many questions, how do I pick just one? "How can I call you now?"

"I've always been here, in the stars and among the flowers. I've come to you in your dreams and reached for your hand many times."

"But I couldn't see you. I didn't know a spirit guide cared about me."

A dreamy haze surrounds her where the edges of her hair and chin blur into golden light. "You have a choice in this world, Primrose. You created walls around your powers and around me and all I could do was wait."

"Until I died. Or did I?"

"You only heard me when the veil had thinned, and you listened."

"Which one is the three-colored man? Is it Ash?"

"I relay the messages I receive. They do not always come with answers."

The petals sway, lulling me into a cozy drift toward calm. I am, however, still me, and hold tight to the worry of it all. "I don't know how to perform visions without touch, nor do I want to."

Though her eyes shine as clear as glass, her beauty remains conventional. Gorgeous, even. "Becoming is painful. You must break down a lifetime of what didn't work and find the person you've always been inside."

Another poppy stem drops from the sky, curled tight like red lips withholding a secret. When the petals open, a vision appears. A memory, I realize. Little silver-haired me sat under a table as my father performed for an audience. I peeked out through the slit between panels. His green hair was like a flame of make believe, his smile grand and wicked. As he waved his arms, the silver flask caught the light. He'd never been without a palmful of liquor attached to his body. One even sat under his pillow.

"Who dares to touch the otherworld?" he yelled. "Step right up and hear your future. If you dare." He spread his fingers wide and swoops his arm across the air.

"This was before Mother used my looks to lure patrons," I say to Gwendolyn.

"Yes." Her light dims, then flares brighter than before. "What do you see?"

I lean close, watching my little face redden with tears springing to my eyes. "It was very late, and I wanted to be in my bed."

A man stepped onstage, coins in hand, carrying a baby on his hip. I smiled at the man's easy gait, the way his hand cradled the baby's back to prevent her from falling. *He must be an excellent Christmas tree decorator*, I thought. He read books to babies knowing they don't understand a word. My mind conjured all the wonder this man put into the world as he sat in the rickety chair my parents had painted gold.

"What does this little girl want?" Gwendolyn asks.

Little me looked off to the side of the stage where Mother slept, an empty flask upon her lap. With a pain in my throat, I say, "Love."

"What happened next?" Gwendolyn asks.

Little me reached through the fabric to touch the baby. "I thought it was smart to read the little one, as grownups sometimes caught me touching them, and Papa would smack me backstage for ruining the show."

Gwendolyn lowers her gaze to the center of the poppy. Or it could be the center of Earth.

Everything before the vision comes into focus. As Father waved his hands over the crystal ball and pretended to lean his ear to the all-knowing glass, I sat deathly still, unable to whisper their futures through the crushing pain in my chest.

Papa swatted my arm. Right then I realized he could have sat me on stage with him to avoid all the lies, but he had to have the spotlight.

"What did you see in that baby's life?" Gwendolyn asks.

As I settle into the memory I had long since buried, the vision fades to black, and the flowers turn to dust. Gwendolyn and I stand together in the white mist, back in my body and out of my mind. "I saw a dozen flashes of her future. Birthdays, her wedding. Reading her poetry at the dining room table. Giving birth to her perfect baby."

"And what was in the background?"

"Her parents."

The light from Gwendolyn's dress drains away, leaving a black gown against the striking lines of her cheekbones and downturned eyes. "Tell me more."

"I couldn't handle the happiness. Her joy was more than I could bear." Realization settles deep into my gut. "Jealousy locked me up, right then and there. I could agree to the dark visions, but not the light."

Gwendolyn wraps me in a hug. It feels real though I know better. Still, I lay my cheek on her shoulder and acknowledge the awful parts of myself I've protected for too long. "I've done this to myself."

"You know, dear, there is nothing more noble than honesty with yourself, even when it hurts. That's what it is to be human."

I hug her, letting touch soothe a wary part of my soul. If only I'd listened for her whispers long ago and heard the voices of those who could guide me.

I pull away, the lingering ache of that memory stinging my skin. "What good does this do now?"

"Maybe you can start to see the light."

Before I can pepper her with every question in my mind, she spins, disappearing into her orb and floating away while the feathery mist around me thickens. The eggy scent of hot springs shifts with the wind, and I am once again alone in the morning sun, grappling with memories.

I glance at the hotel and find Judy in the window. She appears to be watching me. I lift my hand to wave, but a nurse pulls her away from the glass. I pass a trio of women who cross the path beside me. They all stare, which seems ridiculous since they've watched me for several days now. My looks shouldn't still shock them, but often the intrigue grows. One blocks my path. "What are you?"

She speaks with fascination, but I ready myself for the worst. "I am a woman." I don't sidestep or avoid her eyes. Not today. I'm too raw.

"Yes, of course." She rolls her pretty blue eyes. "Do you have some sort of birth defect? Were you damaged?"

They always assume something failed me. "No more damaged than any of you." Undeterred, she reaches for my hair, but I duck. I suddenly realize she is one of Ash's women. Lady, you don't need to be jealous of me.

"You are peculiar," she says with a smile at her two friends who stand there like statues. "What do men see in you?"

I don't have time for these games. "Silly questions by silly little women bore me to death." I sidestep but she leans her shoulder toward mine. I was unprepared and couldn't stop what reached for me. No, no. I must see in this ridiculous woman's mind?

Dropped through a chute and through a sticky film, I pop through to her soul where a vast, empty field of dead wheat gives way to a gray horizon. "Okay, what do you have to show me?" No emotion yet, just space. Exactly how I envisioned her. Up from the ground, spindles of coiled petals shoot up around my boots. Red tendrils cover my shoes and extend toward my ankles. Across the field, shoots of red grow toward the sky.

Hot, white jealousy.

The tendrils and stems creep over me so I run, smashing them all down with my boots as I speed toward the horizon in no particular direction. Ash's voice rings in the distance, telling me to make decisions from want. "A dozen cars!" He yells with a laugh.

I trip. In an instant, the spindles grow over me. I can't move. I'm face down against the dirt as flower ropes tie me down. Then the ground opens, and I fall, caught by a bed of stars. As I bounce in place, a vision appears. After a romp with Ash, she sneaks into his wallet and steals his money.

The truth always shows from the sky.

Back again. I realize the vision took me away for a mere second, and she only threatened to shove me before slipping past. A vision without touch.

"Hey!" I yell back and wait for her to turn. "Careful what you take from people. You never know who is watching."

Her shoulders jerk backward, but I'm already bored with her. I carry on toward the covered patio and past the blacksmith shop, where a man tinkers with metal pieces and car parts. Two well-dressed men cross the room without a glance at the guests. They head straight for the medical ward stairs. I follow until I lose sight of them, their black bags disappearing into the stairwell.

I almost turn away, but Oliver races down the stairs. "Primrose," he whispers. "Come here." He jumps to the floor and waves me over to an alcove between the post office and barber shop. "You've done it. I can't believe it."

"What have I done?"

A man strolls past with a snarl at Oliver's arm, prompting him to roll down his sleeve to cover a large pink patch on his skin. "Judy said you inspired her. She wants to leave the medical ward."

A flash of excitement jolts across my chest. "She does?"

He nods his head. "Just for a break, but that's a start."

"Tell her to come down."

"She has to time it between doses, so she doesn't go through withdrawal."

"And Marion?" I ask.

"She's a tough one. She's staying put. Especially now that those men are here."

"Who are they?"

"The Mayo Brothers. They have some big-time clinic in Minnesota, and they work with Braun on surgical procedures. Today they're cutting into a man's heart."

"We have to get the psychics out of that place."

He swallows while looking around the first floor. "It's awful to watch them disintegrate. Most of them weaken and grow sicker here before returning to facilities or into hiding. They live somewhere between human and psychic."

"You have Braun's ear. Stand up to him. Tell him he's a lunatic who's making them sick."

"Hey, I don't have friends with money on my side, okay? I could lose the only home I've known and my animals. At least she's close where I can take care of her."

Realization hits, as I consider the concern in his eyes, and how he brings gifts to the women upstairs. "Who is it that makes you blush like that?"

He scratches his hairline as his knuckles raise his hat off his scalp then readjusts and wipes his now reddened cheeks. "Judy. I've never told her how I feel."

"Why not?"

He cracks his knuckles. "I shouldn't pressure her while she's dealing with all this."

"Has she ever done a reading on you?"

"My birth parents. They say they want me to move past what's happened and live my life, which is strange seeing as how I've never met them."

My first instinct is not to touch him, and then I remember how that's been a lie. My assumptions about my powers turned out to be a self-built prison, so I take his hand in mine and wait. Pattering taps crawl along my temples, but I don't run away. I sit in the moment and watch his eyes. "Your parents still love you, even from the great beyond. Fear stops me too, you know. Love is really, really scary."

Gwendolyn's deal included me telling the truth. I'm beginning to see why.

He pulls away but smiles to let me know it's not from anger. "I want to help her, I simply don't know how."

Oh, do I understand him. "I've felt that way more times than I can count. I suppose we just do our best." A vision tugs at me, and we aren't anywhere near touching.

"I know that look. Go ahead. Do your reading."

"It's lovely to be understood." We share a smile and bam! I'm in a black night under the faint outline of a dark moon. A beam of light shines on a yellow road where one lone flower grows. I move toward the light and dive into the center, falling past the tunnel of stars where I see Judy kissing a patch of white on Oliver's neck.

And I'm back with a deep inhale, as my lungs drink in gulps of lovely air. I must have stopped breathing for a moment.

"I know," Oliver says. "How my parents died, and how much the animals love me. How there will be a fire in ten years at the hotel."

I didn't see any of that. "I saw you with Judy. You're happy." I see why I held my breath during that vision. I've never seen joy in the stars before, only death. It all felt sort of tenuous and surreal.

"W—What?" His frightened eyes find a speck of excitement. "You saw my future? With her?" His voice ticks up at the last word, but he quickly focuses. "We have to get her out of there. Tonight."

I'm all in for showing a silver that she's loved. "Okay. Tell me what to do."

"The Mayo Brothers will distract Braun, so the timing is perfect. I'll sneak us in, and you convince her to come with us."

"Let's do it." Before I can celebrate, I remember Ash's card game. "What's going to happen to Ash? How bad is the underground?"

"They'll eat him alive and cheers to his death."

"Arrogance will do that to a person." Of the three men, Ash is the one in the most danger right now. Looks like I'm headed to the underground tonight.

Chapter Sixteen

Before I prepare to break Judy from the sanitorium and defend Ash against his own stupidity, I take a moment to reflect on all that has happened since yesterday. Why did Oliver's future go from hazy to clear? *Trust your visions, Primrose.* But this gets harder as I care more. Bathers jump in and out of the outdoor soaking pools with a dunk in cold baths between. We're all hurt and ailing, just searching for that one big fix.

"What are you watching with such intensity?" Finn joins me on the patio. He leans against the wall, petting Otto's indigo neck.

"The strangeness of this place. Look at these travelers who swim in geothermal water. They drink it to heal stomach pain and soak their weary joints. People love the weird and surprising when it suits them."

He joins me, shoulder to shoulder, to watch the guests frolic as if this is all a game. "It's human nature to want a piece of the magic."

Memories of our midnight kiss bring me back to my body and out of the enormous problems facing my night ahead. "You told me fear always wins." I face him. "But I touched you and you trusted me."

He tenses from his jaw to his fists, which stirs an unease inside me. "Yes, we did do that." He exhales through tightened lips.

How can he stand so close, pulsing with want, and still fear me? Though words thrash around in my mind, I say nothing. He's like the sun, rising and setting without ever remaining steady. And I believe I can lasso something so complicated and beautiful. What do I know of love?

"What's it like to see through peoples' souls?" he asks.

His multicolored eyes hold entire universes in them. "Like I'm able to both help and hurt people, but I never know which will win."

When he looks into my eyes, my heart beats into my throat. The way he scans my hair, my eyes, my mouth. "It might not look like it," he says, "but I'd like to find joy again."

"What does joy look like to you?" I ask.

"Like Uncle Henry's suppers." He exhales. "Stars splashed across a clear summer sky. Apple trees in full bloom before the fruit breaks through." He takes another step closer and rests his hand on my hip, his touch deliberate and slow. "Kissing you."

I rest my hands on his shoulders. He pulls me close enough that the weight of his chest feels like the best hug in the world. "Being happy doesn't stop you from grieving," I say.

"No, it starts me living. And that is terrifying." He runs his hand through my hair, and it's like I'm weightless. Like the sky has opened and wrapped me in soft, cornflower blue. He kisses me in a tangled mess of both restraint and desire.

There is no pulsing in my chest warning of danger. There are only our bodies, touching, breathing, kissing. There is only right now. I slide my hand through the thick waves of his overgrown locks. "Life hurts. I used to think I could avoid all that by cutting off experiences and people. All those rules were fabricated lies, and in the end, I still hurt. I just did it alone."

He tucks my hair behind my ear. "And now?"

"Now I have new lessons to learn. Why people hurt themselves, and how I can make it better."

"You aren't responsible for other people, Primrose."

He doesn't know the deal, or why the stakes are so high. He can't understand how it feels to carry a second vision behind my eyes, one where I see into hidden secrets. "Why would I have this gift if I couldn't do a damn thing to change the future?"

He shrugs. "Maybe it's meant to change you, not them."

"I am already changed. Now I have a world full of people who can't see what I see. Marion won't believe she could live happily out there. Ash is about to walk into a disaster because he's too pompous to admit his limitations. Oliver wants so badly to save the women upstairs but can't find the courage to risk his own safety."

"And me?" He tilts his head, waiting for me to reveal all I've seen in him.

"You must mend a broken heart."

I've gone and said the truth out loud. I've brought the darkness to light and admitted I care about the state of his heart.

He stretches his spine tall while watching the hot springs, seemingly trying to wrestle away from the unease in his body. "Nah, there is no mending this." He drags his gaze back to me. "But I can try to walk and breathe with all of it broken."

"That may be the saddest thing I've ever heard."

The way he winces suggests he may need saving as much as Ash. I'm one woman with a galaxy of hurting people to help with only a directive from my spirit guide to light the way.

"Before you decide to fix me, you should know I don't want that." Finn's voice is decisive, strong. "No pity, understand?"

"Yes, I understand." Though I do not want to comply. I could kiss away the pain if he'd only let me.

"Now, how are we going to get Ash out of this mess?" he asks.

His emotional shifts from high to low and intimate to distant leave me on unsteady footing. My feelings for him only grow by the minute. "Right, so I want to go to Pendleton with him. I can read the room and get an idea of the secrets he is up against."

"Yes, we should stick together."

"Also, Judy wants to leave the ward for a while. Oliver will take her away for a few hours and I need to help."

"I thought it was her choice to leave or stay?"

"In theory it is. Braun has her on a medication schedule that's terrifying. When she's due for another dose, her body revolts. Shakes, sweats, mood swings. It's like watching my father all over again."

Finn nods. "Okay. Looks like we have a full day ahead of us."

"You care what happens to them?"

"I care about you." This time, when he reaches for my hand, his touch is tender, hesitant. "If you go, I go."

I realize with sudden clarity that I don't need him healed. I need him close, in all his difficult truth. For that, as Gwendolyn said, is what it means to be human.

***

While Finn spends the afternoon trying to convince Ash not to go forward with the card game, I make my way back to the sanitorium, where a nurse opens the door and scurries away to a wayward scream. Marion isn't in her room, so I consider heading for Judy so I can solidify our plan, but Braun's office is wide open, and the light is on. I stop just shy of his door. I lean my back against the wall to gather myself before he sees me.

"Are you going to come in?" he asks.

I slink around the doorway to find Braun sitting on his desk, puffing away on his pipe as cherry tobacco fills the room.

"You would like access to Marion, I assume?" He bites down on the pipe, a harsh clang of teeth on hardened clay.

"Yes."

He drops his pipe to his desk and stands, his eyes narrowed and his brow tight. All I can hear is that damned metronome. Tick. Tick. Tick. That would drive me mad. I suppose he's already there.

"You know our deal." He paces around the room for a full minute then comes to a rigid stop. "You failed to rid me of Mr. Sterling, and I had to deal with him myself. You want time with the women here, you'll pay in examinations."

What more can he do to me? I've already learned my limitations. "Please, begin." I say it as a direction and not a request.

He rolls over a tray with a tumbler of liquid and next to it, a syringe of emerald medicine. "An emerald elixir tinged with magic from the hot springs and the spirit realm. This is going to change the world," he says.

A powerful green drug that breaks apart those on the periphery of society. Psychics, mystics, mediums, shamans. "I see. You've not just been experimenting on them, you've used their power to create something sinister."

"Your kind sees things I do not. Think of all we could accomplish here."

"Careful what you wish for, old man." I look past the syringe and grab the tumbler. The liquid looks like muddled spinach and smells like cider vinegar. "What is it?"

He nears my face, close enough that I can see the black rim around his hazel eyes. "Opium."

Tick. Tick.

He lifts the syringe of glowing green liquid and waves it in front of me.

All I see is misery. My father's debauchery. Russell's eyes. The girl's broken limbs. The bartender's sliced neck.

Tick. Tick.

"Your connection to otherworldly voices makes you vulnerable and dangerous, a very interesting combination." He rolls the syringe between his fingers so the light glints off the needle's metal tip. "Marion was very sick when she came to me. This little vial dulls her pain. Her first month here she didn't stop screaming. Look at her now."

"Is near-death weakness an improvement?"

"You will have to ask her." He places the syringe down with gentle fingers.

This volley of jabs solves nothing. "Where is she?"

"Consulting with our visiting surgeons." Before I can ask why she needs surgery, Braun has moved on. "Tell me what you see in your visions."

No one has ever asked for details. Not even my parents. "First, I feel their emotions. I walk along a yellow road with red poppies that show me their deepest feelings, which is generally terrifying. Then I dive into the sky. Sometimes stars catch me, sometimes I plummet. But I always see their big secret. Past, present. Future."

"I see."

The oddest sensation grows in my throat. A tickle or an itch, bordering on a scratch. "Coming back to my body hurts. Headaches, usually." Speaking of headaches, my skull turns cold and achy. Underneath my intense dislike of this man lies the frail notion that he could say something to help me wrangle this unmanageable task. To help me find my power.

He taps a pen against his lip. "I have a theory. About the hair." His eyes don't leave mine. "The spirits need to know how to find you. Secrets and souls can pick you out of a crowd, reaching for the one with the odd hair that shines like chrome."

Souls need nothing but to exist. These things are felt, not seen. I don't bother to explain that to Dr. Braun. "And the eyes?"

"Yours are remarkable." He steps close. Too close. "They keep your body gentle. Weak to outside influences. Your clear eyes allow the secrets of the universe to find their way home."

"That sounds more fairy tale than science."

"Ah, yes. But what is science without a bit of magic?" He extends his arm, clears his throat, and bows. When he stands tall, the syringe is back in his hand, and right in front of my face.

"No." He examines my expression. "You will not jab me with that thing."

"This is the answer to your troubles, Miss Whittaker." He doesn't hide frustration very well.

"Injecting drugs into my veins will help nothing. My troubles lie in the disconnect between what my soul knows and the limitations of my human body." I slide from the table, standing tall with arms straight. "Your little green drug will not enter my body. Ever."

Silence mixed with metronome. Maddening.

He taps his foot in time to the ticking. "Judy told me about your father." He pauses to watch for any flinch, but I don't give him the satisfaction. "Alcoholism should never be treated with opioids, as then we force the addict onto yet another addiction."

"I'm certain you know nothing of my tragedy."

"Oh, but I do." He waves a hand, at what I can't tell. "My mother took everything available to her. Laudanum, whisky. Morphine. Disease of a nervous character." His jaw pulses. "She needed support, not an ignorant doctor who only saw an eccentric woman who needed to be compliant."

"How could you turn around and do the same to these women that you saw done to her?"

He slams his fist on his desk, arm shaking. "I give them agency!"

I glance at the door to see how fast I can make it out of here.

He smooths his vest against his chest. "I'm giving them a choice when no one else will. They are not victims, and neither are you. I'm working to cure your ailment and lessen the pain you live with, and this is my most noble act."

"Noble?"

"Yes." His voice steadies.

"You want to take away the thing that makes us special. You force them into mania when your drug runs out, leaving their body to beg for more. Nothing about this is noble."

"You've traveled from Portland, escaped an opportunist mother, and trekked across the Oregon landscape to find answers. You've run from your special gift since the day you discovered it."

"It is not the gift that scares me, it's the people who exploit it."

He curls his lips in part disgust, part intrigue. "You are a different kind of psychic. A woman who struggles with loss. Betrayal. Parents who used you for your talents and left you trusting only yourself in the world."

"That isn't unique."

"Yes, but your response to this trauma is." His pants seem to hang off his narrow waist. I wonder, suddenly, if he doesn't eat enough. "You've developed such extreme empathy it paralyzes you. You appear cold when really, you care too much." His mouth opens and curves into an almost-smile. "Their hurt is your hurt."

I resist his words that cut to the heart of me. He's seen inside my soul with no psychic powers. My vulnerability is now exposed, and this madman knows more about me than I ever will. It's unsettling.

"You have both human and psychic powers." He crosses his arms, satisfied with his genius. "But you won't act on them because of fear. Fascinating."

If I could mold a suit of armor around me and threaten him with a sword, I would challenge him to a duel. I would slide the blade through his stomach and save every person on this floor. I could no more find armor than I could change the future. Helpless, once again.

He walks to the door, opens it, and leaves me just enough room to slide past. The darkness doesn't call me when I brush my shoulder against his chest. His soul remains locked down, hard and bitter. Thank God.

"These women are my responsibility," he says. "I could protect you too, if you'd let me."

"The only thing I care about right now is protecting them from *you*."

He stares with a blank face then slams the door.

Marion's room is still dark and empty. I arrive at Judy's door, ready to throw her over my shoulder and drag her away, but she isn't here. I'm standing in this sanitorium with a body full of rage and a heart full of good deeds, with no one to save.

All my fight has drained away, and in its place sits a fragile girl pretending to be a woman of the stars.

Chapter Seventeen

As a midnight card game looms in the distance, I settle into the unease of truth. So many notions shattered since this morning and yet, I still can't see how to use these visions for good. Gwendolyn helped me see how childish ideas worked to protect me from the scary world, and Dr. Braun shoved that fear right in my face. All I can think of is dragging Judy out of Braun's control. She's given us a window and I plan to kick the glass down.

"Primrose." Finn slides into a chair next to me in the solarium. "Bad news. Ash refuses to back down from the card game. He's blinded, the poor guy."

"Blinded to what?"

"Seems to me his father will never see him as competent or exceptional, so why bother?"

I keep my sights on Oliver as he closes the animal pens at the base of the bluff. "I don't know, he won't learn that lesson until he learns it." Oliver pets the long muzzle of an aging horse, pressing his forehead to the animal's. "Ash has only ever known a life of chasing affection. Somewhere along the way he'll decide he doesn't need it, but only by doing the wrong thing over and over."

"Is that what you're doing?" he asks.

For some reason, I don't bristle at his pointed question. "Probably."

He stretches his arms long, and lets his hands come to rest behind his head. "Yeah, me too."

I could sit here in this moment forever. What if Finn is my three-colored man, and all I have to do to save him is fall for his dreamy smile and landscape eyes.

Oliver pokes his head into the solarium. With overalls and a neck covered in dirt, I can imagine he doesn't spend much time around the guests. "Come on." I grab Finn's sleeve to lead him over to the door. We step outside into the golden hour of Oregon autumn days, late afternoon under a marigold light.

"Judy's next dose is at four o'clock. Just ten minutes from now," he says. "We probably only have a few hours, but I hope we can show her life outside the ward and convince her to fight."

Finn scratches his neck. "I don't understand why she's still there. Is she sick?"

Oliver shakes his head. "Braun has a way with people. He makes them believe they will fall apart without his help. Now Judy is stuck needing this drug to keep her stable."

My meeting with Braun floods back to my memory. He has vision like I do, just in a different way. He knows how to manipulate and control, two things I hope to never learn. "I'll do my best."

"What about Ash?" Finn asks. "He has to get to Pendleton by midnight."

Oliver checks the sun level. "It takes a little more than an hour to get there. We'll have plenty of time. Does he have any idea what he's getting into?"

"No," Finn and I say in unison.

"There's no describing it, really. It's dark and suffocating, and full of unexpected debauchery. I hate it there." Oliver grimaces. "He'll never survive with that linen suit and manicured hands. He's about to come face to face with Braun's favorite whisky-swigging cowboys."

"We have to protect him," I say.

Finn shrugs. "He is an awfully soft fellow. He doesn't stand a chance against the kind of men who run poker games underground."

"It's decided," Oliver says. "I'm going. I'll at least keep him from upsetting the wrong people."

Hunger rises inside me that only a vision can satiate. Like I've tasted a drop of water after a drought, and I might wither if I don't find more. Noises rumble as people meander by. Are souls offering up stories, unsolicited?

Finn reaches for my hand. "Is something wrong, Primrose?"

With a hard blink, I shake away their voices, determined to keep every unbearable soul away. If I open myself to every voice that reaches its hands for me, I'd live as nothing but a servant to the world. In service to everyone but myself. "No, nothing." I force a smile and don't let go.

Oliver jingles his keys that dangle from his hip. "Let's go."

Once again, we climb the stairs. Oliver freezes at the door, hesitant to slide the key in the lock. "What if we make it worse for her?"

Judy doesn't leave her room. She's locked inside on a routine of injections, teetering on madness. "She doesn't know what's beyond these walls," I tell him. "And she never will if we don't show her."

Poor Oliver. He must adore those animals because humans are so very difficult to love at times. He unlocks the door. Just as I expected, Miss Strauss greets us with her *get off my ward* scowl. "It isn't visiting hours."

"Judy asked us here," Oliver says with a trembling voice.

"No, she certainly did not." Judy peeks out from her room but shuts the door when Strauss locks eyes with her.

"Isn't this a voluntary hospital," Finn asks.

"Of course it is," she snaps.

"Then step aside." He has no stake in this game, and I love him for his forwardness.

"My job is to protect my patients. You disrupt her wellbeing. Get out." She points behind us but can't do much more than yell. "I will fetch the doctor and have you banned from the premises."

All that time Finn spends around Ash has him adopting the swagger. "Fine. Mr. Sterling will have your doors shuttered and the doctor's practice evicted."

Strauss's soul, seemingly weakened, reaches for me with such voracity that I don't even think to fight it. Through the veil and into her land of yellow sunshine and bright blooming flowers. This is not what I expected. Excitement and calm surround me.

"Strauss? Why is your soul so beautiful and your attitude so sour?"

Something knocks me on the side of my head, sending me to the hard bricks. When I sit up, the view is the same, but the flowers have turned varied shades of gray. Sunlight drains away. A flicker of light opens just out of arm's reach. I crawl toward the burst over dried flowers that crush to powder under my palms and knees. In the light, a figure forms. Braun.

The ground below tips up, rolling me forward toward the light. I tumble down and through the blast, falling past an image of Miss Strauss's bedroom on the first floor. A veritable wallpaper of newspaper clippings and photographs, all of Dr. Braun.

Once again, I've returned, noting a bulge under her dress at the level of her heart. My head swims but doesn't ache like usual. I step close enough to whisper in her ear. She flinches but doesn't pull away.

"You were once a bright, eager student, until Dr. Braun stole you away. He made you believe you were special. He even kissed you once in a drunken mistake. You've watched your world narrow and darken as he grows further from your grasp. He despises you, and yet, you still carry a photograph of him against your skin to always keep him close."

Her eyes widen. She stutters a bit, then steps away, turning her shoulders from my gaze. "Do as you must. I will alert the doctor to your presence."

She walks away with a softer gait, head hung low. Unrequited, obsessive love.

"What did you say to her?" Finn asks.

"The truth."

Oliver hesitates, his eyes shut and neck taut. I reach out to touch his arm without a thought that I may stir his soul. I can touch to show kindness now. What a revelation. "Hey, we'll do this together."

We hurry down the hall toward Judy's room. While Finn keeps watch, we work on Judy.

Oliver sits next to her on the bed, his hands placed softly on his lap. "It's time to go. We're excited to take you out of here for a while."

Judy picks at her fingernails. She stares out the window with a longing that makes my heart ache. "No doctor. No nurses," she says. "All that breezy air."

"How long have you been in here," I ask.

She drops her head but looks up at Oliver who answers for her. "A year."

"At first, I liked the safety here. I'm comfortable in these walls, where people understand me." Her cheeks redden. "Then he began to fix me. Spirits don't own my time anymore, which I've always wanted. But out there, it always seems like the protection would go away. They'll come for me again."

"Judy, if you can't leave these four walls, you aren't healed." She read my father, selfish bastard that he is. "And his drugs have made you sick."

"I know." She doesn't resist, like I expected her to. "I want to feel the air on my skin. I want to meet the animals."

Judy and Oliver exchange smiles, which unlocks something inside me. They care for each other but fear roars between them like an ugly beast.

"Braun is talking to Strauss," Finn says.

I kneel in front of Judy and hold her hands. "Do this for me."

"For you?"

"We can show Marion how to fight for her life. Help me save her."

"Here he comes." Finn backs into the room, standing between us and the doorway.

Dr. Braun saunters in, Strauss hot on his heels. "What do we have here? A party?"

I step forward. "Judy wants to spend time with us downstairs." His smirk sends me somewhere near enraged. "You always say it's her choice."

"I do say that, don't I?" He cracks his knuckles and stares out the window. "But Judy knows what awaits her out there, don't you, my girl?"

"She isn't your girl," I say, my voice sharper than I intend. "Stop trying to intimidate her."

"I do not take orders from a psychic who cannot regulate her own visions." He stares at Oliver, who slides away from Judy and stands next to me. Braun takes his spot on her bed. "I know best. You know that, don't you?" Judy nods. "Good girl."

Finn steps forward, chest puffed, but I know a fight will spook her. "Judy, we want you to experience a bit of time with music and food and laughter. A little dancing, maybe. We'll bring you back upstairs any time you wish."

Dr. Braun snaps without turning his gaze away from Judy. Strauss comes running, lifting a vile out of her pocket. "I could give you a little something extra so you feel good." He points to the vial without a needle. Green liquid, as always. "If you are in distress, it's the doctorly thing to do."

"Why don't you want her to leave, Braun?" Finn asks. "Afraid she'll discover there's a life outside where you don't control her?"

Braun waves the vial in front of Judy's eyes, then runs the glass down her jaw and neck. The way he taunts her sends chills up my spine. "She makes the choices here, not me."

Oliver breathes heavy, watching Braun seduce her with drugs. "Stop," he says.

Good job, Oliver. Find that voice.

"I will protect her." His hands shake, but he pushes forward anyway and shoves Braun's hand away. "Judy, you can do this. I will be there with you every second." He reaches his hand for her, standing firm while she considers her choice.

Braun glares at them both, as does Strauss, but Judy looks into Oliver's eyes and reaches for his hand. Their eyes don't leave each other as she stands, and they walk toward us.

Braun doesn't stop them. "I'll be waiting here for when you need me. And I promise, you'll need me."

I look back at the doctor and his nurse, vowing to protect everyone from this monster. Finn pulls me away and we leave the medical ward behind Oliver and Judy, hand in hand, stepping with hesitation into a new world.

"It's sweet, isn't it?" I ask Finn. "He cares for her so much."

"So much he ignored his own fear to take a chance on someone else's happiness." Finn's gentle smile and beautiful eyes center me. "That's what men do when love finds them."

***

As the boys play cards, I invite Judy into my room. She sits at the vanity, her hair in a bun on the back of her head. She's pale and weak, but there's a simple beauty to her entire face. I remove her bun and brush her hair, smoothing the ends with oil. Her remaining silver isn't bright, but still catches the light.

"I don't touch people much," she says.

"That seems to be a feature with our kind." She seems to enjoy the bristles along her scalp, so I scrape them slowly from her part to her neck, sliding my other hand along the silky strands.

"Why did you think touch made visions?" she asks, her eyes closed.

"I guess I could control my fear by pushing people away." Ouch. To say the words aloud is to really feel them—and they carry a sting I wasn't prepared for.

"Yeah. Me too." I slide open a tin of pink makeup and pat color on her lips and cheeks. She looks from the mirror over to me. "You can't save Marion, and I doubt you can save me."

I keep blending the pigment into her skin. "I've decided not to listen to cant's anymore."

"And that's why we've been waiting for you."

I drop my hands into my lap. "What will happen?"

She shrugs. "Marion will die. I will take enough emerald opium to eradicate my power. You'll save the world from Braun's evil."

"I can't say I care about saving the world. I care about saving you. And the men I've met along this journey." I rub the pad of my pink finger on my opposite palm in circles to remove the stain. "I care so much now, I suppose this is what I've tried to avoid all these years."

"Even the drug hasn't stopped how I care," she says. Tears line her eyes. "My heart skips when Oliver visits. Over the year, I've wasted away. Still, the way he looks at me has never changed. I'd love to be the person he deserves."

"By curing your visions?"

"Yes. When the dead find me, I'm scared and angry. Distracted. I can't go anywhere without a dead person hovering in my space. All this pressure is bigger than I can manage."

"Who knew a big heart makes for a lonely life?"

"Every psychic who ever lived." She examines her reflection. "I look pretty."

"You started pretty. This is just fun for tonight." I tuck her hair behind her ear. "We're going to get you out of there."

"I know. You will once I'm healed."

"What if you keep your power?" I shouldn't have said that. Not when she's so fragile. "I mean, I'm learning to live with visions, maybe you can too."

"Oh, Primrose." She sighs as if she knows things I do not. "You think you can control the world. You can't stop what's coming, but you can learn to let go. That's where your power is."

"And how do you know that?"

"Your father's spirit told me. He's an asshole, but he's right."

A knock on the door disrupts our conversation, which leaves me worried for me more than her. I open the door to find all three men dressed for the evening and ready to escort us to the dance hall. Ash checks his watch, too concerned with the time to notice anything else.

Judy steps forward as Oliver swallows his excitement. "Do you think Clara can see us now?" he asks.

"Yes. Let's not disappoint her."

They walk down the hall arm in arm, Ash checking his reflection in every mirror and window we pass. Finn slips his hand into mine. "We did it."

"Let's enjoy the moment. Who knows how long it will last before the next disaster."

We step into the dancehall, just as glittery and dreamy as the last time I was here. This time, Finn's touch doesn't scare me. Judy hesitates then holds Oliver's hand tight as her eyes glitter brighter than I've seen. Ash finds the woman who steals from him, pulling her behind a palm to kiss her neck.

Finn holds me in a dance position, eye to eye. "When you've saved us all, what then?"

His question rattles me. "I don't know. Find more people to save?" I suppose I've always known I need to fix who's hurting. Avoiding my visions as I have has only made me the loneliest woman on the planet.

"For now, we dance." He spins me to the dance floor as a whir of lights and smiles fly past. After an hour of spins and touch and pure joy, I come to a breathless halt against the window, heaving and laughing to Finn's silly jokes.

My elation falls when I notice Judy with Ash's flask in hand, chugging his expensive liquor like its water. "Oh no."

Ash has disappeared with the woman for the entire hour, returning with a dopey gaze yet still checking his watch. Oliver doesn't catch on that Judy has guzzled some illegal liquor, and here we stand, as the clock ticks ever nearer toward midnight, considering what's next.

"Time for a journey," Ash says.

Judy's nerves have calmed. She kisses Oliver's cheek. "I want to go with you."

"Oh, no," Oliver says. "We're going to the underground. It's incredibly dangerous."

She shrugs, a manic wildness in her eyes. "Yeah, and I have the voices of the dead on my side. Let's go."

"You'll need your meds," he says.

She slips a tin out of her pocket. "I thought ahead."

She brought her own opium injection, stolen from the mad doctor. We follow her to the front of the hotel, where Ash's giant automobile awaits. Everyone piles in, but I stay behind to check Ash's state of mind. "How are you feeling?"

"Fine. Just fine." He is not at all fine. He's terrified.

"You don't have to do this."

"Neither do you." He pats his jacket to find his flask missing but seems too distracted to question it.

"Why did you bring your father's land deeds here?"

The way he looks away, like a little boy, makes me want to hug him. I would, too, if I weren't waiting for an answer. He's so lost.

"No matter." He smooths his hair at his temples. "Protection," he admits with reluctance. "Money is the only way out of anything, and I thought, maybe…" I remain silent and unmoving to coax out the terrified kid with big dreams. "If I could use his assets to make my own money, I could buy land and buildings. Businesses where I can lead how I want, doing things that matter. Whatever that means."

I place my hand on his arm just soft enough to disrupt his sleeve against his skin. "Ash, that woman you dance with. She's stealing from you."

"I know."

I can't comprehend what he's saying. "You know, and you still sleep with her?"

"Primrose, look at this group." He gestures to the car. "You're all unique and interesting. It's no wonder you all found someone to hold you and promise to care for you. I am generic. Seems fitting that I need to pay a woman for attention."

I open my mouth to shake him back to sense. To scream that he is kind and generous and deserving of all the love in the world. He holds up his hand and calmly says, "Do not teach me something you have yet to learn."

He opens the door, and I slide in, next to Finn but between him and Ash. Oliver and Judy laugh and hold hands in the back seat. We stare ahead as we leave Hot Lake and drive toward Pendleton in the dead of night. The eerie stillness of the black sky settles into the car, and we don't speak. We become the lost souls who seek out someone to hear their cries. I am the yellow road and poppies and cluster of stars, for I am the lost and the found, and everything in between.

Chapter Eighteen

After an hour in silence, we approach Main Street in Pendleton. Ash's hands grip the steering wheel tight enough to whiten his knuckles. We pass through heavy brick alleyways and buildings like stone tombs. Ash rolls the car into place near an empty sidewalk. We climb out into the breezy air as streetlights light the concrete walkways. The faded red image of a finger points to the underground.

Oliver stops at a corner, gripping Judy's hand. "Around there is one entrance. Follow me and don't talk to anyone."

Under Oliver's feet are purple glass blocks embedded in the sidewalk. "What's with the purple squares?" I ask.

"Purple prism glass. They let in light," Oliver says.

People crawl through darkened tunnels in a purple haze playing secret card games and tossing back liquor.

We cross two more mysterious glass grids that glow like amethyst, then approach a painted finger that advertises baths for ten cents. Something rains to the ground.

Girls hang out of windows, breasts pressed to their chins. They toss another handful of something at us. I bend down and retrieve metal and mother-of-pearl buttons. A not-so-subtle suggestion for the men to undress them. I've read a few prostitutes over the years. Their fear is secondary, it seems, to all other emotions.

"Come visit the cozy rooms, boys," one girl says. She twists out the window like a creeping vine.

"Not now, Betty." Oliver leads us down a set of concrete steps as piano music clangs from inside. Oliver opens the door into the grimiest bar I've ever seen. Darkened by low hanging beams, the room stinks of wet wood and cigars. We walk across muddy, creaking wood planks, the floor both sloshy and sticky.

A breathless panic grips my chest. My neck itches like a rash as souls groan and screech for me. Finn places his hand on my waist, a gentle reminder to stay here. Keep these people's poppy roads far away from me.

A bartender nods to Oliver as he wipes off gold shavings from his bar. Some sort of payment from the colorful patrons. "Hey kid, haven't seen you in a while."

Oliver pulls his shoulders back. "We're here for the red room."

"Yes, I heard something about that." He scowls at Ash, examining his suit. "You here to sell me something?"

"No," he says, indignantly. "I am here for the red room."

I'm fairly certain he doesn't know what the red room is, but poor Ash is working hard to keep control.

"You?" The bartender holds back a laugh.

Ash sighs loudly. "Take me to the card room at once."

The bartender's eyes go wide, and the piano player stops mid keystroke.

Oliver leans to Ash and whispers. "That's not how things are done. Now shut up and order a drink."

I can almost see Ash racking his brain to determine what in his father's teachings could equip him for this situation. "Fine," Ash says. "Whisky."

Finn leans close to my ear. "They're going to eat him alive down here."

"It's good we're here then." A test, of sorts, to see if my visions can protect him. Or anyone, for that matter.

The room hums with energy. Table lanterns cast domes of heavy amber light and shadows crawl up to the ceiling. Something deep in the underground whispers to me. I feel it in my bones.

"Judy, how do I stand in a room full of people and not let their souls overtake me?"

"Drugs."

I shove her arm playfully. "Stop. That's not funny."

"Well, it's the only thing that quiets the dead. Numb my spirit detection with opium and only suffer breakdowns if I miss a dose." She must notice my shocked face because she smiles and nudges me. "You stop focusing on them and keep your attention on yourself."

"What do you mean?"

"This right here." She lays her palm flat on my sternum, fingers pressed over my collar bone. "Stay in your body. Find power in yourself and stop worrying so much what other people have to say."

The voices do control me. They always have.

"Some will still find you. The stubborn ones always do. Or the neediest. God, the way the lost ones crawl inside you. It's enough to make one live in a sanitorium with a mad scientist." She winks and slides a shot of gin over, swallowing it without a blink.

"I'm worried about you."

"Nah, don't be. I'm living for once. Besides, you're going to save us all."

Yeah, the girl who lied to herself for two decades and has never recovered from her terrible childhood, she's going to save the world.

"What happens after the drink?" Finn asks.

Oliver scans the room, for what I'm not sure. "When the bartender gives you the nod, we head in. But not a moment before."

"What's back there?" I ask. Curiosity swells inside me, like a throbbing tooth that begs to be yanked from its socket. Voices bounce around my head, picking at my strength one by one.

Oliver scratches his temple. "The Empire Meat Company. You'll need to pay them a fee to pass."

"Naturally," Ash says and throws back his whisky. "Everything has a price."

The bartender waves his hand to Oliver. We follow him past the bar, into a tunnel where glass shines plum-colored light over our heads. The curved ceiling and rock walls leave just enough room for us, and Ash has to duck to clear his head from the stone archways.

I stumble against the wall and play it off as a misstep, but my legs ache and squeeze. All this noise weakens me. Pressure builds strong enough to make my head throb. I imagine the stone walls compressing these psychic visions around me in a pressurized heat until I break.

"Why do people come here?" Finn asks.

"Sundowner laws," Oliver says. "The Chinese aren't allowed outside after dark, and when they do go out, they get harassed and beaten."

Ash freezes in place, bent under a stone that drips water next to his feet. "There are laws for such things? Unfathomable."

We stop in the belly of this dark, wet service tunnel, and stare at Oliver. Sounds murmur around us from all sides in the damp, dingy cave. "Are there really laws just for the Chinese?" I ask.

"Sadly, yes. Wait until you see their living quarters."

"No one could actually live down here," Ash says.

"They build these tunnels and move goods from place to place, so they live here too, protected by the dark. An entire city lives and breathes underfoot."

Finn looks up to a slow drip from a crack in the ceiling. "I can't imagine not seeing daylight."

Oliver nods. "Braun buys powders and bottles from the Chinese men. Sometimes I deliver his finished products back here. I don't ask."

Judy struggles to take a deep breath. "Someone is reaching for me," she whispers. "I don't want it." She looks around and finds a jug. Taking a swig before I can stop her.

"What the hell, Judy?" I pull it from her. "That could be piss in there."

"I smelled it as it went down. Just gin." She squints, holding up her hand as if instructing the spirit to back off.

The tunnel compresses, darker and smaller. We walk through slivers of eggplant light, past walls of blackened basalt rock, and step over a drunken cowboy crumpled in a corner. My breathing rapid, I swallow the sickening desire for release. Like I could scratch my skin open to let my mind breathe with just one brief vision. I stop myself, desperate to hold control for once.

Oliver leads us to a corridor that narrows tighter and tighter. Through a doorway, we step into a parlor with white metal bistro tables. Plush, crimson red cushions cover the matching chairs. Behind a counter two boys hand crank some sort of apparatus.

"What is that?" I ask.

Oliver looks behind the counter and against the corners. "Ice cream."

"Ice cream?" Ash shouts. "Why would anyone come here for that? There are perfectly good parlors above ground."

A group of young women bounce into the cramped parlor with bare shoulders and hair like a windblown afternoon. They gather around Oliver and blow kisses from upturned hands.

"Hey, doll. Haven't seen you around lately." A burgundy-lipped woman pats his cheek. The same prostitute from upstairs.

"Betty, I keep telling you. I'm not interested." Oliver rubs his now rosy-pink neck and walks back to us. "Those are the working girls. They're taking a break from the cozy rooms upstairs."

"I think they like you," Finn says with a smile.

"They like any man with a pulse and a few dollar bills. I sometimes help their patrons escape when the sheriff comes through for a raid. They like to tease me."

Judy doesn't seem jealous. She's too busy rubbing her temples and searching for hidden booze in every corner we turn.

"Don't tell me," Ash says. "I need to buy an ice cream now."

"Yep," Oliver says.

They offer Ash vanilla, their only flavor, handing him a two-inch box and resume smiling at the working girls who laugh and glide their hands over every man that walks through the door.

Ash brings the box and four tiny spoons back to the table. "A box of ice cream?" he snorts. "Whoever heard of such a thing?"

It's unfortunate that he turns pompous when he's nervous. We each take a few bites of the creamy dessert. Not bad for underground confections.

"Enough." Ash slaps his hands on the table. "Take me to the poker game."

"But the butcher," Oliver says.

"I don't care about anyone else. I'm going." He pushes his way through the girls as they paw at his face and shoulders. "Later, girls. Right now, I have a sanitorium to win."

"He's gonna get himself killed," Finn says.

We have a strong man in Finn, a capable one in Oliver, and two psychics to fend off Ash's enemies. I'm also prepared to buffer his stupidity. But the cold stone and hollow tunnels seem to compress around me, tight and suffocating. Judy lifts the tin box from her pocket that holds a green vial capable of liquifying fear. She's nearing time for another shot.

We slip through the group of girls. Oliver tries to stop Ash as he marches past raw meat piled in stacks, undeterred by the sharp air of metallic blood. Ash, hand over his mouth, approaches two young men slicing through half a cow.

"Here." Ash throws a ten-dollar bill on a bucket of ice packed around the meat. "We're going past you to the place I'm not supposed to talk about."

One brother wipes his bloody hand on his mottled apron and reaches for the bill. He nods to Ash who steps between rows of skinned pigs that dangle from hooks in the ceiling. The ominous thudding in my stomach reminds me this will be a lot harder than reading fortunes on a Portland street corner. Ash still believes money is the answer to every question.

Pressure expands in my head as desperate mumbles snake through the air. I imagine crawling into a vision to rest in someone's starry night—before my head splits like a cracked watermelon.

We near a door half the normal size. Oliver turns to us and says, "Follow my lead."

Ash fidgets, shifting his weight back and forth between his feet, like a boxer about to take to the ring. "I'm ready."

Oliver knocks once.

My chest tightens with so much force I find it hard to breathe. Something silver catches my eye in a storage nook deep in the recesses of the tunnel. I step away from the door and follow the stream of light into the dingy cavity in the stone wall. A stunning Chinese woman faces me, dark eyes clear and glowing. Her straight black hair waves over her shoulders. The tips shine *silver*.

"Are you?" I can't seem to form words. "You're like me."

She runs past me and disappears. I'm desperate to follow her, but Ash needs me. Her voice trails away as she moves. She's the voice I can't seem to quiet. A silver girl who lives underground. At least she's not another three-colored man.

I can't be certain, but her soul seems to have something important to say. I turn around to find Judy, sleeve tucked into her teeth, biting down as she injects the needle into her elbow. Her eyes roll back and she exhales, collapsing against the wall. I rush to catch her. She looks up at me through glassy eyes. "I just want to be better."

I peek around the corner at the men who wait for a card game, completely unaware that souls swim in misery all around us. "Me too, Judy. Me too."

Chapter Nineteen

Oliver pulls me back to the door, where this group of unsuspecting visitors waits for our chance to save our friend. This may go horribly wrong. He's here to prove something to the world, to his father. But he can't see how we're all here for him. He has us, if he'd just reach out and let us love him.

A tiny window slides open, just like in the speakeasies of Portland. "Password," the man grumbles.

Oliver leans in. "Password."

"Oh, come on," Ash says. "That can't be the answer."

Oliver tilts his head toward the door and the man unlocks it. We step through the increasingly smaller tunnel. He mutters something about how Dr. Braun sent the four of us.

The man opens what looks like a cabinet in the wall, and light floods our cramped tunnel. We step into a lavish set of red rooms. Crimson velvet wallpaper lines the walls and panels of stamped tin ceiling tiles reflect the light from crystal chandeliers. Men play poker at various tables, dressed in pinstripe suits and crisp new hats. They smoke cigars and stare at their opponents like hawks eyeing a fat fish at the water's surface.

I run my fingernails over the skin along my sternum, worried the pressure may explode inside me.

Ash steps up to the glistening, smooth mahogany bar. "My name is Ash Sterling. Where shall I sit?"

The bartender looks him up and down and they stare at each other for so long it's uncomfortable.

Finn grimaces. "What is that smell?"

"Mothballs," I say. "We had them all over our house once after an infestation of pantry moths."

Oliver crosses his arms. "To cover the smell of whisky in case of a raid."

I yank his sleeve. "I think I saw a silver out there. Is she one of us?"

He dismisses me. "I don't know. Tons of people come and go. I haven't met everyone. And besides, I don't want more psychics finding out where I work. That's all we need is more subjects for Braun to manipulate."

But we aren't simply psychics. We are outcasts, shunned for our looks. We can't hide away, much as we've tried.

Ash takes a seat at the big table and slaps down a piece of paper. "One-hundred-dollar ante should cover it." He clears his throat. "Here." He slides the money over with a firm hand.

The men lean back in their chairs. One speaks up. "Dr. Braun sent you?"

"Yes. But I'm here on my behalf, not his."

"Let's get started, Mr. Sterling."

Ash settles into an icy stare; one I've not seen before. He's in his element. All those years learning from his cold, unfeeling father no doubt prepared him to wager a fortune on a rigged game.

Ash plays his hand. I don't understand anything, as they move cards around the table in silence. They speak in side glances and slow blinks, exchanging contempt without uttering a word.

"The night is young," Ash says. "Another twenty dollars." He throws a bill on the table and the men match.

I lean to whisper to Finn. "He's doing well, right?"

"Yes. A little too well."

I focus on Ash and watch the room. For what, I don't know. Gwendolyn's vague instructions left me little to go on, but all three men are here, and my chest burns like a sizzling cigarette. I search the room for some kind of power. Voices from their souls or secrets that beg to be heard, it's how I've protected myself all these years. Well, I've cut myself off from the humans attached to their whispers. Perhaps, that wasn't power at all.

A man slaps down a deed for a bank in town. "Can you match this?"

Ash drains his whisky in one gulp and asks for another. He scratches his nose and raises his eyebrows tall, working hard to focus.

"What's wrong with him?" I whisper.

Oliver shakes his head. "I don't know."

A man's soul grumbles, but I can't focus. Judy has found a bottle to sip from on a table behind us. The concoction of drugs and booze has never gone well, so I ground myself to the moment but reach for her sleeve to yank her back. "Knock it off, Judy. This isn't how we break you from Braun."

"I'm great." Her euphoric voice taunts me. I know how this trip lands.

The eerie scent of smoke crawls through the tiny room, but I try to shake it away. Ash lays a pile of deeds on the table. "Oil fields. Montana, Wyoming, Utah." His words slosh.

"No," Oliver says. "They're playing him. How does he not see it?"

I will myself to feel a vision, whispers—anything. Come on, boots. Start shining. But they don't so much as sparkle. Guns and knives decorate the room and glint from the guard's hip. So much danger in this room, it's muddying my visions. "Judy, do you see anyone? Can you read the dead here to help Ash?"

She rubs her palm across her face in a sloppy swipe as her finger catches on her bottom lip. "Shut up," she mutters. "I'm resting."

"Finn, we're going to have a problem here."

"It won't be the only one." He nods to the table. The men play their hands as Ash's neck heats to crimson. They say things like three of a kind and flush and full house. I don't know what's happening, but

Oliver and Finn bury their faces in their hands. I prepare to fall into a vision, until—

Ash slides forward more papers. "Hotel. Farms in California." The way he speaks conjures images of a stone-cold businessman unloading his entire fortune, and not an eager young man out to build an empire. As if he walked in wanting to lose.

The vision is gone. I step forward but a guard blocks me with a firm hand and deep scowl. A warning rests on that expression I shouldn't question. I tap my toes together. Anger, Primrose. Get angry. Tap, tap. Someone speak to me, dammit.

Judy slumps against my shoulder. I swoop her up and hand her to Oliver. "What do we do with her?" Oliver shrugs, but wraps his arms around her waist, checking her eyes and speaking to her in a hushed tone. They share a smile which, though endearing, proves how incapable we are of managing this.

"That's it, Mr. Sterling. You're done."

"He lost it all," Finn mutters. "Just like that."

Ash tries to lunge for the man across the table, but two guards attack. Fists to Ash's cheek and stomach. He spits blood on the warped floorboard next to his perfectly shined shoe.

Whispers begin from somewhere outside. A woman's voice. It's all I can hear. No, I need a vision here, in this room. Judy wobbles next to me, losing her grip on reality. "What do we do?" I ask.

"Hope he doesn't fight back," Finn says. "There's too many and they have weapons."

The woman's voice sings, high and pretty. No one else can hear, yet this sound drowns out all others. What is she trying to tell me?

A bell rings and I wonder if it's part of my vision, but Finn grabs my hand, pulling me back to our current mess. The men drop Ash to the floor. "Coppers," one says, and they all rush out a hidden door in a cupboard. My head aches something fierce, but I force myself forward to help lift poor Ash from the floor. Swollen eye, bloody nose, busted lip. The belligerent Ash looks nothing like the undaunted man who walked in this room less than ten minutes ago.

We yank his heavy body back through the door we came through. "I couldn't help him." Tears spring to my eyes and he brings his hand to my cheek with a sad smile. "I failed."

"That was a losing battle from the start." Tucked in a damp, dark corner, Finn wipes Ash's bloody face with a handkerchief. "He'll have to sleep it off. We can't carry him up the stairs."

Oliver holds Judy who is semi-coherent but nowhere near stable. "The cops are coming through, but they're more concerned about the card game. We should be okay."

"I saw a woman with silver hair. I think she can help us. Oliver, you okay to watch them both?" Between Judy and Ash, the poor guy has his hands full. He nods, seemingly grateful to watch over these two vulnerable souls.

Finn holds my hand. "You go, I go."

We head into the darkness in the direction I saw the woman flee. We step through puddles as pots clang somewhere nearby. A deep pit of failure presses into my stomach as Gwendolyn's deal waves a disappointing finger my way. This isn't just about what I get at the end. Ash deserves happiness. We all do.

Finn wraps his arm around my shoulder and pulls me tight. "What are you going to ask her?"

"Why only her roots are silver, and why she's been singing to me since the moment I stepped underground."

We trip over uneven stones into a curved corner devoid of purple prism glass—or any light for that matter. The air is cold and damp, and that clanging noise has grown louder.

"There," Finn says.

We walk up to a framed square cut out of stones, like a window without glass. Inside, lanterns fill the space with low light the color of mustard, like the sallow skin of a man I once read who was dying of liver disease.

"What is this place?" I ask.

A wall of beds stacked three pallets high on a dirt floor and the cobweb-covered rafters. This place is uninhabitable. "They sleep here," Finn says.

"How can anyone live down here?" An older Chinese man sleeps, curled on a pallet. He has no pillow, no blanket, and his shoes are still tied on his feet. A pot simmers on a wood stove as another man stirs what I can assume from the smell to be cabbage soup.

Carvings of Chinese symbols decorate most of the wood, the language of lonely men far from their homeland. In the corner, smoke blows from a desperately dark room like the devil's breath.

The woman steps right in front of us. Her silver tips glimmer in the dim light. "Your hair," she says. "Your eyes."

"You've been calling to me all night."

"I didn't know who was listening." She shakes her head, focusing on my every movement.

Her pale skin against her black hair is strikingly beautiful, and the way the stones frame her feels like an art piece. I step forward into the meager light and pull my silver hair forward over my shoulders.

She trails her gaze along my hair from root to tip. "It's beautiful."

We hold the moment, connected by hair and eyes that have found their match, and the magic that plays inside us like a silent symphony.

"Do you live here?" I ask.

"I'm the cook for the working girls upstairs. Honestly, it's the best job in town. I come down to speak with the men and tell stories. Though it's dark and musty, there's something magic about being with people who understand me. I lost my family years ago, so speaking the language with them gives me a sense of home." She looks over her shoulder and smiles. "Besides, I bring them leftovers."

They've built a home down here as best they could because us white people don't want to see their humanity. I've seen our future, and I fear this country may never stop this sort of hate.

Finn points to the back of the living quarters. "What's behind all that smoke?"

"Oh that. That's the opium den.

That must be where Oliver barters with powders in the name of Braun's grand scheme. "Our friend didn't fare well at the poker game. Can you help us find a place for him to rest?"

She examines my face. "Do you… see things?"

"Yes. Dreams and past and futures. I always have."

She gasps, the way I did when I first learned of Judy and Marion. When I first saw another girl with silver hair. We're connected by a thread of loneliness, us silver psychics.

She ducks out from the makeshift room. "Come on." We follow her as the long, tattered ends of her linen dress smack against the stone walls. "My name is Lin," she says as she winds through the darkened space ahead of us.

We slide past men carrying crates and bags of who knows what. Lin ducks and spins through every black corner like a dragonfly through a thicket of trees. She knows every turn and bend in these tunnels.

We arrive at the door where Ash remains crumpled in Oliver's lap, right next to Judy. "What happened to these two?" Lin asks. She bends down to examine Judy who snores on Oliver's shoulder, then evaluates Ash's eyes. She tips his chin up with the gentle hook of her finger. Ash peeks open his non-swollen eye. They hold their gaze for a suspended moment, locked in hazy wonderment.

Ash finds a smile through a pained grimace. "Mr. Ash Sterling, at your service."

She smirks. "You are at no one's service right now. Come. You all can stay upstairs for the night in the brothel."

He nods with a dopey grin, and everyone helps maneuver Ash and Judy and their floppy limbs through the tightened hallways. Finn carries much of Ash's weight, guiding him through Lin's path.

Ash halts, a pained smile toward Finn. "You're quite capable. I see what Primrose sees in you, old chap."

"I'm twenty-four, Ash. Now quit talking. You'll run out of breath." Their two bodies lean on each other, one tall and lean, the other fit and breathtakingly strong. They stop so Ash may take breaths and allow his pangs to pass, but still they walk on, together.

We follow Lin up two flights, with a quick moment out in daylight. The sun, dreary under oyster clouds, is enough to blind me after the darkness of the underground. Oliver grabs my arm and leads me inside, but I can't see a thing. I feel around the hazy shapes and once again curse these damn eyes.

Lin opens the door out of the kitchen. "I'll show you the rooms." She leads us down the hall past a cacophony of groans and heavy breathing as headboards knock against walls. Oliver's eyes are as large as full moons, and I bite back a grin. His sheltered existence is foreign to me, as I've seen the souls of prostitutes and lonely men alike. Thankfully shutters cover the windows to the hallway.

Shining maple floors and an elegant crimson runner fill the space with unexpected comfort. A piano chimes in another room as girls sing and laugh. My eyes have fully adjusted now as our weary group stumbles around for a soft place to land for a few hours.

Lin shows us to the end of the hall. "Here." Two beds with floral bedding match the pink rosebud wallpaper. Finn lowers Ash to one bed who squints at the bedside lamp with pink fringe and tassels. "Where am I?"

I recoil from his busted face that I failed to stop. "A brothel."

"Naturally." His eyes flutter backward, and he sinks into the blush-colored bed.

Oliver lays Judy in the second bed, his hand behind her neck to guide her to the pillow. He removes her shoes and tucks in her feet, sliding the blanket up to cover her shoulders before smoothing her hair back from her eyes. "I'll sleep in the chair to watch over them both."

"Will she be okay until morning?"

"It'll be close, but as long as we get back first thing in the morning, she can stick close to her med schedule."

Lin opens another door to a room with one queen bed and a vase of wild daisies on the nightstand. "These are the working girls' quarters," she says. "I'll have them bunk two to a room tonight."

"Thank you." Her stares don't unnerve me like normal ones do. "Why have you been singing to me all night?"

She tips the ends of her hair up between her second and third finger. "My mother would sing. It took me years to realize she wasn't moving her lips. I could hear her thoughts." She looks back up at me with a bright, tight-lipped smile. "Isn't that lovely?"

"Yes, it sure is."

She drops her hair. "When she fell ill, she sent me to America to join my cousins. I could still hear her sing, all the way across the world. Until one day, the sound faded to silence. Ever since, I sing in my head, hoping she can hear me from wherever she is."

Finn leans his shoulder against the wall with a sorrowful thud, his eyes shining with tears. "I hate when their voices fade."

"Yes," she says, knowing somehow that he speaks of memories and not psychic gifts.

Her soul hasn't reached for me yet, leaving me with the idea that there's something to learn here. There seems to always be something to learn.

"I can patch up Ash, but the girl's in trouble."

I slide my fingers from the bridge of my nose along my eyebrows to steady my focus. I hope one more dose is enough to get her through the night. "She needs more help than we can give."

The door clicks shut as she leaves to attend to the badly beaten Ash. "So much loss," Finn says.

I run my fingers along a rose-colored shawl draped over the closet door to avoid the sadness in his eyes. "You joined our adventure when all you wanted was to work Uncle Henry's farm in silence. Somewhere inside, you believe you can heal that broken heart of yours."

He runs his hands through his mess of hair. "Believe is a strong word."

His cheeks. Why I stare at his cheeks, I don't know. But they're sharp and high and warmed to a terra-cotta red. His eyes are big and bright and multicolored little earths of grassy land and water. But I reach for his cheeks, and kiss along the curve under his eye.

Not a bit of me bristles at the notion he's put his faith in me. Gwendolyn's deal is but a memory right now as all I see is a man who makes me believe in the notion of home. "I was wrong. Touch doesn't elicit visions. I made that all up, apparently. A wistful story I told myself as a scared little girl. I was afraid of the good things, you see. Good was dangerous and lonely."

Finn's hand glides to my waist, such a light brush that my entire body tingles. We stay there, cheek to cheek, hands discovering how intimate honesty can be.

He breathes into my ear with a deep and controlled exhale. I graze his skin with my lips, desperate to taste his kiss again. When he pulls back to look at me, something cracks open. like sunshine floods my insides and blasts all the darkness away.

He presses his mouth to mine, soft at first, then hungrier, deeper. His touch makes me forget I'm a psychic. *Just like magic.*

He pulls away and smiles as he drags his eyes open slowly. "Will you do something for me?"

My heart races, grateful to be useful for something. "Yes."

He lifts my hand to his forehead and runs my fingers through his hair. "I'm ready to cut my hair."

A moment passes while I cradle his head and he slides his hand from mine, where the longing inside turns tangible. Loneliness sprouts to the surface and finds a bit of sunlight. "I'll get the scissors."

Chapter Twenty

Finn found a toiletry kit in the men's bathroom. We've gathered a towel and brush, scissors, a comb, and a razor. "I've only ever cut my mother's hair," I say. "And I cut it unevenly on purpose."

"Hopefully I'll get better service," he says with a smile.

A knock on the door. I can hear Oliver clear his throat. "Sorry to bother you, but Ash is awake, and he's pretty upset. He's asking to see you, Primrose."

Finn runs his fingers along my arm. "Go ahead. I'll wait."

I open the door and follow Oliver to their room to find Ash on his bed, forearm over his eyes. His hair is a matted mess and his skin shines in unnerving shades of crimson and purple.

I sit next to him and glance up at Oliver. "How is he?"

Ash slides one hand aside so he can see me, then rubs his face, forgetting he's been bloodied. "I hurt."

"Where?"

"Everywhere I have skin."

"I should have stopped you. I'm so sorry this happened." Another day, another failure.

He waves a hand in the air at nothing. "It's not your fault. I'm ruined."

"You're not ruined, Ash. You made a mistake."

"This is much more than a mistake. It's stupidity of the highest order. This is proof I don't belong in my family." He rolls over and groans. Oliver lowers his head and walks off to check on Judy again. "I was so stupid." Ash scratches his neck hard enough to leave bright red lines from his nails. "I let Braun manipulate me. I believed I could outsmart him and return to New York with buckets of money." Ash drags himself up, his head bobbing, too heavy for his neck. "They put something in my drink."

Whispers. This vision isn't for me or because I'm forced into it. This vision is for him, a brand-new feeling. "Ash?" I touch his lumpy, swollen cheek. In an instant, I'm shot onto the long yellow road. I tumble from the force but don't fall. Poppies grow up from the cracks between bricks. They push their way through, disrupting the ground like an earthquake. My sparkly boots teeter on the uneven road. A vine spirals overhead. I reach for the thick green rope as it flies me through the air in a rush of freedom.

Nothing shoots me through the sky because I let go. I drop, knowing something will catch me. I fall past the stars with a glimpse into Ash's dark soul. Clarity.

Back in my body, I breathe with surprising ease. Coming home didn't hurt.

"Your eyes rolled back again. I hate when you do that."

I pull my hand from his face. "You know what you were doing tonight."

"Like hell I did. If I would have done a single thing right, I'd have a handful of money right now."

"No." I glance over at Oliver who strokes Judy's cheek as she smiles at him in and out of sleep. "You walked into the fire because you knew you'd be burned."

He turns toward me as awareness dances across his face. "What are you talking about?"

"What you really want isn't money and land, but you believe it's the only thing that matters. You want love. Acceptance. Home. It's what we're all here for."

"I could have all that if I could just get out of my father's grip."

"Don't you see? You threw a bomb into your life because you didn't have the strength to choose destruction. You need freedom, and this disaster just handed you that." I shrug. "In the most unfortunate way."

"I let those men steal my money and beat me so my father would walk away from me?"

His soul, while a genuine mystery to himself, spoke to me with clarity. Sabotage for self-preservation. He never wanted my help.

He dabs his split lip. "I'm not sure which is more painful," he says. "Wanting love you'll never find or ruining yourself in the process."

"I understand you more than you know."

Lin cracks the door open, holding a tray of tea and medical supplies to tend to his wounds. "May I?" she asks.

Ash sits up straighter and attempts to force open his bulging eye. "Please."

Lin places down the tray dabbing a towel into the water and over his brow. Ash keeps his eyes on her, not seeming to notice her silver tips, and definitely not hearing the song in her mind.

I step back into our room to find Finn examining a handful of hair pulled forward over his eyes, perhaps saying goodbye to all the protection his loneliness provided.

"Ash is in for a long night," I say.

He flops his hair back to expose his eyes. "The man sure makes things harder for himself."

"Yes, he really does." I unload the grooming kit and prepare the comb and scissors. "Is that what I do too?" I don't dare look at him when I ask the question I already know the answer to.

He stands and walks up behind me, his shoulders pulled back and head tall. "Maybe we all do."

Our reflection in the mirror lights half my face with hazy sunlight that has filtered through the curtain. "I came to Hot Lake to find more clairvoyants. I wanted a family. Somehow, I landed in an impossible scenario where everyone's survival rests on my shoulders."

He moves my hair over my shoulder and smooths it against my back. "You don't need to save anyone but yourself."

I turn from the mirror, too tired of the reflection staring back at me. "My spirit guide made a deal. I can live with pain-free visions and do good with this thing I never asked for. But I have to save a three-colored man."

He rubs my back without even a hitch when I admit this to him. "That's me, right?" He cocks his head in awareness. "But also, Ash and Oliver."

"I'm sorry I didn't tell you." I hesitate to reveal too much. "A deal with death doesn't seem like such a big deal anymore because this moment is real and you're real and all of this terrifies me."

He glides his fingers over my cheek. "Reality is more terrifying than the fantastical will ever be."

He kisses the back of my hand, and the world seems to soften around me. "Gwendolyn, my spirit guide, told me that becoming is painful. Maybe this is what she meant."

"Nothing great ever got there by an easy road," he says. "So says Uncle Henry every time I tired of farmwork."

"Are you certain you want this?" I'm not just speaking of hair. My deepest question lies in whether he can let go of all that's destroyed him.

With a head toss to loosen his wild locks, he hands me the scissors. "I'm ready."

He sits down, and I lay a towel over his shoulders. "Seems a shame to get rid of all this gorgeous color."

"I don't need it anymore."

With my cupped palm I scoop water from a bowl at the bedside. His skin rises with goosebumps when the cold water drips down his neck. I comb through his thick, copper locks that remind me of a trail of pennies. Slow and patient, I'm careful to avoid the tender spots on his scalp. They're mostly healed with no fresh wounds to speak of.

The comb slides through the bands of soft hair, and I take the scissors to a large hunk of it. I wait to see if he'll flinch or pull back, but he does neither as I snip and slice away years of open sores and quiet agony. The way he closes his eyes and leans his head back in complete trust. The intimacy of it all is almost too much to bear.

He looks down at the scattered hair around his feet as I carefully use a blade to shave his neck and the soft skin behind his ear. When I'm finished, I remove the towel and brush off the small, silky hairs from his shoulders. I hand him a mirror.

"You can see my eyes," he says.

"And what a view it is."

His blue eye reminds me of a thunderstorm. The other, earth and pine needles.

He wraps his hand around my wrist, his other hand cresting my hip as he pulls me close. I lower to his lap and slide my fingers around his neck, watching as he leans his head back and smiles. He trails the back of his fingers down my chin and neck, fingertips skimming my breastbone. "I never expected this," he says. "You make happiness seem possible."

The intensity of a sharp comeback rolls up strong while I almost quip that it was simply a haircut, but the moment is too pure for jokes. Too important for fear veiled as wit. This was so much more than a haircut.

With firm control, he pulls my hips into his and kisses between my breasts. His short hair reflects a lighter shade of copper, more red in the glitter of sunlight.

Feeling like I might burst, I grab his head and press my lips to his. My mind goes numb in the most incredible way. His soul remains quiet. No whispers, as his body is too busy talking.

He pulls back my hair, cradling it at the base of my neck.

I stare into his eyes and unbutton my dress, my heart pounding against my hand. Gold flecks pepper his irises. It's like staring into a new world every time I look at them. "Back at the farm I met a quiet, hurting man who wanted nothing to do with the silver-haired psychic."

He pulls his shirt over his head, his arms rippling with muscles. "We're not on the farm anymore."

Filled with nerves and hunger, I bring his hands to my dress, guiding him to gather the skirt. He lifts the dress over my head, his fingers grazing my waist and ribs. In the few times I've been with men, I've never felt the soft brush of fingertips or the intense hold of a gaze. Finn has changed all that.

He lifts me as if it's nothing, wraps my legs around his hips, and carries me to the bed, laying me softly on the pillow. His fingers glide along my waist and the curve along my buttocks. Around my hip and between my legs. I lean back and moan, grabbing his hair in my palms as desire swallows me.

I want more. As the rest of our clothing gets thrown against the wall, I pull him on top of me. Memories of visions and spirit guides and saving people rest far away while I open myself to being a woman whose powers do not define her.

He presses into me, gentle but firm. We move and roll together, eyes locked in a fierce stare until my body tightens and releases, and finally, floats. All those years I've craved touch, I was, in fact, longing for only this kind of touch. We groan together, breathless and tangled in each other. He takes me somewhere new, somewhere magical. As my body explodes, our eyes remain locked. Afterwards, my skin tingles with newness and possibility.

He covers us with a blanket. Kisses on the curve of my breasts send me aching for him again. "I don't feel like a psychic in charge of saving the world," I say.

"What do you feel like?" He lays next to me, propped on his elbow and stroking my hair.

"Like a woman who is glad she didn't die."

The weather has turned gray, a summer storm rolling in. The plaster under the window has chipped, a crack running from the ceiling to the floor. I turn back to Finn, to hide from the chill that rushes through the window.

Fear taunts me from the periphery, a warning that knocks on my ribcage like a caged animal. I press into Finn's neck and close my eyes, desperate to hold onto this moment a little longer, before life crashes back to me. Save the three-colored man. Save the women in the sanitorium. Stop Braun from drugging every psychic in the country. I can't do it all, much as I ache to do so. Perhaps I'll fail at every turn, but I won't know until I try.

We are most definitely no longer on the farm.

Chapter Twenty-One

I wake to a soft, dreamy haze, Finn's naked arms wrapped around me. But as soon as my eyes open, fear emerges as knowing settles on my skin. Danger closes in. I feel it everywhere—like a fever.

My breath trembles and I slide from his sleepy embrace. Something calls to me. Stars whisper and beg, colliding with each other in a frantic cry for help. Lin's songs call to me, their words freckling the dark morning light.

Her cries pull me down the hallway, past the kitchen and bathrooms. Beyond the tall windows of the cozy rooms then through the parlor, with its silent piano. Cowered in a corner, I find Lin, tucked into a ball and crying.

"Lin?"

Her eyes glow powdery white in the dark, like moonstones nestled in black sand. Dark purple streams bleed from her lower lids. Tears the color of bruises. Marion's advice crashes into me. I'll know I'm on the right path when I see purple tears.

She can barely form a whisper. "I won't cry in front of people. My tears scare everyone."

"Just like my hair."

"I can hide my tips, but these?" She doesn't wipe her eggplant tears as they roll over her lips and down her chin. "The more I hold them back, the darker they get. They sting."

"Oh, Lin." I wipe her greasy, viscous tears. They stain my fingers. "When I avoid reading futures, my chest hurts and my head aches. Your tears are probably tied to your powers."

"How can crying be a power?"

"What made you cry?"

"That man!" She throws her hand up with a nod toward Ash and Oliver's door.

"What did Ash do? I'll kill him if he hurt you."

"No." As her tears lessen, they leave streaks of purple along her cheeks. "He made me feel seen. Despite his busted face, he wanted to know about my childhood in China and what my family was like. He asked how to say beautiful in Chinese. I can't fall for a rich, white man. I can't want what I cannot have."

"Why can't you want him?" She shakes her head. "Lin, can I read you, please? Your songs have haunted me since we walked in here, and I might be able to teach you something."

After examining every detail of my facial expression.

I hold her hands in mine and welcome her starry night. Though I no longer need touch, it still eases the connection, and I venture to guess that she fears this just as I do. Her soul drags me through a slick tunnel so fast I bump my head. My feet pierce the veil, and I'm back on my honeycomb road. Only this time, the sticky honey is blood.

I'm sinking, like quicksand. A flower extends its hand and wraps around my waist to pull me out. But it isn't a poppy. It's a black calla lily, petals coiled tight. The bright green stem wraps around my waist, my arms, my neck. I can't breathe.

The flower pulls me from the river of blood and tosses me into the blackness, but stars catch me, thank goodness. I stare below and watch Lin's last moments. Her strangled, tortured last breaths... from Braun's emerald opium.

Back with a shove into my body, holding Lin's hands, staring into her purple flooded lids. We are connected. She's shown me what happens if I fail.

"What do you see?" she asks.

Damn this deal. "There's a doctor an hour from here at Hot Lake Sanitorium. He's developing a drug to fight psychic phenomena." Just tell her the hard truth and be done with it. "The emerald opium will kill thousands of our kind, including you."

Her shoulders soften but her hands remain squeezed over mine. It's all to gain the reward at the end, I remind myself. A peaceful life for me and anyone under the threat of Braun's evil.

"Why?" she asks.

I could say how he believes he is purifying the world and curing our pain. How he wants infamy, seduced by the allure of groundbreaking medicine. He studies the occult to turn our powers against us. I don't know why he does it. These are only conjectures. "I don't know."

"Am I dying now? Because I feel like I'm dying."

I sit in the memory of her soul once again. What did I feel? The real her bled out of the soil and sent me down a river of loss. It all feels so familiar. My chest spasms, forcing a deep breath as I shoot my eyes open. "You ignore your source power, and your fear will eventually drown you."

"My source power?"

My left ear rings into a high-pitched squeal. No amount of pressure from my finger below my temple lessens the tightness. Gwendolyn pops into my mind and in no time, a tiny gold dot floats around in the darkness.

"Trust your visions," Gwendolyn whispers. "You know the answers. They've always been inside you."

"Lin?" The ringing fades. The dot has disappeared. "What happens if you stop singing?"

She drops her hands to her lap. "I hear things."

"What kind of things?"

Her tips glow bright silver, and the tiniest pinpoint of white appears in the center of her dark eyes. "I hear thoughts." She pinches the bridge of her nose. "In moments of closeness, especially."

"You sing to override the noise."

"My mother did too. I would rather hear her sing and hum than listen to how a neighbor called her a whore or a stranger's distaste for my difficulty talking. I was a quiet child."

"Understandable."

"Mr. Sterling, he said lovely things in his thoughts. He thinks I would never love a man like him. I quieted the singing for a few moments to listen to his mind."

I avoided touch and Lin sings. The wild things we do to avoid the truth of who we are. "Quieting your gift is killing you."

"The men in the underground understand magic. They speak Chinese in their thoughts and don't question that I understand them. I miss my language so deeply it hurts."

I can't fathom losing who we are, our connection. "Those writings on their beds and on scrolls. What do they say?"

"Stories, mostly. The one on the wall is a Chinese proverb. Life and death are preordained; wealth and status are in the hands of fate."

Something rings in my head as if a bell clangs to alert my mind. "Free will."

"It's a loose translation. I believe the men need a reminder that they still have some say in their future."

Oliver's vision. That's why I can't see his future. It's wrapped up in Judy's and mine. Oliver will have no life if I can't save the woman he loves, and I would then lose Marion and Braun would prevail. Every choice I make ripples through my world, sending quakes to disrupt the natural order of things. But what is set in ink and what spaces remain blank?

As the sun creaks its way into the sky and the window shades a deep pink, something clangs in Ash's room. I glance back, knowing something is about to turn.

Oliver bursts through the door, wide-eyed and out of breath.

"Shit," I mutter. "Oliver?"

He tracks my voice. "Primrose? She's gone. I fell asleep in the chair and when I woke, her bed was empty." He looks around the room and down the stairs as if she may be hiding.

With horrific realization, I stand and hurry toward him. "I know where she might be."

Lin shoos us down the stairs. "I'll keep an eye on Mr. Sterling."

We fly down the back stairs, out into the street, and back into the underground. Through quiet tunnels and past the purple haze, over drunken ranchers and cowboys passed out in pools of drool. We pass the Chinese quarters, where every man is awake, brewing tea and playing cards.

I grab Oliver's sleeve and point to the back room. "There."

"The opium den?" He gasps. We may be too late.

Memories of Braun's opium needle from Lin's reading slither into my mind. The drug slid into her veins like rain through sidewalk cracks.

We hook arms and run past the card game, under the hanging baskets. A man's soul beckons me, but I fight the whispers. No time.

The blackened rocks ooze darkness, while the windowless stone room closes tighter and lower near the den. We pass carvings painted in black, telling stories created by men's memories. Smoke trails from the corner carrying an odor I can't place. Like burned molasses, sweetness gone terribly wrong. We choke on the scent but move forward, hands over our mouths.

We push past the man at the door and past the rickety pallets filled with sleeping men, toward the dingy, suffocating corner.

The black stone room with a slanted ceiling is enough to send me into a panic. Sweet smoke crowds the air but through the white puffs are a dozen cowboys and businessmen asleep on dirty beds. Makeshift toilets sit at the foot of every pallet where men lie on their backs, necks propped up by wooden blocks. "What the hell is this?"

"The blocks keep their windpipe open so they don't choke," Oliver says, stepping carefully to avoid any limbs. "Dammit, Judy. Please don't be here."

I swallow my fear which only rises again like a tide, swelling larger with each breath. So far just men in a cloud of forbidden smoke. The room compresses around me, growing smaller and tighter.

We reach the last bed. We paw our way around as the hard mat creaks under our hands. Through the smoke, Judy's angelic face appears, holding a long, thin pipe made from redwood and decorated with brass and copper. Elegant and so out of place.

A man takes a pea-sized ball of sticky paste into the bowl at the end positioned over an oil lamp.

"Stop." I reach for him, but Judy knocks me away. She places the pipe in her mouth and reclines back. "Get away from me."

Oliver can't stop. He touches her cheek. "It's me."

"I don't want you here." She kicks him to the hard, cold ground.

The opium bubbles and swells into a golden ball just like Gwendolyn's orb. Smoke crawls from the opening and into Judy's mouth.

"Judy, this is too much." I grab the pipe in my fist and yank, but she shoves me with far too much strength, and my back slams against the wall.

She inhales the vapors. Her lungs crackle, like shattering glass. The man mutters something in Chinese, but I can't understand him. I search his face and see only concern.

I cough with shallow inhales of perfumy smoke that crawl and slither into my insides like worms. The vapor expands and grows.

"Please," I beg. "Stop."

Judy ignores us both. She smiles in extreme euphoria like air itself is money and her body needs the riches.

I inhale to survive but cough between shots of sweet candy air. I catch Oliver's gaze. We nod, knowing she'll fight, but we can't let her fall like this. I shove the pipe out of the way as Oliver lifts her from the pallet. She writhes but seems too sedated to fight.

"I'm sorry," the man says. "She paid." Lord only knows where she found money.

We stumble out of the den, Oliver carrying a sagging Judy. We fumble into walls, desperate for clear air. By the time we reach the stairs, Oliver drops to the bottom step to collect his strength. "I can't breathe," he says. "My head."

"Don't stop." I need to crawl. Hands and knees knock from one step to another, an eternity to reach the brothel's door. Oliver manages to stumble up the flight as Judy remains deathly silent.

On my knees, I turn the knob to the kitchen. Lin opens the door as I fall face first to her feet. "The opium," I say. "It made us sick."

Oliver lowers Judy to the kitchen floor. Ash and Finn run in, sliding toward us huddled around her. She's pale and sweating.

"Oh, God," Ash says, his swollen face somehow worse than yesterday. "She needs help."

"There are no doctors here," Lin says. "The only ones in town refuse to touch anything from the underground."

"We have to get back to Braun. He's the only one who can help her."

Finn touches Ash's arm. "I'll drive. You can't see out of either of those swollen eyes." Ash hands him the keys and we all lift Judy as Lin gathers our belongings. We make our way down to the car and slide her onto Oliver's lap. He cradles her, staring down at her ghostly skin.

Lin touches Ash's cheek before he turns away. "Goodbye."

Finn peels away from the brothel, spitting dust in every direction. Through the cloud, Lin lifts her hand in a wave. Purple tears appear just before she slides from view.

We drive in silence, Finn focused and speeding faster than this car should ever travel. Oliver shakes but rubs Judy's shoulders to hold the life in her. She's quiet, her breathing slowed. Every time I turn back, I worry she'll have turned blue.

"We should have never taken her," Oliver says.

We don't correct him because we all know he's right. She was safer in Braun's clutches on a steady stream of emerald injections.

Finn on my left and Ash on my right, I lean into my vision. She will live. *She will.*

To break the silence Ash asks, "Did Lin have purple tears?"

Lin's singing hides her true talent. Her path to happiness. "Yes. She has visions, just like me. We have psychic powers, Ash."

It hits me with clarity that we cannot be everything we want if we don't accept who we really are.

He grimaces, taking a deep inhale of afternoon air tinged with fear. "I still don't think I can believe in magic," he says.

"Even after everything you've seen?" Finn asks.

"I choose to see facts and logic," Ash says.

"And what happens if you believe in fairy tales?" I ask.

He slides his hands down the front of his thighs. "Then I will have discovered that my entire life has been a lie. And that's something my fragile heart cannot take."

Finn reaches across to hold my hand. What I wouldn't give to have a taste of Lin's powers right now. I'd listen to all our thoughts and fears, and I'd hold space for Judy's darkest murmurs that hold her prisoner.

The car thunders toward La Grande with two silver psychics and our three-colored friends. We're all searching for something only the emerald world of Hot Lake can offer. I can't help but think back to the moment we all boarded the train hoping for a grand adventure.

I stare at my friends and imagine who to save. The balmy wind flutters my hair, and I know none of it matters if I don't stop Braun from more of this torture.

It's time I commit to this deal with my whole heart, isn't it, Gwendolyn?

A ball of gold light rolls along the roadside. Inside, the faint outline of myself appears like a snow globe, lost in emerald light. To save Judy, to save any of these men beside me, first I must save what I've always feared: my unfiltered, unapologetic power.

Chapter Twenty-Two

After an intense hour in Ash's car where Judy nearly stopped breathing twice, we screech into the steamy air of Hot Lake. Oliver rubs his knuckles on her sternum, his eyes frantic. "We're here, Judy. Stay with us."

The car has barely stopped rolling when we drag her out, every second precious to keep her alive. We must hand her over to Braun, the man who put her in this nightmare. We're moving backward, traveling deeper into Braun's madness rather than escaping it.

Ash and Finn take turns carrying her. Though she's a sprite of a thing, her limp body makes for awkward movements as her head keeps flopping around. The men hold the back of her head against their chests in one of the most tender things I've ever seen.

We open doors and clear pathways through horrified spectators as Judy's lips glow pale blue. The commotion must have alerted the ward because Strauss is at the sanitorium door when we arrive.

"Good heavens." Her lack of nasty insults worries me. She hurries down the hall, yelling for Dr. Braun as she throws open the door to what looks like an exam room. Finn lays Judy's fragile body on the table as Strauss checks her skin and pulse.

Dr. Braun slides into the sterile, intensely bright room. "What did you do?" He posed the question to all of us. We back up to give them room to work, watching in silence. Braun's voice drops to a growl as he tears open a bag and prepares a syringe of some sort. "You could have killed her."

He injects her lifeless arm while Strauss covers her with a blanket and rubs her sternum. Oliver rocks next to me, his eyes closed, unable to watch. I touch his arm but can't bring myself to say anything.

"Get out," Braun says with a dark calm in his voice.

We head out into the hallway, but I remain at the door to glimpse any movement from Judy. Strauss blocks my view, forcing me to stare down her disappointed scowl, and slams the door in my face.

"He's right," Oliver says. "We could have killed her.

"She wanted to leave," I say. "I didn't know how bad it was." Or, I refused to see it. I should have seen the signs. The drastic changes in her personality, the skin problems. I've seen it all before. My father almost died multiple times before he actually did.

Marion wheels herself out, stronger than usual. "What happened?"

The men look to me. "Judy. She took too much opium and chased it with too much alcohol."

"Oh." Her eyes brighten, surprisingly unfazed. "Right on track."

"You've seen this in the future, haven't you?" I ask.

"Yes." She smiles at Finn and Ash on either side of her.

"Will she live?" Oliver asks.

"I think so. But I've never seen Braun's future. He's never let me in." She puts her fingers to her mouth and blows a high-pitched whistle. Clara skips into the hallway, smile beaming when she sees the lot of us. "Clara, I need you to tell me what they're saying inside the exam room."

She crosses her arms. "It'll cost you."

"Why, you little swindler," Ash says. "Yes, fine. I'll smuggle in all the chocolate pudding you want. Now, look."

She jumps for joy, then turns to face the door.

Ash elbows me. "You can't be serious. That little girl can't hear through doors."

Clara clears her throat. "Medication administered. Judy's body is trembling, shaking the metal table. Oh!" Clara cringes. "They turned her on her side and she's retching now. A lot."

"She'll be okay?" I ask Marion.

"She'll live. But she's far from okay."

Clara holds up her hand. "Braun is barking orders at Strauss. He just threw a towel on the floor and told her to clean up the mess." I almost feel sorry for Strauss. Almost. Clara continues. "Miss Whittaker has ruined everything." All eyes turn to me. "That woman has all the makings of the perfect subject. Exceptional talent, strong-willed. No family to protect her. Her hair is pure silver. Undiluted power. I'd trade in all these women for a shot at examining her."

Braun has all these women held as prisoners. Dependent on him. And still, he would turn them away for a shot at my mind. Why? Finn slides his hand behind my back.

Clara remains focused. "Strauss asked him what to do about their addictions. She's angry with him. Says he ruined us. He says he tried but can't find the final compound to eradicate, *what does that mean*, their disease." Clara bounces between voices. "Don't stop now. You can't stop now." She turns her head to the side, voice lowered. "Primrose is the answer to the compound." She slides to the side. "He's coming." Clara ducks behind an open door, out of sight.

The door creaks open. Braun stands tall, undeterred by a hallway full of people concerned for the sick woman on his exam table. "You've all made a grave mistake," he says. "She'll live, no thanks to any of you."

Finn elbows Oliver to stand up to Braun, but he shakes his head. "She doesn't want to live here," Finn says. "You're keeping them like hostages."

Braun slinks out of the room, eyeing us like a schoolteacher. "Are you aware what happens to silvers out in the world? I'm certain Primrose can tell you. Shunned. Mocked. Attacked. At Hot Lake, these special, talented beings are the stars. The center of innovative research. Each one works to help the next, a community that does not exist out in your world."

It's why I came here. All I've ever wanted was a friend who looks like me, who understands this gift, and how to do good with the messages we see. In a drunken stupor, Mother once told me I had Aunt

Vanessa's hands. What a strange thing I've held onto, the notion that her disappearing sister shared something with me. The silver hair and clear eyes were one thing, but every day, I would reach for something and think, a piece of my human body looks like someone who isn't drunk or high.

This thought leads to too many memories of sleeping alone in tents and watching my fragile parents stumble around, hitting walls.

Ash throws his hands out, attempting to fix the situation, as if he can. "Release them, Braun."

"I don't believe you have any jurisdiction here any longer." Braun pulls back his shoulders but still can't make himself eye to eye with six-foot-two Ash. "The game went my way, did it not?"

"You cheated."

Braun shrugs. "We played a game, and you lost. You have one week to draw up the papers and leave." He turns to Oliver. "I should have known you'd fail me. Bravery was never your strong suit. Hand over your keys." He lifts his chin, his gaze sharp enough to cut glass. "Now all of you, get the hell out."

Marion waves goodbye, no fear in her eyes. We leave the white-walled sanitorium that smells of ammonia and smoke, and step into the hotel of greenery and mint-colored caramels where ladies paint and gentlemen smoke cigars. We pass groups of women along the windows who play Bridge and enjoy full tea service, uninterested in the goings on of the mad doctor upstairs.

"Why won't you stand up to the man?" Ash asks as he throws his hand in the air.

"I can't lose my job," Oliver says. "Those animals need me."

"One day, you'll need to make a choice. If you love Judy as you claim to, you'd sacrifice everything. She's dying while you're playing farmer."

"Hey, Ash. Back off." I pull him back. "We're all trying here."

"Forget this place," Finn says. "Let's steal them away and take them to real doctors. We'll report Braun and get this place shut down."

"We can't." They turn to face me. Much as I hate to admit this, Braun has everyone by the throat. "He's turned the residents into addicts, hooked on his medicine. He's probably the only one who knows how to keep them alive. Some fancy surgeons are here doing research with him, which means he has the funds to squash us."

"No one has more funds than my father. I'll instruct him to shut this place down."

"After you lost all his property?" Finn asks.

Ash's bravado falters. "Oh, right." He grows pale at the mention of it.

Oliver juts his chin forward. "Don't care enough to fight, huh?"

"Okay, stop." I push the men away from each other by their chests. "Let me think." I don't need to think. I know exactly what I must do. Marion was right, our futures are connected, and I'm the only one who can stop Braun because my mind is clear. All this time I've run away from people who use drugs or booze, but these are who I understand the most. I fear this has been the purpose of my talents all along.

"I need to admit myself."

"To the sanitorium?" Finn asks. "No. No way I'm letting you do that."

"I don't need your permission. You heard what Clara said. Braun wants my mind. He'll let the others go. And I'm not going to take his medicine. I'll let him test my psychic powers until he cares more about me than them. It's the only way out."

"No," Ash and Oliver say in unison.

"Just give me a few days. I think I can convince him. It will take me reading his soul, which he guards tightly. He'll discover something new about us—I'll make certain he does—and that will take over. I'll convince the women to leave of their own accord. And I will need you to have a plan to get them to hospitals immediately."

"I don't like this at all," Ash says.

"You can't fix this with money or brute force. I can fix it, but only from the inside. And only with trust in each other."

Twenty-two years old and I'm just now discovering how to be human. How to be the me who exists outside of visions and stars and honeycomb roads and magic boots. Inside Braun's emerald city of opium, I'll have to learn how to be all of me, all at once.

Chapter Twenty-Three

A mere ten minutes after I've declared my plan for the sanitorium, the men have put their foot down. That didn't take long. When will they understand I'm through allowing others to decide my fate? If I can't save the women upstairs, nothing else matters.

Ash paces the solarium. "We'll leave. All of us. We'll swoop the residents up and drag them out in the middle of the night if we must." His red face shines under the sunlight streaming through the windows. "Braun doesn't live here, does he? We can steal everyone when he's distracted.

"Then what?" I ask. "We're now responsible for sick patients while Braun fills his sanitorium with more psychics? No. I have to stop him."

The men glance at each other again like I'm a toddler caught in a lie. They all think they know what I need.

Finn tilts his head. "Walk away."

"No. Everything is on my shoulders, not yours." I step away and lean against the wall, out of the direct light to protect my eyes.

"We just want to help," Ash says.

"I don't need help." He flinches but I carry on. "You're avoiding going back to face your father after losing his fortune at a card game. You don't have the money you did yesterday, Oliver has probably lost his job, and Judy died for a few minutes up there. Any power we had is gone. It's up to me now."

"You've seen silver girls leave here, right?" Finn asks Oliver.

"Yes, but in terrible shape. They often go to other facilities when he's done with them, or they search for opium anywhere they can." He takes a pained breath. "Like Judy did."

"They don't understand he only cares about using them." I throw my head back to aim my voice toward the humming pipes on the ceiling. "That's right, Clara. I'm talking about you." Guaranteed she's listening. If not for Braun, then for her own entertainment.

Oliver rubs his arm as the white patch on his hand warms to pink. "He'll break you too, Primrose."

"That's a risk I'm willing to take."

Ash's lying tease of a dance partner waves at him from the corner of the solarium where she sips on iced hot springs water. A strange attraction here at Hot Lake. He smiles but doesn't leave us. Not yet.

"You're too good for her." It's the absolute truth.

Finn reaches for me, shaking his head. "I can't let you get hurt."

I settle my hands on his shoulders. "Please understand. I've been useless all these years. Terrified of this darkness inside me that makes people use me. This is my turn to do something right. My powers on my terms."

His hands settle on my waist, soft and loving. "How will you break him?"

"Only one way I know how to stop people. Fly through their souls to see their deepest secret. He has a weakness and I'm going to find it."

"What will happen to you?"

"If anything gets dangerous, I'll send Clara for you, okay?"

A bird watching group gathers around us, preparing their hats for an afternoon picnic. They crowd us into the corner next to a giant palm. Ash watches the beautiful people dressed in their white linen and leather boots. He longs to be one of them even though he already is.

"We need to trust her," Finn says.

"It's my fault Judy got sick," Oliver says. "I'll help any way I can."

"The only one at fault old friend, is Braun." He slaps Oliver's shoulder. "A bloody mess he's created." I realize what Ash does. He takes on the persona of his father when he needs strength. Models his movements and dialogue to show the control he doesn't feel inside.

"Ash, is your father British?"

"Yes. How did you know?"

I smile. "Simply a guess."

"The only way I'll agree to this is if you send Clara to us for regular updates," Finn says. "You say the word and we'll break down the doors to save you."

I want to resist and attempt this on my own, but as I stare into the faces of these three men who've changed my life, I come to the realization that this is what family means. Sacrifice and trust and letting people love you. "Yes, I agree."

"When do you hand yourself over?" Ash asks.

After I discover the secret to my internal power? No, not enough time. "Tomorrow, I guess." I need time to plan.

Ash inhales while gazing up at the pipes in the ceiling. "Do they really pump boiling water through those things? It is a marvel. Well, Primrose. Please know how lovely you've been. You inspire me to be a better human, and I fear I may feel responsible for your predicament." His neck reddens and eyes turn glassy. "With that, I shall take my leave. A pretty woman wants to steal my money and use my body, and I do not wish to spend my afternoon anywhere else but that horrid woman's bed." He bows. "Adieu."

"I need a bit of time to myself," I tell Finn. What I really need is advice from my nonexistent but slowly redeeming spirit guide. Details of my psychic self remain hidden.

"Okay." He kisses me on the cheek with a lingering hold before he pulls away. "I'll find you for supper. Oliver, let's get those animals fed and clean, yes?"

Oliver, ever the worried soul, grabs his overalls and nods. "I'd like the help." He dips his head in my direction. "I'm so sorry, Primrose."

"Say nothing more, Oliver. We're going to help them all." If I held on to every disaster I've inadvertently caused, I would never get out of bed. I almost didn't many times.

Once the men are off on their perspective endeavors, I walk through the hotel's entrance into the chilled autumn afternoon as the quaking aspens rattle their golden leaves in the breeze. Chickens cluck by, on their way back to Oliver's feed bucket, no doubt. Steam from the lake floats around me, obscuring my view of the hotel with thick, white mist.

"Gwendolyn?" I whisper.

I peer through the haze but see nothing. The geyser spews from the lake as green minerals shimmer through the milky water, reminding me how odd this entire place is.

Far away, a tiny speck of light spins like a pinwheel. I expect her orb to grow, but the dot floats away, and in its place emerges a bright white stork.

"Gwendolyn, explain yourself." The bird steps past me through the cloud into clear air. "Storks don't even live in Oregon!"

Behind me, a voice. "The stork was injured and Braun brought him back. He doesn't fly." I step through the marshy ground to find the source of the familiar voice. "The stork represents beginnings. A new life." As if on cue, the steam parts and standing alone, hand pressed to his neck, is…

"Russell?"

"At least there is no shortage of interesting animals here at Hot Lake. How are the boots treating you?" he asks.

"Great." I tip back on my heels. "I'm still trying to figure out what all this means."

"Your visions, you mean?"

"No Russell, the emerald popcorn they sell in the confectionery. Yes, of course my psychic powers."

He throws his hands up. "Okay, okay. Were you always this touchy?"

"I'm tired." His heavy eyes and thinned face give him a haunted aura. The bag he wears around his shoulder hangs at his bony hip. "Are you okay?"

He waves me to follow toward the church. "Has the great one turned you into an all-knowing psychic medium yet?"

"He hasn't killed anyone, and neither have I, so I'll take that as a win." I'll just keep that terrifying situation with Judy to myself.

He still rubs his knuckles into the center of his chest. Worse than before.

He opens the door to the church and steps inside. I follow. A tilted, crumbling roof hangs over a fireplace with bricks and pebbles strewn like dappled sunlight. Stained-glass like rainbows bathes the dark room in a surprising kaleidoscope of color. In the window, the same prism as in Russell's shop.

Under the window sits a green metal box.

"What is that?" I ask.

"You ask a lot of questions." Russell approaches the box and stares out the colored glass panels.

"Did you come back for me?"

"Sorry to disappoint you, but no." He places his trembling hands on the box. "I came here for me."

"What happened with you and Braun?" I ask. "He won't talk about you."

"Oh, that." He lifts the box to his chest like it's a plush pillow and not hard metal. "I disappointed him."

"Because you wouldn't let him control you?"

"Something like that." He slides to the floor, back against the rough wood wall, metal box on his lap. I can see his chest thump from where I stand at the front pew. "I can see what's inside people," he says. "Disease, bad blood, growths. If they hear voices or their eyesight is going. I see it all."

Damn, I knew I felt a connection to him. "I know what it's like to be used." I sit down against the foot of the bench that's split down the middle and lean my head back. "You could make him the best doctor in the world."

"Yeah. Until he discovered something bigger with me as a test subject, and sadly, one of the first recipients of his discovery."

I tuck my knees against my chest, tight enough to rest my chin on them. "You're the only one I've met that isn't a girl with silver hair."

"Yeah. I've met men like me, but we're afraid. Definitely more afraid than the women. We have trouble with our emotions, so we stay in hiding. Ignore who we are."

"Some women do that too." Ahem, this girl fabricated an entire vision of death to cope with it all. "Don't you just want to burst, having all that magic bottled up inside you?"

Russell bites his lip. "Yes. That's why I dull myself with the green stuff. And why I became a chemist."

"You want to find another way. One that doesn't drain the life from you like opium does," I say.

"I haven't had much luck."

I hesitate as something bubbles to the surface. A thought I hadn't wanted to entertain before. But now, with Russell right here, I burn to ask. "If you know he's a user—" I say it hesitantly, like stepping over the floor after you've swept up broken glass. "Why did you send me here?"

"You asked, remember?"

"But you offered the boots." I lift my toes to the light to watch them sparkle. "How did you know they would change me?"

"Things become magic when we desire them to be. You needed to believe." He scratches the inflamed rash on his neck. "Just because I failed, doesn't mean you will."

Tears flood my eyes. I could end up just like him when Braun gets his claws into me.

"Watch." He places his hand on mine and closes his eyes. "Headaches. They're only partly due to your visions. You'll need to work on neck stiffness. And your lungs are prone to infections and pneumonia. You should watch that. Otherwise, fit as a fiddle."

"How did you…" I pull away from his touch. He could tell me I have a bleed or a tumor. Who wants to know that? This must be why we struggle with the purpose of it all. "You told me you didn't have powers anymore," I say.

"I don't have the desire to do readings anymore. That's close enough."

"You lied to me." I shove his foot, which kicks loose the deep, humming whisper of his soul. I felt it when he nudged me, and again when my foot touched his, but I fight the creeping sensation of spiders across my forehead.

"I told you what you wanted to hear." He fiddles with the silver hinge that holds the box closed. "There's a place that houses psychics just like you. I may not see in your soul, but loneliness was killing you like a disease. That much was obvious."

He opens the lid and sighs. Green light shines from inside, casting a sheer, emerald luminescence on his gaunt face. He lifts a cloth band from the box and uses his teeth to bind it around the meat on his sinewy arm, then taps the blood vessel in the crook of his elbow that pulses thick and blue.

He retrieves a syringe from the box and slides it into his blood vessel. Thumb pressed on the tip, he pushes slowly with his head leaned back and face filled with relief.

"Why is that here?" I ask.

"He leaves it for me. So he doesn't have to see me." He licks his lips and stops talking to enjoy his cloud-filled euphoria. "I have enough for a month."

"Why does he do that for you?"

"Because without it, I need a hospital. I've almost died twice."

I lean back against the pew, stomach coiled in knots.

"It's true. Withdrawal from the stuff turns me feral. I could tear the flesh from a rat with my teeth and swallow like it's saltwater taffy."

He must be joking. "That didn't really happen."

"No, you're right." He shoots a little more from the needle. "It was a squirrel."

My heart thrashes in my chest. No way could I ever do something like that.

"You think you're better than me, right? That you'd never go wild or let him give you the opium." He slides the needle from his elbow and releases a pleasurable groan. "You will. I thought I could help people too." He bends his elbow and leans back with eyes closed. "Turns out, this is the only thing I need."

"Do you see poppies and honeycomb roads?" I ask.

He twitches a few times and smiles. "I see only white and feel the answers."

Sadness stretches through me, into every corner. He's fighting to erase himself and all but succeeding. "I'll hand myself over to Braun tomorrow. I'll be his next subject."

"Don't do it." He doesn't even try to meet my eyes.

"I have to. Everyone here is under some sort of spell. He's going to kill innocent people."

"Living under his madness will make you want to die."

"I've spent most of my life there." I stand and inch my way toward the door, unable to tolerate any more of his warnings or his deadened eyes.

"The boots," he shouts. "They belonged to your Aunt Vanessa."

If anything in my life has ever turned me to ice, it's this. "What?" I want to run away and never return, but my boots tell a story. They were *hers*. "You know her?"

"Knew her," he says. "She died."

All the air escapes my lungs. I always thought I'd find her. My magic aunt who understood me and could teach me. That dream falls like dust around me. "How?"

"I told you this place does something to people." His voice is unemotional, like a contrived version of happy. "She was here when I was. Her powers were unique. She could make any man fall in love with her."

"Yes, I've heard." I don't move any closer than the doorway, but I hang onto his every word.

"The irony was, she didn't want men, if you get my drift. She kept falling for women who didn't want her. Loneliness kills us all, eventually."

My mind grapples with what he's told me, like pawing around for a lamp in the pitch black. Mother swam in jealousy over Vanessa's useless, painful power.

He releases a long, drawn-out sigh. "A psychic test went wrong, I guess. Dr. Braun used machines then with electricity and wires. We were in the field right outside this door, using the sun to power emeralds as he brewed his drug. The blast blew off the side of this church, swirled like a cyclone, and dropped on Vanessa."

This church where we stand. "This place killed her?"

"Braun had the side of the house patched but no one comes in here. Too many ghosts.

I stifle a gasp. "You watched her die?"

"Her silver boots stuck out from the torn wall, pristine and sparkling next to her crumpled body," he says with a little too much calm. "She knew she was risking her life, but she was so lonely. She told me that if anything happened to her, I was to find her niece, Primrose Whittaker. The boots were a sign she was with you. It only took ten years to find you."

"But we found you in the chemist shop."

"Did you?" he asks with a snicker. "She knew we'd cross paths. I moved on with my life and Portland is the only place to make a viable chemist shop. I knew she was right as magic happens in odd ways. Why I still believe in any of it is a damn mystery."

It's all too much. Vanessa was here, hurting the whole time? "She tried to change herself?" I swallow hard and think of every gay person I've read who just wanted to be loved. That seems to be all anyone wants.

"She was a lot like Oliver. She realized early on that she was fine the way she was. So, she liked women. Who doesn't?" His eyes grow dopey and soft. "She stayed for the same reason you are. We all think we can save the world. But Primrose, none of us have stopped him. You're no different."

But I am different. I've lived with needles and drugs and the aftermath of addiction. "I don't understand, how did Vanessa get men to fall at her feet?"

"Oh, same as you. She read their souls. Except, she saw their deepest shame. When she helped to soothe them, they developed some sort of attachment to her. Dr. Freud should have studied her."

"Could she not read women?"

"She could. Quite well." He forces his tired body to stand, joints cracking as he rolls his spine tall. He swaps the box of vials for an empty one. The green one from his chemist's shop. That's why he yelled at me for touching it. It's traded out every month for a fresh set of horrors. "Listen, I was a teenager. A real messed-up kid, you know? I didn't know much, but I could tell she wasn't going to leave without something very important."

"What was that?"

Russell drags his feet in a leisurely stroll toward the door as I follow. As if nothing in the world could bother him. The drug erased his frantic eyes. It does that. Buffs the edge of fear by dulling the will to live.

"She was here to save the one person who had her heart," he says.

"Oh, God." I snap the pieces in place, horrified by the truth of it all. "It wasn't—"

"Marion." He shuts the door, box tucked in the bag slung over his shoulder.

"That's why she stopped trying to fix herself. She fell in love." Another piece clicks into place. "Marion's been here for *ten years*?"

"Yeah," he says with a heavy sigh. "Now I know you'll just work harder to save her, but we've all tried. Even Vanessa. Give it up, Primrose. Get out while you can." He shivers despite standing in a solid patch of sunshine.

"You're still here. He owns you, Russell."

"Exactly." He tightens his jacket and glances at the hotel with, what is it, sadness, disdain? He forces a smile and walks away toward the train stop.

Vanessa gave Russell the boots to give to me. Marion knew I would arrive and play some part in stopping Braun. My role here has been brewing for years, before I even knew how to live with psychic visions. I'm here to carry on Vanessa's legacy and complete what she couldn't. Free the love of her life.

The aunt I never met died a decade ago and set my life in motion from afar. That vague memory returns, being twelve and feeling something but being too afraid to listen. Was that her passing over?

Now, I'll ask again, Miss Gwendolyn. Who the hell is the three-colored man?

Chapter Twenty-Four

One night to prepare for a test to my soul. I've always known the truth, somewhere, deep in the marrow of my bones, that the bricks of my yellow road were laid long before I arrived. That the destination, the dark end of that road, had been defined for centuries. Fate, if you will.

In my darkest moments, my mind has slipped into the thing I didn't want to believe or listen to. I came into this world whole and who I will always be—an outsider with eyes to the darkness, connected to thousands of souls who terrify me. The fear of it all sent me into a fabricated notion of death at twenty-two. A fable written by a child scared to open the depths of herself to the world, so she wrote her own rules in a pen with invisible ink.

It's time I face the truth of who that little girl was before the world forced her into hiding.

"Gwendolyn?"

Dried paint and turpentine fill the dark art room with their chemical scent, and I wait for the orb to appear. Women use this room to fill their time rather than explore the stories inside them. Keep them entertained. It's a motto my parents always used. A distracted person cannot see the truth that stares them down.

That tiny dot spins toward me from somewhere not inside or out. Somehow both here and not here, Gwendolyn arrives in a puff of glittering mist, dressed in a gown of gold that clangs like glass as she moves. "Dear." She places her hand on my cheek. There is something real about her touch. Her fingers press into my skin, warm and soft.

"Why me?" I ask.

She runs her hand down my hair, twirling the silver tips around her fingers. "We aren't chosen, Primrose, we simply are."

"Are what?" The biting edge to my voice reminds me to breathe. She's my guide, here to help.

"The stars, the universe. Our powers are a portal to the other world. Messages flow through us to help those existing here. You're here to help this world and thus, must be part of it."

Memories flow through my mind. Waiting for death as a child, dreaming of the sweet release from this life I never asked for, knowing that would mean defeat, spitting in the face of everyone who came before me. "I'm trying." My voice quakes.

"I know you are. Just look around. You have friendship and love, hope for a future, all since you accepted your place here."

"You've always been with me? Since I was a baby?" The idea is too painful to feel. Loving arms to hold me, someone to drop wishes over my little eyelashes. Various women at fairs rocked me and clothed me while my parents lived their lives. I suppose I'm still hoping for strangers to save me.

"I've been with you since the day you were born. Maybe even before."

"I couldn't see you." Another failure. A self-inflicted wound.

"You weren't ready. You are now." Her dress shimmers in bright gold, stark against her chrome hair, like a metallic sun and moon spinning together. "I know you have questions, and you will discover those answers soon enough."

"Why won't you tell me?"

"You're here to learn, Primrose. Just as I was." A smudged layer of light buzzes around her. "My time on Earth was difficult. The mistakes I made were unforgivable." Her eyebrows tighten, seemingly from the pang of a bad memory. "But I learned, and now I've taken that knowledge to guide you."

I wonder for a moment who she was on Earth, but I have more pressing questions. "So guide me. Tell me who the man with three colors is."

"The answer to that riddle will do nothing to help you solve it."

"That doesn't make any sense."

"The adventure is where we learn, not the end point. The missteps and failures along the way tear the fabric we've held in front of our eyes for years."

"Useful, clear visions will come to me when I learn this stupid lesson?"

Her icy blue eyes stare into my depths, sending a chill straight through me. "My advice to you is this. Sit in your truth. Love greatly. It's the only balm for a broken heart." She lifts her hand with an open palm and blows gold dust over my face. In the dust's light, an image forms. Me, cheek against Marion's belly. I'm hugging her and she's crying.

"I'm not supposed to read my future," I say as Gwendolyn's orb forms around her.

"There are no rules here, my dear." She hovers, her light shining bright enough to make me wince. I lift my hand to block the shine. "Tell the truth. Love big."

The light disappears in a flash, and I'm left staring at the tip of my boots standing over a stain of splashed, watery paint on the checkered linoleum.

No rules? If that's true, I can use my visions to discover who to save, and what lies ahead of me. Do I really want to know?

***

I can no longer ignore what lies ahead. The women upstairs need me, and every moment I wait is another step closer to their end. Marion's older, wiser. Her visions are stronger than mine. If she sees her death, who am I to think I can stop it?

Love big, Gwendolyn told me.

After a nighttime walk to think, I return to my room to find Finn asleep on my bed, shoes resting neatly under the window. The moonlight glistens on his cheekbone. His short hair no longer hides his face which now rests like a painting on the crisp, white pillowcase.

I lower quietly, as the bed creaks under my weight. I sit in the crook of his hips as a wave of desire overtakes me. Desire to lie close to him and rest in his arms in a time and place where I can breathe. To live a life with him beyond riddles and heartache.

He stirs awake and runs his hands through my hair. "Where have you been?"

"Trying to find answers." The heat from his hand softens my neck and I lean my cheek toward his touch.

"Have you found any?" he asks.

"Maybe. But not the kind I needed."

Finn rolls to his back and places one hand behind his head which presses his muscles together and accentuates the lean curves of his powerful arms. His shirt is off, and his chest glistens in the moonlight. That well of sadness tugs at his eyes again.

Before he can shut himself away, I reach for him. Hover my hand above the warmth of his chest. *Don't pull away*, I think, as if I can force him to love me. I press my palm to the valley between his chest muscles where his sternum holds the soft patter of his heartbeat. He exhales. "Aren't you afraid?" he asks.

"Yes," I say without a beat of hesitation. "Mostly afraid of losing everyone."

He hasn't touched me yet. He's let my hand spread across his chest in acceptance, but nothing hints at affection yet, so I press lightly against his sternum.

"We're all afraid he'll hurt you." A slight hitch in his breathing makes my heart ache.

"He may try, but I'll never agree to his medicine." Years of living in the consequences of needles and strange liquids have altered me. I'm on alert for signs I may become like them. I slide my hand up his neck and cup his jaw.

Since I cut his hair, his eyes seem wider, his skin brighter. To me, he's alive. To him, exposed. "Do you now why I don't speak much since… the accident?"

"Why?"

"My father read poetry to us at night, and my mother sang. Farm life in Kansas was loud and fun, after all the hard work died down for the day." He half closes his eyes, seeming to flinch with the memory. "After it all, I couldn't handle the prayers and hugs and chatter, as if life would ever be okay again. I became silent so I didn't have to live."

If I could hug away all the hurt, I'd wrap him in my arms and never let go. Tell the truth and love big. "I knew when I saw you on the porch that you were hurting. You woke me up too. I had been floating through life hiding and waiting for some sweet release from the pain of it all." I flash back to when we sat on the rooftop staring at the moon. "You trusted me."

"I still do."

We lock eyes, holding this tenuous moment between us in all its tenderness. Finally, like a gasp of air, he reaches for me. He pulls me close, igniting a heat in my belly that pushes out all the worry. I straddle him, my hips pressed to his, my hands cupped around his clenched jaw. He sits up, hands gripping my waist, his lips parted and gaze inviting. When I press my mouth to his, all the heat inside crawls its way to my skin, our tongues searching for a secret. Our bodies feel charged, like a summer storm about to fizzle through the sky.

The ridges of his back raise firm under my palms. He slips off my baby blue dress and I remove my boots, the sparkly things I believed were magic. They were simply a legacy that holds wishes for my future. I don't know, maybe that is magic. Clothes strewn on the floor, we press our bodies together and forget everything before and after our touch.

His broken heart and my lost soul searching for a place to call home.

We tangle and sigh and groan into each other's necks. We escape to a place that's so real, I don't need a vision. We find the truth laid bare in our sheets.

As I nestle in his arms, our bodies spent and calm, I think of the pain in knowing how much we must hold to be human. I can fall in love with a man whose touch is deeper than even my poppy-lined road, and long to make a difference in this crazy world, and open my arms to new friends, and be the changemaker I've always known was inside me.

Finn breathes a heavy sigh into my neck. "Can you save them from here?"

I wrap his arms tighter around me until I sink under his embrace. "No, but I wish I could."

"Five days," he says with a whisper so soft it hums. "I'm breaking down the door in five days."

I could protest, demand to do this on my own. Ultimately, I may need more help than I could imagine. "Promise?" He pulls me into a kiss with just enough force to answer without words.

We slip into slumber under the silvery light of an autumn sky. When I wake, I can no longer ignore the crawl across my forehead and the whispers in the air. Braun's soul is teasing me from the sanitorium, coaxing me to step into a world that killed my aunt.

I slip from Finn's arms and watch him sleep for a few moments before dressing and tying my boots in preparation. I brush my hair and teeth by the early morning light and take a deep breath. *See you in five days*, I whisper to him. I like to think he can hear me in his slumber.

The hotel is quiet and somber, as if it knows where I'm about to journey. I suppose she has seen it all, this building. Death, pain, illness, joy. New beginnings and moments of revelation. Past the walls of green floral paper and over the popping wood planks of the sitting room. I pass under dim sconces and pools of amber light, and I ascend the stairs under that sign that I hope to one day burn.

With two hard knocks, I wait for someone to let me in. He knows I'm coming, Clara made sure of that. Quiet so heavy it blisters my calm. I bite back the desire to run back to Finn's arms. The door handle turns and a lock clicks open.

Dr. Braun says nothing but extends his hand to welcome me inside. I take his hand and let the whispers of his soul speak to me, knowing the answers rest somewhere in that deep cavern I'll need to traverse.

I'll do it for Vanessa. This is the only way forward, and there is no place like the home I've constructed in my heart. Can't stop now.

Chapter Twenty-Five

Braun leaves me outside his office for a deathly long hour. It's early morning with no sounds but the faraway clank of metal behind several closed doors. My body has lost all softness from Finn's touch, now trying to find a dulled edge on this hard, metal chair. I had to check my control at the door so he could feel powerful.

Play the part of a doe-eyed psychic he'll be dying to mold. Destruction may be a side effect of his ambition, but I don't care to understand his motives when Marion and Judy fade more by the day.

Strauss emerges from the staff-only room, her eyes heavy and filled with tiny red veins. "Come." I stand and follow. her shoes squeak against the linoleum, her tight bun unmoving despite her purposeful strides. One long smear of blood sits like a hand swipe across her dress pocket. The hallway grows darker and tighter.

Strauss opens the door and directs me inside. "This will be your room."

I explore the space, what's here to see, anyway. Sterile, cold. Peeling paint in one corner by the ceiling. I try to crack the window, but it's glued shut. "Am I a prisoner now?" I ask.

She seems taken aback by this question. "Why are you here?"

"I think you know more than you let on."

Her skin puckers at the corners of her eyes. She could be thirty or fifty. Hard to tell when the weight of years of unappreciated labor rest on her bony limbs, her thinned hair and glassy eyes.

"I was friends with your Aunt Vanessa," she says with a quick shot to meet my eyes before turning toward the window again. "Before things grew ugly here, she was the first to donate herself to the science of psychic medicine. She believed in Dr. Braun like I do."

"How did you know she was my aunt?"

"The name." She shrugs, returning her focus to the spurt of hot springs water below. "And that Russell sent you. We all have a past here, Miss Whittaker, one you cannot disrupt."

"You watched Marion die a slow death. I think you're living a very different existence here than the psychics you hurt."

Her jaw twitches but she doesn't flinch. "If that is all you see, you aren't looking close enough." She nods to the foot of the bed where a cream linen nightgown sits folded into a perfect square. She turns toward the door but stops as she reaches for the handle. "I would fight to send you away, but the doctor believes you are his answer."

"Why would he believe that so fiercely?"

"Marion told him your future. He expects you to provide the missing answers to his drug. After your contribution here, we will lose Marion, but the doctor will gain everything he has ever wanted."

There's sadness in her voice, which I can't quite place. Her soul vibrates the air as it reaches me, but before I can decide whether to read her, she's gone. Alone in a locked ward for those society has cast aside, what with their silver hair and wild notions of magic. A quiet burning smolders at the back of my neck. An unsettling blend of mystic knowing and my earthly understanding of what I'm up against.

"Primrose." Judy's thready voice catches my attention. She's pale with a sheen of misty sweat across her cheeks.

"Are you okay?" I rush to her side, but she waves me away.

"It was stupid of me, wasn't it?" She forces a sad laugh. "To think I could really live out there with you and Oliver, what a dummy."

"No, Judy." I lay my hand on her shoulder and try not to gasp from how her bones creak under my fingertips. "We're gonna get you out. I'm here."

"Oh, you lovely thing." As if she's ninety on her death bed. "It's too late. I'll hold on until Braun finds the cure. You're the ticket, you know."

"So people keep telling me."

"Come on." She shuffles away in her hospital gown and slippers, her spine bent forward. I don't need to ask where we're going as we step right through the door marked *Viewing Area.*

Glass. Like a hellish snow globe, clear panels surround the room, above and below, with bench seating along the walls. It smells of burnt flesh and bleach, turning me lightheaded.

"I hate it in here."

"Then why are we sitting in this horrid place?"

She leans forward and points to the bubble of rounded glass in the floor. "That's why."

A trio of doctors covered in white cloths and aprons and facemasks stand over a body. I lean closer to see Marion, her body covered by a sheet, sleeping or in a drug-induced haze. "What are they doing to her?" I'm not sure I shouldn't break through the glass and fight them off with my bare hands.

"What they always do." Judy tightens her fist and trembles hard for a few moments. She holds up her hand and groans but recovers enough to speak. "They fixed a botched surgery from a decade ago and go back in every year to cut out scarring or some such thing."

"What kind of botched surgery?"

She finds me with her haunting gaze. "You don't want to know."

"This room is to watch her surgery?"

"It's for visiting doctors. They watch his technique, I guess." Her breathing picks up, and she pulls at her hair.

"Judy, maybe you should lie down."

"No!" With a hard gasp, she nods once. I lower back to the seat reluctantly. "Marion wants me here. She's terrified of the medicine that knocks her out. Having me watch makes her less afraid. I stay. So do you."

"Fine." The men tighten gloves as Strauss and another nurse prepare a tray of blades and needles. "He isn't going to cut her, is he?"

"You obviously don't grasp the idea of surgery." Her eyelids fall heavy, but she forces them open again. "After a while, all the cuts seem normal. The blood just looks like water."

"I'm certain that isn't true." As they move a sheet aside, they keep her covered and only expose her belly. They rub some sort of solution over her skin which is scarred and puckered from so many incisions. "This can't be good for her."

"It's not," she says. "It heals her stomach pains for a few months though. If you ask me, Braun gets more out of it than she does."

"How so?" I lean forward again but recoil when they bring the blade to her abdomen. Not Judy. She watches with unnerving calm.

"They explore things in her belly. Research her organs to discover what makes a psychic."

"I can't imagine they find answers in our stomachs."

"Doesn't stop them from looking." I don't hear the tearing of her flesh as anticipated, but only the muttering between surgeons. I dare to lean forward at the same time Braun looks up. He locks eyes with me. Something in his gaze suggests pride. As if his commitment to our ailments should impress me. I am only horrified.

"Don't worry," Judy says. "The smells will fade soon enough. After a few days here, you'll be just like us. Residents waiting for magic to find us.

I run my hands along the bench, wondering if Vanessa sat here, watching Braun cut into the body of the woman she loved. I scan Judy's arm to search for the dark purple bruises and thickened scars my father always had, but she simply looks bony and so, so small. No marks from the doctor. No sign that she's been drugged into oblivion.

"Hey Judy?"

"Yeah?"

"Can we see our own futures?"

Judy considers that question while watching for any sign of difficulty down below. "I guess so. But they aren't clear. Who knows if we can trust anything about ourselves."

I think back to the night of my birthday, how I welcomed death and feared life with visions. And here I am, voluntarily locked in a sanitorium surgery viewing of the woman I'm hell bent on saving.

I long to ask Vanessa what she would want me to do, and if she knew that sending me here would lead to Marion's death. All of this muddies together in my mind. The three men pop into my thoughts. Ash, the surprisingly gentle man who can't think for himself. Oliver, the sweet soul who can't find the courage he needs to survive in this world. And Finn, the man with the tricolored eyes and a broken heart. One of them will save me, won't they? When I lean in hard to my visions, I see nothing but me on a yellow road, holding a lone poppy.

Our visions aren't clear because we're too close. I have no answers here. All I have is the choice to try, love big, and tell the truth.

Oh, Gwendolyn. I'm in one hell of a big mess.

Chapter Twenty-Six

Morning in the sanitorium greets me with ticking clocks and crashing trays. The smack of shoes across the linoleum hallway. Perched on the railing outside my window that does not open, a bright, shining Otto stares at me. He tilts his little bird head as pronounced blinks seem to question what I'm doing up here.

The door flies open as Strauss kicks the lower corner with her heel. "The doctor will see you in thirty minutes." She glances out the window. "Damn bird. You will receive fresh air on the patio every afternoon, weather permitting. Otto will be there as he always is."

She doesn't wait for me to respond before clicking the door shut. I try to conjure possibilities of what Braun will do to me. Physical exams? Cognitive tests? If that man straps me to a surgical table, I'll fight for my life.

They take personal hygiene very seriously in this place. Toothbrush, toothpaste, hairbrush, washcloth and soap, all lined up, labeled, and numbered for suggested sequence. It seems odd to change out of one linen gown into another, but I said goodbye to my dress and boots the moment I agreed to Braun's testing.

I click my door open to find a tray of breakfast. I pick at the roll as I note all the empty rooms next to mine. Clara appears in a perfectly sunny blush dress and a peach cardigan.

"The patients with physical ailments bore him," she says. "He likes the ones like us. Silvers are far more interesting."

We're his own little circus of caged animals, complete with filed down fangs so we don't hurt the spectators. "This place used to be full. Where did they go?"

She shrugs, both hands up at her shoulders. "He sent them away to focus on you."

Braun's little parrot. He must feed her a whole host of lies. "He makes questionable choices."

She twirls the corner of her cardigan around her pointer finger. "You won't help either of them. No one ever does. Besides, I doubt he'll find the cure for us."

"Why do you only use your powers to help Braun?"

She scratches her palm. "I watch everyone. But there's nothing else I can offer. At least Braun gives me a purpose. And the butterscotch is pretty good."

I smile. "You don't take his opium, do you?"

"No!" She shakes her head. "I think you're all stupid for doing that."

"You might be right, Clara. But as you get older, these things we see become torture. It all gets so complicated." Maybe she has the right idea by living small, finding joy in one purpose, even if it is for something awful.

"I know he's using me." She waits for me to catch her eyes. "For my eyesight. I don't care because at least now I have a home. The orphanage called me a witch, and no one ever wanted a silver girl. Here I have Judy and the other girls, a whole bakery downstairs and hot springs to swim in. Dr. Braun even hosts nights with parlor games and magic shows."

I can imagine when you've spent your life alone, even a sanitorium can feel like home.

For the first time, I miss my predictable and simple fortune-teller life.

I stare into Clara's bright eyes. How she must see the world since she can view anything she wants. "You may feel you have a home, but you are nothing more than a tool for him to use. He's lying to you, Clara."

"He tells me the same thing about you."

Braun has convinced her I'm the enemy. He's the one feeding her butterscotch and giving her this magical place to live where her talents are useful. I know I won't win that fight. Not yet. Her little soul reaches for me, a bright singing voice that rings toward me, louder and louder, until I'm sucked into blackness, plopped into a field of poppies. They're soft as clouds, swaying ever so gently underneath me.

The sun shines brightly over the rolling hills of ruby blooms. Their crinkled, papery petals brush my cheeks and forehead. Exploding color against the baby blue sky reminds me of childhood dreams. Where imagination bleeds into visions we aren't supposed to see. I remember living here, where the world seems fantastical, and brilliantly new. Before traveling shows and girls tumbling down stairs.

Stems reach up to stabilize me on either side as I stand. I could fall asleep right here and never wake, but a green castle glitters in the distance, charming me with its glass towers. I step closer for a good glimpse.

In a moment, I recognize the feeling. There is no castle, no great emerald city where a wizard waits to fix us all. There is only the hope of a time and place where we can live without pain. The hills turn to sand which sends me sliding into the black sky below. The stars twinkle above, and I wonder if I'm actually falling, or suspended in the glittering sky.

Clara can see anything she wants, which means she sees things she shouldn't. Things she isn't ready to understand. Much like me as a child, she sees needles injected into someone's arm. She sees passionate kisses and explosive fights, a woman burning a cigarette into her thigh, and the headmistress of the orphanage begging Dr. Braun to take the little defect. She sees it all before she has developed the maturity to understand how fragile we all are.

With a drop, I land back in my body, free of headaches or heartache. This vision simply is, without judgement.

"You had a vision," she says with surprise. "People don't read me. I'm too young. My soul doesn't matter."

I bend down and look into her big eyes shining under thick, dark eyebrows. "You always matter."

Her childlike face fades, appearing older right somehow. Perhaps her immaturity is a ruse. A protective shield against the hurt. She doesn't spin or twirl. She swallows hard, lifting her head tall before turning back toward her room.

I step toward Judy's door, but Strauss appears, pointing at the clock on the wall. I reach Braun's office. The door is open, and he sits straight-backed at his desk. Tobacco fills the air with stifling smoke like a burning cherry tree. I step inside. He straightens his lab coat, cool as ice.

Otto appears at Braun's window. I wonder if he's keeping an eye on me while I'm here.

"You're looking well." He turns to Otto. "And your little peacock too."

I run my fingers along the books on his shelves. Read so many times, the titles have worn away. "What happens now?"

He places his spectacles, perfectly folded, on his desk. His pipe smolders alone in its holder. "Well, that's up to you."

"Is it?" I can no longer hide the edge in my voice. "You think I'll be the answer to your little riddle. I will offer the missing piece to your dreams of opium magic."

"I don't think, I know."

All I've learned over the past few days swirls around in my head and I must choose what to share. "Your experiments killed my Aunt Vanessa."

He puffs his lips while looking down at his desk. "That was an unfortunate day. I regret convincing her to stay. It's why I make sure you all know you can leave any time you want."

"The locked doors say otherwise."

"That is for protection. Hotel guests would visit our residents as if they were an attraction." His nostrils flare. "I will not have our good work tarnished by bored vacationers."

His soul has been locked down my entire time here. Answers elude me, but everything I need to know rests in what he doesn't reveal. "I never met her," I say. "Though I desperately wanted to."

"You've met her. You simply don't remember." He slides his chair back softly and walks around his desk. "Around the time you began to walk, your parents demanded Vanessa travel with them in a new show."

I've heard rumblings of this from my mother. I welcome the image of Vanessa holding me as a baby. Did she know I would grow to be a psychic just like her? "She was smart. She wouldn't let my parents exploit her talents. I wish I would have been that strong."

He sighs so deeply his chest rattles. "She had talents well beyond the metaphysical, but she was so sad. So lost."

How does he know so much about her, I wonder. I despised him an hour ago and here I sit, sympathy blooming in my chest for the man I should hate.

He leans against his desk, legs outstretched and ankles crossed. "I've spent the better part of the last twenty years researching your kind. One thing you all have in common is the desire to save people. The broken ones especially."

I've stopped seeing a doctor, or an expert in metaphysical science. Before me is a man reaching for something he can't have. Do I dare see him as little more than a flawed human? What a dangerous prospect. Still, the moment begs for a question I need an answer to.

"Why is it so painful?" I ask.

He pauses, as if he knows how I've softened to him. "Pain is our body's way of communicating. Calling attention to the dangers that lurk inside."

Otto is gone, and now the sun lights the bluff behind the hotel gold. "Is my power a danger?"

He nods thoughtfully. "It can be." He pulls up a chair next to me, inching closer with every bit of this conversation. "Marion lost the love of her life and her health years ago, Judy longs for a normal existence despite this world beating her up every step of the way. The pain isn't in the power, it's in the people who won't accept you."

His words unlock a place inside me I've never wanted to see. The sad acceptance that in every way, I've always been a foundling, a girl touched by magic that could do amazing things if the world wasn't so afraid of me.

He's right. All I want is to save people. Weakness spreads through me, seeping into every crack, and I remind myself why I'm here. Break Braun. Stop him.

I rub my hands together until they're warm. "Tell me about Russell."

Braun's eye twitches. "What about him?"

"He never really left, did he?" I hold his gaze. Success. He's failed Russell somehow. "He's addicted to your opium, just like the rest of them."

"I'm working to help them. You're the answer to it all."

"You hear that from all the readings, right? Judy's heard it from the dead, and Marion's told you she'll die when I find my power. Is this a truth you've conjured with pieces from the people you've ruined?"

His fingers lace together and with a slow stretch, he pops his knuckles then crosses his arms, his eyes never leaving mine. "Vanessa told me before she died that Russell will deliver me her niece, the woman who would one day stand before me with answers. You would become the missing link to my greatest purpose here. She saw it in you the day you were born."

So many questions linger, including why she would want me to help him. But something more personal grips my attention. "She knew I was like her, and she still left."

"We all make our choices, Primrose. She was magical, but one power eluded her."

"The power to fix Marion."

He nods once. We both stare forward at the loudest sound in the sanitorium, Braun's metronome. "Insight and truth will only take you so far. I helped her damaged body. We were going to cure her pain."

This is all too familiar. As I strive to be a changemaker and use visions to help people, everyone around me dies or shatters apart one sharp rip at a time. "What happened to Marion?"

"That is something you will need to ask her."

I stand and walk around the chair, scanning the wall, for what I'm not sure, but a moving distraction feels better than staring at that damn needle bouncing side to side. Outside the window, Otto reappears, his glossy blue neck tall as can be. I place my hand flat on the window warmed from the sun.

"Dr. Braun?" I turn to face him. He's still slumped in the chair, eyes tracking the bob of the needle. He grunts. "I'll never take your opium. Ever."

"I know." Yet another bit of my future he's been told. What else is he hiding? "We begin today," he says, his voice empty and hard. "Come to my exam room in one hour. Now go."

My hand slips from the window. I walk behind Braun. I've said something to upset him. Good. I'll need to crawl under the layers of protection he's built so I can unearth all he has hidden. As I step out of his stuffy office, a chill grips my neck. We're both chasing visions and answers, and in the end, only one will survive.

It better be me.

Chapter Twenty-Seven

I've sent Clara with word to Finn that I've only spoken to Dr. Braun and viewed a surgery. All is well. But is it?

In the hour before I find out what Braun has planned for me, I have but one thing to do. Marion's door is open. She's sitting in her chair by the window, as always. Speaking to my reflection, she says, "I used to be a dancer."

"Oh? What kind?" I step inside, holding space and waiting to see how much she'll let me in.

"Ballet." Her cheeks brighten when she says the word. "I was a glorious performer."

I could ask questions like I'm dying to, but something tells me to call on what little patience I have and allow her room to speak.

After a long minute of closed eyes and the hint of a grin, she wheels to face me. The wasted muscles of her arms barely find enough force to spin one wheel forward. "You know about Vanessa."

"Yes."

She places her hands in her lap, fiddling with her fingers. "Clara just left."

"Ah. So you listened to my conversation with Dr. Braun."

"Of course we did. There was very little excitement around here before you."

I look out the window at the same view she has stared at through seasons and years. "Is he evil?"

"Now that is a complicated question. He is wrong and deluded and misguided, and the end game of his life's work is eradication of our power. He wasn't always this way."

"He wants to kill all of us?"

"Well, he wants to eliminate our visions, which is the same thing, in a way."

"Why?"

She lifts a tiny cup of water to her mouth with a trembling hand. I reach to steady her wrist, which she allows. "I don't know." She lets me place the cup down for her. "I've never read his soul. Not for lack of trying."

"He's learned to shut us out," I say. "I know the answer to stopping him is in a reading. It's why I'm here now."

"I believe you will succeed." She drags the thinned blanket higher on her lap to cover her swollen belly.

"Tell me about her, please."

"She was radiant. Bold. The loudest woman in any room." Her eyes lighten, the memories of love and affection brighter than the pain of her body. "Vanessa loved you from afar. She wanted so badly to rescue you from all the shows and fairs your parents dragged you through."

"She could have, you know. I would have left in a heartbeat for even just one day of someone who loved me."

"She couldn't."

I walk to the window, hiding my gathering tears. "She was too busy searching out cures with the resident madman to care about the lost silver girl who wanted to die."

"Come here." Her voice is forceful, surprising for how she can barely summon the strength to cough. I walk toward her and sit on the bed. "Vanessa saw your future. She saw all our futures." She curls her finger to indicate to lean closer. I do and she whispers so Clara has difficulty hearing. "You're here to stop him. If she intervened, you'd never be able to fulfill your purpose. You're going to save the entire psychic population."

"He thinks I'm here to offer answers to his drug."

"Both are potential outcomes. We've seen each ending in multiple readings."

I stand and ball my fists, trying not to raise my voice. "Are you telling me the future isn't clear? What kind of vision is that?"

"Our visions aren't everything. There is always free will."

I rub my fingers to my temples in small circles, trying to grasp what she's telling me. "Some three-colored man needs saved, Vanessa sent me here to rescue you, and somehow this leads to saving every psychic in the world?"

She reaches her hand for me. I resist, but the younger me ached for these moments so deeply, I feel like I owe that little girl. I grasp her hand as gently as I can. "Darling, you aren't going to save me," she says.

A truth I refuse to believe. "Did Vanessa know you'd die when I arrived?"

"We've always known. My purpose was to stay alive long enough to guide you since Vanessa could not." She clasps my hand in both of hers, her skin surprisingly velvet- like. "I don't know about the three-colored man, but if that's what you spirit guide told you, they're related. Listen to me. You must read Braun's soul, but Vanessa did once and said she would never be the same."

I should ask more, but my heart can only feel one thing right now. "I wish I could have hugged her." My knees want to give way. I fight the urge to fall apart right here on Marion's lap. "What happened to you, Marion?"

She lets her hands slide from mine. "Surgery gone wrong. I died on the table, they say. Lost blood, cut vessels, damaged organs. I don't understand it all." She smooths her hair back above her ear.

"What kind of surgery? Were they trying to fix something?"

"No, dear. They were trying to take something." The tightness in her lower lip spreads across her jaw which dimples her cheeks. "My parents ordered my reproductive organs removed. To prevent any more like me."

Sometimes quiet is the loudest sound you've ever heard. I could die from this feeling. I've never heard of something so awful. "Your visions or—" Good God, I don't want to say it. "Your proclivities for women?"

"Both." She lowers her eyes. "I am defective."

"That's wrong, Marion."

"I know. But Dr. Braun saved me from the hospital who did it. They were horrible to me. He brought me here. I met Vanessa and had a year that healed my soul. I agreed to help with this plan because I loved her so." Her eyes fill with thick tears. "The opium helped for a while. But somewhere along the way, I began needing the drug. Needing it like I need air. What once soothed me became a horror."

"He keeps dosing it out."

"What else can he do? Without that emerald injection, we turn wild, screaming in pain. You saw Judy. That was nothing compared to what could happen." She wipes her eyes. Clears her throat. "He'll keep working until he perfects the formula. Eliminate our visions. With our consent, of course."

What tough decisions the two of them must have made. I imagine them holding hands deep into the night, joining powers to glimpse the future, knowing each of their ends. "If he succeeds, he'll sell this medicine to the world. Outsiders made normal to satisfy the masses. Doesn't he understand what could happen when humans get their hands on this?"

"No," she says. "And you aren't going to tell him. Neither are you, Clara." She speaks to the wall. "If he questions the outcome, he'll stop."

"That's good, right? Maybe we can reason with him. He doesn't want to hurt us."

"No," she says with finality. "We need the medicine to cure Judy. Once we have the cure, what you find in your visions can alter the course of the future. You'll discover the answers in your poppies and on your yellow road."

"You know what's in my readings?"

"Vee had the same." Oh, she had a nickname. The sound of that brings into focus her as a human and not just a larger-than-life character I've conjured in my dreams. The ache of that bruise may never heal. My Aunt Vee.

"All this rests on your shoulders. I'm sorry, but this won't be easy," she says.

"Nothing ever is."

Strauss pushes open the door, needle in hand. "It's time."

Marion rolls her sleeve back over her unimaginably thin forearm. Strauss injects her. Just like that. Strauss nods to me. "Hurry it up, girl. We're ready for you in the exam room."

Once she leaves, Marion holds her arm as guilt washes over her face. "What began as a hope is now something ugly and intolerable. This medicine is like a deep breath of air at a near drowning. Braun's emerald potion swims through my veins, icy, then warm. Droplets of this comfort push into the holes I've made in my life. All the dark and ugly places disappear and all I feel is calm. Until the terror sets in, which it will soon enough."

I could ask her why she hurts herself, but I already know the answer. Life has a way of killing us in quiet heartbeats of time, so subtly we don't notice we've bled out.

***

The exam room's white walls gleam. One giant metal light buzzes overhead as I dangle my feet off the pale blue table Strauss has cranked high enough that I meet Braun's eyes. The bare room is off-putting enough to prevent readings, something he crafted meticulously. He's spent years protecting what's in his soul, but I must push my way in.

"Tell me about your worst reading," Braun asks, motioning to Strauss to take notes. He's stands close, examining my every facial twitch, my every blink.

"I can't choose just one."

"Your recent worst reading."

The woman with the dead twins flutters back to me, but worse than that was the bartender I kissed. Worse because I intervened and made everything worse. "A bartender in a speakeasy." He notes my wince. "He'll kill himself next year."

"I see. Do you always read their futures?"

"Their future, their past. Everything in between. I read their emotions first, then comes their truth." Dissecting my visions like this sends tremors through me, like I shouldn't be trying to apply science to magic.

He glances at Strauss, interest piqued. "Fascinating." He shines an offensive light in my delicate eyes, but I shove him away. "Sorry." But he is not sorry. "No one has ever looked at their emotions first. You're unique."

That wasn't a compliment. "It's the easiest to read. I simply sit inside and feel."

"This bartender, what did he feel like?"

I think of his aggressive touch, our hurried kiss, and that makes my body ache for Finn. A dent to my armor. No, weakness will not serve me. "Deep, endless sadness. He wanted to kill himself, but never had the plan or the will. Until I gave him one."

A spark of sympathy flames in his eyes. "Your reading ignited his worst impulses."

My mouth goes dry, and I am once again the helpless girl with a psychic defect. "Yes." Desperate not to be who I once was, I blurt out, "I've never wanted to eliminate my visions."

He lowers his chin, staring at me over the top of his spectacles. "Go on."

"I've hated this life from the very beginning. The things I see, the horrors I feel. But never once have I wished it away. I've only wished to love my silver hair and use these visions to do something good."

Still face, no expression, but he puffs his lips ever so slightly. I lean in, reaching for his soul as it hovers, just out of my reach. "Your parents only ever taught you to fear." No, he's trying to push me away, force me to let go of his soul. Don't fall for it, Primrose. He holds the pause, presumably sensing my discomfort. "They taught you to be useful. Manipulated and used you while the little girl attached to those visions cried out for parents to love her. You hated and desperately loved them, didn't you?"

"I was a kid." Instead of reaching, I'm now on the defensive, shoving him away.

"A special child who didn't belong in their world. Even now, you never feel accepted. You're lost and empty, looking for someone to love you."

Nurse Strauss clears her throat. Even she seems uncomfortable with this exchange.

"Stop." I say it as an order, though I know he won't obey.

A sickening glimmer flutters in his eye. "You believe you can read anyone. Save everyone, yes?" He places his spectacles in Strauss's hand, steps back, and extends his arms. "Go ahead. Read me. It's the one thing you've yet to accomplish here."

His body is open, but his mind remains completely shut. "You won't let me."

"Come now. You're a talented woman. If you can't read everyone in the room, you may just shrivel and die. So go, then! Read me."

My heartbeat pounds in my ears. I can't read him while my mind is full of memories, a wasteland of failures. "Why did you say all those things first?"

"Read my soul, Primrose." He drops his arms and narrows his gaze to mine. "Forget everything and read me, dammit."

I swallow and blink, trying to find something to ground me to the moment. I'm all shaken and unsteady. How do I read someone when I feel like this? "It was easier when I wanted to die."

"Easier how?" His voice remains strong and uncaring.

"Because I didn't care about me. I had room to care for others. Space to feel their emotions."

His face lights, just a little. "Shut it down and read me, you pathetic little girl."

My head thumps as my vision turns wavy. I reach for his emotions, but the ease of visions I've always known has disappeared. His soul hums a taunting tune. I shut my eyes tight enough to sting. My breathing quickens as I pull all my strength toward the rigid man.

"Read me!" He shouts so loud my neck quakes.

A scream escapes me in a near-feral release of rage. I jump down and reach both my hands for his shoulders, where I grab his shirt in my fists and howl through tears at his stoic face. He isn't surprised or frightened. He simply closes his eyes.

Like the kick of a mule, I'm shot through his soul. No bubble-like veil this time. I spin through a cyclone of yellow and blue and green, nauseous and begging to be set free. I'm too crushed to speak, so I think hard. *Show me your soul.*

Before I can focus, I'm splayed out on a dirt road, long-dead corn fields all around me. The air is so heavy. I cup my hand over my eyes, looking for something. Anything. "I'm here. Show me what you hold so close."

Though I keep walking, the view does not change. The sun beats high in the sky so hot I struggle to catch my breath. He's still hiding. Why?

Shame. That's all I feel in this eternal summer. It's the season's end when all the goods are gone, and only shells remain to bake in the blaze of heat. Shame with claws and fangs, eating away at any hope of a reprieve.

The ground feels spongy under my boots. I lean down to feel the springy earth. I grab hold and peel back a sheet of dried dirt to find a patch of moss underneath. Brilliant green. I peel away another layer as poppies spring up. Underneath, there must be something more. I pull back again, but darkness reaches its hands through and grabs me by the throat. No peeling or yanking stops the black tendrils from extending their vines around my windpipe.

Stars flutter across my vision as panic sets in. Is this his terror, or mine?

The tendrils yank me through the ground where I dangle by a noose of poppy stems. A flash appears of Braun as a young man. Lonely. Inferior. Out to prove his worth to a family who saw nothing but a defect. He married for money to please his father but left her to pursue something bigger. He abandoned a son. I can't breathe. The vision fades just then. I reach out, not ready to let go, but I may die if I stay.

The vines release me, and I fall past a watery image. The darkness obscures her face, but I know who she is. I feel her.

Here I am again, back in my body, gasping for air. My vision fades in and out as my throat stings. Braun's face appears before me in a cloudy haze and slap his cheek as hard as I can before I collapse into darkness.

***

I come to consciousness on my knees on the cold white tile, my head in a toilet. The intensity of stomach cramps makes it hard to breathe, and I grasp the cold porcelain in between bouts of retching.

What the hell is happening?

A cool washcloth touches my neck. A glorious shot of cool balm to soothe this aching pain inside me. "Help."

"I'm right here."

I lift my heavy head from the toilet. "Strauss?" I flinch though my fear is unwarranted. She slides to the floor next to me, head against the tile wall. I stare at her, my head resting on my forearm. "What are you doing?"

"I may dislike you but I'm still a nurse."

Another wave clutches my stomach in spasms though nothing releases. My head pounds like it could split in two. "What's wrong with me?"

"Braun's only been read once before, and it ended in this same reaction."

Strauss hands me a cup of water to rinse my mouth. I swish and spit, then slide to the floor in a heap. My body grows cold as though icicles dangle from my inner core. My head shivers hard enough to shake my eyeballs. "Everything hurts," I say.

"You were hallucinating," she says. "We had to restrain you until you calmed down."

The watery view of the bathroom fills me with unease, all white and boxy. "Vanessa," I say.

"Yes. Vanessa was the last to read him. And she reacted worse than you."

The cold tiles quell my nausea, pressed like blocks of ice to my cheek. Silver strands of Strauss's hair catch my attention in her dark blonde bun. I've never been this close to her. "He loved her," I say. "Unrequited and obsessive."

Strauss rolls her eyes to the ceiling. "Vanessa never loved him back, yet he watched her and studied her. He dreamed about kissing her while all she wanted was Marion. And here I was, ready and willing to love every part of that broken man."

Vanessa and Strauss. An unlikely friendship, indeed. "Why are you still here?"

She laughs, a sad, accepting sound. "I suppose I hope that someday he'll see me."

"He can't even see himself, Strauss." I try to stand but stop when I reach all fours, too weak to move any farther. Strauss places her hand on my arm. "Sit back. You need rest."

I can't believe I missed it. "Of course he loved her. It was her superpower." Braun fell in love with my aunt, working to fix her so she would return his affections, all while she used him for this overarching purpose. To lay the groundwork for me.

"His obsession was never strong enough to break her."

I rub my palm over the splitting pain in my forehead. "Why do we get sick when we read him?"

"I don't know."

Her easy answer suggests she has a theory. "You have an idea."

She turns toward me, the lines around her mouth and at the edges of her eyes more pronounced than I had noticed before. "I think you're both caught up with his soul somehow. You've both occupied his mind for years now."

He knew I'd be here someday. Vanessa and her niece were both mysteries to conquer.

"You see the problems with his opium, I know you do."

She lifts my wrist to check my pulse. "I believe in his brilliance. But I took an oath as a nurse." She lays my hand back in my lap. "He cares more than you realize."

"Marion told me he wasn't always like this."

Strauss could be a completely different person right now for how her face has changed.

She lifts me into a wheelchair, not rough but not gentle either. Weakness forces me to wrap my arms around her so she can lift my body weight. "Why do you hate me?" I ask into her shoulder.

"I don't hate you." She sighs as she lowers my spent body into place. "Dr. Braun might seem powerful and strong, but he's actually quite fragile." Maybe she can save him, she thinks. She smooths the blanket over my legs. "He'll discover great things, but this quest with psychics has done something to his mind."

Whispers crawl over my forehead like ants. There's something more for me to know. I grab Strauss's wrist and stare into her eyes. My psychic body shoots through a black tube. I expect honeycomb, but I land directly in her stars.

Surrounded by snow, hailstones drop around me. The stars form a net and cover me so I can see through the growing blizzard.

Strauss's sister came to Braun's practice in Minnesota. Her twin. They were eighteen. He saved her from a terrible fever and inflamed joints. The sister ended up drinking herself into an early grave, but Strauss attended nursing school and followed him across the country to Oregon to become his personal nurse.

I glimpse enough before the stars drop me back into my dry, trembling body. "Strauss?"

"What is it?" She asks, annoyed.

"Thank you for caring for me."

She clears her throat and wriggles from my grasp. She thinks Braun is wasting his time with magic. He should cure typhoid or consumption—diseases that really matter. Still, she's found something close to caring for all of us silver girls.

"You're welcome."

She wheels me into the hall, past the empty rooms and the two psychics left as they wither, grasping for any drop of opium. I'm so close. The answers form at my fingertips, but I'm still missing something big. Obvious.

Braun is unraveling. Even Strauss questions his motives. Something deeper drives him, but I'm not sure I can live through another trip through his soul to discover what that is. I long to run downstairs and collapse into Finn's arms.

Gwendolyn set me on this journey for a reason. Vanessa sacrificed so much in the hope of my future. But my head hasn't stopped thumping. And so I fade to sleep in the late afternoon sunshine, staring at the steam rising from the boiling lake.

Chapter Twenty-Eight

The exam room again. Blaring light buzzes overhead, flowing heat onto my scalp. My body hasn't recovered from yesterday. Braun's soul left a stain on mine, a diseased core with its seeds intact. Heaven knows what will grow from that rot.

And yet, I'm here again, anticipating another trip through the veil.

Braun and Strauss enter, clipboard in hand. Braun retrieves a pen from his pocket but fumbles with it. His trusty nurse picks it up from the ground and hands it back. Is he nervous? Good. So am I.

"You read me," he says. His disheveled hair sticks up in patches and his eyes have that glassy look when one doesn't sleep enough. "Tell me what you saw."

I glance at Strauss, though I'm not sure why. "You were married once."

"Yes." His eye twitches. "Wretched woman."

"But you fell in love with a woman you could not have, and that only made you want her more." He's already teetering. I'll push him with the truth, that was Gwendolyn's advice. Tell the truth of my visions.

He turns sideways with a little wobble and eyes me from the side. "Go on."

"You loved Vanessa, but she loved Marion. It drove you mad with jealousy. Things started out innocently enough. You set out to learn about her psychic powers, but the closer you got, the more you developed an unhealthy obsession for her."

I know I'm taking a tremendous risk with this blatant truth, but I'll do anything to avoid going inside his poppy path again.

"She smelled of lilacs. All the time, every season. Even in the dead of winter, there it was, fucking lilacs." He swipes a metal cup from the counter, throwing it against the wall. The clang makes both Strauss and myself jump. "She moved like a goddess." His voice lightens into a wistful sigh. "I had to cure her."

"Cure her from what, exactly?" I ask.

"Not what you think. I'm not a monster." He rakes his fingers through his hair trying to smooth the wild. "She snuck into Marion's room every night. I could no sooner change her attraction to women than I could turn her into a frog."

Strauss won't look at him. She rubs her chest just above her heart.

"She did not want this burden." He rubs his chin with both hands. "She didn't want men bothering her."

"Men like you?" I ask.

"No. I'm not like other men." His disgust rests just on the surface now. "We had a friendship. She respected me. She wanted freedom and begged me to find a cure. I would have flown to the moon if she'd asked."

"Is that why you do all this, because of a promise to her?"

"It started that way." He rolls his reddened eyes to the ceiling. "Come." We follow him through several doors as he slides open a wall panel. We step into his marble sanctuary flooded with bright green light.

"I found the answer here," he says. "Combining emerald light with opium softened the pain of their visions. The powers dulled. I knew it would change medicine."

"But look what you've done, Braun." They keep us in linen gowns and socks for a reason. To feel soft and helpless against the big doctor. "You've made them sick."

"I know." He paces as he rubs his temples with trembling fingers. "I'm close. I can almost feel the answer when you're near, just as Vanessa told me would happen. You saw something in my soul. What was it?"

I stumble back but a cold, hard wall stops me. "I don't know. I only saw your twisted obsession for my aunt. And a baby you abandoned."

"I'm trying to atone for that!" He steps closer, his top lip in a snarl. "You had to have seen what I don't. Tell me."

Strauss watches, feet widened. I can only hope she will intervene if this turns ugly. "You were an angry boy. Your family dismissed you as strange."

"The world always dismisses geniuses." He shakes his fist at his side, his hair loosening again and his face taut and shiny. "More."

I force my mind back to the vision, but nothing turns up. Nothing that would give him the key to his opium problem. "I don't know."

"Yes, you do!" He grabs me and shakes. His fingers grip my arm hard enough to leave bruises. "Tell me." He presses so hard my back aches. Strauss grabs him, trying to pull him away. I can't find what he wants.

The panic inside me reaches for some kind of answer. "Shame," I scream, breathless.

He stops shaking me but keeps his grip on my arms. "What?"

"I felt a deep shame. Stronger than anything I've experienced in visions." He lightens his grip but doesn't let go. "You know what you've done is horrid. You've turned these innocent people into addicts, and now you either watch them die or find the thing that turns your opium into a super drug that cures us lost clairvoyants."

Strauss yanks on his sweater. "Doctor, please. You've never hurt a patient."

Not intentionally, I suppose.

Finally, he releases me. I gasp for air as fear floods my arms and knees in a rush of weakness. He steps away and holds his hand out under the green light. "Yes, I am ashamed. My life's work is beyond my reach, and I've risked every patient here for this dream." He curls his fingers and turns his palm down, examining the light. "I need you to show me how to fix this. If I can't cure them, this will have been all for naught."

I can't understand how emerald light does anything. My father presented with all the same symptoms from some solution he traded in an alley somewhere. "It's not the light."

He drops his hand and looks at Strauss. "Yes, it has to be. I purchased thousands of dollars of emeralds to alter the solution."

"It's fucking opium, Braun." I slide myself from the wall, my socks slick against the shining white tile floor. "It makes people forget what they hate about themselves. It tricks them into believing a lie."

"But mine is special." His eyes glimmer, almost childlike. Too hopeful for the horrors we're discussing.

"No, it isn't." Maybe I can convince him to abandon this insane idea. "Your green medicine is nothing but snake oil."

"How dare you?" He clenches his jaw tight.

"She didn't mean that," Strauss says. "She's just scared."

"I meant every word." I walk around the table where his glass orb sits. "We don't need crystal balls or tarot cards to read people. This is all nonsense."

He drags his fingertips over the glass. "The answer was always in the occult. I need to understand your power."

I pick up the crystal ball which is heavy and cold in my hands. "Then stop wasting time on this joke." I open my grip and let the ball fall to the ground. It doesn't shatter. The thick glass cracks in half, leaving a crater in the tile floor. "You will never have our power."

"Is that what you think? That I want to steal your psychic knowing?" He walks around the circle as I do to maintain space between us. "I am not doing this for me, Miss Whittaker."

His wild eyes keep me believing he could turn at any moment. "Vanessa is gone."

"Oh, don't I know it." He scratches his fingernails across the tabletop. "I've never been the same since she died."

"Marion and Judy. You need to stop for their sake."

"They made their choices," he says. "My research benefits everyone." His upper lip beads with sweat. "You saw it, I know you did.

My drug will take over the world. I will cure the disease known as spiritualism and rid the world of the pain inflicted on you." He waves his arms as if he is a preacher and we are his congregation. "I will be the man to save you, Primrose."

Despite what Marion predicts, I didn't see any of that in his soul. "I don't need saving."

He drops his arms, a relieved smile cast across his face. "We all have needs larger than we alone can manage."

Strauss cracks a little, so subtly only I notice. For her, this is all for the love of a man and a fading dream of greatness.

"And you, Dr. Braun. Your needs can only be filled when the world deems you a genius. You never loved Vanessa, you only cared about holding the thing you couldn't force. Control and power blind you."

He looks far away, lost in a memory, it seems. "Shame." He holds his hands up on either side of his head. "It was right here I discovered the emerald light. Right here I found the compound that dulled power. I remember." He shakes his head in a figure eight, exaggerated and a little terrifying, like some of the show mystics I came across over the years. "My shame held me back. It stopped me from reaching deeper." He gasps in delight. "That's it."

He's possessed by the spirit world or losing his mind. Or worse, he's discovered something at my hands. Just as I feared. "You'll kill us all."

"Sacrifices must be made, Miss Whittaker." He smooths his hands across his chest. "Strauss, we have work to do."

I shoot her a glance, beg her to stand up to him. She's questioning everything, I can see it in her eyes. But alas, she says, "Yes, doctor."

"Now." He motions for Strauss to open the door to the hallway. "Get out of my sanctuary."

Who am I to stop a man possessed by his own demons?

***

I don't have a moment to rest. I barge into Marion's room in a frenzy, wondering how in the hell she's spent a decade in this box.

"I know how to stop Braun, or at least who can help me stop him."

Marion smiles. "You've reached your moment, Primrose. Vanessa would be so proud."

"This is no time for acceptance. Marion, you die at the end of this." A clawing ache grabs my chest. "My spirit guide said we have free will. You can live and Judy can thrive, and we can stop this insanity from ever taking hold."

"And how are we going to do that?" she asks.

"Well, I'm not sure. But I have an idea. Where's Judy? I haven't seen her all day."

"Good question. She normally visits by noon." She glances at the clock on the wall. "Shit. It's three." She rolls herself forward and I hold open the door. We race down the hall. The lights are off and a passing cloud obscures the sun, leaving Judy's room gray and shaded. The bed is empty and unmade.

"Judy?" I ask.

A groan from under the window. I hurry around the bed, Marion in tow, to find Judy huddled against the wall. Every part of her body is shaking. Her neck trembles so fast her hair shakes.

"Oh, Judy." I kneel next to her and place my hand on her arm. "I'll call for Strauss."

"No!" Her voice carries a desperation I've only heard in the saddest of souls. "Make it stop. I can't do this anymore. Please." She buries her face in her arms. Marion rolls close and leans forward to whisper.

"Honey, the only way is to get another shot."

"No." She cries between words in a strangled hitch for air. "I can't anymore. I don't want to live like this." She twitches so violently I consider placing a pillow behind her to protect her head. "Marion, you stay," she says. "Let me die. Take me, Primrose." She clutches my sleeve in her bony fist. "Take my stupid power because I don't want it."

"I need you to live," I tell her.

"This isn't living. Every time I think I can beat this, my body turns on me. I grow sicker every day and beg for another injection." Tears stream down her pale cheekbones that shine through the gray afternoon. "My body always hurts," she says between sobs. "I'm so scared, Primrose."

I slide next to her and wrap my arms around her shoulders. She collapses in my lap. I lay my hand over her forehead, wishing I could exchange all my psychic powers for the chance to heal her. "We're going to get through this," I say.

She rolls her head up to face me, snot running down her nose, cheeks damp. "Stop trying to fix us all. Fix yourself."

She pushes me away and curls on her side on the cold floor. I could reach for her, but I'm too stunned. Her words rattle around in my head like an empty bottle, clanging against every memory and emotion, leaving bruises on everything.

Marion motions for me to walk to the door.

"We can't leave her like this."

"She has to choose what to do next," Marion says with far too much calm. "It's not our decision to make."

I stand but consider reaching for Judy again. She looks up with dead eyes. "Your father is here again." The painful acceptance in her voice worries the hell out of me. "He says to leave. You won't stop Braun, and we'll all die anyway. He wants me to say you're broken just like me."

It takes everything I have just to breathe in and out and prevent a fall to the floor. "Bastard."

Marion tugs at my sleeve, so I drag myself out to the hallway. "She's in pain and scared. You can't listen to her."

"Should I listen to my father?"

"Your addict father who never loved you? No, I should think that's a voice to ignore."

I fall back against the wall, my head hung low. "I couldn't save my parents. Hell, I couldn't even save myself. So I unleashed all this on everyone I met. The men downstairs, you two. All to patch some part of myself that will never heal. He's right. I am broken." I reach for a chair nearby and collapse as tears prickle the backs of my eyes.

Marion rolls closer and reaches for my hand. "All this is bigger than you. It's unfair, isn't it? We never asked for this. I lost my greatest love and waited here for her niece. I promised her."

How selfish I must sound in the face of her deep loss. "I'm so sorry."

"Don't apologize. Don't cower, and don't run."

I press my thumb into the space between my eyes to dull the ache from restrained tears. "I have nothing but visions."

She lifts my chin. "And that's enough. Stop trying to save everyone else and work on you."

"My spirit guide said to tell the truth and love big."

"Yes. You must face your fear. And trust your power."

"Ah, trust." Just the word makes my skin crawl. "My visions killed my father, and my mother used me to manipulate everyone in our lives. She would force me to read futures on men she liked and lie about their bravery and all the fortunes they'd find." I drop my gaze through a side eye. "They were never rich or brave."

"You never learned to let people in, but it's time now. Love big sounds a lot like trust doesn't it?"

"How do I let go, Marion? How do I let people hurt themselves?"

She considers how to answer that. I presume she doesn't have an answer. "Vee and I met you in our visions. We hugged you and showered you with love. I know you couldn't feel it, but we did. We've loved you from afar for years."

What I wouldn't have given to feel their presence. I try to speak, but tears rest so close to the surface, they wash away any words.

"She saw your future and mine when she held you as a baby. She built her life on you, and in a way, so have I." Marion steps closer and brings me into an embrace. I press my cheek to her damaged abdomen which is surprisingly soft, and I wrap my arms around her waist.

"I'll hug you now, in person. To make up for all the time we lost." I imagine Vanessa here too, the woman I will never meet, but who has changed me in every way. Marion sniffs back tears. This was my vision, which tells me we're near the end. I'm not ready.

I could have stayed in her embrace for years. Decades. But what is life but a series of goodbyes. "You see visions in golden threads?"

"Yes. Like a moving picture."

"You watch it happen? You don't touch it or live in it?"

She almost smiles with an awareness that I'm close to something. "Vanessa would remark on that too." She grows weak and sits back down with a thud. "You both dip inside. You become their emotions and move around in their souls. Few clairvoyants can do that."

I look up, too afraid to admit what I've realized. "Is it possible?"

"To alter his soul from the inside? Vee tried. It caused her to have seizures. You can't change the future, Primrose. All you can do is use your visions to help prepare."

Of course that would be the answer. If I discovered a way to save people, I would have done it long ago. Judy whimpers on the other side of the wall. "Can't we help her?"

"Coming down from the drug is the worst pain I've ever felt. It's why I take low doses more often." She leans back to glance inside the doorway. "Judy's dose is too high. She likes the flight she takes when it hits." Marion rubs her belly. "When I die, promise me you'll look after her? I've seen her future. The years after she heals will be really hard."

"I promise." I've hunched over now, worried what Braun is doing in his secret rooms. He had an epiphany because of me, just as he knew he would. "Why do his readings make me sick?"

"Because you become him, and his soul is compromised. He's hiding a very dark secret we've never been able to uncover." A commotion catches our attention at the window in an alcove. "Go on. I'll watch over Judy. She'll beg Strauss for another shot any minute now."

"Wait." I grab her armrests, staring into her soulful, dark eyes. "How does this end? Why do you have to die?"

"I don't have to. I want to. My life was over years ago." She rolls backward, turns, and heads toward Judy's whimpers.

I freeze in place, eyes closed and wanting to cry. Can I stop any of this?

At the window that opens to an unusable balcony, an unlikely duo flops over the railing. Ash and Finn walk to the glass, crowbar in hand. Their focused smiles warm my heart. They're going to break me free.

Ash fiddles with the thing, trying to break the seal, but launching himself to his backside. Finn grabs the bar and manhandles the stuck window until it pops open and a gust of fresh air hits my face.

"Hi."

He reaches in and grabs my cheek, planting a deep kiss on me. "Can we drag you out of here yet?" he asks.

"It's only been twenty-four hours."

Ash jumps up. "I'm okay!"

"I haven't found the answers yet. It will all be over if he finds you here." Thank goodness they're preoccupied with his experiments.

Finn runs his hand down my cheek and neck. "He fired Oliver."

"What? Who's going to take care of the animals?"

Ash looks past me with a grimace. "The man is mad. He's kicked out the customers. The hotel staff have gone home. He tried to have us removed but we wouldn't go. The police were kind enough to take a bribe. It may be all the money I have left, but it was worth it to be here with you." He speaks to us both, which I find so endearing I consider jumping out this window and down their ladder.

"You're the only two in the entire hotel?"

"Yeah, it's creepy as all get out," Finn says. "The cops will come again tomorrow. Please let us take you out of here."

His words almost break me, but a deep moan from Judy's room centers me again. "I can't. Not yet."

"Fine." Finn crawls inside the window and crouches next to me.

"What are you doing?"

Ash smiles. "This was our contingent plan. If you refuse, we force our way in. I'm grateful to be of use for once."

They're so full of love I wonder how my life has changed so drastically in a few weeks. "I need your help."

Ash's eyes light up. "Anything."

"Braun is losing it. He remembers a moment in his experiments where he missed something. I need to know what and there's only one person who can tell me. Can you get to Portland tonight?"

"Yes! Finn taught me how to turn on a car without a key. I'll take one of Braun's. Oh, this will be exciting."

"Great. Go to the apothecary on Burnside and find Russell North. Tell him I sent you."

Finn reaches his hand out to shake Ash's. "Drive safe old friend."

They share a firm handshake and exchange smiles. A surprise moment of brotherhood. "Will do," Ash says. "My father may disown me after tonight." His nervous laugh suggests he isn't ready to face the consequences yet.

"Hey, where is Oliver now?"

Ash blushes. "He went to Pendleton. Lin can help him cut off his opioid powder supply."

"Oh, good idea."

"Lin." Ash floats for a moment with her memory. "I'm off then to save the day." He shakes his fist in the air, smiles, then shuts the window. He escapes over the ledge, and I wrap my arms around Finn.

"I'm glad you're here."

"How's everything going?" he asks.

"Not great. Judy's sicker than I've ever seen, Marion is ready to die, and one reading on Braun sent me into a mini-coma."

He helps me up and kisses my forehead. "I'm not a psychic, but I will do anything I can to help."

"We're in for a long night." I hold his hand as we peek down the hall. Strauss clops toward Judy's room so we duck back into the alcove, backs pressed against the wall.

"Now, now, dear," Strauss says to Judy. "I'm here."

Judy sighs, a marker she's taken the medicine. I lower my eyes. She has to stop at some point. When will it be enough? "Strauss?" she asks. "I hate myself."

Silence. Not even Braun's trusty assistant can fix that.

Finn tightens his grip on my hand. Once Strauss returns to the experiment sections of the sanitorium, I lead Finn to a spare room at the far end of the hall. "They won't find us here. At least for a few hours."

He shuts the door. "So, Primrose, what's our plan?"

"Braun may have his super drug by morning light. He may already have it, the medicine that can wipe out our psychic powers." I drop to the bed and watch the steam dissipate into clear wind. "The secret he's hiding rests in another reading. I'm not sure I can survive another trip through his soul."

Finn sits next to me. "Do you really have to risk yourself to save people you don't know?"

I lean my head on his shoulder. "It's not just them, I'm saving myself. If I don't have my poppies and my yellow road, I may as well die right now."

He lifts my chin and kisses me in the light of the setting sun. "Uncle Henry says adventure will bring you home." He runs his finger along my jaw. "Loving you may be the most terrifying adventure of my life, but maybe we could find home together."

"Yeah, maybe we can."

I settle into his chest with visions of our future, a life I can only have when Marion dies. When I prove myself worthy of this gift and take a trip into the darkest soul imaginable. I may not make it out alive. Vanessa didn't.

Everything comes back to my visions. My final test. The moment my life has been careening toward since Vanessa held me as a baby. Now I have reasons to live. Love, friendship, loyalty.

Face my fear. Finn is like all the touch I've never had all in one place. And all that love scares the hell out of me.

Chapter Twenty-Nine

I shouldn't have let Finn stay. He could ruin everything. But I want him close to hold my hand if I wake from a seizure after attempting another jump into Braun's madness. And here we lay for the past four hours, pretending the night won't end in catastrophe.

I whisper as we lay on the bed together, his breath on my neck. "Reading Braun's soul make me sick. I can't do it again."

"It makes you sick?"

"It did. It happened when my aunt tried to read him too." I roll on my back to stare up at his multicolored eyes. "Marion thinks it's because I don't just see a vision. I become it."

"Hm." His cheeks glisten in the shadowed light of evening. "I don't know how these things work, but if you become the horrid things he holds in his soul, wouldn't that sicken a normal person?"

"I suppose it could." He drags his fingers across my temple. "You know, I'm still held down by messages from my dead father. Fear rules my every move, and I can't stop it."

"I don't think we can," he says.

"Well, that's encouraging."

"I mean it." He finds little ways to touch my skin and stroke my hair, every moment telling me in every way to return to him. "I'm scared all the time. Too much, to be honest." His eyes drop. "But I'm more scared of losing you than I am of moving on."

"Gwendolyn tells me to tell the truth. Over and over, it's her only advice."

"Are you frightened to tell the truth?"

"Hell yes, I'm scared. What horror will I unleash on the world? Would you want to know when you'll die or how you may lose everything? These are the things I see."

"Wait, you only see bad things?"

"Yes." I push myself up into a long sit. "There has to be more, doesn't there?"

"I'd avoid visions too."

"Fear." I jump up, lace my boots, and pace the room. "I'm preventing myself from seeing the good because I approach every reading with fear."

"I doubt it's your fault, Primrose. There's no guidebook for this."

I grab his shoulders. "Can I?"

"Go ahead." He smiles, complete trust that I won't ruin him.

A light hum lulls me from my consciousness. I hold tight to his touch and his smell and slip into his soul full of love. I land in a soft poppy. My legs and arms hang over the side, a velvety hammock to cradle my languid body. The sun shines like a summer morning. Pink blossoms flutter around me from the apple trees that sway in the breeze.

"Finn?" I don't fear because I know he will respond. He lifts me by my hands, teetering me forward until I'm standing on the yellow road with him. A clear path, a waiting journey.

"You can see into the parts we hide," he says. "All this was here before you but covered by rain and hail. An eternal storm drenched all this color."

Happiness blooms in my chest. The farmhouse waits in the distance. "I couldn't see all this joy," I say. "I was too busy finding the pain."

"That's why hurt people reach for you."

"There's less fear in the darkness. Somehow, hope is the most terrifying of all."

He pulls me into a dance, holding me gently at my waist. With one hard spin, he sends me out of his hands and into a yellow pool. I splash through but the water turns to air. As I dangle among the stars, I watch Finn and I share a kiss on the farmhouse rooftop under a giant harvest moon. But then he falls to his side, his face pale and his mouth slack. Before I can see more, my vision goes black.

With a blink, I'm back, staring at Finn with memories of our future on my skin. Our supposed future. We still have free will. "Well?" he asks.

"I saw our life together. It was magic. But something could go wrong. You might get sick." The memory swirls in my mind, refusing to retreat. "I don't know, somehow I can stop it."

"But we were happy?"

"Very." I hold onto the way I felt when I landed on that poppy. "I went in open to the truth, hoping for good." The statement lingers, growing larger in the silence. "Oh, God. I control what they show me. How did I not see this before?"

"Are you saying you make the visions?"

"No, not at all. But if I want to see the truth, I can't shut out any possibility. I have to get myself right before I jump. That way they can't hurt me. I can't assign judgments to the things I see. They are just moments of truth, that's all." I grab his hand. "Come on."

The second we step into the dimly lit hallway, I know something is wrong. It's too quiet. The walls hold years of patients in now empty rooms and faded green halls.

"I need to do this myself." Before he can protest, I point to a doorway. "Here. The viewing area. Stay out of sight and you can watch through the glass."

"What in the world does one watch in the viewing area?"

"Surgeries." He looks faint, eyes rolled to the ceiling. "Don't worry, I won't allow any surgery. But please, let me deal with this."

"Fine." He sneaks into the viewing room and crawls over to the edge where he can see down. "There's no one in here."

"Not yet. Be patient."

I shut the door and notice Judy's door open. Her lights are off. Same with Marion. Where the hell is everyone? Braun's office is empty. His exam room is dark too. The damn sanctuary. I reach for the handle, knowing somehow that everything changes once I open this door.

"Primrose," Braun says. "I've been expecting you."

He's too eager. "What are you doing in here?"

"Waiting for you to finish your little rendezvous in the storage room." He dips his head to the side. "Yes, I know Finn's here trying to break you out. There's no need. You don't want to leave. Not until you've discovered my secret."

"Dammit, Clara."

"Don't be too hard on the girl. She's impressionable. Her powers are pure."

His light tone doesn't match the sinister look in his eyes. "What do you mean, pure?"

"Did you know, Primrose, that Vanessa's greatest strength was her confidence?" He fiddles with a new glass orb under the now silver moonlight. "She could read any man without hesitation. Lay bare their worst impulses and render them useless fools. And she didn't bat an eye."

"How was that her biggest strength?"

"Life hadn't broken her. Parts of her, yes. But she didn't care for men." His arms swing wildly as he swoops across the floor. "Don't you see? Her visions simply existed. No emotions to get in the way."

Shit. He discovered the truth before I did.

"It's life that ruins you." He lifts a vial to the moonlight and shakes it, watching it bubble. "I was wasting the drug on the wrong subjects and losing the battle for answers."

No Strauss in this cold room. Braun's eyes are bright and ice cold. "Where are they?"

"Come, my dear Primrose. To the exam room. I have a surprise for you."

Through the hidden door and down the hall, we descend into the bright white exam room. Judy and Marion sit in wheelchairs, writhing and sweating.

I rush to their side and press my hand to Marion's cold, slick cheek. "Marion? What happened?"

She shakes, teeth gritted, her face twisted into contortions. "He's withholding meds."

Braun really has cracked. I hold her hand and Judy's, their pain somehow thundering through our touch and up through my arms. My mind races through options. I could steal medicine. Beat Strauss until she agrees to help. Where is that disaster of a woman?

"I was far too ashamed, you see." Braun dons an apron of sorts, and a pair of gloves. "I couldn't see it. Until you saw my soul. Shame held me back."

"Braun, don't do this." I release their hands and wipe their sweat on my thighs. The last thing I want is to be close to this man, yet I force my feet to move closer. "You don't want to hurt them."

"Hurt them?" His eyes turn wild. "I'm going to heal them."

"Look at them!" I throw my hand out as if yelling can force him to hear me. He can hardly see me. "You became a doctor to help. You took an oath, for Christ's sake."

He prepares his solutions as his right hand trembles. "Shut up and watch me eliminate their disease."

The women are now doubled over in pain, gasping for air. "You can't. If you take away their visions, you'll kill them."

He places the vial down and steps toward me, fist raised near his cheekbone. "The only reason I let you stay is because you will want this too. Don't you see? I will heal you. I am extending my grace to you because you've played your part." Saliva gathers in the corner of his mouth. Just one corner. "Vanessa sent you here. She told me you would answer my years-long question, and you did. I promised to reward you with the final product. Inject you with the cure. I have made a vaccine to prevent the onset of psychic powers. There will be no more suffering."

His poisonous eyes turn unhuman. "What was the answer, then?"

"Vaccines resemble an infection. I tried to kill the disease when I should have been replicating it." He reaches for my face like he wants to touch me but stops just shy of my cheek. "You were right. Shame kept me from accepting the occult into my heart. But I have now, and I understand. I held a seance." He massages the air around my face as my every muscle tightens to resist his touch. "The dead spoke to me. I saw a bright light, and the compound appeared, written in stardust across the night."

He couldn't have turned magic overnight. Our powers have been with us since birth. We live every day with the results of looking different. He is not one of us. "Even if you spoke with the dead, you can't understand how we live. The things we see."

"Of course not." His smile makes my skin crawl. His shoulders tighten high near his ears and remain there as he spins toward the women panting and crying in their wheelchairs. "I can fix you because I am not burdened by your restraints." He slides over, chest to chest with me. He breathes onto my mouth, "I am your hero."

Strauss opens the door just as I imagine stabbing Braun in the eye with his own scalpel. I've never considered myself a violent person, but he could kill my friends and eradicate psychic powers forever. I connect with Strauss's eyes, pleading for her to stop the doctor.

Braun looks at her, tongue pressed to his upper teeth. "My trusty nurse. You've always been with me." The unsaid lingers like an unpleasant taste. He means, don't turn on me now. He reaches for her, but she hesitates. She stares at her tray of medicine, then over at the women. Her eyes seem to burn with regret. Please, broomstick. Do the right thing.

"I—I can't see how this will help, doctor." She swallows hard, trying to catch her breath.

He places his finger under her chin. No, Strauss. Don't fall for it. He gazes into her adoring eyes, and I know it's all over. She's followed him for years. She presses her hand to her chest, again over her heart. "We will become famous. Together."

Strauss nods and places her tray down on the table next to his vials. "Don't," I whisper to her. "Please."

Marion is coughing now and Judy wheezes. "Medicine," Judy cries. "Now."

Braun blocks me from running to them. "They will be fine. Better than fine. They will be normal and happy."

Only one of Braun's eyelids hangs heavy, partially closed. Before I can think, I've reared my arm back. My fist lands square on his droopy eye. Through stinging knuckles, I reach for the scalpel he's so carefully placed on his exam table. I hesitate, but Judy's anguished cry mobilizes my rage.

One slash. I don't care where. Just as I widen my stance, I note Braun's eyes. They dart to the side of me. A hand reaches across my face and holds a cloth against my mouth and nose. The biting, acidic smell swallows me. I drop the blade to the floor. My knees go weak. Judy and Marion grow blurry as Marion reaches a hand toward me.

My body weight crumbles, and the lights go dark.

Chapter Thirty

Arms around my torso. It's the first thing I feel as my eyes shoot open, and I gasp for a deep inhale of delicious air. I wake mid-swing, throwing punches at the air. It all floods back. Braun, the scalpel. Judy and Marion strapped to tables, begging for medicine.

An arm appears around me, so I bite.

"Stop!"

Strauss. I can tell from the scent of menthol. "Get off me, you hag!" A giant wave overtakes me, and my knees give way. My woozy head threatens to go dark again.

"Calm down," she says as she restrains me. I can't fucking move. Who knew she had all these muscles hidden under that bony frame? She's dragging me down the hall, I think. All I see are white tiles and my vision is still blurry.

"I need to slash that monster's hands off," I say through gritted teeth.

She pushes open a door with her backside and drags me across the tiles. She whips me around to face the showers, but I throw my feet up and lock my legs on the wall. "Let go!"

She struggles but holds me so tight, I can't tell if she's got me in a hug or a chokehold. With one foot she hooks my knee and drags my leg down to the ground and breaks my strength like a crushed Tinker Toy. She shoves me in the shower and turns the water on.

Frigid water blasts my face and body. She holds me by her foot on my chest. I grab her foot and knock her to the tiles. I'm not strong but the slippery ceramic helps me drag her into the shower. Now I've got her in a bearhug.

"You're so stupid, Primrose," she yells in between gulps. "How can you be so powerful and so blind?"

My hands are too cold and weak to hold her. She slides back and I throw my hand up, prepared to punch her if needed. I look around for more of her ether, knowing that could take me out again.

"Don't," she pleads.

We heave and stare at each other as the shower douses the white tiles. No green in this room. She reaches up and turns off the water, but it still drips and tinkles around us. "Let me back to the exam room," I say, blinking my drenched eyes.

"You need to know the truth first."

I wipe my face, suddenly refreshed from the cold water and rush of frozen air across my skin. I lick a drop that rolls over my lip. "Fine. Hurry. I need to help them."

"They're fine. I shot them with a microdose when the doctor wasn't looking." She rubs her eyes. "You can't kill him."

Finally, enough air in my lungs. Feeling returns to my fingers. "I beg to differ."

"Please, just listen." After I roll my eyes, I force some form of a nod. She throws a towel at me. I wipe my face and wait. She reaches through the top of her nurse's uniform and pulls out a picture from her dress. She shakes the water away and turns it to show me. Damp and blurred is a young Strauss, Braun's arm around her.

"This was my first day as his nurse. I'd never felt so proud in all my life. I've been chasing this man ever since. The idea of his greatness, his approval."

"Choose better men." She can't help but laugh a bit at this. "That's why you touch your chest? That damn picture?"

"Yes." She holds it up and stares with such disappointed heartbreak in her gaze I almost feel sorry for her. "Somewhere along the way he lost what made him great."

"Can you get to the point, please? I may have another fight on my hands any minute and I need to prepare."

"Vanessa told me what our future will be. All of us." She blurts out the thought, strained at the end.

"Vanessa would never tell you."

She rolls her head to look at me with a fleck of that younger woman inside, the one who wanted to do good in the world. "We had our disagreements. She was loud and bossy, and hated my affection for Dr. Braun."

"Loud is another way of saying brave, in my opinion."

"Yeah," she says. "I tend to agree." She flashes a smile. "I've known for years that her niece would arrive one day. Russell would send her with those damn boots. And here you are."

"What else did she tell you?"

Strauss flicks her fingernail across the photograph. "I'm to help Braun while ensuring you don't hurt him."

"Now I know you're talking nonsense." I throw the towel at her. "You need some of that ether."

She slaps the photograph on the counter above her and turns to face me. I can see on her face how serious she is. "Braun has a part to play. Someday, he will discover a cure for a terrible disease. One we don't even know about yet. His research here leads to something bigger."

"Maybe I don't care if he saves people."

"You should," she says. "Because Finn will fall sick with it, and without the medicine, he won't make it."

I stare at the doused hospital gown and soggy socks on my feet. My vision. Finn fell over. He was sick and I couldn't stop it. My hair drips down my back, sending a chill through my very core.

"Primrose?" Strauss waits for me to say something, but I'm too consumed by the thought of a world without Finn.

"What do you get out of this?" I ask.

She's quiet for a long moment. "I'll die too."

"Vanessa told you that?"

"Marion saw my death as well, but she didn't have the specifics." She rolls herself up out of the puddled water, speaking down toward me. "Vanessa saw it in her Braun reading. Right before she had a seizure."

"She spent years putting together the pieces. The doctor, Rusell, Marion, and me." Strauss's tired body has worn from years of work and the solid belief in a man who would only hurt her at every turn. "She knew how she would end, didn't she?"

"She gave Marion a ring that morning. Told her she would see her on the other side."

The cold finally settles into my bones. "I won't let him hurt them."

"Then you just handed Finn and myself a death sentence." She lifts the photograph. "I don't know how you live with all that knowledge in your head. All the truth of what will become of us. It's too painful for little old me." Ater a rigid hesitation, she rips the photo in two and drops the pieces on the floor before turning to walk out.

The room feels somehow both giant and compressed all at once.

I drop my head and cry. Wet and cold. I can't summon the fight. "It's not fair," I mutter. "I shouldn't have to decide who lives and who dies."

"You don't decide." A voice rings through the shower room, echoing around me. I lift my head and wipe away tears.

"Gwendolyn."

She reaches for me and blasts the room in a gold glow. "I've been in these moments a few times in my life," she says. Her silver hair rests in a sweep across her shoulder, with a rosette above her ear. Her dress, a simple frock of pink. "The moment where you want to give up is precisely the one where you need to believe."

"Believe in what?" I still hold her hands as her touch warms me to my core. "That good will prevail? That I can find love and embrace psychic visions where no one dies at my hands? I can't anymore. Every choice I make will hurt someone."

"That is life, my dear."

"No, it's not the same, and you know that." I yank my hands away. "You know the answer and you float in and out of my mind, speaking in riddles while I watch the women I care for writhe in pain."

"You cannot force them to do anything, Primrose." Her voice grows in strength, loud and firm. "We all make our choices."

"Then I choose nothing." A buzzing, gilded light surrounds my head as her presence fills me with love. I'm never alone because I carry her with me. "I can't want this anymore."

"We do not choose who we are. Our parents, our childhood, they are out of our control. But now that you've lived and learned, you get to choose what you do. Don't turn away from what makes you powerful."

Her eyes glisten in the light. Tears gather and she breathes hard and fast. "Why do you care what I do?"

"I am your sprit guide. My concern is not what you do, just that you do it for the right reasons. You've almost conquered your fear. Don't stop now."

I reach my arms out to find the wall but all I feel is cloud and light. "I need out. Let me out."

"You are so close, Primrose." Her image fades. "Everything you need to save the three-colored man is already inside you."

"Oh God, the three-colored man again?" I swipe her image away. "Get me out!" I shove the door open and find myself in the shadowed darkness of an empty hallway. When I turn back, there is only an empty room with a torn photograph in the pool of water on the tile floor.

Judy and Marion need me. Finn hides in the gallery, for what I don't know. I'm holding this place together by my fingernails and I'm about to crash through the glass.

A tickle at my ankles startles me. I jump back but my eyes adjust. "Otto?"

He rubs his little bird head on my hand, so I lower down and pet his bright blue neck. "How did you get in here, buddy?"

While I scratch his neck, he looks directly into my eyes.

"Don't look at me like that." He doesn't even blink. Do birds blink? He simply stares long enough to make me uncomfortable.

Ash burst through the door, crowbar raised above his head. "I did it!" He bows when he sees me. "I went on an adventure, found your friend, and broke into the sanitorium. Bloody hell, I love living on the edge."

Russell stumbles up the stairs, even more gaunt and pale than before. "Russell, what the hell happened?" We catch him as his knees give way.

"I tried to go without the drug," Russell says. "Stupid."

"I'm sorry to bring you here. Let's find you a place to rest."

"No." He forces his spine straight. "Ash says you need me, and I want to be here."

"Vanessa told you I would, didn't she."

"Boots and come running when you call. They were my only instructions." His knees buckle, but he recovers. "I'm all right."

"Russell, you're sick."

I exchange glances with Ash, who recoils from Otto. "Why did you come?" he asks Russell.

He pushes back to lean on the wall and drops his face in his hands. "I can't stay away from this damn place." He dips his head and rakes his fingers through his dark hair, flopping it forward and hanging down toward the ground. Deep in his roots is a patch of silver and gold. Silver, gold, and black.

"Russell?" He lifts his head, holding my gaze with desperate eyes. "You're here so I can save you. You're the man with three colors."

Chapter Thirty-One

No time to ponder how or why I will save Russell, because we all hear a blood-curdling scream from the exam room.

We help Russell who has found some bit of strength as Otto waddles behind us. Finn bangs against the glass. "That bastard locked me in here." The door muffles his voice. He shakes the door again and again, but it won't budge.

"He left the sanitorium open but kept you in here?"

Russell speaks up. "He expected us but Finn isn't supposed to be here."

A twist in the expected outcome. "No one expected me to bring him?" I ask.

"He wasn't part of the vision." He shakes his head and shrugs. "Free will changes things. An unexpected wrinkle in the prophecy."

"Who screamed?" Finn asks.

"I don't know. But I'll find the key and come back for you."

He places his hand on the glass, and I do the same, as if we can feel each other's touch through space. If Finn threw a wrinkle in this future, maybe I can too.

We head through the doorway to Braun's empty exam room. The door is open to the surgery center. With both terror and anticipation, I gather myself to step into his arena. Judy and Marion lie on tables, strapped down. Their sleepy eyes hang heavy, and their heads roll around.

Braun stands in the center, a spotlight around him. "Welcome!" He looks up to the viewing area. "Your little boyfriend threw a wrench in my plans. I locked him in and will force him to watch our glorious moment together." He turns to Russell. "I knew you would come."

"You've been waiting for this for years," Russell says. "One bewitching woman tells you it's so, and you commit to eradication." He pushes away from us. "But you've been after this your entire life, haven't you?"

Braun moves toward us with a great drag of his foot. Is he trying to be theatrical? "I tried for so long, didn't I?" He laughs in between maniacal gasps. "These women know what I can do. They've drunk the hot springs and fed their blood with my opium, and now they beg for my mercy." He sneers at Russell. "If only you were that grateful."

Ash steps forward, hands on his hips. "Now, that is especially rude. This has gone on long enough!" Ash towers over meek Braun and I wonder if he might pop the doctor right in the same place I did where a bruise has already formed. But Strauss appears behind Ash and covers his mouth until he falls to the floor.

"You and your ether again?" I ask. Strauss drags Ash by extended arms across the floor and places a pillow under his head. "How generous of you."

Braun holds up his hand. "But wait. You're going to love this." He opens the door that leads to his sanctuary. Clara pokes her face around the doorway. Her usual childlike excitement has faded and, in its place, a worried scowl. She steps inside and shuffles her feet toward Braun. "I'm ready."

"That's a good girl." He turns to us, his hands resting on her shoulders. I have an overwhelming urge to break his finger joints. "Say hello to our first subject."

What the hell is happening here? Vanessa wouldn't want any of this. I stumble forward, my hand reaching for Clara. "Stop."

"Shh, Primrose," Braun instructs. "This is Clara's choice, not yours."

"She's a kid," I plead.

Russell drags himself forward next to me. "That's why he chose her."

"Ah! This is correct." He wraps his arm around her shoulder. Her big eyes plead for me to help. "She is so pure and unaffected by the outside world. She believes in her gift, don't you, Clara?"

"Yes, I do."

"You see, when we stood in my sanctuary all those years ago, Russell, I felt such shame for trying to change you. It blinded me. Vanessa knew I would arrive here, but I could not admit to myself that I must break laws and ethics to bring this drug to life. Now, because of you, Primrose, I have the cure." He lifts a vial from the pocket of his lab coat. "I had to be unafraid."

How can Braun and I be careening toward the same lesson? I glance up at Finn, who is pacing the viewing area, trying to find a way free.

Braun extends his hand toward Strauss. She takes the vial and prepares the liquid. She stops a few times, hopefully to consider what she's about to be part of.

Russell inches closer to Clara as I plead for any way to stop this madness. "You can't do this. You don't know what this drug does to us. It will turn her from innocent girl to hungry beast who will devour anyone for another taste of relief."

"Vanessa wanted me here with you," I say to Russell. "Why?"

"To answer that, you'll have to go somewhere you've been fighting."

The place none of us want to go. "Braun's soul."

"With me." We glance back at Judy and Marion barely hanging on. "We'll find answers together."

"You read sickness. How do you expect to get into his soul?"

"Vanessa was convinced our power is more than what we know or understand. She said I could piggyback on your ability."

I can't imagine this will work, but I wink at Clara and grab Russell's hand. Braun's annoyance froths from his scowl. "Hurry it up, Strauss!"

Together, we shove Clara out of the way and wrap Braun in a hug. His bony frame and tobacco-scented hair activate my dread, but it is precisely that feeling that makes me pull him in harder. I close my eyes and squeeze Russell's hand tighter.

And together, Russell and I tumble through the icy, black chute of our psychic world. We land in a howling wind kicking up dust around a yellow road that leads to darkness.

"Russell, what do we need to find here?"

"I lied to myself." He grabs both my hands. "I said I wanted relief, but I only cared about the drug. I wanted opium to pump through my veins and wash out every bit of pain. To wash *me* away." Russell's hand trembles against mine. "I sent you to Braun's emerald city so you could defeat him. I wanted you to save *me*," he says.

"Why didn't you tell me. I could have helped earlier."

He shakes out his hair, exposing the metallic hues deep at his roots. "You had lessons to learn before you could help me."

"I can't fix an opium addiction." Trust me, I've tried. "I'm lost here."

"Your spirit guide sent you to save me, that is correct. But there's more that you don't know."

"I'm tired of secrets and we don't have much time." The wind howls in my ears and whips my hair against my face.

He holds up his hand to shield his eyes. "I could identify every sickness, and I did. Typhoid, rheumatism, alcoholism. He used me to become a better doctor, and I let him."

"Why?"

The wind halts, fluttering dust to the ground around our feet. Stars drop and sway over our heads. Gold light flutters against darkness, just like the dragonflies that tickled my arms at the apple farm.

"Look harder."

I close my eyes and listen. Approval. Disappointment. I feel the ache in my chest of failure. I feel the way I did as a girl, wanting my father to see me.

Awareness hits me. "You're the baby he abandoned."

Russell collapses, his head shaking slowly side to side. "I'm too afraid to read his soul."

I help him stand. "We do it together, okay?"

In this world, he appears strong, his eyes clear. A glimpse of what he could be without the shackles of that drug. We link arms and stand firm as a thunderous cloud rolls toward us, frizzled with electric lightning.

"What is it, father?" Russell yells. "Bring it to me!"

The storm rages toward us, louder and faster, but we don't run away. We don't cower. When the rain and hail and thunder rock our bodies, our hands split apart, caught only by grasping fingertips. "I feel it!" I yell though I can't open my eyes to see Russell. "He wants to hurt us for failing him. Is he really this evil?"

"No," he says. "Something's wrong. It's like this storm is some devil waiting to swallow him."

I can't see my stars. The wind is too intense. I cover my face with my arm but hold tight to Russell's hand.

"Wait." Russell pulls me close and walks into the center of howling darkness, deeper and deeper into the smell of rot. "There, do you see it? How did I miss it?"

"Is that…"

And just like that, the storm clears, and Russell slips from my grasp. Back to his physical body. A few moments of Earth time felt like an eternity in that blizzard of a vision.

There's something to see still. A hum pulls me away from Russell, into another trance. I'm back in a vision. As I run down the yellow brick road, my silver boots flicker and spit metallic light. My soft, glittery sky awaits. I launch into the black night, falling without the thumping grip of fear.

The brightest star deep in the sky flickers. As if it's been waiting for me.

The star grows and wraps me in a golden hug of light. "I see it." Fear can no longer stop me from being the woman I've been searching for. Gwendolyn is the answer.

I click my toes together over and over. "Maybe this is home."

My one giant, bright star doesn't drop me like I think it will. It hovers and seems to wink before tossing me back into the inky sky. I land back in my body in Braun's surgery center, not with a thud, but with a floating ease and no headache to speak of.

The room steadies, Braun and Russell and the silver girls unmoving.

A hand presses against mine. I turn to see Gwendolyn. She wraps me in her golden circle and smiles. Her dress shimmers like stardust. Champagne tulle embroidered with emerald crystals.

"You know the truth now," she says.

"Yes, I felt it. I feel it now too."

She runs her hand through my hair.

"You saved me, didn't you, Aunt Vanessa." My stars showed me everything. She returned the night of my twenty-second birthday to save me from the darkness.

"I have always been with you. In human form and then, when you turned twelve, in spirit form."

The light around me glows so bright I have to squint. No flowers or yellow roads or emerald castles—just light. "Why couldn't you come back to me as Vanessa and tell me all this?"

"Gwendolyn was my first girlfriend. She was a glamorous actress who wore ballgowns and diamonds." Her skirt fluffs as a gust of wind blasts us. "I couldn't tell you the answer, for you wouldn't have discovered the depths of your power. We don't learn from the successes nearly as much as the failures."

I pace, working out what I saw in my vision, my one bright, relentless hope of a star. Wind circles around us as gold particles spin and flutter. Without fear, I can see it all so clearly. "You sent me here to save Russell so he could heal Braun."

"A peaceful life full of love is all I've wanted for you. Our people need to live. This was the only way."

Our hair flies up, a mess of silver strings bound together. Her hands fade to translucent. "No, don't leave."

"I will never leave you." Her entire being disappears and rubies clang to the ground.

Returned to my body, I gasp for air, hands gripped to my knees for stability. Russell shakes my shoulders. "Stand up, Primrose."

I force myself up and look into Braun's eyes. "You will not inject them."

He grins by only lifting the center of his upper lips. "Strauss, don't give it to him. You know he'll hurt someone."

She lowers her hand, softened by Russell's pleading gaze. Braun yanks the vial from her. I run to Clara and grab her around her trunk to drag her away. Just as I do, Braun knocks Russell to the floor and runs toward the women. I scream "No!" so loud that Clara covers her ears, but it's too late. Braun slams the needle into Marion's arm, injecting the solution into her veins. I shove Clara back to Strauss and run. I grab Braun by his lab coat and throw him down.

He rolls me to my back and presses my shoulders into the tile floor. "I did it," he yells. "Leave me be! I no longer need any of you."

A giant crash forces us to roll away from each other. I cover my head with my hands as Finn drops through the gallery in a storm of glass. He lands on the surgery table with a crash, then bounces to the floor in a clatter of metal as instruments fly.

Finn forces his way up, holding his shoulder in obvious pain. But that doesn't stop him. Braun grabs another prepared injection and races toward Judy. Finn rushes at him, head down, straight into his chest, as the needle spins through the air and lands with a crash on the ground.

"Stop," Russell says calmly.

"You always were a traitor." He holds his ribs with a wince. "I know the compound. I'll just make more."

"No, you won't." In walks Oliver and Lin. She pushes her way forward as Oliver rushes to Judy's side. "I've told every opium dealer in Oregon not to deal with you. Most didn't like you anyway."

The entire room stares in shock. Braun backs up, forming a plan to steal what's left of his super drug. "Strauss, come. Let's begin anew."

"No." She looks at me without a smile so much as a definitive nod. She walks past him to attend to Judy and Marion. "I will be performing my nurse duties."

Finn checks Marion's pulse.

Braun seethes his way toward Russell. "I am in charge here, not you."

"Technically, you're my father, but we share only blood. I am not you."

Braun throws his head back as his hand slides to a pile of strewn surgical instruments. "You kept your mother's name."

"You left when I was a baby to pursue your dreams. At all costs, you told her. Looks like you are a man of your word."

Braun fiddles over the instruments and finds the last vial. He holds it in his sweating palm. "I did this all for you. For us."

I can see how badly Russell wants that drug. Maybe it's the high, or maybe he wants to heal. He rolls back his sleeve. "Give me the needle."

"Russell, stop." I yank him back, but he pushes me away. "I've always wanted this. Just fix me and let me live without this pain."

Braun taps the tube while holding it to the light. "That's my boy. This is my last dose."

"Don't." I push Braun back and stand between the two of them. "I'll do anything to stop you."

"No, you won't," Russell says. "You won't hurt him. That would risk too many people, wouldn't it?" He looks over at Finn who approaches, blood trickling down his temple from one of many cuts across his face and arms.

"My directive was to save you, Russell, and that is what I'll do."

"It's me he wants, Primrose." Russell's sad, accepting eyes seem to have lost all fight. "He's done with you."

Braun lifts his hand, poised for injection. "You can finally become something spectacular, son. We can fight mysticism together. It will be our legacy."

He reaches for Russell's arm. I throw my weight toward Braun and wrestle with his hand. He faces the needle toward my thigh, pressing to reach my skin. I slam the heel of my boot onto his foot just as Finn rips his hands away from me. He punches Braun hard in the face, enough to send his head spinning. Russell grabs the vial and aims it for his elbow, but I rip it from his fingers, swing around, and land the needle right in Braun's chest.

He gasps. I hold my finger over the plunger, my hands trembling so hard I nearly jerk the needle out of place.

Russell lays a hand on my shoulder. "He's sick."

My hand remains locked around the syringe. Braun's heavy eye reminds me of what I saw in my vision, and I adjust to the intensity of the moment. I loosen my grip and step back. Finn grabs my arm to steady me. Braun plucks the needle from his chest. "You could have killed me, Miss Whittaker. Why didn't you?"

"You're sick, just as your son said. You have a brain tumor that is slow growing but pressing on parts of your brain that affect mood and judgment. This evil isn't you."

Braun doesn't believe me. He stumbles up to standing. "No, that can't be."

"We saw it in your soul." Russell clears his throat. "It's why your right eye hangs heavy, and you drop things. I was too caught up in my need for your drug that I couldn't see it until we went inside."

He rubs his head. "No, I just created a groundbreaking medicine." He stumbles to a chair, checking his hands by moving them back and forth. "I can't. But I… this isn't how the prophecy was supposed to go."

"You need surgery, or you will die." Russell stares at the vial on the ground. Without hesitation, I smash it with my boot.

"You still have life ahead of you, Braun, but it can't be with psychics," I say. "You've done enough damage and it's time to make things right. Reconnect to the reason you started this journey."

Ash groans himself awake, happy to find himself in Lin's lap as she strokes his hair. "Well," he says. "Glad I could take care of the situation here."

Clara is hiding in the corner, head buried in her arms. I help her up. "It's okay, sweetheart. It's all over."

Her bright eyes catch the light as they grow wide with fear. "Don't make me a subject."

"You won't be. I promise."

Strauss drops a stethoscope on the floor. "She's gone."

The entire room moves toward the tables where Marion lies still and lifeless. Her pale face and blue lips take my breath away. One arm dangles off the side of the table so I pick it up and lay it on her swollen belly. "Rest now." Something gold catches the light. Around her neck rests a chain holding a simple gold ring. "Aunt Vee is waiting for you on the other side."

Everyone bows their heads. Silence takes over the room, the only sound that of crunching glass under our feet.

One by one, we all turn to Braun. He meets eyes with Russell. "I didn't want to kill anyone." He stumbles back and falls to a chair, head hung down between his knees.

Strauss lifts a sheet over Marion's face. "Goodbye, sweet Marion. It's been a pleasure to be your nurse. And your friend." She rests her hand on her chest where a photo once rested. "Goodnight."

"And Judy?"

"She's stable, but we need to transport her to a hospital." Strauss monitors Judy closely.

I lay my hand on Strauss's shoulder. "What will you do now?"

"I suppose I'll still follow him, hoping he can find his way back to who he once was. I believe we all can."

"Back home to who we're meant to be," I say.

We gather in the hallway as Russell stares at his father from the doorway.

"You know, Primrose," Oliver says, "You gave us the strength to face our fears. I found the courage to stand up to Braun. Ash stood up to his father. Just today he phoned him to say he isn't coming home to New York. And even Finn found himself a way to mend his broken heart."

I lace my fingers through Finn's. "No, all my visions did was help you see what was already inside you."

One Year Later

Late October nights carry a chill, announcing the creep into the cold months of fall. The most magical time of night is the moment the sun falls behind the mountains and the moon appears like a gift, dangling from an inky sky. Birds sing and life is simple with apple cider and morning biscuits.

Two gold orbs float in my periphery. I smile at them both, Vanessa and Marion, joint spirit guides of goodness who live beside me.

As I climb the ladder to the farmhouse's rooftop, my skin floats with the breeze, anticipating Finn's arms around my waist and in my hair.

"Hi," he says.

"Hi." We made it back here, against all odds. I fought my way through fear to find the simplest of moments worth living for. I'd like to say I'm clear and whole, but the sanitorium still haunts my dreams.

Finn slides his hand under my hair and rubs my neck as we watch Otto strut through the corn fields below.

Judy and Oliver live in the guesthouse. Clara lives with a widow down the road. She has made quite a name for herself with the ladies of the surrounding farms. She listens in on conversations and has the entire town in a gossip frenzy, much to her delight. Uncle Henry finds the new, hectic life at the farm quite enjoyable. Oliver manages the animals while Finn tends to the crops.

Ash pokes his head up above the roofline as he fumbles to the top of the ladder. He wobbles but catches himself. "Honestly, why do you two sit up here in the dusty air? Not to mention the threat of falling to your death."

"It's only one story, Ash," Finn says. "Worst that'll happen is a broken bone."

"Well, I certainly don't want that either."

"What can we do for you, Ash?" I ask.

"Just came to say goodbye." He stares over his shoulder at Lin who waves from down below. They live in Portland but attend dinner here once a month. Uncle Henry had to craft a bigger table to fit us all. "We're going to take some apple butter to the neighbors on our way home."

Ash is attending law school in January. His first goal will be to fight sundowner laws. His father disowned him, and it was the best thing that's ever happened to him.

"You've become the unofficial mayor of this place," Finn says.

"Well, someone has to bring city fun into these country estates." He loses his footing and slips from view. From below we hear, "I'm fine!"

Finn tucks my hair behind my ear. "I hear Russell and Braun are doing well."

"They are."

Braun's surgery was a success, performed by his friends from the Mayo Clinic. Russell opened a legitimate pharmacy with Braun's clinic in the back. Russell helps heal what formal medicine cannot. Braun's work with opium will lead to another discovery eventually, and he's hard at work researching dangerous diseases. He has no desire to change us anymore. It's been a struggle to get to know the man he was before the tumor changed him. He even indulges us in a magic show when we get together. He's become interested in Houdini and learned card tricks and parlor games. We all find it silly, but we allow him to entertain us.

"Is Russell still seeing his doctor?"

"Yes." Both Russell and Judy went through extensive treatment to rid their bodies of the drug. I've never witnessed something so terrible. They lost everything and had to claw their way back to life. "He still struggles and wants the drug, but the doctor meets him weekly. He's fumbling through. I guess we all are."

Strauss, ever the loyal subject, followed Braun but she found a nice man to settle down with. She works as Dr. Braun's nurse, acting as his conscience. She keeps him in line and returns home to her husband, a gentle man who lets her call the shots.

Hot Lake is now a flourishing hotel under Ash's father's direction, with only remnants of metaphysical power clinging to the walls. Some guests claim to see flashes of silver in the hallways and green shadows when the sun hits the windows.

"Guess what I saw when I went to Russell's shop the other day," I say with a smile.

"What?" Finn asks.

"It appears Silver Lily is back."

He cocks his head with the hint of a smirk. "You've got to be kidding."

"My mother stood right there on a street corner, dressed in black, handing out fortunes for a dollar each. She even has a display now with homemade jewelry."

The woman finally found her calling. As I've always said, no one cares about the truth, they just want the lie to help them through their difficult lives.

"What did you tell her?"

"That I'm happy." The starry night twinkles above us. "I told her she can have the lies, because I'm all about farm life now. She was always Silver Lily."

I run my hand along Finn's golden cheeks and stare at his vibrant three-toned eyes. He leans in and kisses me, soft and slow. His affections are never rushed, never forced.

"I'm so glad we found our way here together," Finn says.

"There really is nowhere like the home we build."

The moon shines in all its silver glory. "I love when the moon is low like this," Finn says. "Tomorrow will be a harvest moon."

A memory rattles my brain. "A harvest moon?"

"Yes. Common at this time of year. A giant, strawberry-colored sphere that seems to dust the earth."

The bartender from last year will kill himself tomorrow. I can't intervene, but I can make sure he knows someone cares. "Want to come to the city with me tomorrow?"

"I'll go anywhere with you."

I still wear Vanessa's boots, though I know the only magic in them is how they brought me to Hot Lake. When I tap them together, the sheen catches the light, reminding me to trust. I have a new relationship with my visions. They aren't so scary when they don't define me.

Finn kisses me again, and the world fades away. All the worry and pain that can be set aside when I need to just live and breathe as Primrose, a woman who sees things. I died that night of my birthday. The old me fell asleep and a new woman awoke. As Gwendolyn once told me, the answer wasn't a prize at the end. It was the lesson I learned along the way.

I learned no one is without fear, and everyone needs more love.

Author's Note

Sometimes, I write a story from the strangest historical finds. In my travels through my home state of Oregon, I discovered Hot Lake Hotel in La Grande. This hotel did not have a typical past. Built in 1864, Hot Lake Resort was named for the thermal springs that heated the lake. Once a thriving resort on one of the rail lines, they leased the third floor to a doctor who managed a sixty-bed medical ward, complete with experimental medicine and a surgical viewing area. By the 1920s, this place was a thriving resort complete with stables, a ballroom, post office, blacksmith, confectionary and more, while laboratories and experimental medicine bubbled upstairs.

This just begged for a supernatural story.

The doctor in this book is in no way reflective of the doctor who practiced at Hot Lake, as Dr. Braun is fully fictional. As I began to write Primrose and her fortune teller life, the hotel became the strange, wonderful background to her story, rooted in factual history. They were the first to use geothermal energy for heating and used the boiling lake water for medicinal purposes. The real doctor dabbled in the occult, and local children would boil eggs in the hot springs for their lunch. Rumors remain that the Mayo Brothers visited the sanitorium to participate in surgeries.

I visited the hotel while writing this book, expecting to be greeted by ghosts, but felt only a sad energy that this building had once been a glorious and strange masterpiece that suffered from fires and years of disrepair. A local family has worked hard to bring it back to its former glory, and you can stay in the hotel while enjoying the hot springs.

As for Primrose, this story took so many iterations, I lost count. She took me three years to complete, as the *Wizard of Oz* reimagining didn't take shape until well into my rough draft. Also inspired by the production and movie *Wicked*, I wanted to tell the story of a lonely woman with an odd look, who must find the strength do what's right, while treated as the ultimate outsider.

In everything I do, Eleanor Roosevelt whispers to me in the background. One of my favorite Eleanor quotes rings so true for this project. "When you have decided what is right, what you feel must be done, have the courage to stand alone and be counted." Other badass historical women who inspired this story are Nellie Bly, who committed herself to a women's asylum to expose the cruel conditions, and Dorothy Parker, who influenced Primrose's snarky wit.

I will be forever grateful to Black Rose Writing for supporting my experiments in genre and seeing this project to completion. This story took many turns, but the most pivotal was with the help of Irene Cooper, an incredibly talented author, poet, and writing teacher here in Central Oregon. She taught me use poetry in the tiniest of moments, which has forever changed my approach to storytelling.

The women writers who surround me make this journey worth taking. Sayword, Jen, Samantha, Lisa, and the women of the Eleventh Chapter. I cannot imagine doing this without them.

And always, my husband Mike remains my biggest supporter. From helping me edit newsletters, to listening to me work out character issues and plot holes, to celebrating my every win, his belief in me has never wavered.

Thank you, readers, for taking this journey with me into the fantastical, where history and magic convene. I strive to always bring you the best stories I can create, working to fill the pages with heart.

Book Club Questions

1. Identify the *Wizard of Oz* imagery. Which characters can you see represented from the original L. Frank Baum series? Which themes are similar to *Wicked*?
2. Primrose created a false narrative about herself and her power. Why did she do this, and how did she drag herself out of that mindset?
3. How did her relationships with the three men change her view of herself? What roles did they play in her journey?
4. The themes of the book touch on social injustice and the notion that we can be "whole" if we simply change the thing that makes us different. What current social difficulties could this represent?
5. Discuss the ways Primrose built a web of lies around her psychic powers to protect her heart.
6. What role does Dr. Braun play in Primrose's growth? How was the "evil" character able to dig into her biggest fears and, ultimately, lead her to grow?
7. Primrose differed from her peers. She never wanted to eliminate her talents. How did her past give her the strength to fight Braun's opium, and remain steadfast in believing in herself, even when all seemed lost?
8. Discuss who Primrose started as, and how she changed over the course of her journey. How did the opening scene differ from the ending scene?
9. What current societal issue does Dr. Braun represent with his quest for power and justification of terrible deeds?

About the Author

Kerry Chaput is a multi-award-winning historical fiction author who writes of daring women with loads of adventure and a splash of magic. Born in California, she now calls the Pacific Northwest home, where she spends her days hitting the trails, chasing historical rabbit holes, and feeding her addiction to espresso and doggy cuddles. Explore more stories from women's history at www.kerrywrites.com.

Other Titles by Kerry Chaput

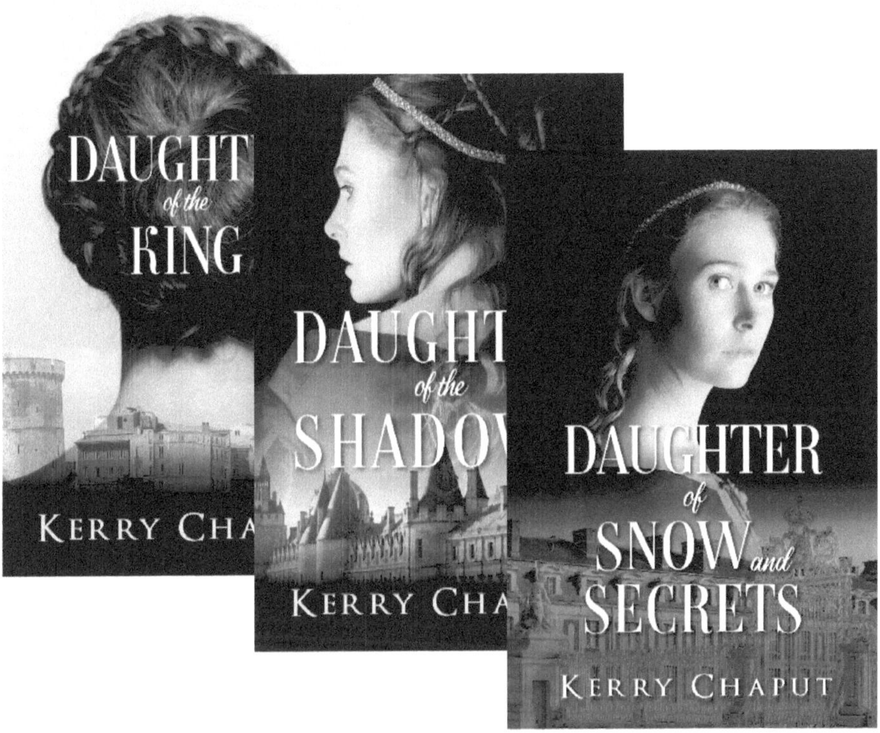

Note from Kerry Chaput

Word-of-mouth is crucial for any author to succeed. If you enjoyed *The Death of Primrose Whittaker*, please leave a review online—anywhere you are able. Even if it's just a sentence or two. It would make all the difference and would be very much appreciated.

Thanks!
Kerry Chaput

We hope you enjoyed reading this title from:

<u>www.blackrosewriting.com</u>

Subscribe to our mailing list – *The Rosevine* – and receive **FREE** books, daily
deals, and stay current with news about upcoming
releases and our hottest authors.
Scan the QR code below to sign up.

Already a subscriber? Please accept a sincere thank you for being a fan of
Black Rose Writing authors.

View other Black Rose Writing titles at
<u>www.blackrosewriting.com/books</u> and use promo code
PRINT to receive a **20% discount** when purchasing.